A Shadow in Time

Book III of The Twisted Boeman Collection

I0678231

A. Ryan MacGibbon

@thewritersembrace

Copyright

Dedicated to Dad,
whose most precious gift to me, was his *time*

"!kcab nruT !kcab nruT !kcab nruT
.ton si … emit tub ,elbisrever si cisum ehT"

Jeff Lynne

Part 1
The End of the Beginning

1

Kelly Christopher sat in a cold interrogation room, his wrists shackled to a silver metal table as the detective across from him paused the video playing from the laptop before him. Without saying a word, Detective Frank McDowell—*once a colleague and friend, now his interrogator*—sat back in his chair, posture upright, hands placed firmly on the table, a position of power Kelly understood well, having been on the other side of the table during cross-examinations many times before. He knew the charade well. Frank would linger, letting the tension build as the revelations of the security footage sunk in, then in a comforting and friendly tone, he would ask if that was *indeed* Kelly recorded by the security footage.

Kelly had interviewed enough crooks and junkies to know that no one ever confessed to a crime outright, especially without a lawyer present. They would usually ramble, get angry, or try and come up with some sort of easily disputable alibi, and that's if they even remembered committing the crime in the first place, many of the hopped up on drugs and other substances. But not in all of Kelly's years of interrogation had he seen evidence as damning and irrefutable as what he just sat through. And he knew Frank knew it too.

"So," Frank said, breaking the silence, calm and collectively, as if they were having a friendly BBQ like they did not but a few weeks back in the dying heat of late September.

"That was you right, at the Halifax Ferry Terminal, on the morning of October the 8th at precisely 6:53 am?"

Kelly didn't respond.

Did Frank really think he was capable of doing such a thing? Jesus.

They'd been colleagues for nearly fifteen years, friends for even longer, going all the way back to high school. They played beer league together on Tuesday nights, shot pool at Dooley's every second Saturday. *Christ*, Frank stood at his wedding for God's sake.

Obviously he was innocent.

He wasn't even there!

Of course—*even Kelly had to admit*—the evidence was heavily stacked against him. Watching the man in the video, Kelly couldn't find one feature, not *one single mannerism* that suggested it wasn't him. It was like watching yourself play a part in a movie, the star of a dramatic crime-thriller. Only, this wasn't fiction, and the man in the video—*that wasn't him.*

Even the clothes the man wore were identical to what he was wearing now. But Kelly was never at the ferry station. He saw what happened on the news, rushed out the door and arrived at the station by *7:58 AM.*

To be arrested at 7:59 AM.

What do they think he did, shot up the ferry terminal then walked straight to the police station? After *all* these years, did they *honestly* believe he was that stupid, or that heinous? Apparently, they did, because here he was nine hours later, handcuffed within his own station, getting questioned by his closest friend about the murder of a fellow officer, Zoe Stevens.

"Kelly. I'll ask again. This morning at precisely 6:53 am, did you shoot and kill Officer Zoe Stevens while she was on duty at the Halifax Ferry Terminal?"

"Frank—" he couldn't believe the words coming from Frank's mouth. The fact that he could believe such a terrible thing placed their years of friendship into question. It was as if he didn't even know the guy sitting across from him, interrogating him like he was some kind of murderer.

"Answer the question, please. Did you—"

"Of course I didn't shoot Zoe. I'm not a *God damn* killer, Frank! Jesus Christ." Kelly took a calming breath in a desperate attempt to keep his cool.

Another officer stood guard inside the room at the lone exit door. Officer Riley was a newer addition to the force, but a great addition. He was always first to respond in any situation, whether it be a joke at a party or a soothing line to calm the nerves of jittery suspects. Kelly knew his type, and knew it wouldn't be long before he climbed the chain of command.

To his left, along the pale grey walls of the purposely-boring design of the interrogation room, was a plate of one-way glass, and he had a lingering suspicion that every officer in the force was standing behind it—*and then some.*

All of them knew Zoe.

All of them knew him.

Half of them wanted him dead.

Zoe was dead.

They think he did it.

Kelly knew he didn't.

"Do you plead innocent?" Frank asked coldly.

"I *am* innocent!" Kelly harshly stated, his voice choked up, partially by rage, somewhat by anguish.

Frank took his reading glasses off, rubbed his temples with his thumb and middle finger, took a quick breather, then placed them back on the tip of his nose, signalling he wasn't quite finished—*not yet.*

They'd been at this for over three hours already. Kelly had been cuffed to the table for four. He hadn't talked to his wife, Donna, since this morning, and he hadn't spoken to a lawyer during the entire process. He wanted—*no*—he *needed* to sit eye-to-eye with Frank and tell him straight to his face that he was an innocent man. Yet, no matter how many times he pleaded, no matter how many times he shouted it to the skies, Frank carried on with his investigation, determined to prove that his best friend was the monster the security footage revealed him to be. Kelly would have guessed Frank would be defending him, looking for alibis, but the recently gained animosity and mounting exhaustion clearly clouded his judgement.

Hell, if the roles had been swapped and Kelly was the interrogator and Frank the suspected murderer, and he saw the evidence presented to him over the last half-day, he'd probably believe it too. *For* Zoe's sake—*as well as her husband Jessie*—Kelly would have brought Frank down with all his might.

But that's if Frank did it.

Kelly didn't do it.

He knew he didn't do it.

He wasn't even there.

At 6:53 am, Kelly was just hopping out of his bed next to his wife Donna in their Dartmouth home a skip across the harbour from Halifax. He *certainly* wasn't at the Halifax terminal, and he *most definitely* wasn't there to gun down one of his own in blue. Not once had Kelly ever been in a gunfight before. *Thank God for that.* He was sure that Donna had told them he was innocent a thousand and one times, if she even knew what was going on, which she probably didn't. Kelly doubted if any details were shared with the public.

A cop killing a cop?

In one of the busiest morning places in the city?

It was unheard of for Nova Scotia.

That sort of stuff just didn't happen here.

"Let's watch again," Frank said, grabbing the laptop and rewinding the silent security footage from the terminal.

"I don't want to watch it again, Frank. *It wasn't me.*" They had shoved that video down his throat what must have been a half dozen times already, replaying the shooting over and over again as if trying to torture him into admitting his false crime.

"I don't care," Frank responded, turning the laptop screen back toward Kelly and clicking play on the 23-second video:

The ferry had just pulled into the terminal, opening its doors for the early morning passengers to make their way off to work. About a hundred men, women and children marched out, most of them dressed in formal clothing, the men wearing suits and ties, the women with purses and shoulder bags, and the children with backpacks ready for school. Several men wore expensive watches that complimented their slicked-back hair, while a few others sported beige trousers, a single-toned dress shirt and a simple tie. The women displayed mostly formal dress pants and professional-looking tops, a few of them dressed casually, most of them in their most proper office attire. In the centre of the crowd, a split was made by people avoiding the ragged man in a large green overcoat asking for change as they walked by. The camera had surprisingly high-quality as compared to your average run-of-the-mill security footage. To the pixel, one could make out the complex patterns on the women's blouses, the colours on the children's backpacks, or even the words on the homeless man's sign. His plea simply read, "Spare a dime, if you've the time," written in black sharpie on a cardboard backing.

Standing over at the far wall by the vending machines, watching over the commuting business-folk as they marched in, was

Officer Zoe Stevens, dressed in her blue uniform, gun latched on her right hip, the badge clearly visible on the front of her body-armour, as well as a few stripes and badges. Next to her, a man placed a coin into the vending machine, popping out a red-bull and cracking it open as he made his way back to the exiting crowd.

Kelly knew what happened next. He knew it down to the millisecond. The video had been played for him so many times that he could play the entire video in his head forwards and backwards, and worse off, he knew what the damning evidence meant for him. It meant a lifetime sentence if he didn't come up with some kind of alibi, or if more evidence wasn't dug up in the meantime. Even though he didn't do it, it was the perfect set-up. The evidence against him was just too strong. *He was wholeheartedly screwed.*

"Turn it off, Frank."

No response.

Frank had two modes, alternating between each like a light switch in a dark basement. Those modes were *'cop'* mode, and *'Frank'* mode. *'Frank'* mode was pleasant. It was a *'have a few beers, watch the game, enjoy a medium-rare steak'* mode. Pretty typical, but respectable, and well suited for his lifestyle. His other biological setting was *'cop'* mode, which was why Kelly respected Frank as much as he did, and why Frank performed his job so well. He was stern, steadfast, and always got the job done, whether it was guiding traffic during a power outage, or yanking an abusive husband off his bruised wife in a low-lying neighbourhood. At 8:30 sharp, *'Frank'* mode switched to *'cop'* mode, and once the shift was over at 16:30, Frank was back again at the turn of the clock.

Right now, he was in *'cop'* mode, and Kelly doubted he'd ever see the other side of his partner again, at least not any time soon. Not while there was a case to be had. And the lack of response to his demand proved it so. The video played on:

Walking through the main doors, facing directly toward the camera, dressed in a button-up blue and white checkered dress shirt, blue jeans, and black work-boots, the gold badge clipped clearly on his belt, was Kelly Christopher—or at least, the man identically resembling Kelly. He stood behind a young blonde woman in a knee-length skirt and strategically unbuttoned dress-shirt, the harbour visible in the reflection of the glass behind him as he walked through the main entrance. Kelly looked almost identical to what he did now. His thinning hair was a little bit messier, and his shirt was buttoned down, revealing some dark chest hair and a gold chain. It looked as if he'd just been through a long night of drinking at Bearly's. Besides that, it may as well have been Kelly himself. His gun was even holstered on the left side—Kelly being a left-handed shot.

The mystery man was barely a few steps through the main doors when he unholstered his pistol, drawing it like a cowboy in an old western film, revealing his SIG Sauer P226, the station's standard issue firearm—one he'd never fired before while on duty.

It was crystal clear in the video.

There was no mistaking what happened next.

The Kelly doppelganger drew his pistol, raised it into the air, and fired a single round into the roof, a bit of rubble and dust falling from the ceiling onto the panicked civilians. Everyone in their formal workwear ducked, cowered, and dashed in seemingly random directions to find cover. Then, while everyone was bowing in self-defence, fleeing away from the shooter in the crowd, the Kelly look-alike lowered his gun, lined up the barrel with his left eye, holding it firmly with both

7

hands just as he learned in training, and fired a single shot directly at Officer Stevens, dropping her instantly as the bullet broke through her eye-socket, lodging somewhere into her skull.

Zoe instantly dropped, her drawn firearm crashing to the floor beside her, plummeting to a bitter end as muted screams and shouts filled the terminal lobby, the security footage completely silent.

What happened next was unclear. It looked as if some sort of explosion detonated within the building, a shockwave bowling over the crowds of cowering bystanders, knocking out every camera within the building.

The video stopped, a black-and-white static haze filling the computer screen. Frank grabbed the laptop once again, turning it back toward him and shutting the lid as his gaze shifted back to Kelly. This time Kelly didn't wait for Frank to ask his questions. It was his turn to start.

"No matter how many times you show me that video, I'll give you the same answer. I *did not* shoot and kill Officer Zoe Stevens. I swear it on my life. I swear it on Donna's life. Jesus Christ, Frank, you've got to believe me. We've been friends since before I can remember. You know me. I would *never* do that. You must know that, right? I'm no murderer."

Frank stared directly at Kelly, studying him. Detailing the exhaustion under Kelly's eyes, and the nervous twitch of his nose like a high stakes poker match.

Kelly simply stared back, regarding the well-maintained goatee and wrinkled cheeks of Frank's experienced face. His brown eyes and thick brow matched his hair and jacket as the interview progressed ahead. From somewhere behind the one-way window, a man coughed.

"Kelly, " Frank said, in a similar tone one might use to command a rowdy child to sit down and behave. "I've been a cop for a long time. Same as you. What usually happens here? What do you think is going to come from this?"

Even though it was a question, Kelly knew what Frank meant, and elected to dodge the query.

"It wasn't me."

"What...happens...next?"

"Frank..."

"Answer the question, Kelly." Frank dialled his *"cop"* mode up to the next level, his voice filled with rage, the veins visible on his tanned neck. Frank was walking out of here with one answer and one answer only, but Kelly wasn't going to give it to him. There was no response he could provide that would vindicate his innocence *and* satisfy Frank's incessant determination to put his best friend behind bars.

"You know what happens here, Frank? Since you've already decided my fate, why don't I tell you what happens next. I spend the next couple months rotting in the pound, pissing a half-yard away from my bed, all the while you and the other hotheads out there build up some bullshit case against me, making up stories on how *'I acted a bit strange a few weeks back,'* or how *'something seemed a bit off about Kelly, didn't it,'* or some other fabricated bullshit like that. Meanwhile, the actual murderer is out their free as a bird, most likely hiding somewhere between here and Vancouver, sipping a cold beer and laughing as he watches the news and updates over the next couple months—*a free man.* Of course, this will probably be sped up a little, won't it? Good. I can't wait to meet my cellmate. Who do you think it'll be, a pedophile, or some cross-eyed junkie? Or maybe someone we locked up already, that would be fantastic, wouldn't it? I'm sure you'd get a kick out of that, wouldn't you, Frank, you asshole."

Frank didn't bat an eye. The expression on his face could have been that of a world-tour poker player like on ESPN. He simply stood up, grabbed his papers, notebook, the laptop, and turned toward the exit, his back facing Kelly. But before he left, just had his hand reached the handle, he turned back, mowing down Kelly with his interrogation eyes.

"One more thing," Frank said, following it up with a question from left-field. "What kind of bomb did you use? Was it timed? Or did you detonate it yourself? Or was there another culprit not stupid enough to get caught on film like you?"

"Go to hell."

Frank left, free to come and go as he pleased.

Kelly remained behind, chained to the table, alone with his thoughts, the image of his doppelganger shooting Zoe in the face replaying over and over in his mind like a bad dream stuck on repeat.

He knew he was innocent.

His best friend and partner did not.

The entire station wanted his head on a spike.

Kelly almost believed the film himself, if not for the fact that he knew *exactly* where he was at the time of the shooting, even though no one seemed to believe him. Whoever was framing him, the stranger knew precisely what he was doing, orchestrating the perfect set-up and getting Kelly blamed for the atrocity.

This was as bad as it gets, he thought to himself as he sat on the cold metal interrogation chair, alone, countless eyes staring at him through the one-way mirror.

He couldn't have been more wrong.

2

Donna Christopher was pouring a second cup of coffee when Kelly walked into the kitchen and sat down in his usual spot at the dining table, giving her his routine morning smile. She returned the gesture back to her husband, who somehow looked nearly as he did when they first met twelve years ago—*minus the added thirty pounds*—

—*and thinning hair*—

—*and aging skin*—

—*and chubby stomach*—

—*and maybe a few other things*—

Donna didn't think they'd had the perfect marriage—*perfection was impossible*—but she did think they had the next best thing. Except for the odd verbal scrap, they had it pretty good. She loved him—*and he loved her*. It was more than she'd ever hoped for growing up in a quaint Nova Scotia fishing village.

The only thing missing from their life were a few little kids stomping around their overly-empty-sized home. It wasn't like they hadn't tried. About three years after their wedding, after a few extravagant vacations and too many nights out, they finally decided it was time. For over a year, they tried repeatedly testing to see if *this* was it. But their dreams never transpired. There were hospital tests, sex counselling, and even a few small-town spiritual gurus, not that they helped much. No matter how much effort they put in, they just couldn't seem to plant the seed.

Then suddenly—*after many more attempts and even a few dry spells*—thirty transitioned to forty, and the drive just seemed to fade away. There was still the odd attempt, but by this point, they knew there would be no result. It just seemed like it wasn't meant to be. And that was *okay*. Disappointing, but Donna and Kelly had accepted it, shifting their priorities elsewhere. Kelly climbed the chain of command quickly at the city-station, while Donna was already Vice Principal at the local high school, and currently, the most likely candidate to take over as principal once the current principal, Brian Sanders, retired.

Yes, except for the lack of children, things were pretty good for Kelly and Donna. The summers brought two-month long trips to their timeshare in Florida, and the winters brought the odd impromptu treks to wherever they pleased. Last year it was Cuba. This year they were going to do a five-day tour of the Ireland hillsides and castles. *Life was good.*

Donna poured a packet of sugar and a splash of cream into Kelly's coffee, then placed it on the table in front of him, giving him a quick kiss on the forehead before sitting next to him as they fought off the morning sludge.

"How'd you sleep, dear?" Donna asked, sipping another hot gulp.

"Good. Not long enough, though. You?"

"Not bad. Could have been better, I guess." That was a lie. She slept terribly throughout the night. Tomorrow was 'inspection day' at the school, where a few board members would pop by and take a quick tour of the premises to make sure everything was still in order. Of course, it was, so Donna knew she had nothing to be worried about. Yet, she worried none the less, that's just who she was. "Anything big planned today, dear?"

"Just the usual," Kelly responded, his eyes still glued to the morning news, their grogginess still slowly fading away.

Donna grabbed her phone and began scrolling through social media, seeing what her digital friends had been up to during the late hours of the night. And as always, the answer was, *'not much'*, so she quickly flipped over to the New York Times app and started reading a few articles before going upstairs to get ready. There were a few editorials like "*When 'Get Out' is a President's National Security Strategy*," and "*Seeking Ukraine Aid Records, House Subpoenas White House Budget Office and Pentagon.*" Donna wasn't in the mood to read about American politics, so she switched back to social media and continued to doom-scroll a little while longer. After a few more minutes of their regular routine, Donna slipped her phone back into her housecoat pocket, grabbed her half-filled mug, and made her way up toward the bedroom, leaving her husband behind to the whispers of the morning sports and weather.

There was nothing overly special about their house. It probably looked similar to every other house in their crammed subdivision.

They had a kitchen with white cabinets and simple decorations.

They had a living room with an oversized TV and one too many couches.

They had a master bedroom, along with a few spares for the rare guest.

And they had an attached garage, overloaded with boxes, dusty bikes, and Kelly's car to boot.

Every now and then they would discuss the possibility of downgrading to something a little smaller, but without kids, they lacked the motivation to find another home. This one was plenty big enough, the mortgage was manageable, and except for the odd tune-up here and there, the house gave them no problems they couldn't handle themselves. It was hard to find something to complain about. *Maybe they could have used a few more decorative wall hangings.*

Donna slipped off her robe, the frosty air brushing across her exposed skin. To her surprise, a cool autumn breeze was leaking in through their open bedroom window. She made her way over to the window and closed it tight—*surprised it was open in the first place*—the baseboard heaters working overtime to combat the chilly breeze. Spinning around, she noticed Kelly's gun and badge sitting next to their bed on his nightstand. *She sighed.* He knew she hated seeing the gun in the bedroom, *especially* in plain sight. The gun safe was right next to his bed, how hard was it to quickly tuck them inside after work? Apparently, it was very hard, because this was the third time this month that he left it lying there—*despite it being against the law.*

After another lengthy sip of coffee to warm up, Donna slipped on a pair of mismatched panties and a bra, covering them up with a professional looking pair of grey dress pants and a purple top to compliment the purple flats she planned on wearing today to work. She then made the mistake of looking at herself in the mirror, her tired eyes matching the rest of her not yet beautified face. Of course, Kelly would tell her she was beautiful any way she looked—*and she loved that about him*—but she always held high standards for herself. It was most likely that delicate balance of grace and authority which allowed her to climb to the vice-principal position so rapidly—*that, and not having to spend half her morning forcing non-existent children to rise out of bed.* Donna shook her gaze from the mirror, grabbed her now nearly drained coffee, and made her way to the bathroom.

But she wouldn't go in unaccompanied.

She was surprised to find her husband hovering over the sink, staring back at her like she had just caught him in the middle of some seedy act.

"Jesus," Donna said, startled, "you startled me half to death, I nearly screamed. You must have snuck in right behind me."

Donna looked up at her husband, towering about nine inches above her average five-foot-four frame. Kelly was a tall man. It was one of the reasons she became so attracted to him in the first place. But he seemed far from his usual dapper self.

His hair was messy.

His shirt was unbuttoned.

His gold chain hung loosely around his neck.

And a hint of body odour radiated off him gently.

She grabbed her hairbrush to start fighting the knots out of her hair, Kelly still standing next to her by the sink, just sort of staring at her like a googling child in a candy shop.

"Well," she said while striking the comb across her head, "are you going to get ready for work, or are you just going to stand there and gaze at perfection?" She smiled at him. He looked extra tired this morning—*even more than usual*—the bags under his eyes were heavy. "I thought you said you slept well?"

"Huh?" Kelly responded, buttoning up his shirt and suddenly kicking into gear.

"Never mind," Donna put the brush down, grabbing her foundation from the medicine cabinet instead for a little touch-up. "What're you doing in here anyway? I thought you were all ready?" Donna waited for his response, then after a few seconds, she stopped applying the foundation and looked back at Kelly, looking slightly dazed and confused. "Hun?"

"Uh yeah. Sorry. Daydreaming." He gave a weak smile, then answered again. "I—um—forgot to put on deodorant."

That explains the smell, she thought to herself, but decided against cracking a joke. Something about Kelly seemed just a tad off. "You alright?" she asked as she padded her face with her foam pad.

"Right as rain," he answered in his usual tone. "Right as rain."

"Alright," she said, unconvinced, but too distracted to push further. "I'm going to finish up in here, but I'll come downstairs and say goodbye before I go. And dear, please don't leave your gun on the nightstand."

"Oh, okay." Kelly acknowledged, "Sorry."

Then he was on his way.

Before he left the bathroom, he turned back to her and whispered, "*I love you.*"

That caught Donna off guard. She knew he loved her—*that was nothing but obvious*—but rarely he said it without her prompting him to, not in the master bathroom while getting ready for work—*and especially not after she nagged him about leaving his firearm out* "You do something bad?" she said half-jokingly, continuing to beautify her face.

Kelly smiled at her and gave an ominous, "Not yet."

Then he was gone.

She knew she married an oddball.

But it was *her* oddball, and she loved him with all her heart.

She'd bear his kids—*if only she could.*

It only took a few more minutes to finish up in the bathroom before she made her way back downstairs, where Kelly was back sitting in his usual spot, watching the *actual* news on the television this time instead of sports highlights.

She hated watching the news in the morning.

It was always so negative and disheartening—*a terrible way to start off the day.*

"You fixed your hair, I see," she said, pouring the rest of the coffee into her travel mug.

"Huh?"

"Never mind, did you—"

"Shh," Kelly cut her off, and she felt her temper rise, but that lasted as long as it took her to turn her attention toward the counter-top television.

On the T.V. was the usual morning reporter, Casey Evertt. She was standing by the main doors of the Halifax Ferry Terminal, which had been taped off with bright yellow police tape, the words '*DO NOT CROSS*' written in repeating bold black lettering across each side. That specific terminal was a short skip across the harbour from them, a mere 14-minute ferry ride from their local station.

"Turn it up," she said, Kelly already way ahead of her.

The reporter on the television continued to speak.

"*...standing next to me is Chief Superintendent Donald McNeil. Chief, what are you able to tell us so far.*"

The superintendent was fully geared in body armour and uniform, his hands grabbing the armour-straps at breast level as he responded to the reporters' questions, looking confident and authoritative in front of the cameras.

"*We don't know much at this point. And what we do know for now is confidential to protect the victims and their family...*"

Victims—Donna didn't like the sound of that.

"*What we do know, is that the suspect is still at large, and we are currently all-hands-on-deck right now trying to track him down. In the meantime, it's advised that residents stay away from the downtown area until the perpetrator is caught. We will be keeping frequent updates on our social media platforms. Also, the ferry service will be suspended until further notice.*"

In the background behind the interview, a handful of cops stepped out of the ferry terminal entrance—*one of them in tears*. Donna recognized the young officer as Jessica. She didn't know her well enough to remember her last name, but spoke to her in brief a few times during the semi-annual *Big Blue BBQ*.

"Jesus Kelly, you better go." Donna didn't have to say it twice. He was already up and out of his chair, searching desperately for his badge and gun. "Did you forget? They're on your nightstand?"

Kelly didn't respond.

He darted quickly out of the kitchen and up the stairs, and before Donna could blink, he was back down with his badge clipped on his right side, and his gun on the left. He grabbed his brown coat and tossed it on, his standard-issue weapon still clearly visible below his jacket.

"Why"? he said, muttering to himself as he scrambled to put his boots on.

"Why, what? Donna asked, standing nervously in the doorway of the kitchen, facing the front door.

"Why didn't they call me?" Kelly had one boot on, then grabbed for the other.

"Don't curse. What are you going to do?"

"Sorry," Kelly said, slipping on his other boot. "I'm going straight to the station to help, even though they don't seem to need it.

"Alright. Please be safe." Donna's nerves were trembling. She had a terrible feeling about all of this. She was always nervous about her husband's profession. All it would take was one bad day, one mistake, and suddenly she'd be a widow, a pity-case, with all her neighbours bringing her flowers and tin foiled suppers, like that would even come close to filling the void of a half-empty bed. She shook the negative thoughts from her head.

He'd be fine.

"I will." Kelly ran across the floor, gave Donna a long hard kiss, grabbed his car keys from a hook on the wall—*then he was gone—and she was alone.*

Suddenly grabbing her coffee and combing her hair didn't seem all that important anymore. But she still had a job to do, and this was the price she paid for marrying a man of the law. She knew from the moment they married that there would be days like today.

It still didn't make it any easier though.

So—*with that in mind*—Donna continued with her morning routine, leaving the news turned loud as they provided vague details and constant repeating updates, the words *"If you have any information, please call (902)-237-0916,"* constantly scrolling across a yellow banner at the bottom of the screen.

Another twenty minutes rushed by as Donna's distracted routine came to a close. She was just slipping on her purple flats when her cellphone rang in her pocket.

The number was blocked.

Her stomach sank.

But she answered anyway.

"Hello?" she whispered, her voice quiet and shaky.

A man's voice resonated through, with a drowning cluster of other voices and noises clearly audible from the background, like they were calling from the center of a large social gathering. "Is this Mrs. Donna Christopher?"

"Speaking."

"Hi, this is officer James Dunphy of the Halifax Police Department, calling on behalf of your husband, Detective Kelly Christopher."

Oh Christ...

Is this how they'd do it?

With a phone call?

No folded flag at the door?

No special visit from Chief Superintendent Donald McNeil?

Donna closed her eyes and waited for the bad news.

"Mrs. Christopher, I'm going to need you to come to the station."

Managing to fight the frog in her throat, Donna responded, uttering a couple of pitiful words. "Is he alive?"

There was a slight pause, then the young man responded once again. "He's alright, ma'am. Are you able to drive, or do we need to send a cruiser."

She breathed a partial sigh of relief, still confused about why they needed her down at the station. "What's this about?" she said, able to speak a little more clearly.

"You'll be briefed at the station, ma'am."

Donna didn't like that answer.

At work, Donna had years of experience dealing with delinquent teenagers and trouble makers. Whenever one of them acted out at school, the teachers sent the bad apples to her office. She wasn't an overly intimidating lady at first glance, but if someone got her riled up or upset in any sense of the word, Donna could go toe-to-toe with the best of them—*and getting no information from someone presumably half her age while her husband was on the case of what sounded like a pressing situation was certainly making her angry.*

"Listen, buddy. I've been married to a cop a lot longer than you've been one. So cut the *crap.* Why on earth does my husband need me at the station, and why isn't he calling me himself? What the *hell* is going on?"

There was another pause.

Donna could hear the phone shifting hands. Then a different voice answered, one that Donna recognized instantly. *It was Frank,* one of their closest friends, and Kelly's longtime partner on the force.

"Donna?" Frank asked from across the line, his voice audibly weary.

"Frank? What's going on? Where's Kelly?"

"He's locked up, Donna."

Locked up?

What did he mean by 'locked up'?

"I don't understand—" she responded, holding back the rage she had just so readily communicated with the previous cadet.

Donna could hear Frank breathing on the other side of the line as she waited for what felt like an eternity for a response, his breath slightly louder than the hustle-and-bustle behind him at the station.

"Frank? What do you—"

"He killed her, Donna." He said it so quick that she barely had time to process before he began again, uttering words that couldn't possibly be true. "It was Kelly. I'm sure of it. I don't know why, but he gunned down one of our own. He killed Zoe. We have proof. It's undeniable."

Now he definitely wasn't making sense.

Kelly killed Zoe?

What the hell was he going on about?

She could no longer control her rage, not even for Frank's sake.

"For Christ's sake Frank, what do you—"

Frank hung up, the dead dial tone echoing along with his words in her head as she stood alone, a lost and empty stare resting on her pale face. After a second's pause, her mind flustered with confusion, anger, and rejection, she dropped the phone into her pocket, grabbed her car keys, wiped away the tears, and immediately made her way to the car.

Donna backed out of the lot and drove directly to the station, barely following the rules of the road as she sped across the MacDonald Bridge toward Halifax. The next time she'd see her husband, it would be through a mirrored glass pane, and he'd be shackled to an interrogation table.

The uniformed traitor.

Donna's incarcerated husband.
The cop killer.

3

When Frank McDowell stepped out of his black Dodge Charger outside the Halifax Ferry Terminal—*a sleek-looking ghost car he had earned the privilege of driving a few years back*—the crime-scene was already littered with bystanders, news crews, paramedics, and a few other officers. The perimeter was only just being assembled, the yellow tape stretching out from lamppost to lamppost as it diverted unwanted foot traffic away from the entrance doors of the ferry terminal station. To his right, a pair of ambulances attended to the needs of a few injured bystanders. A couple civilians were wrapped in thermal blankets, while a few more were being interviewed by Officer John Morrison. Frank would read the notes later; but first, he wanted to familiarize himself with the scene and try and get a feel for what he was dealing with.

The first thing he observed were the shattered windows, the shards of glass scattered across the wooden planks of the Halifax boardwalk, blown outward from the explosion originating from inside the building. There was no word yet on the cause of the explosion, but incredibly enough, no civilians were killed in the blast.

There had only been one fatality this morning, and the explosion was not the cause.

Not one inch of his body wanted to step foot into the Halifax Terminal. Staying away somehow made the grim reality less real.

He knew whose body awaited him there.

He got the call only twelve minutes earlier that there had been a shooting, as well as some sort of small explosion, and that one of their officers was down. The 10-999 had been called out across the radio just as Frank was rolling out of his driveway to head to work. Further information followed as he drove directly to the scene from Dartmouth, warning anyone in the area that the shooter hadn't yet been caught and was still on the prowl somewhere in the city. His heart sank when Zoe's name was dropped over the broadband, confirming the fatality of one of Frank's favourite up-and-coming officers. He still didn't believe it, the reality not yet sinking in as he mentally prepared himself for what kind of scene he was about to investigate.

Frank slammed the door of his cruiser, and a few news-cameras clicked to his right, the flashes partially visible on the dark-rainy morning. The reporters were a little closer than he'd like. He didn't want any of those vultures snapping a shot of poor Zoe resting lifeless inside. She was too good of an officer to deserve that—*too genuine of a person to be treated just like another story for the curious masses.*

"Hey, Officer Morrison," Frank yelled over the crowd. "Get them to expand the perimeter. Push them back ten more yards."

Morrison nodded, tucked his black book back into his breast pocket, then motioned for a few other officers to push back the spectators and camera crews.

Frank thought about calling his partner Kelly but figured he had already been alerted and was probably on his way. Kelly was good like that—*always there when you needed him.* Not once in the past—*which included many years of duty*—had Kelly *ever* disappointed. He was an ideal partner, and a good friend. He didn't know what he'd do if Kelly were lying dead and gunned in there like a wild animal. Frank considered anyone in blue a brother or sister to him, and to lose one of their own wasn't something he was prepared to cope with, but losing Kelly would be a whole other level.

One step at a time, Frank thought to himself, making his way to the lobby entrance.

He pushed through the onlooking crowd, making his way to the front of the line, lifting the newly placed crossing-tape over his head, and stepping into what was now *his* territory.

He took a long breath and prepared himself for what was to come next. Frank had seen plenty of crime scenes in his day, but not once had he seen someone he recognized in this sort of scenario. If that ever happened—not that it ever did—the protocol was to assign another detective without an immediate connection to the victim. Of course, what was the protocol when the victim was connected to every available member of staff? The answer—*they sent the most experienced detective they had*—and so here stood Frank, about to step into the hornet's nest.

Frank didn't have to walk far into the terminal to find her.

Lying motionless on the ground across the foyer near a pair of vending machines, surrounded by numbered yellow pylons and a drying pool of blood, was Officer Zoe Stevens.

Christ.

He was not prepared for this.

There's no way he was mentally equipped to lead this investigation.

But who else was there?

There was no one.

It had to be him.

This was *his* crime scene, having no choice but to stay strong and rigid to help everyone around him stay focused. If he fell apart, what kind of message was he sending to those around him? Instead of crumbling, Frank swallowed his despair, took another long, relaxing breath, and walked over to Zoe's body, where Officer Price was taking as many photos of the scene as he could.

Her body was still.

She rested face up.

Her knees had buckled backwards.

Her arms were still and outstretched.

Next to her, Zoe's pistol rested on the ground, half-soaked in mist streaming in from the vacant window space, mixing with the watered-down blood oozing directly from her left eye—*at least, where her eye should have been.*

The bullet had torn clean through, lodging somewhere in the darkness of her skull. Frank could tell the shot didn't make a clean pass-through due to the lack of splatter printed on the wall behind her.

It was only a couple of weeks ago that Frank had hosted one of his *Big Blue Barbecues.* Nearly the entire force had attended—*except for those on duty and a few others with previous engagements.* Kelly had managed the grill while Frank and his wife Cecilia shuffled from guest to guest, shaking hands and enjoying a few cold ones with friends and strangers alike. Zoe had been there, along with her new husband, Jessie. This was the first time Frank had met Jessie. Frank and Cecilia sat with the newlyweds in their outdoor lounge by the pool, munching away on a few perfectly cooked burgers and enjoying each other's company. Zoe was keen to learn, asking Frank a half-dozen questions about his career path, about how he came to be a lead-detective, and if the job compared to what it was portrayed as in the movies. Frank didn't watch too many movies, but he assumed detectives in the films had a bit more excitement than himself. Zoe was smart, attractive, and a great officer, never once late for a shift, nor one to back down from a challenge.

She was born to be a cop.

Why did it have to be her?

It didn't matter now.

The only thing that mattered was catching the lowlife that did it.

And that started now.

"Price," Frank said, diverting his pale attention from Zoe's lifeless body. "You alright?"

Price lowered his camera, clearly in a state of distraught as he fought forward to perform his job—*for Zoe.* "I'm alright. It's just *messed up.*"

"I know."

"It could have been any one of us. She didn't deserve this."

"No one does." Frank fought back the pounding anguish in his chest. *Especially Zoe.*

Frank peered up at the wall above Zoe. Towering just above the vending machines was a single security camera, covered in curved black glass, facing the waiting area toward the main lobby. The bullet had originated from somewhere in that direction, so assuming the surveillance system functioned, they should be able to get a clear image of the culprit right away.

"Anyone grab the security footage yet?"

"Paul went a few minutes ago. You just missed him. The janitor brought him up."

"Which way?"

Price pointed toward a set of stairs with the words 'STAFF ONLY' written across the door in bold print. Frank nodded, then left Price to continue taking photographs. Frank knew he needed to inspect the scene, but he needed to get away from Zoe's body for the time being—*even if only for a few minutes.* He made his way across the eerily empty room, and up the set of stairs to the second level. Following the signs, it didn't take long to find the security room, where Officer Paul Collins and the janitor stood inside, eyes fixated on the security tapes.

Frank knocked on the open doorframe lightly, careful not to scare the two men inside the room. Everyone would be a little jittery now, and Frank didn't feel like startling anyone with a gun strapped to their hip—*even if they were trained*. The two of them turned to face Frank in the doorway. Paul's face was pale and vacant—*a strange sight for someone who was typically so lively and always ready with a joke*. He was one of those guys that always found a way to be the centre of attention—*the perfect guest to invite to Frank's barbeques*. He was a veteran on the force, nearly putting his second decade behind him. But right now, it looked as if he'd seen a ghost.

"Shit," Officer Paul Collins muttered, clearly meaning to keep that to himself.

"What is it?" Frank replied.

"Uh," Paul choked on his own words, staring blankly at his superior officer as if he'd never seen him before in his life. "You're going to want to see this, Frank."

They must have got a hit.

Maybe it was going to be easier to catch this guy than he thought. He couldn't wait to slam this filth behind bars, or better yet, get the chance to shoot him down himself.

Lord knows the scum deserved it.

He stepped toward the monitors in the windowless room, standing alongside Paul as the janitor vacated the room, leaving the officers to their job. Paul was about to hit play when he shifted his gaze back to Frank.

"This is going to be hard to watch."

Frank knew that.

Not one piece of him wanted to watch the footage of Zoe getting shot—but if it meant capturing the shooter, then this is what it took.

"Play it," Frank ordered.

Paul pressed the space bar, and the video began.

Not in twenty lifetimes could Frank have prepared himself for what he saw next.

It couldn't be true.

It wasn't possible.

Yet here it was.

The impossible captured on film.

Clear as day on the monitor, Frank watched as his partner Kelly Christopher stormed through the entryway doors of the ferry terminal, trudged against the crowd in a jagged and forceful manner, pulled out his standard-issue P226, and murdered their friend and colleague, Zoe Stevens like a dog in the street.

He couldn't believe it.

It just couldn't be him.

The man probably just *resembled* Kelly but wasn't really him. Frank must have been mistaken. His best friend and partner would *never* do something like that in a million years. Collins played the tape several more times, and each time Frank watched it, his heart dropped further and further into his chest.

The footage was of immaculate quality, a rare occurrence in his line of work. The video was at least 1080p, every detail and aspect perceptible down to a single pixel. The shooter drew the gun with his left hand, firing a quick round into the air, his gold badge clipped clearly onto the front of his belt. The crowd ducked, the only two standing being Zoe, from which Frank could only see the backside of, and the man resembling Kelly, who was now aiming the barrel directly at Zoe's head. Not but a few seconds passed between the first shot and the next, the bullet connecting with the left side of Zoe's head, dropping her instantly in camera's view. And standing before her, on the other side of the foyer, was inexcusably and undeniably his partner, Kelly Christopher, plainly visible as if he were standing right here in the claustrophobic room next to Frank and Officer Collins.

"Jesus Christ." A rush of confusion overtook Frank, his balance waning, his thoughts scattering. He sat slowly into the chair next to him, unable to breathe, think, or swear, looking for any reason to prove what he just saw wrong.

He couldn't.

Instead, as the room began to spin and his vision began to tunnel, he puked into the wastebasket resting on the floor next to him.

"Are you alright, sir?" Officer Collins asked, pausing the video and tending to his superior officer.

"I..."

"I know." He paused a moment, letting Frank catch his breath. "What do we do about it? Do I call it in?"

Frank thought about it for a moment, struggling to search for reason amongst the madness. If it was true, if Kelly *was* indeed the son-of-a-bitch that shot Zoe, then he was the most dangerous man in the city. And if they called it in, he'd know instantly.

"No." Frank struggled to his feet, his anger and grief barely overcome by his sense of *duty* and commitment to avenging Zoe. "No radios. I'll call H.Q. directly and fill them in. You go gather every officer you can find downstairs, tell them we're on a full-scale manhunt for detective Kelly Christopher, and that he's presumed armed and dangerous."

Officer Collins nodded, wasting no time at all, making his way to the door before getting reeled back by Frank one last time.

"And Paul, we'll get to the bottom of this. I promise you that."

Of course, Frank was talking to himself.

If what Frank saw was real, if his best friend—*his partner*—was truly a cop killer, then he was going to tear his whole life apart. Frank was going to bring the entire weight of the Halifax Regional Police down on top of him.

He was going to take him down.

He was going to destroy Kelly Christopher.

A Shadow in Time

4

The rain was only just beginning to fall when Kelly Christopher entered his attached garage, fuming over the lack of communication between the station and himself. He still couldn't believe they didn't call him. Sure, he wasn't on duty yet; but for a shooting to happen right here under *his* jurisdiction, there wasn't a chance he didn't want to be fully involved, helping in any way he could, bringing down those responsible, if they hadn't been caught yet already.

He was only a few steps into the garage, heading to his cruiser parked on the far side when a throbbing headache sliced across his head like a dagger. A searing pain raced across his skull, the stress of the situation clearly taking its toll right away, stopping him in his tracks for a moment as he felt his vision twist and stomach turn. He felt like he had just been slammed in the head with a bag of bricks, his balance waning, his brain throbbing. He rubbed the skin above his eyebrow, placing pressure on where it hurt most in a feeble attempt to soothe the pain as the spontaneous migraine slowly ran its course in the dimness of his cluttered garage.

As he fought the migraine's stranglehold on his thoughts, it sounded almost like a voice had seeped through the persistent throbbing, whispering inside his head a single phrase...

...you're...next...

Then as fast as the migraine had risen, it vanished, the searing pain washing away like a footprint in the sand, his vision traversing back to normal, his thoughts crawling back to silence.

Kelly took a deep breath, letting his stress dissipate with a heavy exhale.

"*Everything's okay,*" he whispered to himself as he swung his car door open and hopped in. "*Don't let it get to you.*"

The radio immediately started playing the second he started the car. The familiar voice of CBC host Craig Clarke began talking through his car's speakers, accounting the events of the shooting, warning those on their way to work to avoid the area and the streets surrounding it. Apparently, there had been a total shutdown in the area, and talk of some sort of explosion at the Halifax Ferry Terminal, the commuting cars left in total gridlock on the surrounding streets. Kelly didn't think that would affect his drive to work, cutting across MacDonald Bridge connecting Dartmouth to Halifax.

Immediately Kelly was off to the police station where he could finally get a debrief on whatever was going on.

Not even Frank had reached out to him.

Not even a text.

First a shooting, now talk of an explosion!?

He was going to have some choice words for his colleagues when he rolled in, his walkie remaining utterly silent throughout his entire trip, like the entire communication system was down and out.

Radio host Clarke switched topics to the usual garbage, spewing information about some unrelated politics of The United States—as if that had any relevance to the city of Halifax right now, where a murderer was apparently on the loose.

It only took a few minutes to reach MacDonald Bridge from his place, and only a couple more to get to Halifax on the other side where the police station resided. A few cop cars raced by him across the bridge with their sirens blaring, the rest of the vehicles pulling off to one side to let them pass, a mere couple inches separating the side-view mirrors of the police cruisers and passenger vehicles. Kelly tried to catch a glimpse of who was on duty, but they sped by too fast for him to see.

Was the perp on the Dartmouth side?

He couldn't imagine that the ferry was operating after the shooting.

How would he get across?

He supposed he'd get a briefing soon enough.

Just not in the way he thought.

Kelly pulled off the bridge, driving a few more blocks through the north end, then pulled into the headquarters, where there were barely any cruisers on hand. It seemed that nearly the entire precinct was on the streets, hunting down *whoever* it was they were looking for. Maybe they had a hit, or at worst, some sort of rough description from the witnesses. It had been almost an hour since the shooting—*if CBC's information was reliable.* The incident occurred sometime before 7:00 AM. Kelly still couldn't believe that an hour had passed without receiving a call. He was beyond pissed.

Pulling into his designated parking spot near the entrance, Kelly zipped up his jacket, covering his firearm and badge, flicked off the engine, and made his way out toward the entrance doors. Kelly marched up the empty steps of the station and pushed open the double doors, facing the immediately noticeable hustle and bustle of his long-serving HQ—*marking the moment his entire life would be flipped upside down.*

It was as if the entire world had stopped to stare at him.

Every officer. Every rookie. Every single person.

They all dropped what they were doing, all standing in silence as they stared directly at Kelly Christopher, standing in the entrance of the police quarters.

It was silent.

It was still.

Kelly knew something was up.

The silence wouldn't last for long.

Two cops jumped him from either side as a third drew his gun, pointing the barrel directly at Kelly's chest as if he was public-enemy number one.

He didn't know how true that was.

Before Kelly could blink, one of the younger officers— *known loosely to Kelly as Officer O'Reilly*—seized his hands on Kelly's shoulders, slew-footing him from behind and slamming him down to the ground. Kelly landed on his elbow and chest, struggling to fight back as the other officer began pinning his arm behind his back, barely able to restrain Kelly and his rage. One of the officers pressed his knee like a blade into Kelly's spine, securing him to the ground with the entire weight of his armoured body. Within seconds, the two cops were twisting his arms around, slapping their cuffs on his wrists and holding him down like a rabid dog.

Then came the Charter of Rights and Freedoms. Kelly barely heard a thing, the officer's words muffled by rage and dismay.

"Kelly Christopher, you are charged with the murder of Officer Zoe Stevens. You have the right to remain silent. You have the...."

His heart dropped to the depths of his chest, the bewildered eyes of his colleagues and friends watching in silence as he was hauled across the station.

The murder of Officer Zoe Stevens?

What was he talking about?

Zoe was...dead?

Kelly felt a massive knot develop in his stomach, his mind repeating the words of Officer O'Reilly as he was forcefully dragged behind the processing counter and toward the cells.

Murder...? Zoe...? Dead...?

It didn't make any sense.

Not a single person in the station heard his pleas for help or irritable exasperation, as if *all* those decorative years of service and advocacy meant *nothing* to his colleagues, who watched him as if he were just another criminal to be processed.

The feeling of abandonment would continue for hours as they left him in the dark solitude of his cell, the same cell whereby night's edge, his entire reality would be turned inside-out and backwards.

Kelly didn't know it, but over the next twenty-four-or-so hours, the brazen accusation of the murder of Officer Zoe Stevens, his backstabbing friends and colleagues, and the stinging resentment that was building up inside him would be the   *least*   of   his   already   mounting   problems.

5

It had only been eight minutes since Frank McDowell called the headquarters, when they dialled him back to share the news. He was downstairs at the ferry terminal when they called, beginning to ask a few of the shaken witnesses what they had seen, praying that one of them might have another perspective or video that would prove the atrocious reality he was about to face wrong, that Kelly was somehow in the right, and wasn't the barbaric murderer the security footage showed him to be. So far, Frank was getting anywhere, but he'd keep trying. He'd scrounge up every detail available.

When he answered the phone, it was Sergeant Major Mickey Nelson on the line. Before Frank could even say hello, the Sergeant cut in.

"We got him, Frank. He's here."

Frank was confused.

They caught Kelly?

They only just found out he was the culprit.

How could they have possibly caught him so fast?

It was like the Sergeant was reading his mind because he answered that question too.

"He just walked in, Frank. Like it was another day of work. One of the rookies took him down, read him his rights. He's locked up for processing now. You better get down here."

"He just walked in?"

"Yes. It doesn't make any sense."

He was damn right.

It didn't make any sense.

Why would Kelly simply go back to the office, knowing what would happen to him if he did?

"We'll wait for you before digging any further. And Frank, one of the boys checked his gun. There are two shots missing."

Sergeant Mickey didn't wait for a response. He hung up the phone, leaving Frank to stand alone in the glass-ridden lobby of the Halifax Ferry Terminal, surrounded by the rest of the squad, each one of them listening to the words he shared with the Sergeant Major, all within eyesight of Zoe's corpse, still warm, lying motionless on the ground. Without acknowledging any of the other officers, Frank stormed out of the building, ignored the camera crews and inquisitive civilians, hopped into his cruiser, flicked on the sirens, and drove back to the office to meet Kelly—*face-to-face.*

6

Kelly waited alone in his own private cell. A large bruise had formed where the cadet had driven his knee into Kelly's back right before they slapped the shackles on his now-swollen wrists. The kid that took him down was barely twenty-five years old but was built like a linebacker for the Saskatchewan Roughriders, Kelly feeling the aftermath of the boy's brutal takedown.

But the physical pain was *nothing* compared to the unsettling irritation he felt from the lack of clarity between the station and himself, the officers not answering any of his questions, leaving him entirely in the dark as he shouted endless profanities from the seclusion of his own private cell. The only info he *did* have was what O'Reilly had said to him just after taking him down.

'You're being arrested for the murder of Zoe Stevens.'
Kelly didn't believe it.
Zoe couldn't be dead.
He liked Zoe.
She was one of the best.
How could they think he was capable of killing her?

Kelly found himself fighting back the tears, the only thing keeping them inside was his wrath.

"Assholes!" He yelled from the confines of his cell. Once this was all cleared up and he got out of this jail cell, he would make sure O'Reilly would get the night shift for the rest of his career. *That's if Kelly didn't get him fired instead.*

But that thought faded, replaced by the image of burying Zoe Stevens beneath the dirt, a folded flag on her coffin, her husband Jessie left alone. She had such a bright future ahead of her—*so much promise.* Kids, her career, there was so much left on the table for her to experience. Now there was nothing, taken away by some twisted monster.

And they think he did this!?

There were no words, no reasoning, only pain and confusion taking the place of sanity's foothold.

Kelly stood up from his rickety prison bed, walking to the bars and yelling down the hallway again for anyone to hear. He cursed, screamed, hollered, begged, and cursed some more, all amounting to nothing. The cell-wing the boys had tossed him in was completely unoccupied, a few walls away from the next prying ear.

Screw it, he thought, laying back down on his overused cot. He wouldn't talk to anyone unless they wanted to speak with him first. Then when they did, Kelly was sure he could clear his name in seconds.

Surely Donna would have already told them about his whereabouts at the time of the shooting. He was home when he found out that someone had even been killed. Wasn't that proof enough? Of course, Kelly didn't have any evidence of being home at the time, just his word-of-mouth. He knew alibis like that never held up in court, but it didn't matter.

Frank would see.

Frank would get him out of this mess.

There's not a chance in hell that Frank would believe he was capable of murdering Zoe. They have been partners for too long—*friends long before that.* They knew each other like the back of their hand, and neither one of them were murderers.

Thinking about the words he'd say about Zoe at her funeral, confident he'd be out of this cell before long. He'd talk about how strong she was, never wavering in the line of duty. She always knew what to do in every situation; a trustworthy officer any cop would be lucky to have as a partner. He'd talk about how he could have seen her grow into the role of Chief Superintendent someday, leading the next generation of female cadets. Of course, that would never happen now. That was taken away from her. And Kelly wouldn't rest until the culprit was captured, locked behind bars just as he was in the killer's stead. But for now, it was merely a waiting game, counting down the minutes until they released him from his cell, along with a formal apology and a few other repercussions he'd have to devise.

Unfortunately, minutes turned into what felt like hours. It was hard to tell how long had *actually* passed, the *idiots* outside leaving him in the cell with nothing but the clothes on his back and the thoughts in his head. Kelly's wrists remained bound, which was certainly against protocol, not that *any* proper procedures had been followed during the disorder. Of course, if he were on the other side of this, tossing the culprit responsible for the death of Zoe Stevens into the slammer, he'd have also made the bastard's stay just about uncomfortable as humanly possible. This thought pissed off Kelly even more, knowing he was in here, while the shooter was still at large, free to run and hide under the veil of Kelly's incarceration.

Every twenty minutes or so, Kelly would stand up from his tiny bed, stretch around the cell, bang on the door a few times, shout through the tiny peep-hole for no-one to hear, then sit back down, waiting for someone to show up and release him. He could barely lie down comfortably, his wrists still bound behind his back, the throbbing pain still ever-present from O'Reilly's massive takedown.

Kelly must have repeated this routine a half dozen times before someone came knocking on the door, the sound of the metal latch releasing from the outside, a familiar face standing before him. Lingering in the open doorway, staring directly at Kelly with an adverse, exhausted look on his face, was Frank.

His broad frame completely blocked the entrance as Kelly rose to his feet to meet him. There was no friendly greeting, no usual handshake, and no welcoming embrace as the two friends—*now foes*—stood face to face in the tiny confines of Kelly's cell.

Kelly felt his temper rise, taking a step toward Frank, ready to explode at his partner for everything he had been through.

"Frank, I don't know what has gotten into you and everyone else, but you take these cuffs off of me at once, and start making some *God damn* sense. There's going to be hell to pay for whatever nonsense you idiots are trying to pull. I mean it, Frank. This is going straight to the top."

Kelly took a breath, the lack of response from Frank making him even more angry.

"Jesus Christ, Frank. Aren't you going to tell me what the hell is going on? I mean, what am I even doing here? I should be out there, catching whoever it was that killed Zoe, not locked up in here like some kind of animal!"

No response.

Kelly turned away, physically fighting the anger within to try and spit out a single calm sentence.

"Frank," he said calmly, clenching his teeth. "Will you at least tell me what this is all about?"

Frank stared him down, scanning him from head-to-toe, carefully observing his mannerisms and twitches—like he was studying his words and demeanour—*like he was investigating him.* Kelly's partner looked to his right, giving a half-hearted nod.

Immediately officer Price and Collins marched in, not speaking a word, not even making eye-contact. Instead, they each grabbed one of Kelly's wrists and hauled him out of the room and down the hallway toward the interrogation room.

To get to the interrogation room, one needed to pass through the main room where ninety percent of the force operated. It was there where Kelly got to see the looks of misery and grief on the faces of everyone at the station, a final confirmation that this truly was a living nightmare, and Zoe was indeed dead. One could have heard a pin drop when he entered the room, the entirety of the force completely stopping what they were doing to stare at him—*to examine him*—and observe as their shackled colleague and lead detective was escorted toward the interrogation room. There must have been over thirty officers scattered across the room, some at their desks, some walking around, every pair of eyes locked upon Kelly as he felt helpless to stare back. Every single person in the silent room watched as Kelly Christopher was dragged against his will into the interrogation room of his own station, the heavy metal door closing behind him and latching shut.

Over the next several hours, the heinous act was revealed to Kelly in the form of security footage from the scene of the crime. The first time he saw the video, his jaw dropped like a hammer on a nail.

The man in the video—*it could have been his twin, if he had one.*

He looked identical in every possible way.

There was no doubt about it; whoever committed the crime must have been trying to frame Kelly for it.

They *had* to have been.

It was too perfect, the crime too obviously executed. The suspect was dead centre in the camera's view, clear as day as he marched in through the entrance doors of the ferry terminal.

The standard-issue pistol was at his left hip, just like Kelly's.

The gold badge on his belt, just like Kelly's.

Even the man's clothes matched Kelly's current attire.

The video wasn't the only evidence they had against Kelly, either.

Apparently, his pistol was missing two rounds from its clip, matching the number of times the shooter fired. Kelly's fingerprints were found at the scene of the crime, imprinted on the front of the entrance doors where he pushed them open with his bare hands. Everything was falling in place against him, the evidence wholly unexplainable and insurmountable as Frank laid everything out on the table. Kelly's only alibi was that Donna had said he was at home during the shooting, confirming what he had already told them. But that was only her word against stacks of damning evidence. Kelly knew their word alone wouldn't hold up in court.

They *did* find camera footage from the MacDonald Bridge of the same make and model of Kelly's car driving across toward the station at about the time he said he crossed—*even the licence plate matched*. But the heavy rain and high winds made it impossible to identify the face of the driver inside, making the evidence almost unusable in a case defending his innocence.

Every domino was stacked to fall entirely against him. Whatever kind of set-up this was, it had been executed flawlessly.

Kelly tried to think of anything else that could buy him some sort of leverage, but the only image running through his mind was the footage of Officer Stevens being brutally gunned down by *his* imposter. He couldn't believe it—*and watching it over and over and over again was pure torture.* To think that his colleagues—*that Frank*—thought he was capable of doing such a thing made it even worse. He kept expecting to wake up from this nightmare, a constant feeling of disbelief trudging over him, but the veil was never lifted, the derangement staying put.

And Frank had ceaseless questions for him, all of which he couldn't answer.

Where did you go after the explosion?

Was there anyone helping you?

Why show up at the station if you knew what was going to happen?

Then the more obvious question…

Why did you do it?

After every empty answer, Frank would note something down in his black book then move on to the next. Kelly knew the drill. He had been on the other side of the interrogation table countless times before. But every open-ended inquiry dangled more and more suspicion in Frank's eyes. Every single question Frank asked was damning, as if they had *already decided* it was Kelly that gunned her down, never once pondering the notion that someone else had done it in his place—*which was the truth no one seemed to want to believe him—or even listen to for that matter.*

This would go on a few more hours, taking a short break for a bland sandwich and glass of tap water brought in from one of the newer officers. Not once did Kelly ask for a lawyer, determined to get through this on his own, to clear his name in the eyes of that law, and the eyes of Frank. It was most likely a terrible decision, not bringing in outside help, but he *was* innocent, and he was going to prove it. He was going to get to the bottom of this, no matter what it took. Of course, that was a lot harder to do when shackled to a table, getting questioned by someone who already had Kelly pinned as a psychotic murderer.

The first round of questions had taken their toll.

Kelly was exhausted, and he didn't seem to be making any headway.

There's only so many curse words one could say in the run of an interrogation before they start to take their toll, and Kelly was pretty sure he invented some new ones for not only Frank, but the officers behind the one-way mirror as well.

After about twenty minutes of sitting alone in the interrogation room in the late evening of October the 8th, he was finally thrown a bone. The heavy metal interrogation room door creaked open, revealing the only face he wanted to see in his moment of dire tribulation—the look of his loving and crying wife, Donna.

She immediately rushed straight to Kelly, wrapping her arms around his aching torso, holding him tight like how a boa-constrictor catches its prey. Tears and mascara streamed down her face, the entirety of the police force surely watching from behind the mirrored glass.

"Kelly, what's going on?" Her voice was hysterical, like she had been holding in her emotions all day, only now being allowed to release them "I know you didn't do it. You couldn't have. Please tell me that wasn't you!" Tears raced down her face, her makeup running alongside. Her hair was a mess, and her eyes were exhausted, just like his. It looked as if she'd been through a two-week bender. *Maybe three.*

"I didn't do it. I promise."

"Oh, I know. I know. I know." Donna released her stranglehold for a moment, looking down at the shackles then bursting back into an array of tears. "How could you have? You were next to me all night. We got up together as always. They just aren't listening to me, Kelly." Finally, Donna released him, walking around and sitting across from him at the table, where Frank had just interrogated him for several hours. Kelly knew everyone was still listening behind the one-way mirror, including Frank, but he didn't care. He was just relieved to have even a minute alone with his wife.

Kelly held back his own exhausted tears, holding strong for them both, even though it proved more difficult than even he anticipated. "What else did you tell them?"

"Well, just that we got up as we usually do. Had our morning coffee and toast, and that you didn't know about the shooting until you saw it on the news, and that you were upset that they didn't call you right away."

"Anything else?"

"Not really. I told them you left around quarter to eight, drove off in your cruiser, and that you were never near Zoe or the ferry terminal".

"And what did they say?"

"Nothing really, Frank just took some notes. "You don't think Frank honestly believes you'd be capable of killing Zoe, do you? You're practically brothers. He must know you'd never do that."

Kelly looked directly toward the one-way mirror to give his answer, knowing Frank would be listening from the other side, "You'd think so." He shifted his attention back toward Donna. "When you go home tonight, see if you can't find any evidence that I was home this morning, at the time of the shooting."

"Like what?" Donna said, finally halting the tears.

Kelly thought for a moment, thinking about his regular morning routine. There weren't really any moments that came with a time stamp.

"I don't know. Maybe there's a setting on the T.V. to see what time I turned it on? Or maybe the coffee pot? Although I'd doubt it."

"I'll check anyway. Anything else?"

Kelly thought for a moment. There was only one last thing that popped into his mind that she could really help him with. The more and more he tried to think of any evidence he could find to support his case, the more and more he realized how screwed he truly was. Maybe he *should* have called his lawyer...

"Yeah," Kelly said, holding her hands with his on the cold metal table. "Say a prayer for me. I think I'm going to need it."

Neither Donna nor Kelly knew how true that was.

7

Officer Price escorted Donna out of the interrogation room, leaving Kelly alone once again—*but not before enduring some carefully-chosen swear words from the depths of her darkest imagination.* On her departure, Donna didn't lock eyes with a single person.

Not Frank.

Not Price.

Not Collins.

Nobody.

If even one person tried to stop her to talk or sympathize, she felt like she'd rip their head clean off. Luckily, no one was brave enough—*or stupid enough*—to make-face, and she was able to leave without hassle or confrontation.

Donna made her way out of the station, hopped in her car, and drove directly home. She could have run a red light and wouldn't have even noticed. Her mind was completely distracted, replaying the events of today over and over in her head like a broken record. Donna wasn't even thinking about the upcoming school inspection, nor did she even care about calling in to inform her colleagues why she'd been uncharacteristically absent the entire day. However, if even one of them flicked on the news today or scrolled through social media, they'd know in a heartbeat. Kelly's name had been plastered over every single headline, tweet, news report, and everything in between. And if it weren't for the bars of his jail cell, an angry mob would have already executed him on the spot, despite his innocence.

Parked at a red light, she looked down at her phone, her home-screen littered with endless notifications and text messages. She had thirty-seven text messages and twenty-two missed calls, some from family and friends making sure she was alright, but mostly from news-reporters looking to get an inside scoop on the story.

Vultures.

The light turned green, and after a few honks from an asshole behind her, she continued ahead.

A cop accused of killing another cop—*with no apparent motive or reasoning*—that was a story every journalist in the world wanted in their back pocket, a story that was going to make national headlines for sure. And for it to happen in such a normally peaceful and easy-going city, *well it was just unheard of.* She imagined what the headlines would say as she sat behind the wheel of her Civic, the radio silent in the evening light; *Horror in Halifax, Terror at the Terminal, Betrayal in Blue.* They'd come up with something more creative and damning than that, she thought to herself.

She was no reporter.

And Kelly was no killer. She had to find a way to...

"Fuck!"

Donna swerved to the left to avoid a car pulling out in a four-way intersection, their horn blaring as her right bumper narrowly dodged oncoming traffic. She yanked the car back between the lines, her heart racing, her head pounding. In her rearview, she could see that she had just bee-lined through a four-way stop. An accident was the last thing they needed right now.

Her pulse was nearly back to normal as she pulled into their attached garage, the door automatically lowering behind her as she flicked off the engine to her car.

Then—*with no one around to see or judge*—Donna Christopher burst into an uncontrollable stream of tears.

Gripping her hands to the wheel, alone in the damp darkness of their two-car garage, Donna let it all out. Her mascara ran down her already tired face, her tears staining her favourite purple blouse. She didn't care. The insanity of the day was more than she could handle, and there was no one to lean on—no one to comfort her in their darkest hour. She thought about calling her sister but didn't think she could stomach the words. No, for the next ten minutes, she would release everything she had, then when it was all gone, she would get out of her car, walk into her home, and search for anything that might help clear Kelly's name.

One step at a time.

After a few more quiet moments to herself, Donna finally managed to pull herself together, dragging her exhausted body out of the car and into their home. That's when she noticed the horrible messy state the police officers had left their home in. While at the station—*watching Kelly get interrogated and berated through the one-way mirror*—Frank presented a search warrant, informing her there would be a top-to-bottom scouring of their home to search for any incriminating or absolving evidence, asking if she wanted to be present while they searched. Donna declined, wanting to stay at Kelly's side the entire time. Frank nodded, sending a few of his boys to go ahead with the search without her. *And now, coming home to the wake of their investigation, Donna couldn't believe the disastrous state of disarray they left behind.*

Her home had been completely ripped apart, every cupboard opened, every drawer emptied onto the floor. Not a single thing was where it should have been, the officers showing absolutely zero respect for both her and Kelly. It was as if they emptied every individual nook and cranny, tossing its contents across the room like mindless apes. Of course, there was nothing mindless about it. This was their way of enacting revenge for a crime Kelly didn't commit. *So much for being innocent until proven guilty.*

Donna took a shallow breath of irritation, slipping off her shoes and setting them in the now-empty shoe rack, the rest of her footwear scattered across the hallway in seemingly random directions. She didn't bother tackling any of the mess. She was too distraught to even think about cleaning up after the *assholes* that ripped apart her home. Instead, she stepped over the clutter, heading directly toward the kitchen, where the entirety of their cutlery and utensils had been shoved onto their tiled floor. The oven had been left ajar, their pots and pans resting out of place on the counter or floor—*as if Kelly was hiding something beneath the muffin tin.* Their sink was littered with dishrags and plates, a dumping ground for whatever didn't fit on the floor. She bit her lip, fighting the urge to hop back in her car, drive to the station, and smack Frank across his *smug* face with all her strength. For now, there were more important things to do, like finding any sort of alibi that could clear Kelly of this delusion.

After a long search for the television remote—finding it behind a stack of Tupperware containers left in the corner of the room—Donna turned on the twenty-two inch flatscreen sitting on their kitchen counter, flicked over to the 'settings' section searched for any type of user history that might prove Kelly had been home when he said he was. Donna never watched sports, so if she could find proof that the sports channel had been on in the early hours of the morning, it would at least be enough to show Frank and raise some suspicion about the case. She wasn't the best with technology, but from what she could tell, there was nothing on the TV that showed what channels they had watched and when. It was a long shot anyway, she thought, placing down the remote and moving to the next lead.

Their coffee maker was sitting on the floor by the fridge, the cord unplugged and dangling behind it. She raised it back to its usual position on the counter, plugging it in and waiting a couple seconds for the internal system to boot back up. There was a tiny digital screen on the bottom, where you could set the alarm, a timer, the temperature preferences, and a few other minor things. There was nothing she could find that proved Kelly had used it early this morning, even though she knew he had. He was always the one to start the pot in the morning.

She continued this process across the entire house, desperately looking for anything that could help prove Kelly's innocence, despite how much of a long shot it might be. But no matter how hard she searched, she kept coming up empty-handed. There wasn't one single thing he did in his morning routine that came with a timestamp. The towel was still damp from his shower, his coffee mug was still sitting half-full on the now-cluttered kitchen table, and his bed was still left unmade from getting up this morning. Kelly had interacted with all these things during his usual routine, but none of them could prove Kelly had been home during the shooting.

After a few hours of despairing investigation, Donna collapsed onto the sofa in their disordered living room, drained, distressed, and defeated. In Kelly's most dire hour, Donna had been left empty-handed, unable to scrounge even the slightest piece of evidence. She knew Kelly didn't do it. He was no monster. Her husband was as sweet and kindhearted as they came, dedicating his life to saving people, not killing them. She couldn't believe any evidence was even required to prove this. Surely Frank must have known this too, only running through the motions necessary to prove his friend and partner innocent.

There's *no way* Frank believed Kelly was the murderer the news stations were painting him out to be, did he?

Donna wasn't sure anymore, the state of her house proof enough that the station was no longer on her side. But was Frank? Was Frank genuinely going to try and get to the bottom of this, or was he just as blind as the rest of them? Only time would tell if Frank was for or against his lifelong friend and partner. Only time would tell if Kelly would walk from this a free man, or the next victim of a modern-day witch-hunt.

Only time would tell…

.8

... Ten minutes before contact...

Frank McDowell was losing his ability to think straight as he sat exhausted at his desk. The office staff had mostly shifted to the late-night crew, and a few reporters were waiting for any sort of interview so they could build on the *'Story of a Generation'* as they had been calling it. Well, this *story* was tearing Frank apart from the inside out. Even his ordinarily steady demeanour was wearing thin. In the last twelve hours...

...his best friend and partner murdered one of their own with no apparent incentive or motive...

...Donna hated his guts, having received an angry call about his boys tearing their house apart...

...the press was shredding them into pieces...

...and his superiors were calling on him constantly, asking for updates faster than he could come up with them...

It was too much for one man to handle. He had some help from his colleagues, but as far as he was concerned, this was his responsibility to face.

This was his case.

This was his life.

And he was going to get to the bottom of it, even if it killed him, for better or for worse.

But right now, he needed a break. He promised his wife he'd be home by ten, and she said she'd have a hot meal waiting for him, something he desperately needed.

Frank stepped up from his desk, covered in papers, notes, security footage tapes, evidence, and other case-related clutter. His office, which was habitually clean and organized, looked like a tornado had ripped through. There were papers, notes, wrappers, and leftovers everywhere.

Grabbing his refillable mug, Frank exited his office, heading down toward the break room to get what must have been his fifth refill since the interrogation alone. Of course, to get to the break room, you needed to pass by the cells, which were all empty but for two.

One held a guy they picked up a few hours ago for possession of an illicit substance, selling it down in the north end of Halifax. The other held his partner, Kelly, although he supposed it was fair enough to call him his ex-partner now. That traitor wouldn't be carrying his badge again. Frank would make sure of it, assuming he was guilty, which Frank was becoming more and more convinced of as time passed on.

But why do it?

That was the question that left Frank puzzled as he continued his way down the hallway toward the breakroom. There was no rhyme or reason for Kelly to do what he did.

He knew Kelly.

He loved Kelly.

He wasn't the type of man to shoot a cop, especially not without provocation. But he wasn't one to lie either—yet here he was, denying he was ever at the ferry terminal when there was clear-cut evidence he was.

It didn't add up.

He needed to keep digging.

Frank walked by Kelly's cell, the thick metal door standing between his partner and freedom. He doubted Kelly would ever be free again. Any competent judge, given the current evidence, would easily serve Kelly twenty-five years for first-degree murder, which was only one of the crimes Kelly was facing. There was still the matter of the mysterious bomb that went off in the ferry terminal, blowing out the windows and knocking the entire crowd off their feet. There were no traces of an explosion, no scorch marks, and no hazardous substances detected at the scene, yet it was clear that some energetic discharge had transpired. The camera footage had dropped off in wake of the blast.

Frank peeked through the grated peephole of the jail cell door to get a glance at his prisoner—*formerly his friend*. Kelly was lying on his back, staring blankly toward the ceiling. His hands had been released from his shackles after the interrogation on Frank's orders. He was constrained enough within the confines of his cell. There was no reason to torture him further. He *was* a decorated officer not too long ago—even if he was a killer of one now.

Frank didn't think Kelly even noticed him staring in. The holding cells weren't like they were in the movies, where they had steel bars captives could poke their hands through. These cells were built solidly, with heavily insulated steel doors, each equipped with a 12x6 grated peephole so officers could communicate and keep tabs on their prisoners. There was also a small slit where they could pass food through on plastic trays. Most of the time, the tiny cells held drunks, junkies, and brawlers. Rarely did they hold murderers—*and even more rarely did they keep cops as experienced as Detective Christopher.*

Frank realized he wouldn't ever see his friend as a free man again. Kelly would spend the rest of his life rotting in a cell, thinking about the family he tore apart—her family at home, *and* her family at the station—and that pissed Frank off. Maybe he *deserved* to rot. If he was guilty, Frank would see to it that he did.

But why didn't he simply give in to the questions?
It was over for him.

What else did he gain from lying?

Was there someone else involved, or was there something larger at play?

Kelly was a great detective.

One of the best.

Surely, he must know that it's over for him.

He must understand that he's never stepping out of that cell a free man.

Frank stepped away from the cell, unable to bear the sight of his friend in such an incarcerated state. He turned back down the hallway, away from the cellblock and toward the break room, where one of the late-night crew members, Officer Robertson, was sitting, eating a bag of Doritos while reading the paper leftover from the morning. Frank imagined there'd be *a lot* more to read in tomorrow's paper.

The two officers exchanged brief pleasantries, neither of them being overly well acquainted with one another, considering Robertson's recent transfer to this precinct. After their brief *hello*, Frank reloaded the *Keurig* with a shot of Newman's Extra Bold, waiting for his oversized mug to fill for the fifth time today, considering if he should try and talk with Kelly or not on his return, not as a cop, but as a friend. Maybe he could somehow dig up some more information by adding a personal touch. Maybe there was something Kelly could shed some light on, something he didn't want to say on the record. It was a long shot, but at this point, Frank was grasping at straws, looking for *any* sort of clue that could break this case wide open. His detective instincts told him that it was a fool's errand, but he was willing to try anything at this point. Desperation was starting to sink in, and he was getting tired of —

BANG!!

An explosion of immense proportions roared from the prison cells, shaking the building, causing Frank to drop his hot coffee to the ground. Officer Robertson didn't hesitate. By the time Frank's mug came to a rolling stop, Robertson was already at the door, his gun drawn, and his body on the move. Frank did the same, gripping his standard-issue P226 in his hand and making his way toward the source of the blast.

An alarm pounded throughout the building, loudly repeating with ear-piercing consistency as everyone in the police station reacted to the unknown source of the eruption. Frank could hear shouting from down the hallway toward the cellblock, as well as Robertson's radio patching in and out as people hollered inaudible commands through the intercom.

Whatever just happened, it was big.

Without hesitation, Frank sprinted out of the breakroom and down the hallway, Officer Robertson in tow as his temporary backup. They reached the cell-wing in seconds, where smoke and dust swirled around in the dark air. The emergency lights had replaced the overhead lights, the heavy debris cloud blanketing the hallway in thickening darkness. Frank squinted through the dust, covering his mouth with his uniform as the swirling particulates filled his lungs. It was *damn*-near impossible to see what had happened, but from where Frank stood at the edge of the cell blocks, it looked as if one of the cell walls had utterly collapsed.

Was it?

Fuck, it was...

It was Kelly's cell...

Frank dashed down the hallway, uncaring about any structural damage that might have occurred in the blast. Robertson stayed cautiously behind, his gun at the ready as he struggled to see through the dust and smoke.

Frank's first guess was a bomb. But as he got closer, he noticed no residue or fires typical of a blast—*exactly how it had been at the Halifax Ferry Terminal*. The entire ceiling had collapsed along with the load-bearing wall, the dust so thick Frank could barely see the tip of his gun.

"Kelly!" Frank yelled, forcing his way toward the entrance of Kelly's cell, crawling over the settling rubble, half-prepared to find his friend's body covered in stone and brick amongst the blast. It was impossible to tell what had happened, but as he approached the cell, that's when he started to see the aftermath of the explosion. The metal door keeping Kelly locked inside was bent and smashed, curled like a piece of warped tin, resting within the dust on the far side of the hallway as if it had been blown outward, the explosion emanating from within Kelly's cell.

"Jesus," Frank said, coughing as he stepped closer for a better glance, Officer Robertson no longer able to see him through the smoke.

The grit in the air stung against Frank's face, his eyes watering as he fought his way forward. It was getting harder to breathe, the air wholly littered in smoke and residue, but he pushed ahead anyway, needing to find Kelly for himself. It looked as if not only the door had been blasted off, but the entire wall had collapsed, blown outward from within the cell. That wall was reinforced brick. It would take *one hell of an explosion* to knock that down. The closer and closer Frank trudged into the confines of the debris-filled cell, the more and more he expected to find his lifeless partner's body lying buried under the rubble, skin covered in dust and rock and blood.

He prepared himself as he stepped inside, wanting nothing more than for Kelly to be somehow alive and well.

Frank climbed into the centre of the cell and desperately dug through the fallen debris, frantically looking for any signs of life. He scoured Kelly's cell from corner to corner, tossing away broken pipes, clumps of shattered brick, chunks of cement, and shards of metal, searching every square inch of the tiny cell, confirming a truth Frank would never have expected.

Kelly wasn't dead.
Kelly wasn't here.
Kelly had escaped.

Part II
Contact

9

There wasn't enough time in the day for Kelly Christopher to make sense of the chaos that occurred since he woke up this morning. Despite his extensive years working as a detective, there was nothing Kelly could deduce within the last several hours that seemed rational or connected. He didn't know what was worse, the fact that he was locked up for the murder of Zoe Stevens, or that people believed he could do such a thing—*his partner Frank included*. The only person on his side was his wife. Once this was over and he was free—*an outcome that seemed to dwindle by the minute*—Kelly was going to take Donna on an extended vacation, to anywhere of her choosing, and he was going to make his office pay for it. He was going to go after them for that and much more once he had his freedom restored.

But Kelly didn't want to focus on that now, the unending hours of frustration and confusion were starting to take their toll. He was tired, just wanting to get some sleep. He answered too many accusing questions today, and imagined he was in for another long day of interrogations tomorrow as Frank built up his case against him. Kelly knew Frank was a good detective, but was he good enough to see that Kelly didn't do it? *He'd find out soon enough.* It wasn't exactly a thought of comfort, but he still had a little faith left, even though it was waning.

Kelly rested on his lumpy cot within the tiny confines of his holding cell, his consumed mind barely able to keep his eyes open as sleep slowly overtook him.

◇◇◇◇◇

When Kelly opened his eyes, he was no longer resting on the hard bed in his tiny jail cell but was instead standing next to his wardrobe in the familiar surroundings of his home in Dartmouth. The room seemed different than normal, slightly offsetting in a way he couldn't really comprehend. It's like the entire room had been discoloured, varying shades of grey replacing the normally warm tones beige and blue. A dim glow shone in through the windows, Kelly unable to see the street outside, a thick fog obscuring his vision. He had only just begun to grasp his dim surroundings when he heard a heavy breathing sound begin in a low and repetitious manner, echoing from the darkness of their attached bathroom. A deep inhale would be followed by moments of silence, quickly matched with a long scratchy exhale, a faint growl stirring amongst the droning silence.

He tried to peer into the bathroom, but his bathroom was engulfed in the same fog that lingered outside, the incessant gasps repeating themselves in the grey darkness. After a few deep breaths, the bathroom light began to flicker, shimmering erratically as the fog oscillated in obscurity.

Kelly tried to speak out, to call for whatever lurked in the quivering darkness, but his voice fell silent, unable to speak as his gaze remained focused ahead. When his voice failed, he instead tried to step into the bathroom, but no matter how hard he pushed himself, his legs wouldn't budge. They were glued to the floor as the dull breathing continued from beyond the fog.

Slowly, the peculiar grasp that held his legs in place crawled up his body, causing his limbs to sink into paralysis. Kelly was helpless to watch as he waited for the darkness within his shimmering bathroom to reveal itself.

And it wouldn't take long.

Kelly listened as the droning hums of the shadow's breath was slowly replaced by the distant screams of his wife—a voice he could recognize anywhere—shrieking in terror from the ominous fog as Kelly pushed with all his might to reach her—with zero success. His wife's frail whimper echoed across their home, and Kelly remained helpless to watch and wait—and listen.

"No, please, God, no! Stop!" His wife's voice called out, then, with a final shriek of pain, the screams ceased, the silent breathing continuing in its place.

Kelly waited as the faint glow of the bathroom's glimmering grey light shone into their bedroom, his heart racing, his eyes lingering, the fog beginning to spread across the bedroom. The harder Kelly tried to press toward the bathroom—toward his wife—the more he found himself paralyzed, frozen on the spot, unable to break free from the shadow's grasp. He knew she was suffering, he felt it in his core, but there was nothing he could do to help, forlorn to watch, waiting for the unknown to step out from beyond the fog.

After a few more repetitious breaths from the darkness, Kelly began to see the flickering of faint shadows dancing within the grey, followed by the light tapping of footsteps scraping against the bathroom tiles, the shadows growing larger and larger, the breathing becoming louder and louder. Kelly felt his chest tighten—the darkness ready to reveal itself before him.

Then he saw her.

He saw Donna—stepping out from the fog and into the dim glow of the grey light, her shadow flickering on the wall behind her like a silhouette caught in a flame. Blood dripped down from her right eye from a long gash that had been gorged across her cheek up toward her forehead, as if a blade had sliced up the side of her face. Her eyes were as black as night, staring directly at Kelly like a hollow void. Donna's arms were outreaching, as if calling for Kelly to come to her, even though he was helpless to stay put and watch his wife suffer from across the room.

She took a single step toward him, blood falling from her right eye like a streaming tear. Her jaw was unhinged, cracking back and forth in a grinding manner. Kelly could tell she was trying to speak, whispering so dimly that he could barely hear her, Donna's groans growing louder and louder as she slowly inched toward him from the void. Her voice was scratchy, whimpering as if every word resulted in insurmountable torment—yet, she spoke anyway—directly to Kelly— whispering nonsense over and over as blood oozed from her facial gash...

"...no time no time no time no time no time no time..."

Her voice grew louder and louder, traversing from hallow whispers to emphatic shrieks, roaring harsher than any woman should be able to cry. Over and over she screamed at him, repeating the same two words until they became stamped in his brain, her jaw scraping unnaturally from side to side as blood dripped down her cheek and onto the floor below. Kelly couldn't look away--couldn't close his eyes—and couldn't run. He could only watch as his wife's possessed body tormented him to utter madness.

"...no time no time no time no time no time no time..."

Kelly's eyes burst open, his heart throbbing, his skin and hands covered in sweat, the words *no time* bouncing around in his head like jagged stones. *It had all been a nightmare.* Yet, the vividness of the dream lingered, his mind unable to shake the image of his mutilated wife crying to him, as if begging for the pain to end.

It was only a dream, Kelly.

Shake it off.

His blood pressure slowly crept back to normalcy.

It was only a dream.

Somewhere down the hallway, Kelly heard approaching footsteps as he stared blankly into the ceiling. He listened as the steps grew louder, echoing from down the hall, most likely coming from the reception/office area, heading toward the break room or one of the staff bathrooms. Then, when the footsteps were at their loudest, they stopped, and Kelly knew someone was staring at him from outside the cell.

He didn't care who it was.

Not unless he had a full pardon.

Kelly just wanted to be left alone right now, the visions of his wife haunting his mind. He continued to stare at the ceiling, the stranger's breath easy to hear through the grated peephole.

I'm still here, Kelly felt like shouting at the onlooker. *Feel free to piss off now.*

It was like the stranger heard him, and the footsteps began again, teetering off and fading as Kelly continued to stare at the lifeless white ceiling. *Good,* he thought. He felt like an animal at the zoo, locked in his cage for all to observe.

Toss me a treat, and I'll do a trick, he snorted internally.

Pricks.

He closed his eyes, imagining himself lying in his bed at home, Donna snuggled close by his side. What he wouldn't give to be resting beside her right now.

Soon he'd be free of this hell.

They'd finally come to their senses and let him go.

Soon enough.

Kelly heard another breath from behind the locked door—*deep breathing*—sounding like that of an obese slob.

Just go away, Kelly repeated in his mind as another heavy breath whispered through the grate.

Just…go…away…

Another breath, louder.

Another…

Another…

Passing the threshold of irritation, Kelly opened his irritated eyes to face the ceiling—

—something had changed.

The room had grown dark.

Was it lights out already?

That wasn't until 9:30 PM, wasn't it?

Kelly rose from his cot, planting his feet on the cold cell floor. He looked up at the light—*burnt out*—leaving him in darkness.

Typical, he scrutinized.

Kelly walked up to the peepholes and looked through, but from what he could tell, he was alone.

There was no-one there.

Yet, another breath.

Then another.

And another.

Kelly felt his blood pressure slightly rise, the room feeling a tad chillier than average, like the window was left open on a stormy winter's night.

Another breath.

Another…

"Frank? That you?"

Another breath.

Another…

This time it was from behind him.

Kelly could feel the hairs on his wrist rise high into the air, like a sort of static electricity was building all around him.

Of course, that was nonsense.

He was alone in the cell.

He was alone.

Another breath.

A faint smell of rot and decay seemed to rise from the concrete, swirling around the room and lingering in his nostrils. Kelly felt the brush of freezing air across the back of his neck and down his spine.

Then a breath.

Then another.

He turned to face the darkness of the cell, but—*there was nothing.*

His cell was empty.

To his left was his prison cot, and to his right, a metal toilet and pedestal sink bolted to the brick walls. Besides himself and his sanity, that was all that lingered within his barren cell. He reached around to the back of his neck, rubbing it with his trembling hand. It felt cool, almost damp.

Was he losing it?

Kelly walked over to the shallow sink—*shallow so none of the real criminals could drown themselves*—and spun the tap. No water came out. He tried the other valve. *Nothing.*

Was the power out?

That would explain the lights, but there should still be some water in the pipes, shouldn't there?

Another breath.

Kelly froze in his imprisoned tracks.

Another breath.

Another…

Another…

They were growing faster.

They were becoming louder.

They were coming from right behind him.

The smell of putrid decay returned, engulfing the room as if it was being injected into the air from an overhead vent. Kelly's shaking heart pumped through his chest, his fingers trembling, his mind racing. He felt more fear than he ever felt before in his life—*and he didn't even know why.*

Then from behind him, a deep and gentle whisper caressed the hairs at the back of his neck, replacing the ominous breathing that seemed to echo from the void.

The voice was coarse...

The tone was dark...

The words were simple...

"*...no...time...*"

The words that haunted Kelly in his dream twisted their way into reality, bouncing off the cell walls, emanating from directly behind him.

Another breath grazed the back of his in the dark...

Kelly knew—somehow—he was no longer alone.

Against every instinct, Kelly Christopher spun around within the cramped confines of his cell—*and came face to face with a creature that would shatter his preconceived notions of reality.*

It lingered behind him in the shadows.

Its empty face towered above Kelly.

Its hollow eyes stared into the depths of Kelly's soul.

Its body swirled and twisted like a whirlwind of conjoined fog, and its stench flowed off it like a fountain of toxic mist.

Kelly wanted to scream.

He wanted to run.

He wanted to cower and hide.

But all he could do was return its hollow gaze as he found himself alone in a room with a creature that he immediately knew did not belong on this earth.

Kelly found himself in a trance, staring up at the dark translucent being, its shadow-like form slowly beginning to encapsulate him—*devour him—consume him.*

Kelly felt his energy slowly drain from his body, every inch of life squeezing from his pores as the shadow kept him under its paralyzed scowl. He became null and void to the power of the darkness overwhelming him.

His will to fight immediately began to fade...

His drive to survive slowly numbed to an empty shell...

His vision began to wane and shrink until all he could see was guzzling darkness.

Suddenly nothing mattered.

The crime he had been framed for...

The doppelganger in the video...

Zoe's death...

His wife...

It all faded from his mind...

It dissolved in the consuming mist...

But something inside him told him he was still there...

Something deep within kept the flame from being snuffed out for good—*and the flame brought back the warmth that had almost completely vanished.*

Slowly, he felt his blood pumping in his veins...

He felt the thickness of the cool air surrounding him...

He tasted the stench of the creature before him...

Then as fast as it had all faded, it rushed back to him in droves, every sense, every emotion, every fear, it all slammed back into his soul like a thousand bullets fired from a gun.

Kelly released a bellowing scream as he fended off the last of the creature's overwhelming grasp.

Then Kelly was back at the helm.

He had retaken control of his body.

He had retaken control of his mind.

Kelly turned away from the malevolent shadow—*doing his best to fend off the nagging sensation to submit his will to the darkness*—and retreated to the far side of the cell, his hands against the steel door, his knuckles bashing against the cold metal.

He pounded on the heavy steel, knowing the creature was slowly closing in from behind.

He slammed his hands against the door until blood began to drip from his fingers, his screams intense and terrified, his heart pounding from his chest.

Thud after thud, Kelly bashed at the door, wailing as hard as he could for someone to help.

He could feel the room growing colder, the stench rising in his nostrils as he desperately prayed for escape.

He didn't know what it was that lingered beside him...

But he knew it was wicked...

He felt it when it tried to consume him.

There was no doubt in his mind that whatever this creature was, it was evil beyond his darkest imagination.

Please God...Help...Please...

He thought of Donna and Frank.

He thought of the misery of never seeing them again.

Please...Please...

And for the first time in Kelly's short existence on planet earth, his prayer was answered.

The walls confining him within his cell burst outwards as if being yanked apart from the outside, the metal door contorting like cheap rubber and exploding out toward the far side of the hallway. The stone walls he had pounded on only seconds ago crumbled into a rising cloud of rubble and grit, bits and pieces of debris launching out in random directions.

He had no idea what was happening.

It didn't matter.

He now had a way out. And he was going to take it. But the quick sense of relief lasted only moments as the smell of rot and sulphur became even stronger than before within the dusty air.

The creature hissed again, its raspy voice cutting through the debris with a harshness that chilled the air.

"...no...time..."

Kelly did not look back.

He knew what awaited him if did.

Instead, Kelly rose rapidly to his feet, ignored the unknown monster lingering behind him, and pushed his way forward through the falling rocks and dust where his cell wall had stood seconds earlier. He bolted out of the cell, and made his way down the darkened hallway, putting one foot in front of the other as fast as humanly possible.

He would never forget the despair as the creature strove to consume him.

The loneliness...the fear...the emptiness...all originating from the inhuman creature that somehow materialized within his prison cell...all stemming from the cold black darkness pursing him through the rubble...all deriving from the creature, the monster, the darkness...The Entity.

10

Kelly hurried down the dimly lit hallway of the police station, getting as much distance between himself and his cell as he possibly could, never looking back to see .what followed. He didn't know if it was still behind him, whatever *it* was.

He didn't care.

He just knew he needed to get as far away from that monstrosity as he could.

His instincts screamed for him to flee.

Having spent most of his working career at this exact station, Kelly knew the quickest way out of the building. Dead ahead, a doorway would lead into the main room, where processing and reception would be waiting. From there, it was a straight shot toward the exit out of the main double doors across the room, and he wasn't going to let anyone stop him.

Not Frank.

Not that rookie officer that took him down last time, *nobody*.

That shadow wasn't going to get anywhere near him.

He would make sure of it.

Of course, he couldn't have ever anticipated how easy his escape was going to be.

No one could have, because when Kelly pushed through the cellblock doors into the central processing area, where the desks and work stations of almost every officer in the station were held, he was greeted by an unflinching, immobilized crowd.

Waiting directly in front of him, standing scattered across the oversized room, were about ten to fifteen officers—

—and not a single one of them was moving.

No one shouted to seize Kelly, nor did anyone draw a firearm with the intent to shoot. Instead, Kelly found fleet of officers that looked like they had been frozen in time.

They weren't moving.

They weren't budging.

They weren't even breathing.

It was like their bodies were disabled, fixed in place as if the shadow had seized their will to move. Officer Price, McDonald, Butler, not one of them budged, all of them frozen in whatever activity they were doing before all this began.

Kelly seemed the only body able to function. Everyone else was still as a statue. He would have stayed to get a closer look and try to understand, but he knew what the cause of this was—*he knew the devouring sensation that awaited him if he lingered any longer. He still felt it, enduring inside of him like a stagnant infection.*

He felt the shadow's presence, trailing close behind amongst the deadening silence as the putrid stench grew stronger and more intense with each passing moment.

And sure enough, back toward the direction of the collapsed cell, *was the shadow*, skulking ever closer, its translucent body like a misty fog—*a dark ghost*. It was stalking him, inching nearer and nearer, its arm outstretched as if to snatch Kelly, to haul away his mind to the darkness—*this time for good.*

He would not give it the chance.

Kelly burst ahead, dodging the debilitated officers incapacitated at their stations and making his way toward the entrance doors. He kept expecting the officers to react and draw their weapons or reach out and nab him, but they never did. They simply waited in place, utterly oblivious to Kelly's presence.

Their eyes were open, but they did not see...

Some were standing, but they did not move a muscle...

What was going on...

Kelly's heart pounded in his chest.

Nothing made any sense.

Nothing but the fear.

Kelly raced across the paralyzed room, dodging the two-dozen officers and civilians standing between him and freedom. Upon reaching the entrance doors, he looked back to see how much ground he gained on the creature—*and he immediately wished he hadn't.*

Every man...

Every woman...

Every soul...

They had all broken from their frozen trance, each of them rising from their spots at their desks and turning to face Kelly standing at the entrance doors.

And they were not their usual selves.

Each one of them glared directly at Kelly—*their eyes glazed over in a black haze, the whites entirely engulfed in void-like darkness.*

Their limbs began to twist and curl...

Their necks became crooked and bent...

Their bones cracked and curled...

None of them were moving—all remained frozen on the spot as they glared at Kelly with hollow eyes. And in the centre of it all, hovering inches above the ground and drifting slowly toward Kelly, *was the Entity.*

For a moment, the twisted souls remained motionless, each of them fixated on Kelly, each of them corrupted by the *Entity*'s ungodly grasp. Then one by one—*as if conducted by the Entity himself*—the twisted officers and civilians scattered across the room began to scream, replacing the deafening hush with ear-piercing shrieks of pain and terror.

Kelly watched as every person in the room—*many of whom he knew personally*—howled with a sinister tone at the *Entity*'s behest. Kelly forced his hands against his ears to try and muffle the high-pitched shrieks that filled the room. The windows of the office began to shatter—*slowly*. Kelly watched as the cracks in the glass spread up the windowpane, as if watching lightning split across the sky at a fraction of the speed, the endless screams echoing louder than what seemed humanly possible.

Kelly wasn't interested in listening further. He wanted to help them, to somehow release the *Entity*'s grasp over their contorted bodies, but relief from this nightmare was far beyond his reach.

The best thing he could do was run.

To run as far away as he could and never look back.

Kelly sprinted out of the station and into the cold rainy night.

The Entity grimly followed.

11

Frank McDowell emerged from Kelly's empty cell, climbing over fallen bricks, pipes and rubble, the dust lingering thick in the air. Shouting filled the hallway as other officers flooded in, trying to figure out what just happened, their guns drawn.

"It's clear!" Frank yelled, wary of any trigger-happy rookies as he stood half-blocked by the settling debris.

"What's going on?" A voice yelled back from down the hallway. Frank couldn't tell who it was from. "Is anyone hurt?"

"I don't know. And I don't believe so." Frank didn't know how anyone could have survived a blast strong enough to blow a door off its hinges. Kelly was absent from the scene, indicating once again that he was at large. He somehow escaped the blast and slipped by dozens of armed personnel. There was no way Kelly should have been able to walk away from this—*whatever this was.*

Two more officers appeared through the dust, holstering their weapons as Frank did the same, each of them looking at the damage done. The inch-thick metal door had buckled as if it were tin foil. There were thick dents smashed in the centre, and the hinges had been shredded right off the wall. A door-sized dent marred the far wall, and part of the ceiling had collapsed alongside a few support beams. Frank couldn't make heads or tails of it. There was no soot, no burn marks, no remnants of an explosion whatsoever besides the resting rubble. And not a man alive was strong enough to kick this door down.

What the hell happened?

Frank faced the other two officers, who shared his look of disbelief. "Did you see anything? Did you see Kelly?"

Both shook their heads no. "Sir, no-one came this way. At least—sir, there's something else you need to see."

There were two ways out of this building once Kelly exited the cell. To the left was the side emergency exit, but he would have needed to go past the break room to get to it, and Frank had come from that way the second he heard the explosion, and he was certain no-one had passed him. The second exit was through the main doors, but Kelly would have had to walk right by the entirety of the HRM police force and staff. There's *no way* he'd get by unseen.

Where on earth was Kelly?

For now, he'd make sure everyone was safe, assess the damage, and see what the other officers wanted to show him. "What is it?"

The two officers guided Frank and Robertson down the darkened hallway, hoping it would give some illumination toward whatever was going on.

It wouldn't.

The explosion in the cell wasn't the only damage done. The doors leading out from the hallway into the reception area were also knocked off their hinges, and every piece of glass in the room had been shattered, crumbled to pieces and scattered across the floor. Adding to the chaos, the front double doors of had been catapulted from their hinges and rested in the middle of Gottingen Street. Outside, an officer was already redirecting traffic to avoid the scene while two others pulled the doors back to the side of the road.

Frank looked back toward the two officers escorting him. "Are you telling me between the explosion, the hallway door, the main entrance being blown off, and every window getting shattered to bits, that no one saw a *God-damn* thing?"

Both officers shook their heads in response.

Frank felt his temper rise. He was already exhausted enough, barely keeping it together as it was. *Now this*? It was more than he could handle. He took a breath, closing his eyes for a moment to try and calm his frustration.

It wasn't their fault.

Get a grip.

He opened his eyes again, calming himself for his next question. "Is anyone hurt?"

"Not that I'm aware," Officer Price responded.

"Good. Find out what you can. See to any injuries. Robertson, and dispatch two cruisers to Donna Christopher's house and search the place. If I were Kelly, that's where I'd be headed."

The officers looked puzzled, the younger one speaking out to his superior. "Do you really think Kelly did this?"

"We made the mistake of assuming what Kelly would and wouldn't do. I'm not prepared to make that mistake again. Just get it done."

"Yes, sir," They responded in unison, then they were off, leaving Frank to figure out what he was going to do next.

What was he going to do next?

He had no idea.

With the camera footage, Frank thought to himself, making his way to the second security room in less than twenty-four hours. The last time he watched a camera recording, his entire life was spun around on a dime. He wasn't looking forward to sitting through another episode of gruelling footage.

What was he going to see this time?

He didn't even want to guess.

There were no cameras in the cells—*which was considered an invasion of privacy*—but the cell wing certainly held one, as did the reception area and bullpen, so if Kelly was behind these mysterious explosions, then there was no way one of the cameras didn't catch it. *Maybe he did have a partner in crime,* Frank wondered as he made himself comfortable in the security room chair. He rewound the camera footage to just before the explosions and clicked play, staring directly at the camera's view of outside cell #4—*Kelly's cell.* His tired eyes were strained to focus on the tiny computer screen. Unlike the camera at the ferry terminal, the one at the station was of lower quality, with scratchy black-and-white footage instead of high definition colour, a timestamp on the bottom right of the video, and no sound.

Frank watched closely at the cell door, searching for any clues or signs of intrusion, signs that perhaps a third party had somehow broken Kelly out of the cell. He could see himself in the footage, peering in through the grated peephole of the solid metal door moments before the explosion occurred, then walking down the hallway toward the break room out of the camera's view. No one else visited the cell after him.

Then came the explosion.

Although it wasn't as he had been expecting.

There were no flames or fire…

No bomb…

No explosive charge…

The cell door simply seemed to burst outward, as if smashed from the inside by an immense force. Dust and stone quickly spread throughout the hallway as the door landed on the floor, making it nearly impossible for the camera to spot anything entering or exiting the cell. Still, as far as Frank could tell, there was no sign of Kelly ever leaving confinement.

He was there when Frank checked the cell seconds before the blast.

He wasn't there immediately after the explosion.

Then where did he go?

It didn't seem possible.

Frank noted the exact time of the explosion.

20:32:12

Frank transitioned to the second camera's footage. That camera was fastened to the wall of the bullpen, the central processing area. If Kelly exited the cell block, he *must* have gone that way.

Frank clicked play, waiting for Kelly to make his appearance.

But he never did.

Instead, the hallway doors exiting the cell block burst open, as if a humongous gust of wind blew them wide open, the wood doors swinging entirely around and smashing into the wall, barely remaining on their cracked hinges. And again, from what Frank could tell, no one came those the doors. The first people to pass through the frame were the two uniformed officers rushing toward Frank in the cell block, their guns drawn and guard on high alert. He noted the time the doors swung open.

20:32:12.

In a hustle, Frank switched to the third camera's footage—*which was facing the main entrance doors of the police station*—praying it captured something that could make sense of it all, but again, he found no answers. Just as before, the main entrance doors seemed to simply blow off their hinges with no apparent cause whatsoever, landing on the sidewalk and sliding out to the center of the road in the rain. One second the doors were closed, and the next, they were lying on the Gottingen Street fifteen yards away. Frank was unable to make heads or tails of the entire scene. He noted the time in his black book.

20:32:12.

It didn't make any sense.

None whatsoever.

Frank felt his head throb, a sharp pain growing above his left eye, unsure if it was from exhaustion, frustration, lack of coffee—*or too much coffee*. He tried several more camera views before switching to the one that would make his spine run cold.

Frank checked another camera overlooking the processing area from a different angle, viewing most of his colleagues at the time of the blast. He rewound to just before the explosion, watching as his colleagues worked in the usual fashion, typing on their computers, sipping their nightcaps, and conversing amongst themselves, not knowing what was about to happen.

The first explosion was heard at exactly 20:32:12

At that time, everyone was undergoing their regular routine, completely oblivious to what was about to happen.

Frank fast-forwarded the footage exactly one second.

20:32:13

And in exactly one second, everything changed.

Not even one of the officers was facing the explosion at the back of the building.

They now appeared to be facing the main entrance doors toward the front, as if they all had flipped around instantaneously and harmoniously within the span of a single second.

And that wasn't all.

They weren't simply facing the exit.

Their arms were twisted and contorted.

Their jaws were open, as if they were screaming in pain.

And their bodies seemed bent and broken, all of them distorted in warped and unnatural ways.

All of them...

Every single person in the room...

Frank did not know how to respond.

He didn't know what to write.

He didn't understand.

He just stared blankly at the paused security footage, absolutely terrified at the sight before him.

He replayed the footage a few seconds, being left more and more confused each time he watched.

At *20:32:12* they were performing their usual tasks.

At *20:32:13*, everyone was contorted, bent, and screaming in pain.

Then at *20:32:14*, everyone was back to normal, facing the explosion and jumping into action as Frank had done.

It made no sense at all.

And more importantly, it terrified Frank.

It scared Frank to the core.

Frank paused, struggling to rationalize the inexplicable scene before him, but there was nothing he could derive that explained what it was he was looking at.

But that wasn't all.

Frank replayed those unnerving three seconds a few dozen times, and it wasn't until the twenty-seventh iteration, did he see something else that didn't belong. It was hard to tell—*the decade old camera barely able to capture what was going on*—but at the moment of the switch, when every staff member in the bullpen had turned to face the main entrance in their twisted forms, it looked as—*and he was sure this was some sort of smudge or glitch*—but it looked as if there were a drifting shadow hovering in the centre of the room, almost like a bulge of darkness had formed on the lens of the camera. Frank leaned in toward the screen to get a better look, but the quality was too poor to distinguish any features. The smudge *almost* looked like a translucent person—*a shaded mist in the centre of his twisted colleagues.* The shadow was only present for a single frame, appearing the moment the staff switched positions to their twisted forms, and disappearing as they traversed back to normality.

A fierce headache was harshly forming above Frank's left eye, his focus unable to concentrate on the artificial screen any longer, his mind too lost and exhausted to even think. He turned off the screen, casting a final glance at the lingering shadow in the centre of the camera's view, then made his way down to the briefing room to try and see if anyone else saw anything during the attack. He'd keep what he saw in the footage to himself—*at least for now*—until he refreshed his mind and could look at the tape with rejuvenated concentration. For now, Frank would chalk up what he saw in the footage as some sort of glitch in the system, even though every tremor in his aching body warned him that something more sinister was unfolding before his very eyes.

12

onna was alone in her kitchen when the police pounded on her door. She hadn't budged for over thirty minutes, her mind utterly exhausted by the day's events.

Her stomach growled unnoticed. Her head throbbed, but she was too defeated to grab some Tylenol from the medicine cabinet. Donna's mental capacity had withered away. The police had to knock a second time before Donna even reacted, her gaze focused on the barren far wall of her lonely kitchen.

Slowly, Donna rose from the wooden kitchen chair, her body making its way toward the front door, her mind lost somewhere in a scattered haze. At the third pound, Donna unlocked the door, revealing two unfamiliar officers with rain dripping from their caps.

"Ma'am—"

"What do you want," Donna replied, rudely cutting off the officer before he could speak.

"Ma'am, may we come in and have a word?"

Both officers barely looked older than she was. She hadn't seen either of them at any of Frank's BBQs in the past, but there were always new officers coming and going from the station, so it was hard to keep track. In her current state, Donna had little interest in speaking with anyone that wore the badge. As far as she was concerned, they were all gunning to put Kelly behind bars. They had *zero* intention to help her.

They were the enemy.

"You're not welcome here," Donna replied, slowly closing the door in their face.

"Kelly's escaped."

Donna stopped, opening the door again to face the two cops standing in the rain, not fully comprehending the words leaving the officer's mouth. "What did you just say?"

"There was an incident. Some kind of explosion. Kelly's missing."

"What do you mean Kelly *'escaped.'*" The needle of Donna's hysterics had shifted from anguish to agitation, distress to displeasure. "Kelly has no need to run. He's innocent! Why in God's name would he escape?"

Both officers, having been closer to Zoe than Kelly, remained silent. They had both seen the security footage of the shooting and had very little reason to believe Kelly was an innocent man. The only reason they were biting their tongue now was because of their respect for Frank, who told them to be as gentle with Donna as they could. It was a delicate situation no one wanted to be part of.

Donna continued her rant amidst the officer's silence. "So you're telling me he just opened the cell door and waltzed out the front door? Do you honestly expect me to believe that? What did *you* do to him!"

That was the explanation.

It had to be.

Those worthless *pigs* at the station wanted to get even with Kelly, wanted to make sure he suffered for what he *didn't* do.

This was all some sick game.

And she was done with it!

"I want you *out*! Get *out*!

"Ma'am, we're—"

"Now! Get the hell out of my house! *Get out!*" She didn't even look at them. She refused to. Their uniforms were a mockery to her very self. They were intruders in her home, and they made her feel worse than she already had, which five minutes ago she would have thought impossible.

"Donna." The officer said sternly. "We need to investigate the house for your husband. I'm afraid we have to insist."

"Do you have a warrant with you?" When silence answered, Donna knew enough. "Then insist on this." Donna flipped the officers the finger and slammed the door in their face, bursting into tears immediately.

Why was this happening to them?

What did they do to deserve this?

What had they done to deserve such divine punishment?

These were the questions Donna asked herself as she watched the two officers walk back to their cruiser parked on the side of the road in the rain. They hopped into their respective sides and stayed put, scouting the house as if Kelly would be stupid enough to walk down the sidewalk and through the front door.

What are you doing, Kelly?

Where are you?

Unaware within the sanctuary of her home, as she hunkered down under a heavy blanket, somewhere outside on this chilly, drizzly night, *Kelly was running for his life.*

13

No matter how fast Kelly Christopher ran, the stench of rot and decay clung close behind, as if to warn him of the ensuing shadow that pursued him across the city of Halifax. He was almost at the end of the block, sprinting as far as he could away from the police station and dashing toward Halifax's main drag before he made the mistake of looking behind him.

Drifting in the middle of the road—*hovering inches above the blacktop in the darkness of the night*—was the *Entity*. Its head twitched erratically, misty arms contorting, glitching in and out of its visibility. Overhead the streetlights flickered, as if the entire block was short-circuiting in the *Entity*'s dismal presence.

What was that thing?

What did it want?

If Kelly had his gun right now, he'd unload it at the demon.

Would that even do anything?

He didn't know.

He didn't want to get that close.

The shade let out another screech, then blinked in and out of existence once again, disappearing and reappearing like a porch light in a power surge. Kelly barely saw through its near-opaque, shadowy form—*Its dark and translucent body virtually drowning out the world behind it.*

And it was drawing nearer.

Slowly, the spectre inched closer, creeping through the chilly air toward Kelly.

It wanted him.

That much was certain.

Kelly didn't know why, but he felt it his is core. The *Entity* hunted him down like a reaper looking to collect its debt. Kelly had zero interest in finding out what debt he owed, turning away from the shadow and high tailing it in the opposite direction.

He sprinted another block down Gottingen, reaching the intersection where Gottingen met Rainnie Drive. To his right, an SUV was parked at an intersection, its headlights illuminating the paved lines ahead. Kelly couldn't see the driver, the lights blocking his vision in the prophetic darkness, but that SUV was his ticket out of here, and he was going to hitch a ride one way or another. Kelly dashed ahead, his heart racing, his hands still throbbing from pounding on the cell walls, the *Entity* always in tow.

He reached the grey SUV, tapping on the driver side window, pleading for help. An older man sat at the wheel, his thinning hair and creased face showcasing his tired age.

But the man didn't seem to notice Kelly.

He didn't react.

He didn't budge.

He just sat there, staring blankly ahead, oblivious to Kelly and the dire situation he was in, completely ignoring Kelly's heavy thuds on the driver's side window.

In fact, from what Kelly could tell, the driver wasn't moving at all. His gaze didn't shift, his eyes were unblinking, and his focus was unflinching.

Kelly glanced back toward the *Entity*, who was already halfway between himself and the station, inching closer by the second.

"Please—" Kelly cried out to the older driver "—help me!"

Again, no response.

Kelly was alone.

He slowly backed away from the vehicle, eyes fixated on the old man in the driver's seat, utterly oblivious to Kelly's presence and fear.

First, the cops, and now this.

It was as if the entire world was frozen, trapped in time as Kelly fled the *Entity*'s grim pursuit.

And that's when Kelly finally began to clue in on his surroundings.

It wasn't just the driver of the SUV...

It wasn't just the officers in the bullpen...

...The entire world was paralyzed in time...

Kelly cautiously surveyed his surroundings, realizing the extent of his predicament—*always keeping a wary eye on the Entity.*

The whole world was still.

He stared as rain droplets crept past, each a suspended gem trapped in time. They *were* falling—*just incredibly slowly*—so slow that Kelly could have run ten laps around the SUV before a single drop fell to the ground. Kelly reached out, poking a single raindrop from the air, watching it burst into several smaller droplets, each of them barely moving in the suspended sky. Gazing down the road, he could see several cars paused mid-drive, each of them stuck in the middle of the street as if their tires had been halted mid-rotation, still water spinning off the tires at one-hundredth the speed it should.

Kelly felt a chill run down his spine in his realization of the immobilized world around him.

Flags hung mid-wave, as if paused by an absent breeze

Strangers walking along the sidewalk were interrupted mid-step.

Vehicles were still.

Birds were almost motionless.

Aside from himself, everything else appeared frozen in time.

Nothing natural, at least.

There *was* one thing that wasn't entangled in the still sands of time — *the source of it all* — and it crept only twenty yards away in the silence of the night, its twisted arm outreached as it inched ever closer.

Kelly didn't have time to sit and watch the suspended rain, as beautiful and terrifying as it was.

He had to move.

He had to move now.

Kelly sprinted away from the creature, not wanting to be anywhere within sight of whatever it was that materialized within his cell.

What did it want with him?

Where did it come from?

These were questions he didn't even know how to begin to answer as he fled down Gottingen, turning onto Brunswick and high tailing it away from the station.

Where could he go?

Nowhere seemed safe.

Where could he escape something that materialized within his prison cell?

Again, Kelly drew no answer.

He only knew he needed to get as far away as fast as he could.

Halifax was a peculiar port city, unlike any other municipality or town within a thousand miles. To Kelly's left was a steep downward slope that led toward the Halifax Harbour and ferry terminal. Between here and there was the downtown hub, a few dozen pubs, restaurants, stores, and other commodities expected of a harbour front city. To Kelly's right was Citadel hill, an old fortress built in the 18th century and a favourite amongst tourists visiting the city, the elevated grassy hill providing a unique bird's eye view of the slanted city. Dead ahead was the south end of Halifax, an area filled with higher-end residential housing, various universities and a few more shopping locations. The only other direction was North, and he had no interest in retreating toward the station—*toward the Entity.*

So where was Kelly to go?

His home was in Dartmouth, down the hill, and a long skip across the harbour, but the last thing he wanted to do was lead the spectre to his home, to his wife, who Kelly presumed was also somehow frozen in time. *His mind flashed back to the entire squad, shrieking at him under the control of the shadow.* Who knows what else the creature could make them do. He had no intention of bringing that anywhere near the ones he loved—*not if he could help it*. He needed a place to think, a place to try and piece the shattered puzzle together—somewhere with a lot of exits and visibility.

There was one place in Halifax that fit that description nicely.

Kelly ran down Barrington Street, heading south, taking note of all the stillness in an ordinary bustling world. He passed teenagers stuck mid-stride on the sidewalk, frozen in stance mid-stride as they tossed a ball back and forth, the ball barely moving over their heads.

On the hill, a black dog peed on the grass with his owner standing closely by. Kelly could see the urine suspended with the rain, the Pitbull staring blankly off into the distance.

Atop the hill, both the Canadian flag and the Union Jack hung motionless, their ripples stiff within the motionless fabric.

A few cars stood frozen on the evening streets.

Even birds perched atop wires were immobile, locked in place as silent observers.

Kelly grappled with the realization that he was the only one in motion.

Why did the Entity not freeze him with the rest of the world?

Fear was his only companion as Kelly sprinted down Brunswick Street.

What did the Entity want from him in the first place?

He ran, lungs burning, until they threatened to collapse, and then he pushed harder, doing his best to gain ground.

He was.

From what Kelly could tell, the *Entity* was nowhere in sight, lost somewhere over crest of the hill as he continued toward the south end. But that could change at a moment's notice.

Who knew what else this thing was capable of.

Who knew what other secrets it held.

He imagined he would soon find out.

Kelly could see his target destination in the distance, a temporary refuge where he could catch a breath and try to piece together the ensuing madness—the *Halifax Regional Library*.

The Halifax Regional Library, a multi-storied fortress of glass, offered refuge and a panoramic view, with many exits and transparent windows running all the way around the entire building that would allow him a bird's eye view of his surroundings while he tried to collect his thoughts. Kelly wasn't about to confront the *Entity*, but he intended to stay vigilant. The building was modern and contemporary, built more as a community centre than a library. *Made for a new age world*, the mayor said during the grand opening many years ago. It was designed to sit as the heart of the city, a place bursting with traffic, activities, support centres, meeting rooms and study spaces. Today, it would act as a guard tower.

Kelly pushed his way through the front doors of the library, locking them behind him—*as if that would make a difference to the spectre that somehow materialized within his cell.*

Standing inside the main foyer were a dozen stragglers, a few of them clearly homeless upon inspection of their cotton toques and torn fingerless gloves. The other visitors consisted of a pair of children, their parents, and a few solo visitors—*every one of them entirely suspended in time.*

Gasping and panting, Kelly paused within the library's glass walls, a sharp pain emanating from his left side, his breath completely winded, his exhaustion from running halfway across the city settling in.

Catching his breath, Kelly made his way toward the edges of the exterior glass wall, scanning the streets for any sign of the *Entity*. From what he could tell, the spectre was nowhere in sight. For now, he had escaped its clutches.

After a few more cautious scans of the dark outdoors, Kelly examined one of the visitors—*suspended in a walking stance*—at the centre of the library. The man must have been pushing seventy, a coffee mug in one hand, a book in the other, titled *Mickey7*, in bold red font. Kelly stood directly in front of him, observing his eyes, face, and frozen body. He waved his hands before the man's blank stare, but the stranger's pupils stayed locked and wide. He grabbed the book from the stranger's grasp and gave him a few gentle taps on the cheek. Not one action grabbed the man's attention, the stranger entirely unaware of Kelly's presence.

Failing to snap the man out of his paralyzed status, Kelly walked over to one of the librarians sitting behind a desk at a computer. Her hands hovered over the keyboard, his thumb pressing on the space key, but the computer failing to respond. He tapped a few keys, but like the librarian, received no response.

It was hopeless.

No matter how hard Kelly tried, he couldn't snap a single person out of whatever time-locked trance they found themselves in. In a room full of paralyzed souls, *he was truly alone.*

"Now what?" Kelly whispered to himself as he made his way up the stairs to the second floor, with the intention of getting a better view of his surroundings. The second level only had a couple of visitors on it—a man and a woman, younger in age, looking like they were studying for an exam. Each had a matching textbook and were sitting at one of the work stations provided by the library near the corner of the room.

She was looking at the notes.

He was looking at her.

Typical, Kelly chortled to himself, making his way to the north facing window.

There were no solid walls on the exterior of the building. Every outer edge of the library was covered in tinted glass, with only a few areas covered in the typical gyprock and plaster. It provided the perfect place to sit and think while still allowing Kelly to keep a bird's eye view of the surrounding streets. He sat alone at one of the desks, pondering his next move, always keeping a wary eye on the streets below.

What did he know so far?

One—he had been framed for the murder of Zoe Stevens by some sort of doppelganger.

Two—Frank and the rest of the officers believed he was a murderer.

Three—some sort of malevolent creature was hunting him across the city.

And four—Time had slowed down to a near standstill, leaving only him and the Entity to their quarrel.

Could there be more? Kelly thought to himself, realizing he was way over his head.

"What more could happen today?" he pondered, questioning the unseen forces at play. Kelly wouldn't have been surprised if lightning chose that moment to strike him down.

Kelly looked down upon the damp, dark street, toward the intersection where Spring Garden Road connected with Brunswick Street.

Cars stood motionless on the street, trapped in a silent tableau.

Pedestrians were statues on the sidewalks, halted mid-gesture and expression.

And somewhere in the encroaching darkness, the Entity was advancing.

It would only be a matter of time.

Kelly was sure of it.

For now, he needed to use this time to think, to try his best to piece together the insanity that was today.

"Focus. Consider the clues at hand," Kelly urged himself, trying to picture every piece of the puzzle in his head.

There were—his tired eyes scanned the road while his mind scraped for any useful piece of information lost in his mind—*there were the two missing bullets from his gun.* He knew he didn't fire the weapon himself, so whoever tried to frame him for the shooting had to have touched his pistol. Hopefully, that meant whoever handled the weapon before him might have left fingerprints on either the handle or clip. But that was a longshot, and he didn't have the weapon in his possession.

Scratch that lead for now, he decided, continuing to the next thought, always scanning the barren road for any signs of trouble. On the street, a cyclist, frozen mid-turn signal, teetered impossibly without falling. In normal time, the cyclist would have already tumbled. Yet—*seemingly defying physics*—the biker remained suspended, his halted motion keeping him upright on a slanted angle. Kelly couldn't even begin to understand what was going on.

It freaked him out.

He tried not to think about it.

What other clues were there?

Then there was the undeniable evidence of the security footage at the ferry terminal, the video that showed him shooting Zoe. There was no way around that one. Watching it, he almost believed it himself. It was astonishing how the imposter held the gun, pulling it from his left hip with his left arm exactly how Kelly would. The imposter even wore the exact same clothes he wore now. And from what Kelly could tell, the man's face looked identical to his own. He had no siblings, let alone a long-lost twin. Unless his parents had some sort of twin they never told him about, the man in the footage must have been heavily made up to mirror Kelly's appearance.

But why?

Why target Kelly?

It wasn't a stretch to see why Frank or the rest of the station seemed to believe the footage, as proven by the rash around his wrists from the binding handcuffs. His reaction to Zoe lying lifeless on the ground with a bullet in her skull would have been the same as Frank's. It was hard not to react as he did, and Kelly didn't blame him. Had their roles been reversed, witnessing someone who looked like Frank commit the act, Kelly imagined things would have gone down quite similarly to how they had for him. Yet this did nothing to temper his fury at Frank, who believed Kelly capable of such atrocity, capable of shooting down another officer of the law—*their friend*—her gun resting alongside her.

Her gun...

Kelly had seen the photos of the crime scene. They practically tortured him with them, shoving them in his face as he sat handcuffed to the metal interrogation table. He had seen close-up shots where the bullet had lodged in her eye socket, lodging into her skull. There were dozens of photographs of the pools of drying blood spreading where she landed. But lying in the blood, resting motionless on the ground beside her, was Zoe's gun. Kelly remembered the video perfectly—*having seen it repeatedly throughout his interrogation.* Within a count of two seconds, Kelly's imposter fired a shot into the air, then another directly at Zoe, killing her instantly, the entire incident caught on film.

When—in that short amount of time—would Zoe have had time to draw her weapon? Zoe was a great cop—in fact, she was one of the best—but she was also human.

No-one could react that fast.

Not even the best detective in the world could have predicted the shooting.

So why in the world was her weapon out of her holster?

Kelly couldn't believe he missed that earlier.

He really was losing his touch.

And it looked like Frank was too.

Both of them missed what might be his guiding light out of this, that is, if he figured out how to resume time—and survived the *Entity's* pursuit.

And as if on cue, breaking Kelly's thought process and seizing his wary attention, one of the street lights outside began to flicker at the corner of the intersection where Brunswick met Spring Garden.

Then another shimmered.

Then another.

And another.

One by one, the street lights flickered on and off, fluctuating and pulsating as the world around remained lost in time.

105

Then, emerging around the corner and hovering just above the pavement, floating directly toward Kelly Christopher as the streetlights around it burnt away, *was the shadow.*

Kelly sat up from his chair, watching from the second-floor window as the *Entity* drew near, wavering in and out of existence as it glitched across the road, over the sidewalk, and through the heavy glass doors of the Halifax Regional Library.

One by one, the library's lights flickered and died.

The Entity had entered.

14

The Halifax Regional Library was a one-of-a-kind building, like no other in the city. There were five levels, each abundant with activities, books, work stations, coffee shops, a movie theatre, and even more books. The architecture was rectangular of sorts. Each floor was a mirrored loop of itself, with a hollow centre allowing viewers on the top floor to be able to look down and see those standing in the main foyer. The surrounding white walls and glass windows gave it that clean, crisp look—*sort of like an Apple Store, but with books instead of gadgets*. Cutting across the hollow center were white staircases and walkways at horizontal angles, adding to the modern, stylistic design.

Kelly Christopher stood on an interior pedway, overlooking the central void of the library, as he faced down the *Entity* below, hovering on the level below, gazing back with malicious intent, the lights all but drained within the deadened building, leaving the two of them in darkness on a moonless night as Kelly awaited the spectre's next move.

Kelly waited on the second level, looking down the hollow centre toward the shade, who returned the stare with vacant eyes. He waited for the *Entity* to attack, to attempt to take control as it tried back in his cell.

But Kelly had already mapped out his potential escape routes.

There were many exits where Kelly could make his escape. The library's multiple exits had made it an ideal temporary refuge. If the *Entity* floated upward, Kelly would dash to the left for the stairs and make his way out onto the street toward the south end. If it went up on the left staircase, he would take the route to the right, down the other set of stairs and out the main door. From there, it would be a straight shot to downtown Halifax, where Kelly could potentially find another sanctuary. Should the *Entity* collapse the entire structure upon him—*well, then he was just about as screwed as screwed could be.*

But it did none of those things.

The Entity lingered with a menacing patience, as if privy to Kelly's every plan.

"What do you want from me?" Kelly's shout echoed through the empty library, a plea for understanding in the face of the unknown. He waited for a response, but none was given. Kelly didn't even know if this *thing* could communicate, or if it even perceived the world as a human did—*because whatever it was, it couldn't have been any further from human.*

The Entity's response would come soon enough.

First, the lights came back to life, every bulb within the building flickering in and out of existence like a surge of power was pulsating through the building. Then the smell of rot began to rise in the stale air, filling Kelly's nostrils with the same stench that soaked his cell right before his first dance with the *Entity*. He could feel the tension building in the hollow of the library floors, like the air had become dense and heavy, squeezing his skin as he waited for the *Entity* to advance.

As the smell of rot began to suffocate his thoughts, he could feel the *Entity* starting to pull the strings of his mind, like it was somehow trying to take over the reins of his entire body, all while staying distant on the marble floor below. Kelly felt his muscles tighten and his fists clench as he fought the *Entity's* stranglehold on his mind.

A sensation overwhelmed him, a compulsion to surrender his very being. He felt a nagging urge to simply let the Entity float up to take him. The Entity seemed to warp the fabric of his very desires.

Kelly Christopher felt an overwhelming yearning to surrender himself to the darkness. The shadow loomed, intent on crushing Kelly's spirit and forcing his surrender, smothering his will and letting him wither like a snuffed flame. From above, Kelly could see the *Entity* twitching and twisting back and forth as it attempted to devour Kelly once and for all.

Resistance felt futile.

Hope felt empty.

His desires felt like they were no longer his own.

Suddenly Kelly's exit strategies seemed hopeless. All that remained, it seemed, was to accept his fate and *die*.

It was the only thing he wanted.

It was all he yeared for.

It was all he knew.

Then at the apex of the Entity's all-consuming power, it gave its response.

"…ddiiiiiieeeeee…"

And at that moment, as the *Entity* seized complete control of Kelly, dying seemed the only thing left to do. The only thing Kelly wanted in this world was to keel over, lay down, and *die*.

But Donna—

Just before his mind withered to oblivion, the image of his beautiful wife split his shattered mind. Kelly envisioned leaving her alone, leaving her behind in this bleak world, surrendering their future to the black.

Below, the *Entity* ascended, its advance heralding an endgame. As it drew near, Kelly fought to replace the thoughts of rot and decay placed in his mind by the spectre approaching from below, with visions of his wife and the strength of their bond. He battled the dwindling urge to surrender to the dark with the unending desire to return to her, shaking the *Entity's* stranglehold on his mind away, returning focus and control within his veins.

And just like that, Kelly took back the reins.

His thoughts rushed back to him.

His strength was returned to him.

Kelly broke entirely free of the shadow's grasp, the *Entity* letting loose a window-shattering shriek, reverberating across the echoing halls of the near-empty library. The *Entity's* grip had been severed. For a fleeting moment, Kelly reclaimed his freedom.

But the Entity showed no signs of giving up.

The spectre had already risen to the second level of the hollow, hovering high in the air as Kelly backed off near the left side of the library, retreating toward the paralyzed students studying in the corner, the young duo trapped in time, utterly oblivious to the darkness around them. He saw the exit, but the *Entity* had placed itself on the path, blocking Kelly's means of escape.

Slowly, the creature advanced toward him.

Kelly edged backward, the distance between him and the Entity closing rapidly.

"What do you want from me?" he demanded, defiance lacing his voice against the silent *Entity.*

No response.

Only the sickening scent of decay answered him.

Kelly snatched a textbook titled 'Nuclear Physics in a Nutshell' from the table where the young couple sat frozen in study. It was a thick, hardcover textbook, with easily over 300 pages. With all his might, Kelly tossed the textbook directly at the *Entity* lingering ever closer. The text flew directly at its intended target.

But the hardcover never connected.

The book sailed through the *Entity*, as if passing through an insubstantial mist, leaving undisturbed the darkness at its core.

Kelly was in too much of a state of alarm to notice that the book never fell to the ground. Instead, it continued its trajectory, appearing to defy gravity, and connected with a wall on the far side of the library, shattering into over 300 separate fluttering pages.

The quirks of a timeless world played their tricks on Kelly's surroundings, and if he wasn't preoccupied by the supernatural monster floating toward him, he would have been amazed at the sight.

But he had no time for experimentation.

No time for astonishment.

Not when his life was on the line.

And the Entity made it clear that surviving wasn't going to be easy.

The lingering phantom released another death-defying screech, wailing in a high-pitched tone like tires screeching on dry pavement, its ghostly voice nearly piercing Kelly's eardrums. The library's glass walls began to shatter, streamline cracks slowly spreading along the tinted windows like lighting-bolts in slow motion. Kelly watched as the glass panels exploded in sluggish form, each crack speeding across the glass a hundred times slower than it should have.

But it wasn't the Entity's shrieks that terrified Kelly to the core.

It was the ensuing cries, however, that truly sent a chill down Kelly's spine—cries not originating from the shade before him, but from the once-paralyzed strangers all around him, slowly reanimating to life in twisted, corrupted fashion.

Kelly watched as in succession as the once-incapacitated strangers in the library slowly began to move, their limbs contorting in ways that defied anatomy, their necks bending to the side, their eyes fading from white to black. One-by-one, the *Entity* seized control of every innocent soul unfortunate enough to find themselves in the library's shattered glass walls, breaking away from the paralyzed reality of time and joining Kelly in his unfathomable nightmare.

They screamed.

They shrieked.

They cried.

And Kelly knew the Entity had taken control of them all.

Shrieks erupted alarmingly close behind Kelly, followed by the sound of rustling feet and shifting weight. He looked back to see the young university couple sitting at the table. Their eyes had turned from white to an abyssal black, mirroring that of a starless night.

Their bodies were contorted beyond how bones should bend.

Their limbs quivered in a frenzied, unnatural manner.

And they were charging toward Kelly with alarming speed.

Kelly retreated from the study table and watched as the young man—*no older than twenty, with short black hair and a grey Dalhousie University sweater reading 'Dal Engineering*—sprinted toward him alongside the young girl with her blonde ponytail and skin-tight jeans. They both scowled at him like rabid dogs, frothing from their crooked mouths, wanting nothing more than to tear him to shreds, their corrupted eyes filled with hate and rage. The air split with another symphony of shrieks, teeth snapping in a maddening cacophony.

And as Kelly turned to run, he realized it wasn't just the young students that were giving chase.

All over the Library, shrieks and cries echoed in the darkness. Screams of men and women, young and old, all slowly becoming consumed by the *Entity*'s hateful infection. All of them of a single mind, to do the bidding of the shadow and kill Kelly Christopher, who was wise enough to do the only thing he could—

—Run.

Kelly fled from the horde, adrenaline fueling his speed, the cracks in the glass still stretching as the razor-sharp shards began to slowly fall. He retreated up the stairs to the third level, peering over the railing's edge to watch the pack of twisted puppets climbing to the second level where he had just left, all of them looking up with their beady black eyes. There must have been at least ten of them within sight—*not including the two students*—twisting and jerking in inhumane, jagged motions, vying aggressively for the lead as if driven by a sinister contest.

Kelly didn't know if he was fast enough, but he prayed to any god listening to give him the strength to escape—*if an escape eluded him, this place would be his end.*

Kelly was sure of it.

He'd never see Donna again and wouldn't have the chance to clear his name from the dreadful accusations being tossed at him.

That was not an outcome he could accept.

Reaching the third floor, a twisted woman wearing a long red skirt, white top, and thick glasses cut him off, grabbing for his arm as he dodged to the left. Kelly was able to get a close look at her void-like eyes as she lunged at his throat, her blank gaze completely trapping her humanity behind the darkened veil. Her teeth snapped down inches from Kelly's neck, her pink-manicured nails digging into his flesh, sharp as blades.

Kelly cried out as he lowered his shoulder and drove it into her breasts, knocking her back and releasing her grip from his bloodied arms. She fell back a step, regaining her balance as her matte-black eyes remained fixated on her prey. Kelly wouldn't give her the chance to attack again. He took a step forward, throwing the entire weight of his body into hers. The woman staggered backwards, flailing in contorted fashion as she tripped over her heels and fell over the half-railing, tumbling three stories down through the hollow centre of the library. Kelly watched from above as her skull cracked against the hard floor below, splitting open and killing her instantly. Kelly could see the blood from his elevated position already starting to spread across the tiled floor as three more twisted bodies raced past her, hopping over her body and sprinting for the stairs to join the hunt.

There was no time to comprehend what had just happened. The two engineering students sprinted to the third level directly behind Kelly, their eyes filled with murderous intent. The boy in the grey university lunged forward, his hands clawing at the air as Kelly stepped to the left, dodging the rage-filled attack. The boy fell to the floor as his study partner attacked from behind. Kelly swiftly turned and released a punch, clocking the twisted girl squarely in the nose with a right hook, dropping her instantly in a fit of wrath and agony. As she fell, the grey-hooded assailant lunged, seizing Kelly's ankles, clutching his bent fingers on Kelly's pant leg. Kelly delivered a swift kick, jarring the attacker's chin and loosening his grip, allowing Kelly the time to flee. He tried to put as much space between himself and the approaching horde as possible.

Somewhere behind him, another round of shrieks cried out like a symphony of pain, as if the souls of those captured were still inside, crying to be released. Kelly could see the university couple already on their feet, sprinting toward Kelly once again, joined by several other twisted bodies under the *Entity*'s all-consuming control.

Think, Kelly.

Think!

With the library spanning just five levels, Kelly's options were rapidly dwindling. Reaching the fourth level, he was relieved to see no twisted puppets waiting for him. A sign reading 'Local History & Reference' labelled next to a bold-faced '4' was printed on the sidewall.

Think!

Seizing an unoccupied wooden chair by a study table, Kelly hurled it with desperate force toward the two young students who had just arrived atop the stairs, their eyes black to kill, their necks bent to the side, their faces bloodied from their last encounter. The chair soared through the air and connected with the young lad in the *'Dal Engineering'* sweater, shattering upon impact into a spray of wooden fragments, splinters shooting through the air, sticking into the walls around them like darts. The impact sent the young man reeling backward, while his companion let out a wail of agony, her ordinarily beautiful face now riddled with wooden splinters and blood.

Seizing the moment, Kelly charged at the young woman, grabbed her by the neck and slamming her down the stairs alongside her study partner. The girl tumbled all the way to the bottom, roaring in pain as she plummeted.

That's when Kelly saw the rest of them.

A swarm of over twenty contorted figures clambered over the fallen students at the stair's base.

He couldn't fight that many twisted souls.

They would undoubtedly rip him limb from limb in mere moments.

There was also the Entity to deal with.

A sinking realization of his dire situation settled in – he was in deep trouble.

Kelly pressed deeper into the library's interior, running out of options as he desperately searched for refuge. He sprinted toward the emergency stairwell, but two disfigured figures, middle-aged men, emerged abruptly, blocking his path and forcing him to retreat it in the opposite direction. He was on the fourth floor, so a leap down the building's hollow core was tantamount to suicide, which at this point seemed like a better option than getting torn to shreds by the *Entity*'s twisted puppets—*or becoming one of the creatures himself*. He didn't understand why the *Entity* didn't just take over his body just like it had the others within the library's glass walls.

What distinguished him from the rest, immune to its control?

Why was he able to withstand its power?

It didn't matter.

Not now anyway.

Kelly sprinted up the final ascending stairwell leading up to the fifth level which led to a smaller section of the building that looked like an oversized shipping container placed askew atop a glass box. At the top was a bold-faced '5', and a sign that read '*Rooftop Terrace / Fiction Collection.*'

The top floor offered no escape.

There were elevators, but they surely weren't working, and the twisted horde was already at the bottom of the stairwell and gaining ground. There was another set of stairs ahead to the left, a large *EXIT* sign written above it in red lettering.

That was the last exit...

His last chance to escape...

He barely made it three steps before the exit doors busted open from the other side. Three distorted figures burst forth, their gnarled hands swiping just shy of his flesh. Kelly veered sharply, evading the three assailants and sprinted toward a dead end where three glass walls overlooked Spring Garden Road from five stories above.

It wasn't a jump anyone could survive.

He had led himself exactly where he didn't want to go.

He was trapped.

He turned to see the horde of twisted puppets making their approach, blocking his only avenue of escape, the *Entity* hovering slowly behind them.

To his left and right were vacant study cubicles.

Behind him, several glass panes encapsulated him within the confines of the fifth floor.

Was this it?

Was this how he died?

Kelly always pictured himself dying in his bed at an elderly age. Never had he envisioned an end torn asunder by the unnatural grasp of writhing aberrations.

He had to think of a way out.

He couldn't let it end here.

This wasn't the first time Kelly was trapped. Earlier, in the cell, Kelly had been locked in a room alone with the spectre's rotting stench—*yet he was able to escape then, wasn't he?*

What had enabled his escape then?

Time had run out.

The horde was upon him.

Kelly watched as what must have been twenty or more twisted bodies sprinted down the hallway.

Their eyes were black and hollow.

Their limbs were twisted and bent.

Their shrieks were harrowing and full of rage.

There was nothing he could do.

There was nowhere he could run.

The *Entity's* horde quickly charged toward Kelly, the ravenous crowd ready to tear him limb from limb for reasons only God could understand—*and even that, Kelly was doubtful.*

Kelly closed his eyes and waited for the end to come.

Donna and Frank flashed through his mind as Kelly awaited his agonizing end.

He didn't understand why these twisted beings didn't seem to be affected by time's frozen arrow—the Entity likely having something to do with that.

He prayed for silence.

He prayed for stillness.

He prayed for a swift death.

The air seemed to grow thicker.

The clamor of the stampede subdued to a hush.

The hairs on his skin stood stiff all over his body.

With eyes shut, Kelly braced for the inevitable conclusion.

...and he waited...

...and he waited...

...but the end never came...

There was no tearing at the limbs, no teeth sinking into his skin, and no violent massacre at the hands of a demonic mob.

Kelly waited for the end, but the end seemed to remain ever elusive.

Upon opening his eyes, Kelly found himself inches from the contorted visages of dozens—*all staring directly at him with dark and empty eyes, immobilized, as if captured in a photograph.*

Each was ensnared in an eerie stasis.

Their arms were twisted and bent.

Their eyes were blank and hollow.

But their shrieks had subsided.

Their murderous intent had come to a halt.

And Kelly had no idea why.

They were all paralyzed on the spot.

All but one.

The Entity continued its dreaded approach.

The relentless shadow seemed impervious to the suspended march of time.

A sudden weakness overcame Kelly, draining him of vitality. But it wasn't as it was back in the cell. There was no yearning to surrender—no overwhelming desire to keel over and let the *Entity* consume him.

He simply felt weak.

But not weak enough to run.

The twisted souls may have been frozen in place, but the *Entity* was closing in, and Kelly had no intention of sticking around and letting it get anywhere near him.

Once the *Entity* drew near enough—*almost atop of Kelly, reaching out its arm to clutch him within its deathly grasp*—Kelly dodged to the left and beelined it for the distant wall, pushing his drained muscles to their limit. With the twisted horde frozen in place, he could now use the emergency exit as a means of escape. As he dashed through the open doorway, he half expected to be greeted by another brigade of puppets flooding the stairs, blocking him off and ripping him apart—*but there was nothing there to greet him.* To his relief, the stairwell was deserted, granting him a clear passage to freedom. There was no more resistance as he made his way through the Halifax Regional Library's empty foyer, the entrance doors directly ahead.

It looked like he was going to make it.

By some miracle, Kelly was going to survive.

He knew his moment of solace would not last long, but every minute he had to think and process he counted as a blessing.

On the way out of the building, Kelly spotted the lady in the red skirt lying still on the hard ground. Her skull was dented inward, and a large split had formed across her brow where her head had connected with the cold, hard ground.

There was no denying it.

The lady with the red skirt and white blouse was dead.

Despite her being a pawn of the Entity, Kelly had been the one that killed her.

Kelly was a murderer after all.

15

Frank McDowell was sitting in the police station security room, trying to make heads-or-tails of all that had happened in the past fourteen hours, as if he had any hope of connecting the dots together.

The explosion in the cell wing...

The similar explosion in the Halifax Ferry Terminal...

The sudden reversal of all the officers in the security footage...

The dark smudge hovering in the centre of the bullpen...

The murder of Zoe Stevens...It wasn't adding up.

Nothing seemed to make any sense.

Kelly Christopher remained the elusive centerpiece in today's unraveling mysteries—*and he was missing, as if he vanished in thin air.*

Amidst processing the day's bewildering events, there was a gentle knock at the door. It was Officer Thomason, and he was about to add to the *nonsense*-pile.

"Sir..." The young Officer spoke hesitantly, his voice still shaken from the events of downstairs.

"Yes?" Frank replied. "Please tell me you have some good news." *It wasn't.*

"Sir, there's been...*um*..."

"Spit it out." Frank's patience was wearing thin, wearied by the day's turmoil.

"There's been an incident, down at the public library. One person is dead, and two are facing life-threatening injuries. They just called it in."

"What kind of incident?"

"Don't know. But they want whoever we can spare down there at once."

"We don't even know what's happening here, Thomason. From what I can tell, some sort of bomb went off, and Kelly is at large. I need to stay put, why are you telling me this?"

"Sir, I've been asked by McNeil to tell you to take the lead at the library. He's on his way here now."

Of course, Chief Superintendent Donald McNeil, ever the provocateur, had summoned him. Frank respected the man, he was one hell of a decorated cop, and leading the station couldn't have been simple with all the politics and nonsense that went on behind the scenes—*but they didn't always see eye-to-eye.* Frank was criticized by McNeil for not promptly sending officers to the Christopher residence, stating that he was letting his previous attachments get in the way of his job. Frank didn't disagree with him on any particular point, agreeing that there probably should have been a full search of their house right away. Still, it ticked him off that he was getting the full run-around only a few hours after seeing one of his own lying dead at the terminal, shot down in bright daylight by his *ex*-partner. Frank muttered his discontent about the chief's reprimand before heading out to stick his hands in another chaotic situation. It was probably best for Frank to head out now, before the chief came in and blew another gasket at the sight of their torn office.

Another disaster in an already catastrophic day seemed par for the course. Frank gave the nod to Officer Thomason, left the station, hopped in his cruiser alone, and drove to the library, where another whirlwind of chaos awaited him.

Upon arrival, Frank saw that there were already a few other officers at the scene, taking notes and rolling out police lines, just as they had earlier this morning at the scene of Zoe's murder. And just like before, as Frank hopped out of his car, thoroughly beaten down by the events of the day, he was met by a flock of nosey reporters. *Another media frenzy,* he mused, preparing himself to get berated by squawking questions.

"Officer—" one lady called out, holding her iPhone out like a microphone, "—was this an act of terrorism in our neighbourhood?"

Frank, unresponsive, headed straight for the police cordon as another man holding a traditional microphone asked his question.

"Did a bomb *actually* go off at the police headquarters? Any idea who was behind it?"

Frank ignored him.

He was almost at the police line when the final question was asked by a younger lady, pushing her way to the front of the line to ask her question.

"Is this related to the escape of Kelly Christopher?"

Jesus, how did they know about that already. Frank ducked under the tape, leaving the reporters behind. Before disappearing into the crime scene, he turned around to give his generic statement.

"All of your questions will be answered in due time. For now, please step aside and let us do our job unobstructed."

That, of course, spared another flurry of questions, but Frank just ignored them. Now was not the time to talk with the press.

Upon entering the library, Frank was immediately confronted with a young woman being wheeled out by two paramedics, dozens of wooden splinters lodged in her torn face, a bandage covering her left eye, her right arm in a sling. *Frank was not prepared for this.* He could barely concentrate as it was, let alone start another case as high-profile as this.

He pulled out his notebook, jotting down observations as best as his weary eyes could manage. He took note of the girl being wheeled to the ambulance, as well as noted how many panels of glass had shattered within the library, the tiny shards laying across the wet sidewalk outside the building, suggesting an internal force had shattered them. He also noticed a young man in a grey *'Dal Engineering'* sweatshirt being attended to by a second pair of paramedics. He was lying flat on his back with a ventilator strapped to his mouth, his jaw visibly broken. Frank noted the injuries in his notebook.

Investigating further, Frank saw a white sheet covering a body in the centre of the hollow on the main level, a pool of blood soaking around her just as it had been around Zoe. A piece of her red dress poked out from under the stained sheet as a different officer set up a blockade around her, ensuring none of the reporters could get a good photograph through the glass walls outside.

"What happened to her," Frank asked.

"She appears to have fallen." The officer pointed up toward the upper level, drawing Frank's attention to a small bloodstain on one of the railings. Frank acknowledged with a nod, continuing his notetaking. There were about half a dozen witnesses sitting downstairs, all of whom had been at the library before the incident. Frank approached the witnesses.

"Can anyone tell me what happened here?"

The witnesses exchanged glances, offering no answer, as if bewildered by Frank's questions.

He tried again, the silence making him uneasy. "Was there an attack?" Again, no response. He continued to dig for an answer, attempting to stir up some kind of clue or lead. "Did this lady get in a fight with the two kids over there?" Frank pointed over to the paramedics, who were in the process of tossing the boy in the grey university sweater onto a separate stretcher.

No one from the huddled group responded. Their silence and pale faces indicated profound shock. Before Frank was able to ask another question, one of the witnesses finally spoke up. It was an older man, with a bruised right cheek and trembling wrinkled hands.

"Officer, none of us know what happened. We've been trying to figure it out amongst ourselves, but we just can't seem to remember. At one moment, I was downstairs about to check out a book at the front desk. The next thing I remember, I was on the fifth floor alongside everyone else, with a bruise on my face and a severe headache."

Frank looked at the older man, puzzled. If it weren't for the nodding heads of everyone else in agreement, he would have never believed him.

"You mean to tell me that not a single one of you saw what happened? Or even remember anything at all?" Some confirmed with nods, while others remained silent, their gaze fixed on the floor.

"Officer," The older man began to speak again, "I don't know how to explain it. But when I awoke upstairs..." He paused a moment as if trying to find the right words. "...Sir, I've never been so afraid in my entire life, and I have no inkling as to why." This time, the entire group nodded, each one of their faces drained of life and colour.

Frank recorded their statements and contact details before proceeding upstairs, where he would find three more clues to add to the madness.

Clue #1: All lightbulbs and glass panes on the floor were shattered. Even the computer screens had been destroyed, as if some sort of high-frequency bomb detonated, blowing everything to bits.

Clue #2: Across the room lay a black textbook, its pages torn and scattered. It sat motionless on the floor next to the wall, which held a book-sized dent. Frank picked up the detached cover to read it. It was titled *Nuclear Physics in a Nutshell, by*

Carlos A. Bertulani. He dropped it back down onto the floor, taking note of the title.

Clue #3: A set of hand-written notes was sitting damp on a study table next to the opening where the glass window had once been. Upon a quick glance, he saw that at the top, written in pink ink was '4: *General Properties of Nuclei - Magnetic Dipole Moment'*. The content was beyond his immediate understanding, but he suspected a link to the destroyed textbook, so he noted it.

On the third floor, only two clues were obvious. There was a wood chair, lying in a hundred pieces, wooden splinters ejected all around, poking out of the walls and ceiling. He imagined that if he inspected the wooden pieces lodged in the young girl's soft skin, they'd match that of the battered chair. The second clue was a small bloodstain on the railing, the paint chipped ever so slightly, with scratch marks covering the flat top. Frank looked over the edge, facing straight down at the woman covered in the bloodied sheet. *Somehow, the dead woman and the young girl with the splinters are heavily related.*

The next clue was on the fifth floor, where a busted emergency exit door had swung the opposite direction the hinges intended. Frank checked the stairwell quickly, but nothing else stood out to him. The only remaining clue was a faint rancid smell lingering in the air, near where the crowd downstairs had said they'd 'awoken.' The scent was weak, but distinct, matching that of rotting compost or a garbage dump. Frank searched around, but couldn't find the smell's source, like it was materializing out of thin air.

He filed it away as potentially significant for later.

After a brief further search, Frank departed and made his way back down to the main level to ask more questions. Frank interviewed a few more witnesses, all telling him the same story, that they didn't remember a thing, and that they were filled with an overpowering sense of anxiety, as if they were drowning in it. *It didn't make any sense.*

After taking as many notes as possible and interviewing anyone willing to speak to him, Frank finally decided it was time—*for the third time today*—to look at the security footage. Of course, that was going to be a little more complicated. Apparently, the security room for the library wasn't on site. It had been contracted to a third-party company. He'd have to call them and have them send the footage over to the station, which was already undergoing its own turmoil as it was.

Frank found a secluded place to rest on the main floor and rested his head in his hands as he looked out at the falling rain. He'd completed more police work today than he'd finished in the past month, and he was doing it all without a partner. He felt his heart sink, the day's events catching up with him like a tidal wave of aversion as he sat alone in the corner of the library. A wave of anger and remorse overwhelmed him.

What he'd give to have his partner back, wherever he was. He'd give *anything* to prove Kelly was innocent.

Amidst his solitude, he yearned for his partner's vindication.

16

Kelly Christopher fled down Spring Garden toward the still city streets of downtown Halifax, continually moving forward to try and stay a step ahead of the *Entity* undoubtedly lurking somewhere in tow, and to give himself some breathing room to try and figure out whatever the hell was going on.

Around him, the late-night crowd remained perpetually frozen in time on the cold Tuesday evening, the rain mystically suspended in the dreary skies, the cars unmoving on the near-barren streets as their headlights streamed through the paralyzed fog. Pedestrians were motionless, mid-step on the sidewalks, their feet dangling in the air. Above, birds hovered motionlessly near the building-tops, their wings still, their heading postponed.

How was any of this possible?

Kelly continued forward, his head invariably checking back over his shoulder to make sure his newly acquired lurker wasn't about to pounce. From what he could tell, he was alone. This would give Kelly much-needed time to try and make sense of his situation—and to determine how screwed he truly was.

He turned off of Spring Garden and made his way left onto Grafton, greeted by a stationary cyclist and several others suspended mid-stroll, their umbrellas deflecting the fixated raindrops falling from still skies.

Kelly recalled the woman he'd inadvertently caused to fall over the library's railing. He wondered if she was a student, or a mother, or just someone there to enjoy some leisurely time at the library. He rubbed his shoulder, a small bruise forming where it connected with the lady, wondering if it would be long before he joined her in death.

He would fight as long as he could, but Kelly had a sinking feeling that he was running out of time—an ironic thought, considering he literally had all the time in the world.

But time was relative. Kelly was on the *Entity's time* now. *Or was he?*

A tingling sensation seemed to remain ever present under Kelly's skin, like he was still somewhere under that imaginary shallow river, the power still emanating around him.

Could he return to his own timeline?

Was he somehow in control of this?

His priority was to master this temporal anomaly. He recalled his escape from the cell, where panic had turned to power. He had pounded on the walls of the cell, only for them to explode outward, allowing him to escape. No natural human being had the strength to burst through walls that sturdy, but he was no longer in a natural world. Yes, he had pounded on the walls, but instead of exerting the pounding force over a matter of seconds, he exerted it over a matter of nanoseconds. Kelly was no physicist, he always hated math, but he understood the nature of impulse and momentum. That's why a car's hood crumbled in an accident, extending the time the impact was felt by the driver, spreading out the accident over a larger timespan, and saving the driver's life. In the prison cell, the opposite was true. He exerted the impact over a much smaller period of time, and it must have been enough to burst down the wall. He felt like a professor, explaining his concept to a half-asleep class.

Question: If one exerts 1 unit of force over 1 unit of time, what happened when you exert that same amount of force over 1/1000th of that time?

Answer: The cell doors fucking explode outwards.

This phenomenon also accounted for the textbook's flight across the library, defying normal gravity. Once the book left his hand, relative to the ordinary world, it was as if Kelly were throwing it a million miles per hour instead of what it would be with his natural strength. The book flew completely across the library, bursting into loose pages when it connected with the far wall.

Kelly checked over his shoulder.

No indication of the spectre.

For now, he was completely alone in time.

An urge to validate his theory gripped him, that with his newfound place in time, Kelly was now, in some sense, like a superhero. He liked that.

The notion of being a superhero buoyed his spirits momentarily—*but superheroes didn't kill people.*

Kelly had. Two, according to Frank and the rest of the world.

Reality hit as he made his way to Pizza Corner on Grafton Street, the late-night alcoholic's favourite place to grab a cheap slice and pop. In the middle of the intersection, between two pizza shops on either corner, was a stalled pickup truck, driven by what looked like an older construction worker in an orange high-visibility vest and a yellow hard hat.

He approached the worker, who was mid-way through his turn when *time* had come to a near standstill. Kelly got a closer look at the man, his scruffy grey beard matching his wrinkled face and callused hands, filth from his worksite covering his left cheek. Kelly carefully removed the man's hard hat, mindful of his uncertain strength. If his theory was correct, and Kelly had some extraordinary strength as a result of his relatively-superhuman speeds, he would have to be extremely careful when it came to other people. He aimed to avoid any accidental harm to the motionless worker.

After removing the hard hat, Kelly checked the worker's watch, alarmed at what the time read, the second hand unflinching at the 44-second marker.

It was 8:33 PM. Barely a minute had passed between the time he left the station and now. Jesus, he thought, stepping away from the construction worker and his truck. *How was any of this possible?* He wondered if he'd even find out. *All in due time,* he hoped, *even if time wasn't moving.*

But now came the time to test his theory. Kelly held the helmet like a Frisbee, took a heaving step, and whiffed the yellow hardhat toward the stars. He watched as the helmet sped forward. To Kelly, the helmet's flight seemed normal, but to an external viewer, the yellow hardhat was travelling faster than a speeding bullet.

And it didn't drop.

The safety helmet kept going and going into the sky, as if gravity had been reduced to that of the moon, effecting everything but Kelly, the spectre, and those under its foul power. The helmet continued toward the clouds, disappearing from Kelly's sight as he began to understand his own power.

He looked down at his hands, as if they were no longer his own, but belonging to that of a demi-God, absolutely amazed at his newly found strength in time. "I'm basically superman," he said to himself, wanting to test his powers further.

If he was going to get through this alive, he needed to understand what he was capable of. *And what he wasn't.*

He grabbed a few more things from the bed of the construction worker's truck at random. Things like wrenches, pylons, chains, and a few oversized bolts. Kelly whiffed them into the air, watching them as they flew far away and out of sight. He hurled them southeast, over the buildings and toward the ocean so they'd land in the cooling waters of the Atlantic, instead of squishing someone kilometres away in the other direction.

Incredible, he reflected, wondering what other consequences there were within his newly found place in time. He didn't dwell on the physics of his situation. That wasn't even close to his profession. Things go up, and things go down, that was good enough for him—*only, things went a lot further up now.*

As amazing as his newly found strength was, it wasn't worth anything if no one could see it. To the worker in the truck, his helmet may-as-well just disappeared in thin air, Kelly moving too fast for the man even to perceive him. Not one of the souls walking alongside Kelly in the motionless street had any idea he was even there. He was trapped in a non-observable state, hunted by an unfathomable ghost, lost in unexplainable circumstances.

"It couldn't get any worse," he thought aloud, making his way down toward Argyle Street, the pub-capital of Halifax, a road he had spent a little bit too much time on as a rookie officer. There must have been over twenty bars over the next few blocks, and Kelly had been inside every single one, some more than once, some even more than that. Whenever his Red Wings played Frank's Boston Bruins, they'd grab a table at one of the local bars, split a pitcher each, and watch the game, reminiscing about all the stupid decisions they made at that very bar ten years earlier.

Some people could never stay in the same place as they grew up, wanting to expand their horizons and see more of the world. But that wasn't Kelly or Frank. They were two home-grown Nova Scotian boys who were perfectly happy keeping their streets safe and enjoying one too many beers on winter nights. Of course, Kelly doubted they'd ever be back here together again. Even if Kelly got through this unscathed, and managed to prove his innocence, he had a feeling that changes were coming—the kind of changes you don't come back from, the ones that expand your horizons beyond realities understood.

Kelly hoped that wasn't true. He just wanted things to go back to normal. He wanted to feel his wife's arms around him. He wanted to share a beer with his partner and talk about the predictable world of hockey. But as he stood outside in the cold dark air, hunted by a creature not physically possible, completely trapped in time, Kelly didn't think he'd ever see normal again.

"One step at a time, Kelly," he said to himself in a sorrowful tone, reeling himself out of his own dark thoughts.

He closed his eyes, feeling the omnipotent energy pressurize around him, pushing the air against his skin, running across his flesh like gentle electricity. *If one could feel time,* he speculated, *then he imagined this is what it felt like.*

As if guided by some unnatural understanding, just like back in the library, Kelly lifted his arms into the air, feeling the energy flow through him, believing it was himself in control of time, and not time in control of him. It was almost as if he were guiding it—*manipulating it.* A palpable energy swirled around Kelly, as if the air around him was trying to solidify itself, forming into a thick, dense pressure surrounding him. *Then,* like a spark igniting a pocket of methane gas, the entire world burst back to life, the electricity protruding from his body and cascading out into the universe around him.

Time had resumed its natural flow.

Suddenly the wet breeze pressed against his face, and the sound of rain danced along the paved roads. The roar of an overhead plane vibrated through the air, and the sound of a car honking from afar reached Kelly's ears. He looked around at the once again bustling streets of Halifax, watching as lively people strolled down the sidewalks in their umbrellas, hugging the building's edge to stay dry from the falling rain. All around him, ushered by his burst of power, the world had come to life, and for the first time in the longest minute of Kelly's life, he wasn't alone.

He didn't know how—*and he doubted he'd ever be able to understand*—but somehow in the dreary dark of a Nova Scotian night, Kelly Christopher learned that he was able to control the stoppage of time.

A thump sounded beside him as a yellow hardhat hit the sidewalk, cracking the plastic protection and denting the concrete. He picked up the hardhat in two pieces, thankful it didn't just crush his skull in. It was freezing to the touch, and ice had formed around the brim and inside the lid.

Somewhere in the distance, sirens echoed in the night, and the *Entity* tracked Kelly through time and space.

17

Donna had spent the last half hour or so sitting at their kitchen table, her eyes fixated on the news as the disregarded kettle whistled in the background. She barely even heard the metal pot's whistle as news of some sort of incident at the local library crackled through the television speakers. There were no reports of any relation between what happened at the station and the incident at the library. Still, she doubted it was a coincidence that two of the most town-rattling events happened within minutes of each other. And somehow, Kelly was at the centre of it all. She didn't know how, *or why*, but she sensed a deep connection between the events. And she knew he was in trouble.

And she didn't even know where he was.

Donna took a breath, forcing herself to look away from the television to turn off the oven's burner.

Outside in the cold and drizzly night, two officers kept post, sitting in their cruiser and listening to the radio as they remained vigilant for any sign of her husband.

As if he'd be foolish enough to use the front door, Donna thought, drawing back the curtain and making her way to the kitchen table to stay up to date on the news. Her mind lingered on Kelly's whereabouts, wrapped in concern.

There were barely any new updates as the news bounced back and forth between reporters at the police station, and reporters at the local library. There were few confirmations, everything else up in the air for the viewer to ponder over. So far, there were reports of one death, two people in serious condition, and a few more minor injuries. No names had been released, but apparently, the woman that died was only in her early thirties and had been pushed off a balcony at the library.

Was the world going mad?

Madder than it had already been?

Donna didn't want to know the answer. She just wanted her husband back. But there were *zero* reports of Kelly. Every few minutes, a freeze-frame would appear, showing Kelly's mug shot, and for anyone with any information to call in immediately. She prayed for the best, but she did not have a good feeling deep within. It was only a matter of time before Frank or someone called to tell her Kelly was hurt—*or worse.*

Donna erased the thought from her head immediately. She couldn't think like that, not now. Kelly needed her, and she would be ready when he did. For now, she would stay as informed as possible, gluing her eyes to the television and waiting for anything that could ease her mind.

From what she could tell, it seemed like not even the police knew what was going on, leaving very little details for the public as crowds and newscasters gathered around each scene, demanding answers.

Meanwhile, a constant ticker along the bottom of the screen called for any information leading to the recapture and arrest of Kelly Christopher, and that if found, that the public should by no means necessary approach the 'dangerous individual.'

As if Kelly would hurt anyone, Donna thought to herself while watching the flagrant news channel. *It's like everyone forgot all he's done for the city! Like all the time and work he's done over the years didn't matter at all. He wasn't some nefarious criminal. He was her husband and a good man! And there wasn't anything anyone could say or show her that would make her think otherwise. Not even Frank could sway her mind!*

Again, Donna fought back her emotions, slowly becoming a professional at sucking back the pain and keeping a straight face. If Kelly was going to get through this an innocent man, she was going to have to be strong—*she knew that*—even if it was the hardest thing in the world to do.

But fighting the overwhelming urge to break down was more than just mentally draining, it was downright exhausting, like holding up the weight of a thousand boulders upon your shoulders. This was too much for one person to bear alone.

It was right before the next wave of tears fought through when she decided that a warm shower might be a nice distraction. She could barely concentrate on the television anymore—the repetitious and damning mugshots of her husband becoming too difficult to watch on the television screen. So—*with little hesitation*—Donna set down her half-finished tea on the table, grabbed the handheld phone just in case someone called and made her way toward the stairs. But she only took a few steps before halting, turned back, and grabbed the steel kitchen knife sitting on the countertop. She didn't know why, but with all the craziness going on— *well*— it couldn't hurt to keep a weapon close, even if it was only for her ease of mind. *And even if two scummy cops were sitting outside her own home, waiting for their chance to arrest her innocent husband.*

Clenching the oversized chef's knife in one hand, the phone in the other, Donna slowly made her way up the stairs toward their bathroom, turning on every light she came across on the way.

She only made it halfway down the hallway when she noticed the faint smell of rotten eggs simmering through the air. It was barely noticeable, but it was undeniably there, rising through their hallway as if something had crawled under the floorboards and died. She tried following the smell, but it seemed to evaporate after a few seconds, as if it dispersed into nothingness. She searched for a few more seconds, but after coming up with nothing, Donna chalked it up to her tired imagination, and made her way down the hallway, through her bedroom and into their tiny bathroom.

Donna turned on the shower, watching as the hot steam slowly filled up the room. For a moment, Donna sat on the lid of their toilet, merely watching the water tumble into their ceramic tub, the condensing droplets dripping down the tiled walls and dark grey shower curtain.

And then she cried.

And then she cried even more.

She cried in the loneliness of her bathroom.

She cried as if God himself had summoned the tears upon her cheeks.

She cried.

Alone, she cried.

Then once her mind snapped back and the tears had all but evaporated amongst the hot steam of her lonesome bathroom, Donna lowered the knife and phone onto the edge of the bathroom sink next to Kelly's toothbrush, slipped out of her purple blouse and dress pants, and slipped naked into the shower, the hot water dancing off her tired skin, falling gently to her sore feet among the sweat and exhaustion.

The water was hotter than usual, but Donna barely noticed as the steam felt good in her lungs. Grabbing the conditioner, Donna began to lather her hair with the soothing scent of strawberries and cream, rinsing the suds away as the water bled down her scalp, the soap escaping through the stainless-steel drain.

Somewhere downstairs, the squeak of an opening door bounced across the walls, but Donna could not hear it above the shower's song.

She switched to her soap, the fragrance matching that of her conditioner, and began to apply it to her scalp, her wearied hands brushing through her long hair.

Donna didn't hear the sound of a creaking step as the soap ran down her scalp and into her ears and eyes, the slight burning sensation quenched by her sealed eyes.

She reached for her towel, which would normally be hanging over the shower curtain on the far side of the tub— but it wasn't there. Her tired mind had forgotten to grab one before hopping in.

She let the hot water beat against her face, blocking the sound of a gentle step on the hardwood as her bedroom door slowly swayed open.

Turning the shower handles, the water ceased, and Donna swung open the dark grey curtain, her eyes closed, reaching blindly for a spare towel on the far rack. Eventually, her fingertips brushed the organic bamboo cotton of their decorative towels, matching that of the bathroom decor. She gripped the towel, tossing it over her head, drying her hair, and wiping out the burning sensation from her eyes, *blocking the man's view standing in her bathroom doorway, staring at her naked body as the water dripped from her exposed skin.*

It wasn't until she went to tangle her hair in the towel did she notice the officer standing within reach before her.

She didn't scream.

She wanted to, but her startled fear had taken that ability away.

She only mustered the strength for a trembling gasp as she stood naked before him—*her back to the wall*—*her only exit blocked.*

Donna stared directly at the police officer intruding in her bathroom, who was dressed in full uniform, his eyes as black as the void of darkness. His neck was bent awkwardly to the left, and his arms seemed warped beside him. A low humming whisper echoed under his twisted breath, his hands jerking back and forth like he was enduring a mini seizure.

Donna felt her stomach drop and her hope shrink. The faint smell of rot mixed with the steamy air as she lost her voice in terror. She wanted to scream *get the hell out and leave me alone,* but the words never came. She simply stared ahead as the writhing officer took a thrusting step forward. Donna instinctively tried to back away but slipped on the wet-tiled floor and fell backwards into the tub. Her fingers grasped the shower-soaked curtains as she fell, but the plastic rings could not hold her weight, and then came crashing down alongside her. Donna slammed the back of her head against the edge of the porcelain tub. Her vision became shaky, her sense of balance all but lost, feeling like a stun-grenade had detonated an inch in front of her nose. But what she did see in the corner of her hazy vision was the demented officer with the black eyes hovering over her in a shadowy haze, the silver chef's knife gripped firmly in his hand.

That would be the last thing Donna Christopher ever saw.

A. Ryan MacGibbon

Part III
Motive

18

Kelly Christopher was cutting between buildings downtown, keeping on the move as much as he could, constantly looking over his shoulder, always trying to stay a step ahead of the *Entity*. He knew it was out there, lurking somewhere, waiting to make its next move. Kelly still had no idea why the shadow haunted him, or why it was obsessed with tormenting him. He had a handful of guesses, but none of them made sense. Kelly considered that he might somehow already be dead, and that death chasing him in some sort of purgatory—but he didn't remember dying, and he felt rather alive right now, evidenced by his pounding heart and nervous twitch. Kelly wasn't an overly religious person, but he always thought it was possible that there could be a higher power above, that life wasn't just over at the draw of a curtain. And if that were true, if there really was a God as the scriptures say, then surely this *Entity* was the Devil. But Kelly didn't like that explanation either. It was too spiritual, and he was a man of certainty, years of resolvable cases sending him down that path.

There was a case he and Frank had worked on a few years back, one of those cases that stuck with you until the day you died. One day, they got a call over the shortwave that a man living on the outskirts of the city had fired off some shots from his second-story window for no reason other than getting the law's attention. The young couple that called it in said the man was shouting for the police from his bedroom window, waving his gun in the air like a lunatic, and had even fired a few rounds at the couple passing by. This quickly turned into a high-profile case, so the station sent Frank and Kelly to try and manage the situation and utilize their expertise in law enforcement, and if they could, take the gun-waving coward in. The duo obliged and jumped in their cruiser and drove a few miles down St. Margaret's Bay Road and joined the collection of cruisers and swat teams that already had the boarded-up house surrounded. When Frank and Kelly arrived, they were informed that the man inside held his girlfriend hostage, tied up at gunpoint, and that all attempts to calm the man had failed. Honestly, there wasn't much that Kelly or Frank could have done but sit there and watch from behind the cover of their armoured car. A professional negotiator had been en route at the time, but he never would have made it in time. About six minutes after Frank and Kelly showed up at the scene, a few gunshots were fired from the top story window, dinging a few cars, and narrowly missing nearby officers. The man yelled profanities from his home, screaming and hollering things that didn't make a whole lot of sense.

Eventually, Kelly had enough, so he grabbed the loudspeaker from one of the spectating officers and tried to give it a go himself. But before he could even stammer out a few short sentences, two shots were heard from within the house. After several failed attempts at communication and no word of any movement from the spotters surrounding the building, the swat team decided to move in, sneaking through the back and charging in by force.

As it turned out, the attempt was futile. The team was greeted by the thirty-four-year-old man and his tied-up girlfriend, both with their brains splattered across the floor. A hand-written note layered with blood had been left behind on the kitchen counter. It simply read:

I couldn't take it anymore.

Too much of a coward to go alone.
Thanks for nothing.

Kelly would let that note roll around his head for many sleepless nights. In every case he'd had before, there had been a clear motive. Stolen cash was for drugs, a beaten man was due to racism or disagreement, and murder was for revenge. But this— Kelly was never able to pin it down to a definitive motive. The reports later would depict clinical depression, but that didn't explain why he'd take her with him. Maybe he was just insane. Maybe not. Frank had said it was just a single man stepped too far off the edge. But again, that answer didn't satisfy Kelly. Nor would he ever be satisfied.

Some late-night research told Kelly that the man had been an assistant manager at a local grocery market, was mostly liked by all his associates, and never had any written complaints by upper management or customers alike. He had family that loved him, and even his twenty-nine-year-old girlfriend's family never had anything terrible to say about him besides his ambition being a little feeble. They had been together two years without a hint of concern or turbulence. It was as though the man's mind had suddenly severed its connection to reality, cutting off his humanity. Kelly would conclude that it was the one and only case where he came face-to-face with pure oblivion. A motiveless crime, and an example of the culprit watching the world burn just to feel the heat. It was the only time Kelly had seen pure maliciousness in its sincerest form.

Until today.

In the few seconds the *Entity* tried to control him—*as Kelly's mind sunk deep within himself before successfully fighting the urge to surrender*—Kelly had felt pure nothingness, a void he wished upon not even his worst enemy. Even the harshest pain imaginable seemed better than facing the bottomless chasm of nothingness.

That was what the *Entity* was.

A push of oblivion.

A wave of worthlessness.

A black hole from which there was no return.

And Kelly *knew* he had to fight it.

He didn't know why, not really, but he knew he couldn't let this thing win. There was more to this than just his own simple life—*although staying alive was certainly a bonus.* Kelly Christopher didn't know what to do next, but he had a feeling that it somehow revolved around the murder of his friend Zoe Stevens, and the imposter that did it, so the next move was to find clues. He needed to use his newly found time-bending power to try and understand why Zoe's pistol was drawn at the time of the shooting, and who the person was that shot her down in the Halifax Ferry Terminal. Kelly's strength lay in his exceptional detective abilities.

Returning from his thoughts, Kelly raised his head to scan his surroundings and try and spot the *Entity* or any of *its* twisted puppets. There was nothing in sight. Kelly stood in a small park in downtown Halifax, across from City Hall. Behind him was a white church, and dead ahead was a stone memorial, with words of remembrance written across the top:

IN HONOUR OF
THOSE WHO SERVED

IN MEMORY OF
THOSE WHO FELL

1914 1918

1939 1945
1950 1953

Kelly was fortunate it was a rainy day. The darkness and rain helped keep his id*Entity* concealed from the few passersby braving the nasty weather. Time may have returned to normal, but he knew the station would be looking for him in full force. Surely his face would be plastered on every news-channel and billboard across Atlantic Canada, so the fewer people around to see his face, the better. He was surprised at the lack of cruisers patrolling the streets in search of him. He had evaded a few cruisers by hiding in alleyways between buildings, but for someone so accused as he was, he was alarmed there weren't more out on the hunt. Kelly was only vaguely aware of the station's situation. The severity and confusion at the station and the public library eluded him. The troops were running thin, and Kelly would unknowingly use that to his advantage.

After a few moments of pondering, Kelly determined his next move. He was going to head back to the station, attempt to slow down time like before, and collect all the information and clues he could find on Zoe Stevens, and solve this case himself, proving his innocence. He also contemplated raiding the weapons locker and grabbing some sort of firearm to try and protect himself—not that a bullet would do any good against the vaporous spectre. But it would be effective against the twisted puppets, he thought. *It was a last resort.* He'd use his powers first, and if that didn't work, he'd run, and if that failed—*he hoped for his own sake it didn't come to that.*

Kelly was about to make his way back to the station when a flicker of a shadow caught his eye on the far side of the park. At first, he thought it might be the *Entity*, but was relieved to see that it wasn't.

That relief would be short-lived.

Watching him from across the park was what looked like a man, but everything about him sent a chill up Kelly's already stiff spine. The man's neck was warped to one side, his arm outstretched in jagged form, pointing to Kelly's right across the harbour toward Dartmouth, Halifax's rival city. Kelly squinted to get a better look, taking a few cautious steps forward. He gathered the energy around him, preparing to use his unexplained power once again—*assuming he even could.* The figure was clad in ripped jeans and a black leather jacket, matched with long dark hair and a silver earring on his left ear. The twisted man in the darkness simply stared at him, one crooked arm outstretched, *pointing.* His neck jerked rapidly and his body trembling faintly, like a convulsing puppet dangling from invisible strings. A slight glimmer of light shining from a street light streaked across the man's face, illuminating his void-like eyes in the drizzly night. There was no doubt about it. He was under *its* control.

Kelly's gaze swept the area, searching for the *Entity*, ready to sprint in the opposite direction once spotted. But the *Entity* never arrived, only this broken man in his jagged form stood before him. Kelly inched even closer, his investigative mind overwriting caution, like a cat investigating a strange noise in the night. He only needed to take a few steps closer to realize the man was whispering something under his breath. Kelly could see the man's lips repeatedly moving, over and over again as if the *Entity* was trying to communicate with him.

At first, Kelly couldn't make out the words. They were deep, mumbled, and barely audible above the sounds of the city. But the crooked man's words were for him, that much was certain. Kelly cautiously approached until he could make out the *Entity*'s message.

He immediately wished he hadn't.

The Entity's message was undeniable.
The Entity's threat was abundantly clear.

"......*Donna Donna* ......"

*No...*Kelly's stomach suddenly twisted into a knot, his vision caving inward like a collapsing tunnel as the contorted man whispered Donna's name in a low deathly hum. Suddenly, Kelly knew what the man was pointing at. He wasn't just pointing across the harbour. He was pointing directly toward Kelly's home, at Donna's home—*at Donna.*

Kelly didn't even try to suppress his rage, nor did he proceed with caution. He stepped forward, grabbing the bent man's clothes by the tuff, and swung his fist forward, connecting his knuckles with the man's nose. The surge of pain streaked across Kelly's arm, his knuckle feeling like it just split in two, but his anger outweighed his agony, and he swung again, smashing his fist into the man's nose, blood beginning to gush violently.

"Don't you touch her," Kelly screamed at the man as onlookers began to gather around. "Don't you touch my wife!"

Kelly listened as the man winced in pain, not noticing that his eyes had shifted back to their natural whites and blues, Kelly's fury blinding his senses. He swung again, and the man in the black leather jacket cowered, Kelly's knuckle connecting with the man's earring, pushing it into his skin, splitting a tiny gash across his earlobe. Kelly threw a few more punches before realizing there was a crowd of about ten gathering all around. Suddenly, another bystander yanked Kelly away from the man with the silver earring.

Kelly's heart raced as the energy around him pulsed. He felt like he could have exploded, but he held back, attempting to calm himself as he separated his anger from his intention. If it weren't for the younger fellow pulling him off the beaten man, he could have killed him. *He would have killed him*. Looking back, he saw the man he had assaulted—bruised, battered, and bleeding. It was clear the man was no longer under the *Entity's* control, but that didn't matter. The spectre knew where Donna was, and Kelly wasn't going to let a *damn* thing happen to her. Instantly, the bruised-knuckled detective fled away, the onlookers watching him as he ran. A few shouted for him to stay, but he didn't turn back. His direction was resolute.

Kelly dashed down the hill and into the oncoming traffic on Barrington Street, halting the cars in their tracks. Immediately he ran to the driver's side of a black Pontiac, yanking the driver out of his seat and onto the wet asphalt, seizing control of the vehicle. Kelly thought about using his powers and freezing time so he could get to his house in a matter of milliseconds—*relative to everyone else*—but thought against it. The car wouldn't work properly with time frozen, and the *Entity* had proven it was unaffected by Kelly's powers. He would have to do this the old-fashioned way.

19

Frank arrived at a park off Argyle Street completely fatigued, frustrated, and wanting nothing more than to crawl home to his bed. His wife had already texted him a few times, asking when he'd be back. She mentioned a couple of pork chops waiting for him under some tinfoil in the fridge. *What he'd give for a meal that didn't come from a wrapper or vending machine.*

He was about to hop out of his cruiser and head to the centre of the tiny park—*where a small crowd had gathered around some sort of minor disturbance*—when his mobile rang. Frank glanced at the crowd in the park to see that another young officer was already resolving the situation and noting details, so he felt less urge to face another crowd thirsting for answers. There wasn't even a news crew present—guess a minor disturbance didn't amount to two potential terrorist attacks occurring simultaneously.

Deciding to take a moment to himself, Frank answered the call. "Hello?" Frank recognized the number popping up on the screen as the security company that managed the footage of the incident at the library. But it *was* strange that they were calling. Typically, the company would send such footage directly to the station for Frank to view at his leisure. Their call suggested an irregularity.

"Hello. Is this the number for Officer McDowell?"

"Yes, speaking?"

"Hi, yes. This is the chief technician at TopShield Security Systems, Greg Norman. We were just reviewing the footage before sending, and…"

Frank already knew what he was about to say. He saw the same thing happen on the footage at the station. "And it's glitched, almost like it skips ahead, missing all the important bits?"

"—Um, actually. Yes. How did you know that?"

"Lucky guess," Frank said, snickering through his teeth.

"Well, we'll send what we do have down, but I don't know how useful it will be. We really don't know what happened, sir, but we promise we're putting together a full internal investigation."

"Thanks," Frank responded half-heartedly. "Something tells me it's not your fault."

Frank hung up the call, pocketed his mobile, and opened the door to his cruiser, the damp rainy air immediately blowing into his face. He doubted he'd be here long. With everything else going on, a small dispute between two city folk was the least of his worries.

As Frank entered the small park, the extent of the damage was immediately apparent. Sitting on a ledge of the stone fence surrounding the park, was a man, probably not much older than thirty. He wore a black leather jacket and torn jeans, donning a bloody earring on his left ear. But what he was wearing was irrelevant. The man's face was pummelled black and blue, and blood streamed from multiple lacerations. His nose was bent to one side, and his eye had completely swollen over, as if he'd gone a few rounds with a boxer wielding brass knuckles. An older lady sat beside him, holding a handkerchief to his left cheek, the fabric soaked in his blood.

"Has anyone called for an ambulance?" Frank asked, guessing he knew the answer.

"I did," said a younger gentleman standing off to the side. "But it's taking a while."

"There's a lot going on tonight, kid." Frank popped out his black notebook, which was starting to look more like a mad scientist's notepad than that of an ordinarily well-organized detective. He flipped halfway through the book to a fresh page, holding it close to his body to protect his notes from the rain.

"Can you speak?" He asked the battered man, not certain he could. The man nodded a gentle yes, clearly wincing as he did so. "Alright, good. Tell me everything you can. Start from the beginning."

The man attempted to speak, first spitting out some blood, his split lips and missing tooth hindering his speech. Beside him, a lady wiped the blood from his chin, briefly exposing a large gash before reapplying the handkerchief. Eventually, the battered man was able to slug out some words.

"I got jumped," he said, coughing again. His scratchy voice betrayed the struggle to speak.

"We can do this later if you'd like." Frank said, offering the man a chance to heal. "Down at the station—"

"No." The man cut him off. "I'm good," he insisted. Frank admired the man's resilience. "I'm not sure how to explain it, but…"

More coughing.

"…I was headin' back to my apartment yea' see. Then the last thing I remember, I was lying on my back in the park, with some asshole holding me down, wailin' on me like I was nothin'."

Frank jotted down some notes, then asked his usual questions for this type of scenario. "Did he take anything? Keys? Wallet?"

"Not a thing." The man reached into his mouth, twisted his fingers around and pulled out another tooth.

Weird, Frank thought. If it wasn't a mugging, then maybe some sort of revenge? "Did you know the guy?"

"Didn't get a good look at him. By the time I snapped out of it, my eye was already swollen over." The man gestured to his eye with his middle finger, unnecessary given the evident gashes and swollen skin.

"What do you mean, 'snapped out of it'? You mean when the fight was over?"

"Wasn't much of a fight," he said, his voice weak, hinting at his exhaustion. "Officer—" he paused for a second, as if hesitant to speak, then continued anyway, "—I know how this sounds, but it's the truth. I swear."

"Alright?" Frank responded, curious.

"Seriously, I've been clean six years now."

"Tell me what happened."

"Officer, my home, it's in the south end. I was on my way back from work when this happened."

"Okay. What does that have to do with anything?"

"I'm a line cook at a pub on Spring Garden...and I was heading straight home after..."

Frank gave him a puzzled look. Spring Garden and the south end were both in the opposite direction of the park. "What exactly are you trying to say?"

"I'm saying that I don't know how I got here. One second, I'm walking home in the dark, next second I'm getting my face smashed a kilometre away from where I should be. I know it doesn't make sense, but it's the God-honest truth. And like I said, I haven't had a hit for over six years now."

Frank stared at him and contemplated what he said, the motive beginning to mesh together with what the victims were explaining to him at the library. It seemed that every piece of vital information had been erased from existence, either from camera or from memory. It was like there was some divine intervention preventing Frank from performing his duties. Frank felt like he was navigating a case without a lead—*like a ship adrift without a rudder.*

Frank slid his notebook back into his breast pocket and pulled out a photograph in its place. He looked at it for a moment, the picture usually resting on his desk at the station. It showed him and his partner Kelly, both in uniform, each of them holding a Police Exemplary Service Medal for solving a case related to the abduction of a young boy from his mother. Kelly and Frank had put together some of their best work, tracking down a criminal in a white-tinted van all the way to the border of New Brunswick and Québec, arresting him in a small town, saving the boy, and imprisoning the creep—*who, disturbingly, turned out to be the boy's former neighbor with predatory intentions.* The child was returned unscathed to his mother, and the creep was still rotting away in jail alongside other convicted murderers and felons.

Raindrops hit the photo as he rotated it, showing it to the beaten man sitting on the edge of the stone wall. He didn't want to ask the question, but figured it was worth a shot. "Was this the man that attacked you?"

The man studied the photograph for a moment, then turned away, looking back up at Frank with his swollen face. "Like I said, I didn't get a good look at him."

Frank felt a sense of relief, holding out the smallest sliver of hope that his partner and longtime friend was innocent, even though in his heart, he knew that wasn't true. How could it be after watching the footage at the ferry terminal. It was clear as day. But there was still that—

"That was him." The old lady holding the bloodied cloth said. Her voice was certain.

"Ma'am, are you sure?"

"Positive. I saw the man flee down toward Barrington. His face was clear as day in the streetlights."

Jesus Christ, Kelly.

What are you thinking?

Frank was aware of officers breaking under pressure, about them not being able to take the heat anymore, suffering from severe PTSD after drawing their gun on duty— manifesting as domestic abuse, animal abuse, or, in some tragic cases, suicide—never something like this, and never here in Nova Scotia.

This kind of thing just doesn't happen here.

Although it seemed that the events of the day were starting to prove otherwise.

Frank tucked the photograph back in his pocket just as the ambulance arrived. The younger officers guided the paramedics to the scene, who just happened to be the same paramedics at the hospital a half-hour earlier. *They were just as busy as he was,* Frank thought, turning back toward the victim and lady.

Frank expressed his gratitude to the cooperative witnesses, and turned to leave, another puzzling piece added to the already towering stack. But before he was gone, the victim yelled back at him, adding another level of complexity.

"There's one more thing, officer." Frank turned back, listening to the man as he gave his final clue. "I couldn't see the man, but he did speak while thrusting his fists into my face." He gently pushed away from the lady's handkerchief as the paramedics made their way to the victim, the blood still trickling down his face. "He said, 'don't *touch her. Don't touch my wife.'* Then he sprinted away, leaving me for dead."

Frank thanked the witness again, feeling his feet hasten as he made his way back to the cruiser. He ignited the engine, locked his seatbelt in place, and flicked on his sirens before even realizing that in his exhaustion, he had forgotten to also grab the man's name and information.

It *didn't matter*. The boys would grab his details. Besides, there were more pressing matters at hand now. For once, he had a lead.

He knew where Kelly was going. And just like that, Frank was off, the sirens loud, blue and red lights flashing on the side of the buildings in the night.

He was going to take him down once and for all.

·20

Neighbours two blocks down could hear the screech of rubber tires as Kelly Christopher ripped around the corner and slammed on his brakes, coming to a screeching halt before his Dartmouth home as the rain rolled heavily into the night. He knew that he was undoubtedly walking into a trap, that the *Entity* would be waiting for him inside. And if the *Entity* and its puppets weren't there—*which he doubted very much*—then the police would surely be waiting for him. An escaped convict on the loose would mean a cruiser posted outside his house with constant surveillance of the neighbourhood. And as Kelly hopped out of the car and into the chilly rain, he could see that he was right.

Only, there should have been guns drawn on him immediately, with officers yelling for him to *get down* and *show your hands.* But there wasn't any of that. Instead, parked along the curb across the road from his house, was an empty police car, the door open, the warning system within the vehicle beeping loudly over the howling wind. Kelly could hear the radio chatter, dispatch requesting mandatory fifteen-minute updates, receiving no response, which meant in a short while, there would be a plethora of blue uniforms on the streets, searching for their missing cops—*and Kelly.*

He had to be quick.

Or risk stopping time once again—*if he even could.*

Kelly gazed toward his house, noting the front door agape, revealing only darkness within. Not even the porch light was on, as if the electrical line had been cut to his own house.

There was the nagging sense that, if he went through that lonely door, there was no coming back. But his own life was hardly on his mind. Saving Donna was the only goal, whatever the cost. There was only one thing left to do before charging the gates.

He walked over toward the empty police cruiser, the rain soaking the passenger side seat through the open door, the repeating door-ajar alert continually buzzing. The cops were nowhere in sight—*a bad omen*. However, the severity of his escape was a promising sign. A supposedly dangerous criminal on the loose on the day a police officer was killed meant the station wasn't going to take any chances. It meant it would do anything to make sure another officer wasn't harmed. *It meant each car came equipped with an emergency shotgun.*

Kelly reached behind the seat of the cruiser, pulling out a Remington Model 870 12 Gauge pump-action shotgun, with a wooden pump handle, black steel barrel, and four shells. There was more ammo under the seat, but if he needed to fire off that many shots, he was already dead.

He didn't plan on missing.

With the shotgun firmly gripped in his trained hands, Kelly hopped out of the police car and made his way toward his home, stopping a few yards before the porch to try and get a good look inside. Not a soul stirred within the house. There were no missing police officers, no Donna, and as far as he could tell, no *Entity*. Kelly could see nothing.

Silence reigned, broken only by the steady tap of rain against the roof's edge.

Every nerve screamed retreat, yet his heart urged him forward. And forward he would go—*for Donna.*

With his wife in mind, Kelly stepped inside the darkness of his home.

Stepping beyond the welcome mat, Kelly pivoted right, viewing the entirety of his dark and empty living room, checking every corner with the barrel of his 12-gauge, praying he wouldn't have to use it. After ensuring the room where he and Frank had spent many game nights was clear, he proceeded to the kitchen, clearing the guest room and bathroom as he walked by. Like the living room, the kitchen was deserted, with Donna's usual chair pulled away from the empty table. Just a lifetime ago, he had sat at this very table, enjoying his morning coffee, and joking around with Donna, hearing the news of the Terminal shooting over the television, only to be arrested for the murder twenty minutes later. Now here he was, under threat by something supernatural, threatened in his own home, looking for his wife.

What did Kelly and Donna do to deserve this?

What they deserved had nothing to do with it.

It seldom did.

Kelly brushed the thought away, keeping his mind focused on the task at hand. The downstairs was clear, and it was time to move toward the second level.

He climbed the stairs with careful diligence, met by an eerie lull. Not even the smell of rotting stench was present, which remained a good omen for the time being.

At the top of the stairs, Kelly could scarcely make out the tip of his shotgun as he held it ready in the darkness, the wooden butt pushed up against his left shoulder. He kept expecting someone to reach out from the dark and grab the barrel, but it never happened. As far as he knew, he was alone, and the gun never felt so heavy in his sweating hands, the rain in his wet hair dripping down the back of his exposed neck.

He stepped a few more paces ahead, checking each room as quickly and carefully as he could, each one emptier than the last until he reached their master bedroom at the end of the hall.

A faint light from the streetlamp outside filtered through the half-drawn curtains as Kelly stepped into the room. The space was vacant, and for a split-second, he began to lower the shotgun. That is, until he heard the faint click of a step coming from the shadow of their attached bathroom. Kelly instantly raised the shotgun again, standing in the doorway of his bedroom, the barrel aiming shakily toward his bathroom, ready to fire.

"Show yourself!" Kelly demanded, his finger pressed lightly against the trigger. A quiet murmur echoed out of the darkness, the intruder not yet seen.

"Come out slowly!" He commanded again, the shotgun trembling in his hands. He knew there was no alternative exit for whoever was standing in his bathroom.

Kelly didn't have to wait much longer for the stranger to emerge.

A single naked soul stepped out of the bathroom.

Their arms were jagged.

Their neck was grotesquely bent to the side.

Their wedding ring dropped to the floor as their fingers twitched and jolted inharmoniously...

The sight was immediately too much for Kelly to bear as he collapsed to one knee, barely able to hold himself up as he propped his crumbling stance with the barrel of the shotgun.

Standing before him, clearly under the full weight of the *Entity*'s power, with a seven-inch steel knife protruding from her right eye socket, was his wife Donna Christopher, blood gushing down her cheek amongst the engulfing darkness.

A rush of desperate hopelessness constricted Kelly's throat like a wave of poison forcefully injected into his veins.

"No...please...God...why?!" Kelly wailed beyond distress, his heart hemorrhaging in two, leaving nothing but the nothingness around him. He looked up again at Donna, who was slowly inching closer, reaching out as if to blame him for not saving her. Her jaw hung disjointed, cracking with each step she took forward, the bloodied knife lodged in her skull swaying back and forth as she struggled ahead.

Donna was halfway across the room before Kelly found the strength to rise to his feet, dropping his gun and reaching for his wife, grabbing her tight, holding her close as Donna's body became limp, dropping to the floor under Kelly's caring guidance. She was whispering softly, her broken jaw cracking and grinding as she spoke.

So focused on his wife's mutilated form, Kelly failed to hear the pair of shrieks that echoed from downstairs, marking the entrance of the two twisted police officers into his home, creeping slowly toward the stairs. He could only look down at his one-eyed wife, her teeth grinding in her dry mouth as her jaw lurched back and forth, whispering a single phrase that would haunt Kelly until his end.

"...No...Time..."

Then, like cool water quenching a dying fire, Donna ceased her struggles.

She stopped jerking.

And she stopped breathing.

Her one in-tact eye halted its rapid movement, and her arms became as limp as a corpse.

The knife had done its damage.

Donna was dead.

Kelly's shriek was so piercing it could have reached the coastline, his fists clenched, Donna lifeless below his knees. He cursed the *Entity*, the world, himself, and everything in between. And just as he cried out the last of his breath of agony, as if right on queue, two twisted police officers burst out from atop the stairs, crashing into the wall on the far side of the hallway opposite Kelly in the master bedroom. He turned to see Officer

McDougall and another he didn't recognize, each of them clearly under the demented power of the *Entity*. He watched them as they sprinted toward the bedroom in a jagged, twisting motion. Kelly almost didn't move. For a moment, he considered letting them come and take him to the afterlife, forfeiting his now-meaningless presence on this earth. But there was a deeper power burning within his core far more potent than the bending of time, a power that could move mountains, drain oceans, and split the moon itself. More than anything in this world or the next, *Kelly wanted revenge.*

Hastily, Kelly sprang up from the floor, grabbed the shotgun beside his dead wife, and slammed the door shut to his bedroom, just as the two officers came crashing into it from the other side, nearly knocking it off its wooden frame. It held, but Kelly knew it wouldn't be long before they got inside.

But he'd be ready.

Kelly perched himself on the edge of his bed, positioning the shotgun under his shoulder, and waited as the two puppets thrashed and banged at the far side of his bedroom door, his wife's lifeless body lying beside him with a chef's knife sticking out her right eye. He listened to their screams—*not shouts, screams*—like their bodies were under constant internal torture. He wondered if that's what Donna felt—fear, loneliness, never really knowing if Kelly was a murderer or innocent.

No, she knew he was innocent.

She knew him.

She was the only one in the world that did.

And now she was gone.

The bedroom door's hinges started to give way, and Kelly knew it would only be seconds before they got in. Bracing himself, he shifted his gaze from the tragedy beside him to confront the monsters ahead, the shotgun primed in his hands.

It only took a few more good bashes before the bedroom door came crashing down, landing on Donna's stiff legs as the two officers collapsed to the floor atop of it, falling through the splintered doorframe with their twisted bodies. Without hesitation, Kelly pulled the trigger, and Officer McDougall's head was obliterated—*or at least, the twisted body of what was Officer McDougall*. Bits of skull, brain, and blood spattered across the bedroom walls.

Quickly, he shifted the barrel toward the other officer, who was trapped under the now decapitated body of the other puppet, looking up toward Kelly with his soulless eyes, reaching out with his twisted fingers, grabbing at Kelly's black boot. Kelly stood up from the bed, stomping down on the creature's wrist, feeling it snap and slither under his boot. Then, with the butt of the gun, Kelly unleashed his fury, pulverizing the officer's face, squishing it with all his might until there was nothing left to crush. Then, for good measure, Kelly flipped the weapon around, and fired a slug into what was left of the puppet's head, splattering bits of skull and brain onto his hardwood floors, showering himself and his dead wife in the mess. In the darkness, Kelly was spared the sight of his gore-drenched reflection in the vanity mirror.

Kelly scarcely registered the gore that covered him. He was consumed by a mix of incandescent rage and profound misery. He released a shout of frenzy, releasing every emotion he could from his body.

Unfortunately, *the Entity heard everything*.

In the hallway of his home, as if slicing through time and space, the *Entity* materialized, glaring directly at the gore-covered Kelly through the darkness of his own home.

"Go back to hell," Kelly yelled, lifting the shotgun and pumping a round into what would be the gut of a normal human being. The bullets never connected, passing directly through the cloud-like form and connecting with the far wall. Kelly didn't seem to care. He fired his last round, this time at the shadow's head, the bullets cracking against the ceiling behind it. He fired a few more dry clicks before tossing the rifle itself, the weapon passing clean through the shadow and landing on the floor by the stairs.

Suddenly, whispers swarmed Kelly's ears, as if the dead from all corners of the world were speaking to him at once, channelled through the shadow lurking before him.

"...*Kill him. Kill her. Kill him. Kill her. Kill him. Kill her....*"

Over and over, the droning voices of men and women, young and old, whispered threats from thin air into Kelly's mind, like the voices were speaking directly into his mind.

"...*Kill him. Kill her. Kill him. Kill her. Kill him. Kill her....*"

Then it grew worse. The voices shifted and changed, altering from that of strangers to that of familiarity. Suddenly it wasn't the voices of random men and women commanding for him to kill, but the voices of Donna and Zoe, penetrating his thoughts, ruling his mind. He looked down at Donna, silent and motionless on their bedroom floor, splattered in the guts and gore of the officers that were supposed to protect her.

"...*Kill him. Kill her. Kill him. Kill her. Kill him. Kill her....*"

Kelly covered his ears, attempting to block the noises from his mind as they caused his head to swell, feeling like a balloon inflating from the inside. He fought it as hard as he could, feeling that shallow pressure against his skin begin to boil, but it was useless. The *Entity* was taking control; he could *feel* it. The same power that controlled the puppets was slowly infecting his mind. He could feel it, spreading like wildfire doused with gasoline. And if he didn't do something soon, he would be joining his wife on the floor, utterly submissive to the *Entity*'s dark will.

> *He was going to die.*
> *Or at least wish he was dead.*

Kelly made a quick retreat to the window on his left, sliding it open and letting the streetlights and rain pour in from outside, the *Entity* entering the room from behind him, reaching out as the sinister voices grew louder.

"*...Kill him. Kill her. Kill him. Kill her. Kill him. Kill her....*"

For a moment, a paralyzing urge to stop gripped Kelly., his neck growing stiff, his limbs growing numb, the pins-and-needles feeling spreading across his arms, but he shook it off, struggling to get his body out the window to safety. The misery and pain of his wife's death grew more prominent by the minute, thoughts of darkness and suicide squeezing his mind. The rain bounced off his skin, but he barely felt it, a silent numbness overtaking his body as the *Entity* poisoned his very soul.

Fight, Kelly, fight.

Kelly managed to cram his body through the tiny window. He landed on the wet slanted roof and unintentionally slid down on the asphalt panels as the rain guided his fall. He was flung from the roof's edge and plummeted to the ground, landing on the damp grass and mud below. As Kelly put distance between himself and the shadow, the voices faded, and the numbness began to dissipate—*if only for the time being.*

He stood up to his feet, looking back at the *Entity* hovering in the darkness of his bedroom window, glaring down upon him in the night. Kelly stared back, vowing to himself that he'd find a way to get his revenge. He would avenge Donna, the officers he was forced to strike down, and anyone else cut down by the essence of evil tormenting him. Kelly would find a way. He believed it with his empty heart.

But for now, he needed to get away and find some sort of solitude to try and mourn.

He would not get that chance.

Standing behind him, as the rain poured down from the cloud-covered skies, gun drawn and aimed directly at Kelly's chest, was his friend and partner, Frank McDowell.

21

rank pulled up to Kelly's house with his lights and sirens silent just in time to hear two gunshot blasts ring through the night from the second floor of Kelly and Donna's home. He could see the flash in Kelly's bedroom through the hail-drawn curtains, slicing through the rainy night like a bolt of lightning. Frank didn't hesitate. He leapt from his cruiser, drawing his gun with the safety disengaged.

Frank knew he should've called for backup—*going in alone was reckless*—but he felt he didn't have a choice. He had spent too many buzzed nights in Kelly's living room watching the game and enjoying Donna's famous Chili-topped nachos to turn back now. Before him, a black Pontiac sat askew on the curb behind another police cruiser, resting with the door open, the cops nowhere to be seen.

Suddenly a horrible thought popped into Frank's mind. He wondered if the gunshots he heard were the officers striking down his partner. He prayed it wasn't. Not before he could get to the bottom of this. His thoughts were harshly interrupted by two more gunshots, loud enough wake the entire neighbourhood, awoken by the disruptive noise. Frank stood out in the rain, wondering what in God's name was going on. To his right, a man a few decades older than himself, wearing a housecoat and dawning an umbrella, walked down the sidewalk toward him. Frank flashed his badge and ordered the man to return home, not wanting to have to deal with civilians right now.

With his gun ready, Frank began to head toward Kelly's darkened home, his pistol on the ready as he hurried forward. He didn't even make it halfway across the yard when he heard noises from the porch-roof above. His vision of the bedroom window was obstructed, but he heard the sliding sound of Kelly's window opening, then a few harsh thumps, followed by a gentle scraping sound. Not a second later, Frank watched from the front yard as Kelly slid off the damp roof, landing hard onto the wet grass below. Frank was pretty sure Kelly didn't see him, but it allowed Frank to get a good look at his once-partner — *now criminal*. His skin and clothes were covered in — what looked like blood — and Kelly was constantly scanning back toward the roof with vigilant eyes, like something was going to come chasing after him on the roof. Frank was frozen for a moment, never seeing Kelly so distraught and dishevelled as he was, his hair soaking in the heavy showers from above. Visible abrasions marred his arm, and his shirt was torn from sliding down the asphalt shingles, and as Kelly stood up, Frank could clearly see a gentle limp protecting his right ankle.

Jesus, Kelly, what have you done.

Frank raised his gun and pointed it directly at Kelly's chest — *his partner's chest*. There was no need to shout or to tell Kelly to *toss his hands in the air*. Kelly turned and faced Frank, his gaze shifting from the darkness above to Frank's firearm, his eyes already in a state of deep distress. Kelly's gaze met Frank's, his eyes red and swollen, his face smeared with blood — *too much blood for it to be Kelly's alone.*

Frank felt his gun shaking, barely able to aim it at the blood-drenched Kelly before him, his finger holding true on the trigger, ready to fire. *Would he fire?* He didn't know. It was time to get some answers.

"What did you do?" Frank demanded, taking a step toward Kelly, who wasn't even looking at him anymore, but back up toward where he had fallen off the roof. "Look at me!"

Kelly did, visible tears rushing down his face amongst the rain and blood. But he didn't respond, he just stood there silently, a man ready to break down to nothing.

"What—" Frank pressed, his teeth gritted, hand trembling on the trigger, "—did you do, Kelly?"

He watched his partner stumble to speak, barely able to find the words.

"She's—she's—"

Frank's heart sank, his thoughts pinning on Donna, who only last week was sitting next to them, wearing one of Kelly's Red Wing jerseys and taunting Frank as they sat in Kelly's living room, enjoying popcorn, and admiring their newly installed surround sound system.

"Where's Donna?" Frank asked, not wanting to know the answer.

Kelly, in profound distress, couldn't maintain eye contact with Frank, his gaze flitting back and forth.

"Kelly!" He took another step forward, keeping the gun fixated on Kelly's heart.

"She's—she's gone, Frank. I—I couldn't save her."

Frank didn't believe him.

He couldn't *believe* him.

He loved Donna like she was his own family, just as he loved Kelly.

She *couldn't* be gone.

He wouldn't be party to his madness.

"What are you talking about? What's going on?!" He'd never been so confused in his life, unable to fathom Kelly's jumbled words. No response, Kelly just stood there, looking like a lost stray dazed and confused.

Somewhere in the distance, Frank could hear sirens blaring. It wouldn't be long before back-up had arrived, most likely responding to a complaint from one of the surrounding neighbours. Frank felt himself choking from frustration and turmoil, lost somewhere between 'Cop' mode and 'Frank' mode, his two switches, as Kelly had once explained to him. For a moment, he was able to swallow his emotion, shifting back into cop mode as he struggled to brush aside the emotional distraction.

"Where are the two officers?" He pointed the gun at the empty police cruiser parked across the road on the shoulder, the light still on as the door swayed in the wind.

"Dead," Kelly said plainly. "It left me no choice." His voice sounded cold, wavering, as if he expected Frank to understand what he was talking about.

Suddenly, Frank more than ever felt the urge to pull the trigger, to strike down the murderer that had killed one cop already. Now he was claiming to have killed two more and was caught red-handed fleeing the scene. He fought back his emotion, struggling the itch to put a bullet in the cop-killer's head. He no longer saw Kelly as his friend and partner. Whatever happened to that guy, he was gone, replaced by the monster standing before him, covered in blood, sobbing like a madman. Frank wouldn't let this son-of-a-bitch hurt anyone else. He was going to make sure he was locked up forever, and if he couldn't do that, he was going to kill him.

"Get on your knees, Kelly."

No response, Kelly just looked at him, silent, distraught, broken.

"GET ON YOUR KNEES! I won't ask again!" Frank took another step toward Kelly, willing to stand there as long as it took. One way or another, he was going to take Kelly into custody.

But Frank wouldn't get the chance.

Tires screeched from around the corner, headlights shining brightly on Frank and Kelly as a large Ford pickup drifted onto Kelly's road, racing straight toward them. In a matter of seconds, the truck screeched down the road and burst through Kelly's wood-stained fence, slamming on its brakes and sliding across the lawn, the oversized tires ripping up the mud and sods as it skidded along. The dark green truck barreled toward them, unable to halt in time. The left edge of the bumper clipped Frank, propelling him backward and slamming him against Kelly's house, knocking Frank out cold. Kelly was able to dive out of the way, the truck coming to a complete stop inches away from the grey-panelled siding of his home.

Kelly lay upon the grass and mud, staring up at the headlights of the dark-green Ford F-150. He knew that truck, he recognized it from somewhere, but couldn't exactly place it. White striped decal streamed alongside the oversized truck's edges, the windows were tinted ever-so-slightly, and a minor lift-kit had been installed.

Where had he seen that truck before?

It didn't matter where he'd seen that. Not in a million years would Kelly have been able to guess who owned it, because stepping out from behind the wheel, hopping onto the grass with a heavy squish and offering her hand to help Kelly to his feet—*as though the night's harrowing events had never transpired*—living and breathing without a bullet wound in sight, was Officer Zoe Stevens.

And she had only one thing to say to Kelly.

A command he would not take lightly.

"If you want to save your wife, get in."

A Shadow in Time

Part IV
Possessed

22

...Minutes Before Contact...

The coffee cup was warm on Officer Zoe Stevens' cold hands as she patrolled alone throughout the Halifax boardwalk. She was only a few hours into her shift, starting at 4:00 AM and rolling through until noon, yet she was already primed to go home, because starting at noon, Zoe had four days off in a row for the first time in over eight months. She wasn't one of the most senior members of the force, so she still drew the short end of the stick when it came to shift-placement. This was the tail end of her sixth straight day, and she was more than ready to go home with her partner, Jessie. Jessie had also taken the week off to join her in relaxation. They had rented a small Airbnb in Wolfville, a small university town an hour outside Halifax. Their plan was to spend several nights exploring the town, checking out the harvest festival, and partaking in a few wine tours around the famous vineyard valley. The truck was already packed and ready to roll. They had saved up a pretty penny for this little mini vacation, so Zoe planned on milking every cent of it, splurging on locally aged bottles of wine, expensive dinners, and maybe even a bottle of whiskey if she was feeling adventurous enough. And she was looking forward to the sex. Oh yes, she was getting busy every night of the week, she was *damn* sure of that. And she was pretty sure Jessie wouldn't object.

But to do that, she had to get through five more hours of her shift. She knew they were going to be five of the most prolonged, excruciating hours she had ever worked on patrol.

Morning shifts tended to be uneventful. From 4:00 AM to about 6:30 am, there was barely anyone around. There were a few homeless people who slept under the benches along the boardwalk, but she left them alone for the most part. They weren't hurting anyone. Other than that, only the early screeches of seagulls broke the silence, singing before the sun even rose as they awaited their morning supper of food scraps, tiny harbour minnows, garbage, or whatever else they ate.

Zoe made her way north down the Halifax boardwalk, beyond the dormant construction work toward the Halifax Ferry Terminal. She could see the ferry crossing halfway across the harbour, leaving the Dartmouth Ferry Terminal and skimming along the calm morning waters toward the Halifax side. She figured she'd greet the guests outside the terminal, making herself known and providing a welcome distraction during her lengthy shift. The wind was calm, and the skies were cloudy, feeling like rain was on the way. She hoped the rain would hold off for much of their vacation. She wanted nothing but sunshine as she sipped her wine.

Although it wouldn't matter.

Unknown to her, she wouldn't see the vineyards of Wolfville or the fields of harvest.

Fate had something more chaotic planned for Zoe.

At 6:51 am, Zoe approached the ferry terminal entrance, watching as the ferry began its usual docking procedure. She hadn't been on the passenger boat too many times herself, preferring to drive her beast of a truck instead of riding with the ferry folk. She knew it wasn't the best decision for the environment, but she worked hard for that truck. Zoe had always wanted one of her own, and now she had one—*and it was beautiful.* She certainly wasn't going to let it sit quietly in her driveway. She wanted the world to see her polished beauty—*and that there was a badass woman behind the wheel.*

By the time the ferry had docked, gentle raindrops had begun sticking on the terminal's glass windows, dripping down the side as a warning for the weather ahead. Zoe was thankful she got inside before the rain fell and considered staying inside to keep warm for a while. It's not like anything was going on outside, and she wanted just to sit back and enjoy her coffee, praying no commands came piercing through her shoulder-radio.

At 6:52 am, Zoe walked past an old beggar standing in the centre of the crowd, shaking his aluminum tin with a sign reading 'Spare a dime, if you've the time.' His hand shook, and his back was hunched like a laden branch on a Christmas tree. She knew he wasn't supposed to be there, but he wasn't causing any trouble, so she let him stay out of the rain.

Zoe surveyed the passing crowd, her XL Tim's coffee cup a firm presence in her hand., her gun holstered safely on her hip. Everyone was dressed in formal wear, dress ties, pants, shirts, and blouses, all off to their monotonous daily jobs—*whatever they may be*. Zoe may complain about her irregular shifts or long hours, but she sure as hell never wanted to work behind a desk. That just wasn't for her. At least as a cop, she was able to walk outside in the fresh air, see different scenery, and even get in a little bit of excitement occasionally. However, the excitement was far and few between, nothing like the movies, and hardly ever during the wee hours of the morning.

Ahead of Zoe, a young girl dressed in cute pink pants and a Bugs-Bunny T-shirt ran across the crowd with a matching pink backpack, her mother giving chase behind her. It seemed unusually early for school drop-offs, but people had to work with whatever schedules they had. Maybe the little girl would wait at the mother's office, then be taken to school once the time came? *Who knew?* The girl seemed happy, and the mother was flustered. Everything appeared normal as the passengers exited the ferry, heading to their respective jobs.

But the normality wouldn't last.

Because at 6:53 am, the lights began to flicker, flashing in and out as if a power surge rippled across the grid. Zoe looked out the windows at a set of flagpoles resting outside, the flags barely flapping in the gentle breeze, the rain falling heavily in the cool air.

Odd, Zoe mused as the lights cycled from bright to dark and back again. Everyone in the building seemed to stop, looking up toward the lights in the same confusion Zoe found herself in. Zoe was poised to intervene, to calmly urge everyone to keep moving and avoid blocking the exits, but she never got the chance.

Somewhere along the near side of the crowd, a lady screamed. It didn't take long for Zoe to pinpoint the source. The scream had come from the mother of the girl in pink pants, and she was staring directly up toward the ceiling. In fact, everyone had stopped to stare, mumbling amongst themselves as they craned their necks toward the flickering lights. It didn't take long for Officer Stevens to see what they were fixated on, or why no one seemed able to look away, their eyes locked on what hovered above.

In the main lobby, levitating several feet in the air toward the ceiling, was what looked to be a shadow, humanoid in shape, gradually materializing from nothing as the lights flickered faster and faster, some bulbs burning out, others bursting into glass shards showering the faces of businessmen and women standing below. A few of them released a shriek of pain, and that seemed to spark a panic. Suddenly, everyone surged toward the exits as if a distress signal had been flipped in their collective psyche. The homeless man abandoned his coins and sign, heading for the side exit. A few businessmen scattered passed Zoe back toward the ferry, where an emergency exit alarm had been triggered, the siren ringing loudly in the enclosed lobby.

The woman next to Zoe picked up her daughter with the pink backpack, carrying her across the crowd in a mad dash for the main exit.

She wouldn't make it.

Zoe witnessed the woman topple over, collapsing to her knees under the crowd's heedless stampede. That was Zoe's call to action. She dropped her coffee to the floor and dashed through the crowd toward the mother and her daughter.

It was like the crowd no longer cared that she was an officer of the law because she was getting battered and beaten around by the panicking ferry travellers, a few elbows jabbing into her ribs, her boots continually being trampled upon. When she finally made it to the middle of the crowd, struggling mightily against the tide of panic, Zoe was able to find the mother, bruised and battered on the floor. She lowered her hand, grabbing the woman protecting her daughter by her arm, and yanked her to her feet, blood trickling from her ear. The woman didn't even look back to say thanks. She was never given the opportunity. The crowd swept the woman away through the doors like a riptide, forcing her out the main gates into the crisp October air.

Only a few others had stayed to watch the shadow, curiosity overcoming their fear and intuition as it formed overhead in a thickening haze. Zoe could feel dense electricity in the air as she looked above to the dark spectre, levitating above like a translucent storm cloud. Though her heart hammered and her body quivered, Zoe couldn't tear her gaze from the apparition above. She didn't even call it in over the radio. She just stood there amongst a few others at the ferry terminal entrance, staring blankly at the phenomena emerging above. She could hear some of the others whispering, talking to each other as they tried to understand the supernatural essence before them.

Zoe had no words.

She had no way to explain the disturbance, the cause of the panic.

She knew she should run, some instinct poking away at her brain, telling her to flee while she still could. *But she wouldn't.* A drowning curiosity gripped her as it did everyone else still inside. The instinctual panic that drove the majority away screaming did not budge Zoe. Perhaps it was her thick skin or trained aptitude from being a police officer. Whatever it was, it was what would lead to the destruction of Zoe's reality as she knew it.

The shadow formed into a humanoid figure before Zoe's very eyes, warping and bending, twisting and turning, like an invisible wind was moulding the shadow into some sort of translucent dark being. She could see its legs, its arms, and its head, a dark cloudy mass filling up the empty air. It looked almost human, but remained somewhere between earthly and demonic, like a demon ripped from hell—*a shadowy Entity.*

Zoe watched as the *Entity* began to lower from the ceiling, most of the overhead lights shattered in pieces, the rest of them flickering simultaneously. She stood locked in place, helpless to watch as the translucent shade dropped to her level, hovering inches before her nose, its dark swirling face hypnotizing Zoe. Suddenly, her urge to flee drained, and the plans for her Wolfville vacation became a distant memory, as did her thoughts. A painful numbness spread through her, extinguishing any impulse to move, to breathe, to think, or to fight. She felt nothing, as if every shred of will and desire had been ripped from her very soul.

The *Entity* slowly drifted toward her, wrapping around her like a stormy blanket, absorbing her in the darkness. Zoe knew she should run, that she should do everything in her power to resist the spectre overtaking her, but that drive had faded, that fight had died. She was submissive to its power, her will becoming its own, her thoughts all but scattered, wanting nothing more than for the *Entity* to overtake her completely.

Once the *Entity* had completely wrapped its twisted arms around her—*the rest of the crowd helpless to watch*—that's when it began to truly consume her. And unlike the numbness the *Entity* had placed upon her seconds earlier, Zoe felt this pain. It felt as though acid was searing her skin, burning away her flesh and eyes. Zoe could no longer see those standing around her, or the spectre consuming her. She felt only the purest anguish blazing through her soul, the fear spreading fully across her forfeited body, the stench of decay and sulfur flooded her gasping lungs. The world began to fade around her. There were no flickering lights, nor were there screams of terror or whispers of fear.

There was nothing.

A life now imprisoned in the void.

Emptiness.

Loneliness.

Pure oblivion.

Then, as though a veil of darkness had been lifted from her eyes, the world began to creep back to life—*but not the world as Zoe knew it.* It was as if Zoe had endured a millennium in a single instant. The darkness unfurled its intentions.

Visions of twisted souls crowding the busy streets of major cities flashed through Zoe's besieged mind...

Visions of contorted bodies filing the streets of silent intersections...

Visions of black-eyed teenagers tearing apart a screaming woman as they dug their nails into her skin...

Visions of fires raging from city to forest...

Visions of fallen military barricades overrun by twisted hordes of tortured souls, trapped within themselves as their annexed bodies pursued the Entity's bidding...

Then—*as if fast-forwarding a century*—visions of crumbling buildings, overgrown streets, barren fields, and desolate skies melded together. Not even a rat stirred across the cracked streets of humanity's most significant cities as the *Entity* hovered overhead in the obscured sky, surveying its havoc, its nebulous face devoid of emotion.

Zoe Stevens experienced every scream, every act of violence, every shot fired, and every soul torn apart as the atrocious experiences of every man, woman, and child over the next hundred years raced across her mind all at once. A wave of pain and destruction overtook her, shared from the *Entity's* twisted mind to hers.

Time suddenly had no meaning, the space of her reality melting together with these abhorrent thoughts and ordeals. The connection between the *Entity* and her own self began to break, a dizzying rush of rot and agony overwhelming her. She felt her mind fade away, disintegrating into the vast nothingness awaiting Zoe, her relinquished soul dissipated by the darkness consuming it.

Then Zoe was gone, her reality along with it.

23

atsy and Gerald Donaldson were walking the Halifax boardwalk, each clutching an oversized umbrella against the intensifying evening rain. They thought they could get away with a short walk along the harbour-side. The weatherman said the rain wasn't supposed to begin again for another few hours. But as often as Gerald liked to point it out to Patsy—*his wife of forty-nine years and counting*—the weatherman was rarely right. "*Should have trusted the throbbing in my knee,*" he told his wife that before she responded with the generic, "*Your knee is always sore!*"

They bickered as many long-married couples do, yet their happiness was evident. Besides, they wanted a piece of the rare excitement that had occurred down the empty boardwalk at the ferry terminal. Apparently, there had been a shooting, and the ferry terminal had been entirely cordoned off from the public. The Donaldsons decided on a short stroll from their downtown apartment to see if they could get a glimpse of what was going on—*and maybe talk to one of the cute female officers, Gerald would joke to his unamused wife.*

Upon reaching the terminal, they saw that the news had proved correct on this account. The boardwalk was taped off, blockading any spectators as the investigation continued. They had chatted with a fine young officer, who told them there was nothing to worry about, and that the cop-killer had been arrested and was currently locked up, sending the old couple back on their way.

It wasn't a far walk back to their apartment, but they walked slower than most folks. Gerald had only recently recovered from hip-replacement surgery, and his wife had been using a cane for the past few years to get around. *The golden years weren't so golden,* he'd often quip.

But the salty air and fresh breeze did wonders for sore bones. That's why every day, sometimes twice, Gerald and Patsy would take long strolls down the boardwalk. Every day there were new buskers, vacationers, tourists and locals to be seen, and excitement to be had. They had lived in Halifax for their entire lives, long enough to see the buildings go up and the family-run shops get taken down. Yet, every day on the boardwalk, there was something new to be seen. And today would take the cake for the strangest thing they'd ever come across in their seventy-plus years on this earth.

As they hobbled south along the wet Halifax boardwalk, a fair distance away from the ferry terminal, something along the barrier-wall rocks protecting the land from the harbour waters caught their eye. Laying atop the jagged rocks, naked as the day their sons were born, was a woman, looking no older than thirty, completely exposed to the pouring rain.

"Jesus, Mary, and Joseph," Patsy said, covering her mouth with her wrinkled hand, a few diamond rings visible on her arthritis filled fingers. The naked woman rested only a few feet from the edge of the boardwalk, just out of arms reach for Gerald and Patsy. She faced upwards, her breasts taking the bulk of the chilly rain. "Is she alive?" Patsy asked, gazing down at the nudity. Her question was answered by a brief moan, the lady's head rolling from side to side.

Gerald didn't hesitate further. He handed the umbrella to his wife, and against her best advice, clambered over the boardwalk's edge onto the slick rocks sloping down to the slimy harbor. There was no way he should have been doing this in his old age. One fall could ruin the rest of his life. But none of that mattered. The girl was alive, and she would freeze if he did nothing.

From the safety of the boardwalk, Patsy watched anxiously, murmuring silent prayers.

Reaching the naked woman, Gerald reached down, cupping his aged hands under her armpits, and with his weakened strength, dragged her up the slippery black rocks toward the wooden boardwalk. He wasn't as strong as he used to be, straining to hoist the sturdy woman over the boardwalk ledge, but with every ounce of his waning strength, he was able to get her off the rocks.

Patsy helped all she could, looking for anyone nearby that could assist them, but there was no one. The boardwalk was barren as the promise of harsher weather deterred late-afternoon strolls.

Once they got the lady up onto the wooden planks, Gerald slipped off his raincoat, covered the lady's body, and rubbed her arms with his hands to try and get her warm. Her lips had turned blue, and her fingers trembled faintly. Gerald thought she couldn't have been there long, judging by her survival, as hypothermia hadn't yet claimed her. They had walked by only ten minutes earlier, and he was sure he would have seen her lying there on the rocks. She must have appeared only recently, by means known only to God and herself.

Gerald kneeled to the now covered lady, pressing his fingers against her vitals, looking for any signs of consciousness. Any later in the season and she would have been done for, Gerald thought to himself as he hovered over her.

"Miss?" He said, giving her a gentle shake, noticing that her eyes were starting to blink, and her breath was becoming less shallow. "Miss, are you awake?" he asked, shaking her more firmly, wondering if she was hopped up on some sort of drugs, that being the only explanation he could think of toward how she ended up on the rocks.

The woman grunted weakly, showing signs that she was regaining strength. After a few more pokes and prods, with Patsy sheltering them with her umbrella, the woman regained consciousness.

Zoe Stevens awoke freezing to an elderly duo hovering above her, staring down at her like she was some kind of creature at an exhibit. She jolted upwards, her head nearly clocking the older man in the nose. Her body felt as stiff as nails, her head throbbed, and it felt like her gut had been twisted around on a carousel. Her entire body shook uncontrollably, and her back felt like she had just awoken from a bed of stone. For a second, she didn't remember who she was or what was happening. But the disorientation was fleeting.

Suddenly the flashes and visions the *Entity* had tortured her with raced across her fragile mind, images of her friends torn apart by deformed humans, of children ripping out their mothers' throats, darkness preying on the weak, enslaving the strong, and tormenting all rest. She remembered the collapsing abandoned buildings, the raging fires, the depleted military, and worst of all, she remembered the *Entity*, hovering in the centre of it all, controlling his puppets to the world's end—To the death of humanity itself. The puppeteer of the apocalypse.

She sprang up from the frigid ground, and the elderly couple retreated, one of their jackets falling at Zoe's bare feet.

"Please miss, you shouldn't be moving. Wait until help arrives."

She looked toward the man speaking as if he had three heads, somehow recalling the *Entity*'s vision of his death. The image split across her mind, and Zoe could see it as clearly as she saw the man standing in front of him. She remembered his body getting flung off the fourth floor of a harbour-side apartment building, plummeting to his certain death. And standing above on the edge of the balcony, eyes black and limbs contorted, was his elderly wife, submissive to the *Entity's* destructive power.

Zoe didn't know why she had this vision, but she saw it as clear as crystal, as though the *Entity* had implanted the information in her mind.

But where was the death and destruction?

According to the vision, this man died shortly after the Entity's arrival, yet here he stood, alive?

Perhaps it was too early?

Had it not begun?

The end?

Zoe looked over toward the older lady, speaking out for the first time since her body was consumed. "What day is it?" Zoe pressed, her head throbbing with pain.

The old lady stared at Zoe for a moment, puzzled, then told her. "It's October the 8th, my dear."

"And the time?"

"Ma'am?"

"The time, please! What time is it?"

The elderly lady looked down at her gold watch, trembling, studying it with trembling hands, as if she needed her glasses to read it. "My dear, it's 4:54 PM. Don't you think you should go to a hospital?"

"I'm fine." Zoe turned away, heading down the boardwalk toward the parking lot where she parked her police cruiser early in the morning. Before fleeing away, still wearing the older man's thick rain jacket, she turned back toward the elderly couple, struggling to dismiss the vision of the man thrown from the balcony by his contorted wife. She choked out some words, struggling to look each of them in the eye to avoid the *Entity*'s embedded visions.

"Thank you," she breathed softly, then she was off to face her new reality.

24

Zoe had already been walking for over an hour as the rain grew more onerous by the minute. The wind blew louder. The temperature was dropping, and only after what felt like an eternity did Zoe make it to her own, familiar neighbourhood. Dressed in only an old man's long jacket and nothing else, shivering and alone, Zoe had made it halfway across the city walking on her bare feet, receiving wary glances from passersby as if she were a criminal, none of them offering aid while keeping their distance. She didn't care what they thought, though. Zoe was lost in her own thoughts, trying to remember everything exactly as it happened, coming back to her like patchwork as her memories fizzled in and out of her scattered mind.

She remembered the screaming—*the panic*—and the sudden arrival of the *Entity*, hovering above like a storm cloud inside the ferry terminal, bringing death and destruction to everything it touched. Zoe had never felt such petrified silence in all her life, her body helpless to watch as the shadow consumed her, powerless to fight, indifferent toward whatever distorted things it did to her.

She hated that feeling.

Complete and utter submission toward her own twisted fate.

Zoe had always been a strong-willed person. It's why she was such a good police officer. She *always* stood up for herself, getting told on several occasions that the force was not the place for a woman, that she wouldn't be able to support her partner if the going got tough, which it did now and then. But she was always up to the task, never faltering. She was a tough person, but just like the leaves crumbling in the autumn decay, her spark had been extinguished at the presence of the *Entity*, her defiance entirely pulverized.

She didn't understand how she was alive or why she had awakened naked on the damp rocks alongside the Halifax boardwalk. She just knew she had to get home to safety, to warmth—*to Jessie*.

Zoe had met Jessie at a house party, half in the bag, brought together by one of her more insistent friends. He was standing with a group of buddies, sharing a flask, and playing darts against a skewed board when she decided she was intoxicated enough to talk to him. He had been eyeing her all night, she knew that, but she was never any good at introductions, and was keener on letting the boys hit on her rather than the other way around. But there was something about him, like a shiny lure drawing her in. She stumbled up to him, stammered some words she could hardly remember, and then, after a few sips of the flask, challenged him to a game of darts. A single round, where if she got the highest score, he had to take her out on a date. And if he got the highest score, she would down the flask in his hand in one breath. Not the smartest bet looking back on it, but she was happy just to be talking one-on-one with him, his plaid shirt, pearly white smile and well-trimmed beard looking more and more attractive as the night went on. He threw first, shooting a 5, 19, and double 20, for a score of 64, leaving an easily beatable attempt. Or so it seemed until her first dart missed the board entirely, embedding in the wall to the homeowner's dismay. The second throw was better, striking a solid 12, and the third throw bounced off the centre and plummeted to the floor, sticking upright in the hardwood. She wouldn't throw again, and completely blew the bet. But it didn't matter, he didn't make her chug the flask—*although she did put a few good dents into it that night*—and they went out on that date anyway.

Then another.

Then another.

Then before too long, the odd date turned into week-long outings. Before too long after that, the two would move in together, get engaged, married, and live that normal, quaint lifestyle.

How she longed to be enveloped in Jessie's arms, cuddled up at home watching Netflix.

But thoughts of warmth and comfort were long since scattered from her mind, replaced with jitters and anxiety, barren darkness, and cold vacancy. The lingering fear had never left Zoe's side since her encounter with the shadow, the visions twisting inside her brain like an overflowing hard drive. Whatever the spectre did to her, consuming her and tearing her apart from the inside out, it hadn't faded, only growing as she tried to outrun her morbid emotions in the rain.

Zoe turned left onto Mumford Road, approaching her apartment past the Halifax Shopping Centre as her lips tattered to a shivering blue, when she walked by a woman dawning a bright green hooded raincoat, yellow boots, and red pants, resembling a garish color-by-numbers painting. The woman, initially smiling at Zoe, recoiled upon noticing her near-naked state and quickly stepped toward the curb, as if fearing an attack from the disheveled woman. Just as the two women passed each-other, stepping around a large puddle forming on the low-sitting sidewalk, a vision splintered across Zoe's mind, hitting her like a wave of heat and discomfort, racing across her mind as clear as a painting at a local museum.

Suddenly, Zoe wasn't standing on the sidewalk, but in a park, surrounded by trees and late-season grass, the flowers no longer blooming, the sun setting low in the sky. Looking ahead, Zoe watched as the woman in the yellow boots and green jacket sprinted across the narrow stone path, heading directly toward her as three bodies gave immediate chase. The paint-by-numbers woman looked as if she were limping, struggling to keep ahead of the two men and one woman that hunted her down. The hunters looked twisted and bent, their eyes black and empty, their limbs flailing uncontrollably as they gained on their prey. Zoe had no doubt the woman was prey.

The woman was only a few strides away, sprinting directly at Zoe as she threw up her arms to protect herself from immediate contact.

But the bodycheck never came.

The woman passed right through her, as if Zoe wasn't even there, her body completely invisible and intangible, the three twisted hunters passing through her just the same. Zoe was a spectator of this vision, but she was no participant, only able to watch as the three contorted bodies caught up with the paint-by-numbers woman, tearing her down to the ground and clawing away at her like wild animals, their fingernails ripping apart her skin like package paper. Zoe couldn't look, the screams lasting only a few seconds before a final departing gasp, then the sounds of hands digging into dead flesh, blood spraying onto grass and stone.

Then as fast as the vision took over her shaking mind, it disappeared, fading from her imagination like a flash of lightning. Zoe snapped back to reality, shaking the image away and focusing again on the world around her.

The paint-by-numbers woman walked by her on the sidewalk, perfectly fine, her body not torn to shreds, oblivious to the horror that Zoe just experienced.

Zoe struggled to grasp the reality of her recent vision. It felt as real and authentic as any other moment in her life, the gore's intensity as palpable as the surrounding asphalt and houses. This marked the second premonition she had, the first being of the older woman launching her husband from the third story of an apartment building, sending him plummeting to his death.

And these visions wouldn't be her last.

Three more times on the way home, she was tortured with conceptions of death and bloodshed.

One was of a teenager, running across the street as twisted bodies gave chase, only to be struck by an oncoming car, killing him instantly when his skull cracked against the street.

The second featured a mother gruesomely tearing at her baby in a stroller with her teeth, her shirt reading 'One Lucky Hockey Mamma' becoming splattered with her son's blood.

The third was of a middle-aged man, his body becoming consumed by the darkness around him as if his thoughts had scattered to the abyss, leaving a twisted shell in his place. No hands grabbed him, nor did destruction come upon him, his mind simply floated away to the void, leaving one of the *Entity*'s empty capsules in its place.

That was the vision that scared Zoe the most, the one that stuck with her as she quickened her pace home. The fact that the *Entity* could control anyone from afar, the absolute power to pick and choose those that fell under his control, and those that were destroyed by it—*Zoe shuddered at the thought.*

She would encounter no more strangers on the way home. Zoe made sure of it. Every time someone walked toward her on the sidewalk, she'd cross the street to the other side, placing her half-dressed self as far away from them as possible.

She zigzagged across the road several times before reaching her street, her small duplex coming into view. Zoe felt her pace quicken, her exhausted legs practically sprinting toward her front door, not caring if her neighbours saw her in what they would assume was a drunken and crazed state. She just wanted to be home and locked away from the world, apart from the rest of humanity.

Zoe scurried through her front door, spun around, and slammed it quickly behind her. She twisted the lock and collapsed to the floor, her back pressed against the doorframe. Her sinking head rested in her shivering hands. She felt like throwing up, her stomach twisted and turned, her head pounding like a thousand jackhammers. Once the tears began to subside, and her shivering slowed to the warmth of her apartment, she lifted her eyes to her dark home. Not a single switch was on. The only light in the room was coming from the television showcasing the local news as the dim blue glow flickered on her living room walls.

"Jessie?" She yelled, with no response returned. She wished nothing more than for Jessie to be home, waiting for her with open arms. She knew he didn't work today, taking time off for their mini vacation, not that they were going to be taking that now.

So, where was he?

She called his name again, louder, as if the first wasn't loud enough in their tiny 2-bedroom apartment-duplex. "Jessie? Are you here?" She struggled to spit out the words, her throat starting to scratch like a bad cold.

Slowly, Zoe stood up from the hardwood floor, her bare feet and legs wobbling as she rose. Her feet were scratched and bleeding, her hair soaking wet as it pressed on the back of the old man's jacket. Once this was over, she'd find that elderly couple, return the coat and thank them for helping her from whatever was happening to her.

She was about to head toward their bedroom when the television caught her attention. The TV was tuned to The National, where the prime-time hosts delivered the news with grave solemnity.

"...the man accused of the killing of Officer Zoe Stevens is currently behind bars, arrested—get this—after walking into the entrance of the police station, only to be tackled by several officers the moment he stepped in... "

Zoe's eyes were wide open, her face pale, her head pounding in confusion.

I'm not dead? she thought, as an image of her in uniform appeared on the screen, next to Zoe's date of birth and today's date, appearing how it would on the face of a tombstone.

"...The culprit is believed to be an officer at the station himself, although it has yet to be confirmed. Detective Kelly Christopher, once a well-loved man by all, turned killer for reasons yet unknown..."

The pain in Zoe's head escalated beyond anything she'd ever felt before, her heart racing and entire body shaking uncontrollably, stemming both from hypothermia and sheer shock.

Kelly...?
Kelly was a great man.
How could anyone think he was a murderer...?

"...our reporters are on the scene. Zoe's partner, Jessie Stevens, was unavailable for comments. Please stay tuned as we

uncover more information on this grisly story. Our thoughts and prayers are with Stevens family, and those who loved her..."

After a few more comments, the dolled-up anchor changed her story to another war being fought overseas, losing Zoe's attention as she processed what she just heard.

This had to be some kind of major misunderstanding. How could anyone declare Zoe dead without confirmation from her body? She was perfectly alive, living and breathing as she watched her own death be broadcast nationwide.

She would clear up this blunder. Zoe just needed to show her face at the station, proving without a hint of doubt that she was, in fact, alive. But for now, she wanted to find Jessie and tell him she was okay. She needed Jessie now more than ever.

Was she losing her mind?

It sure felt like it.

Zoe stepped over toward the landline, pulled the portable phone out of the receiver and dialled Jessie's cell. She tossed the phone to her ear but didn't have to wait long to get a response. The sound of Jessie's ringtone echoed from their bedroom, down the hall beyond the kitchen.

"Thank Christ", she breathed to herself.

He *was* home, just probably asleep or in the shower.

She pictured his response, seeing her alive and well, standing before him looking like a crazed lunatic wearing an old man's smelly jacket and nothing else. Not really the sexiest image, but Zoe didn't care. She just wanted his body against hers, his hands in her hair.

Zoe tossed the phone on the couch and desperately sprinted toward the bedroom — *toward Jessie.*

But the moment she rushed through her bedroom door, her entire world would come crashing down atop her, shattering her heart and draining the last of her strength. Lying on the bed, still-eyes staring at the empty ceiling, a bottle of pills resting on the carpeted covered floor—*drool and vomit streaming down his tilted cheek*—was Jessie, dead as the souls in her twisted visions.

"Noooo...*God no...*" Zoe howled in agony, her lungs bursting alongside her heart as she ran to him, squeezing his limp body in her arms, aggressively holding him tight and shaking him back and forth as if she could coddle him back to life. She scooped out the vomit from his mouth, tried C.P.R., tried chest compressions, and everything else her training dictated.

But it wasn't enough to restore warmth to his cold skin.
Jessie was dead.
She was alone.

For the next hour, Zoe sat in darkness, cradling Jessie's lifeless body.

She couldn't think.
She couldn't breathe.

Zoe couldn't even look away from him as she struggled to find any reason to be a part of this world. Jessie had turned her whole life around, showing her trust, excitement, love, and so much more. They were two halves of the same whole—*now his half was gone.*

Zoe's eyes kept returning to the small orange pill bottle, which held more than enough pills for her to join Jessie and escape the overwhelming pain and loneliness overwhelming her. The idea consumed her thoughts, leaving no room for joyous memories of their time together. All she could see was her partner, lifeless in her embrace as more and more she wished the same upon herself.

"I want to die," she whispered to Jessie's body. "Just let me die. Please say something. Please. *Please*." She chuckled for a second, the maniacal humour forcing her to release a mad laugh.

I'm already dead.

The news told me.

She started to laugh uncontrollably, knowing the one she loved took his own life just because some asshole—*whether it be those at the station, the news, or whoever else*—told him she was dead.

Complete and utter bullshit.

They want a dead Zoe?

I'll give them exactly that.

She reached down beside the bed and snatched the tiny orange plastic bottle from the ground and looked closely at the tiny white pills that took his life. She wondered how many it would take.

Five?

Ten?

She had no idea.

Zoe's laughter grew more delirious with each passing second.

"I've never done this before," she laughed. *"First time's the charm".*

Zoe emptied the bottle into her palm, eyeing a half-finished bottle of whiskey sitting next to her on their bedside table, one that she had bought for their vacation to Wolfville this weekend, recently used to wash the pills down Jessie's throat.

Now it was her turn.

She grabbed the bottle with her other hand, staring down at the amber-like liquid, knowing it would be the last drink she'd ever have. She wondered if it would numb the pain.

Did Jessie feel any pain?

She'd find out.

Leaning back against the bedframe—*Jessie's body limp and cold on her lap*—Zoe downed a handful of pills, washed it down with a few large gulps of burning whiskey, and waited for the gentle   sleep   to   take   her   away.

25

Zoe awoke with a startling gasp, her stomach churning as though a nuclear bomb had exploded within her. The pain was too much to take, too much to ignore, compelling her to take immediate action. She leapt from the bed, inadvertently causing Jessie's lifeless body to fall to the floor, and sprinted to the toilet, sticking her hands down her throat, forcing her stomach to expel itself into the toilet, now stained with the remnants of her ordeal, the acrid taste of whiskey, pills, and bile lingering in her mouth.

Zoe kneeled on her pink bathroom floor, her arm resting like a lead weight on the toilet seat, puking up her insides, her head pulsating, her body convulsing. Viscous bile trickled down her chin, pooling beneath her as she fought to stay conscious.

Why was she not dead?

Shouldn't she be dead?

For the next few minutes, Zoe clung to the bathroom floor, the room spinning in darkness, her head feeling as if it were cleaved in two, the smell of whiskey and death lingering in the thick air.

Once Zoe spat up all she held, emptying everything inside her she possibly could, she slowly rose back to her feet, pleading to God for merciful release.

He wasn't listening.

Avoiding the bedroom for a moment, and keeping her eyes away from her dead partner, Zoe headed instead toward the kitchen, grabbing a glass of tap-water to rid the taste of burning, wondering how she stood conscious after a half-bottle of pills and few swigs of whiskey.

She didn't even feel drunk.

Nothing had changed, though.

Her mind couldn't escape the crushing loneliness or the image of Jessie lying motionless in their bedroom, or the visions of the town-folk being ripped to shreds by twisted maniacs, or the shadow materializing high above her in the ferry terminal as it consumed her, breaking apart the parts of her that make life worth a damn, destroying her from the inside out.

Somehow it felt like a dream, a horrible nightmare from which there was no waking.

But Zoe knew better.

She knew what she saw and knew the death that waited ahead—*for everyone.*

She wanted no part of it.

As far as Zoe Stevens was concerned, her world was already over. Her own personal apocalypse had run its course. All that remained was for her to abandon ship and sail into the unknown.

But she didn't have the pills to do it, nor the stomach to go through another experience above the toilet seat. And she was impatient. There would be no waiting to drift away. She wanted it to be done quickly—*no distractions, no lingering thoughts, no visions.*

And she knew the perfect way to do it.

Zoe left the water glass in the sink and made her way back to the bedroom, her eyes fixated on Jessie lying face-down on the floor next to their bed as she entered. He looked at peace, and she wanted nothing else but to join him. *Soon enough,* she thought, heading toward their closet, and reaching for a small box resting on the upper shelf, pulling it down.

The box was metallic and tiny, just over half the size of a shoebox, with gold edges and a little three-digit lock-code on the front, the black numbers etched on little brass wheels. She twisted the numbers to reveal the code, *9-1-1*, and popped open the box, revealing a polished Smith and Wesson Model 686 stainless steel revolver. It wasn't as accurate or efficient as her standard-issue P226 firearm, which was locked up safe in her closet, along with spare uniform and body armour, but somehow, the revolver felt more authentic. The steel weapon had belonged to her father before she inherited it, passed down to her after he fell to the sickness, buried outside of town before seeing her graduate and become a cop, following in her father's footsteps.

She imagined how disappointed he'd be if he could see her now. Zoe didn't care, though. The pain was too much, and the visions too unstable. It was more than one small-town woman could handle, and even though Zoe was as strong as they came, *no-one* was *that* strong. She popped open the empty cylinder, clean as a whistle, just as her father had left it.

She walked over to her bedside table, stepped carefully over Jessie's still form, and slid open the drawer, pulling out another brown box, this one smaller and made of cardboard. Inside were about two-dozen dusty .357 rounds.

She would only need one.

Zoe grabbed a single bullet and slid it into its slot, spun the cylinder, and positioned the solitary round for the shot.

There would be no waiting for the quiet embrace of death this time. No, she imagined she wouldn't even hear the shot, her brains being splattered across the wall. *It struck her oddly that her entire being could be wiped away with mere cleaning supplies.*

Oh well, it didn't matter now.

Her decision was irrevocable.

She was going to do it.

She had to.

Zoe sat down on the bed, her feet resting next to Jessie's shoulder. Raising the heavy revolver to her head, she firmly held her finger against the trigger, the butt-end pressed against her temple, without even a hint of indecision. She made sure to point the barrel away from Jessie's body as some sort of final twisted act of love, ensuring she wouldn't mar his body further.

This was right.

This felt right.

Zoe pictured the *Entity* one last time, spreading out amongst the masses like an inevitable plague, twisting and destroying everything it touched.

It was coming.

She knew it.

And she wouldn't be around to see the fireworks when it happened.

The barrel was cold against her skin, and the trigger smooth on her finger.

It was time.

In her head, she counted down the final seconds of her life, gave a quick *I love you* to Jessie, and said goodbye to a terminally ill world.

Three...two...one...

Zoe's eyes were clinched when she pulled the trigger, expecting everything to go black as the bullet tore through her head, ripping it to shreds and ending her unruly torture.

But there was no ear-bursting shot, no bullet tearing through her skull and penetrating the far wall along with her brains and blood. In fact, even though every muscle in her body had every intention to pull the steel trigger, she remained whole, her finger numb on the trigger's edge. Zoe's entire body had become numb, frozen like a statue as she fought with all her might to squeeze the trigger, ending her pain, her torture—*her life*. But no matter how hard she tried to force the shot, she failed.

Zoe Stevens sat at the end of her bed, the cold steel barrel pressed against her head, completely paralyzed, completely paralyzed, no longer the master of her own fate.

Within seconds, whispers began to echo throughout the room—whispers from the voices of Jessie, her father, her mother, Kelly, Frank, amongst many other familiar sounds. They stormed her mind with disharmonious fervor, repeating the same two phrases repeatedly.

"…Kill them. Kill them all. Kill them. Kill them all. Kill them. Kill them all…"

Zoe tried with all her might to scan around her, to identify the source, but her head was locked, compelled to stare at Jessie's motionless form as she listened to his voice whisper deathly commands in her ear.

"…Kill them. Kill them all. Kill them. Kill them all. Kill them. Kill them all…"

Then amongst the whispers, materializing in the air like a gust of rotten wind, came the odours of decay that filled the room with a repulsive stench. The aroma was overwhelming, her nostrils assailed by the scent of decay as she struggled even to shiver, her body a helpless spectator to the unfolding events.

"…Kill them. Kill them all. Kill them. Kill them all. Kill them. Kill them all…"

She willed herself to focus on the revolver, knowing that a mere quarter-inch squeeze of the trigger would liberate her.

But it was a futile attempt, her finger not budging, her body completely still as a hot breath began to blow on the back of her neck from the darkness behind her.

"...*Kill them. Kill them all. Kill them. Kill them all. Kill them. Kill them all...*"

Zoe didn't have to guess as to what lurked at her back as she remained helpless to wait. She knew precisely what had control of her. It was the same darkness that tortured her with these visions, the same foul stench that somehow led to Jessie's untimely death, and the same shadow that promised all others would follow in Jessie's horrible wake.

It was the Entity.

She suddenly felt her mind began to slip away as the *Entity* took complete control, seeping inside her like water filling a sinking ship, tugging at the wires of her soul, Zoe entirely helpless to fight. It only took seconds for the smell of rot to consume her, her body becoming engulfed by an impenetrable darkness, and her mind scattering to the winds of oblivion, the whispers still echoing through the air as they hijacked whatever remained of her deteriorating thoughts.

"...*Kill them. Kill them all. Kill them. Kill them all. Kill them. Kill them all...*"

Then, as all her sinister visions and premonitions converged within the *Entity*'s grasp, Zoe had one final glimpse of the shadow's purpose—a world consumed in darkness, every man, woman, and child locked under the *Entity*'s limitless power, doomed to eternal suffering, subject to the abomination's boundless dominion.

And just before Zoe's consciousness was obliterated into oblivion, she perceived the Entity's method with absolute clarity, as vivid as the tangible world around her. She saw how the Entity's ominous plan was going to unfold. Using Zoe's forfeited body as bait, the Entity was going to disintegrate into the modern world.

And it all began with Kelly Christopher.

Then what was left of Zoe Stevens dissolved back to oblivion, her mind surrendered to the dark maelstrom, her body now a mere vessel for the *Entity*'s malevolent intent.

Part V
A Twisted Reality

26

Kelly rode in the passenger seat of Zoe Stevens' four-door pickup, his body trembling, his hair soaking wet, and his eyes boring into the side of Zoe's head with dagger-like intensity, very much alive and vacant any bullet holes. They had driven for miles already, speeding as far away from the spectre as possible, yet no one had said a single word. Kelly remained still, resting hard against the passenger-side door, glaring at Zoe as if she had risen from the dead— *which, if Kelly wasn't already stirred of sanity's edge, was true.*

He didn't know what to say. His mind was overtaxed, struggling even to comprehend where he was, exhaustion, confusion, and utter distress starting to take its heavy toll. Throughout the entire day, he was haunted by the security footage of a bullet ripping through Zoe's eye. The shooting was as transparent and realistic as anything. Until now, Kelly had no doubt she was dead, the only uncertainty remaining to be the man holding the gun that struck her down. Whatever was going on, it was too much for a small-city detective running on nothing but fumes to handle. He could barely keep his thoughts connected as it was, the swirling chaos closing in all around him as he fought to stay afloat amongst the madness. The only thought that *did* stay connected was that of his wife, a knife half-lodged into her eye-socket, slain by the monster that plagued him. Only yesterday, he had wielded that same knife to chop red onions, peppers, and other vegetables while his wife stirred rice and drank wine while making a simple Pad-Thai stir-fry for dinner, sitting down in the late evening to watch a few episodes of Law & Order. Now the knife was a murder weapon, and no one in the world would believe him if he tried to explain what happened. A single tear ran down his cheek as he stared over at Zoe behind the wheel, focused on the road ahead as she quietly drove them away—*wherever that was.*

Kelly tried to dispel the haunting images of his wife's brutal end, striving to keep them suppressed as he searched for the right questions to ask, wondering if there was any reason or purpose to the hysteria, or if it was just him losing his *damn* mind.

"How..." he began, his voice hindered by a lump in his throat. Kelly swallowed heavily, forcing the words from his mouth. "How are you...*here?*"

Zoe was dressed in full police uniform, her body armour protecting her chest and her standard-issue pistol holstered at her hip, as if she was on duty, and this was all part of the job. On the radio, *The Power of Love* played at low volume on the 'classics' station, a cheery tune for these dark times. Zoe peeked over a few more times before responding, as if she were trying to find the right words to say.

"I'll tell you all I can," she said, her voice quiet, her eyes stern. "But first, let's get somewhere where we can talk. There's a lot to discuss."

Kelly nodded, unsatisfied, forcing his gaze away from Zoe out toward the dark October sky, the rain streaming across the window, the overhead clouds blocking the moon's pale glow.

In the back of the truck, laying across the cushions completely blacked-out and handcuffed was Frank McDowell. Zoe insisted on not taking him, but Kelly couldn't just leave him as another victim of the *Entity's* prowl. Together, they shoved him into the back seat, his head with a slight bump from where it cracked against the house after Zoe slammed him with the truck. She said she was only trying to scare him, but the wheels had slid further than she expected on the damp grass, and the vehicle clocked him on the side, bashing him into the wall of Kelly's home, knocking him out cold. At least that made it easier for them to get him into the truck, away from the *Entity*'s reach, if only for a little while.

Kelly could only imagine the confusion and distress that awaited Frank upon waking. *Probably just as messed up as himself,* Kelly thought, staring blankly at the buildings passing by as they drove toward the industrial area of Dartmouth. He didn't know where they were going, but anywhere was better than back with his dead wife and the shadow that killed her. He prayed Zoe would somehow have an answer as to why he was being tormented by that *thing,* as well as his newly found power to bend time.

Kelly was accustomed to observing the supernatural in films, *not living it.* It always looked so entertaining in the movies, watching the hero battle the villains with their superhuman powers. But the films seldom depicted the pain, the internal turmoil, and the misery that such power brings. They never showed what happened in between the action—*the regret, the despair, the mental-torment.* No, those were features only present in the real world, not that anything that happened over the past day felt *real.* Kelly clung to hope for a miracle, praying that he'd wake from a coma in a hospital bed, induced by a car accident he had on the way to work. He awaited the steady beeping of hospital machines or the comforting touch of a nurse, but they never came, and his nightmare pressed on. He'd have to endure a little longer. He glanced back at Zoe as she turned the truck off the main road onto Dartmouth's back streets. "Have you seen...*it?*" he asked, wondering if it was only him being driven to madness.

"I've seen it," she responded, confirming the *Entity* wasn't a figment of his deteriorating imagination, but a real, existing monstrosity.

"Do you know what it is?" Kelly asked again, forcing away the frog in his throat.

"I'll explain what I know, just hold on."

"Please," Kelly pleaded, unable to wait for answers. His wife was dead, he was accused of murdering the woman currently chauffeuring him around, his best friend and partner was handcuffed in the back seat, and hell itself was pursuing him around the city, tearing him apart at every turn. *He really couldn't wait.* "Please," he said again, forcing her to break the silence.

"Fine," she said, pulling down another side road toward some containment facilities. "But you shouldn't be worried about what it is. You should be more concerned about why it's here."

Kelly looked at her, puzzled.

How did she know why it was here?

How did she know anything at all about the Entity at all?

"Why?" he asked plainly.

Zoe pulled the truck into a storage facility, driving between the units and parking by a garage door with the number *fifteen*, written across in oversized white letters. She shifted the engine into park and turned the key, facing directly toward Kelly, the only sound being the rain tapping on the roof of the truck.

"What it has inflicted upon us, *that Entity*, it wants to unleash upon everyone. He's what you'd call the last breath. The Bible's rapture. Or the Viking's Ragnarök. Or, in more modern terms—*it's the end of the world as we know it.*"

27

Zoe and Kelly dragged Frank's out-of-shape body from the back of the Ford, lifting him up by his limbs and carrying him into storage locker number fifteen, where Zoe had kept some spare furniture and a few boxes from her previous move. The locker looked as if it hadn't been opened in some time. There was dust forming atop the cardboard boxes, and the room smelled of thick mould, like her stuff inside had been stagnant for years.

They positioned Frank upright in an old, dusty kitchen chair and re-cuffed his hands behind his back, knowing he was going to be one pissed-off and confused man when he woke up—*if he woke up.*

"Is he going to be okay?" Kelly asked Zoe, who was already grabbing a duffle bag from the back of the truck.

"He'll be fine. He'll probably have a bit of a headache, though. I have stuff for that." She pulled out a little white Advil bottle from the bag, as well as a few bottles of water.

Kelly's head was pounding, the bags under his eyes growing more massive than the moon's shadow. "Mind if I take one?"

"Go for it," Zoe replied, tossing him the bottle. Coming in from the rain, she yanked the pull-cord of an overhead lightbulb, illuminating the room with a dusty glow. The light flickered a few moments, then finally became steady as the dust began to settle. Zoe slammed the garage door closed, blocking out the orange glow from the city lights, leaving them secluded in her little storage unit. "We should be safe here a while."

"How'd you know that?" Kelly questioned, aware that the *Entity* had been on his trail non-stop for the past two hours—*even longer if you count the pauses in time.*

"Have any better ideas?"

"Fair enough," he responded as he pulled a dusty white sheet off an old love seat and plopped himself down. He could have fallen asleep on the spot, but his racing mind wouldn't allow it, bouncing back and forth from the day's events.

In less than two hours since he first encountered the *Entity* alone in his jail cell, he had been chased across the city, nearly killed at the library, acquired the ability to slow time, lost his wife to its puppets, and killed two possessed police officers, amongst other things—*all seemingly without cause or reason, simply because some supernatural shadow felt like it.*

At least that's how it seemed.

There were answers yet to be uncovered.

Zoe had some explaining to do.

She had already made herself comfortable on another rickety wooden chair, matching the one Frank was cuffed to, sliding off her body armour for now, and resting her pistol on the floor next to her. She popped a few Tylenols herself, chugging a bottle of water before cracking open a second, as if it were an early morning after a long night of drinking.

"Hungover?" Kelly inquired with a half-joke, trying to fill the silence with anything but his dismal thoughts.

"Something like that," she replied.

The low hum of the lightbulb echoed across the cold room, the sound of the rain bouncing off the metal roof barely audible in their muffled space. Somewhere off in the distance, Kelly heard the faint sound of police sirens fading into the night. He grabbed the dusty sheet from the floor and wrapped it around Franks body to keep him warm before resting back down on the soft blue sofa, waiting for Zoe to spill her story.

It was as if she was reading her mind because she was quick to start up the conversation.

"I suppose you have questions," Zoe asked, staring over at Kelly sitting on the couch.

"More than a few," although Kelly didn't really know where to begin.

Did he start with Zoe's supposed death...

...his alleged murder...?

...his wife...?

...the spectre...?

There were so many gaps in his thoughts that so many stones were left unturned. But he wanted to get this conversation started, if only to distract his thoughts from the scene left behind in his bedroom. "Start with you." He said bluntly. "How did you get tangled in all this?"

She nodded, acknowledging his question, and preparing her answer. "I'll tell you. I'll explain everything and how I came to know it," Zoe's voice became firm, as if she were dreading what was to follow. "But I need you to keep an open mind. There's a lot more to this than you can possibly imagine."

Kelly was more than willing to keep an open mind after the events of today. If the *Entity* truly existed—*and he wasn't becoming deranged*— then anything was possible. "Shoot. I'll try my best to follow."

"Alright." Zoe took a sip of water and began her story by immediately throwing Kelly for a loop. "I'll rip off the band aid first. I'm not the Zoe you think I am." She paused, waiting for Kelly's response, but he just sat back and listened, waiting for it to all make sense. "I'm from...and I know how this sounds, but it's the truth. I swear on my life. I'm from...a parallel universe."

Kelly gave the only appropriate response to Zoe's claim. "Bullshit."

"Now—*you said you'd keep an open mind.*"

"Yeah... if you'd said you had a twin or someone faked the footage, I would have believed you. But a parallel universe—*what does that even mean?*"

"Well—" Zoe took a calming breath, "—if you'd let me fully explain, I'd tell you."

"Fine. Sorry. Go ahead." Kelly already knew none of this was going to make any sense, but he'd do his best to follow. Zoe continued.

"I first met this, *Entity*, earlier this morning. 6:53 AM, to be exact. I was on duty like any other day, counting down the minutes to shift's end so Jessie and I could take a well-needed break. I was patrolling the ferry terminal down at the docks when that—*thing*—appeared out of nowhere. It was like watching a dark thunderhead form out of thin air, growing and twisting high above the floor. There was so much screaming, so much fear. The smart ones made their way toward the exit, but me, being the 'brave police officer'..." Zoe motioned air quotes as she continued her story, "...I stayed, watching as the *Entity* took control of everyone around it, me included. I think you know what I mean by '*control*'."

Kelly nodded, having run into the *Entity*'s puppets more than he'd have liked already.

"When the *Entity* appeared, I happened to be the closest to him, so I guess that makes me the lucky winner. The lottery of a *bloody* lifetime. He lowered himself toward me..."

Kelly listened as Zoe's voice shifted from a conversational tone to that of a scared child, which unnerved him because Zoe was usually such as a strong-willed woman.

"..I...I couldn't move. It was as if I had been paralyzed. And the *Entity*, it felt like he was devouring me from the inside—*sucking away my soul*, consuming me entirely, tearing at my skin like acid, breaking my mind apart like dynamite."

"I know the feeling," Kelly consoled, trying to share the despair. *Only he was able to break away from the Entity's grasp somehow*. Probably sheer luck.

"No...not like this; you don't. Because if you did, I doubt you'd be here right now talking to me." Zoe gulped down some more water, her fingers trembling slightly as Frank remained unconscious beside them. "I saw...everything..."

"Everything? What do you mean, 'everything?'"

"It felt as if my mind and the *Entity*'s merged into one. For a moment, I saw *every single god-damn thing* he was going to do, almost like it was a dark destiny unfolding before my very eyes. I witnessed every child's scream, every woman's death, and every man's possession by the *Entity*'s unlimited reach. It stretched across the globe like a plague, infecting everyone and everything it touched, with no hope of solace or escape. Nowhere to run, nowhere to hide. Only death, or worse. There are billions of souls on this planet, and I experienced the death of every last one of them—*all at once*."

Kelly was silent, listening attentively as she recounted the apocalypse to detail, explaining how she experienced the death of every single person she now came across, their twisted futures unfolding in front of her, as if it were being projected from a television screen before her very eyes. The details were gruesome, the specifics too granular to be fabricated. The fear in her stare and the jitter in her speech convinced Kelly she was telling the truth.

"It was as though I experienced every moment in time simultaneously, from the first breath of the *Entity* to the last gasp of mankind." Zoe started to cry, a pair of tears rushing down her cheek before brushing them away with her sleeve.

"Look, Kelly. I don't know how I know these things, but I do. It's as though the *Entity*'s thoughts were imprinted onto mine, intertwining *its* intentions with my own. And I know from the bottom of my heart, that everything I held dear back in my Universe...it's going to be destroyed by that twisted creature, if it hasn't already. Everyone I've ever known and loved is going to die, and there's *nothing* I can do about it because I'm trapped here in a world that's not my own. And worse, I know if we don't do something about it, soon, the same thing that's happening to my Universe... it's going to happen to this timeline as well."

Kelly struggled to tie together the pieces of the puzzle, his mind attempting to comprehend too many confusing concepts all at once.

Multiple universes?

Separate timelines?

End-of-the-world events?

It was all too much. And now their Universe was in peril as well? How were two inner-city cops going to fight something powerful enough to cross the boundaries of time and space? He already knew bullets did nothing to hurt the *Entity*, so what else could they do? Kelly needed a moment to process what he had just heard.

"Okay," he said, slowing things down. "How do you know this isn't your universe?"

"Have you ever gone to a party, a BBQ, or somewhere similar and felt out of place?" Zoe took another sip of water, spilling a bit on her uniform before continuing. "Well, multiply that feeling by a thousand, and that's how I feel every second here. It's like every atom in my body is trying to reject this place. Not to mention, when the *Entity* took over my body, it was like a rush of twisted information spread across my mind all at once. I can't remember it all, but I can recall fragments, and when I woke up naked on the Halifax harbour rocks, I knew for sure I was out of my element. I don't know how else to explain it, other than I know it as certain as I know there's air in my lungs and fish in the sea."

Kelly didn't press further. There was no lie in her voice, no stutter in her speech. Besides, who would come up with such a crazy story just to be lying about it in the first place? Not Zoe Stevens, she never beat around the bush, and she was telling the truth. Of that, Kelly was certain. He switched subjects, taking the spotlight off Zoe and shifting to the monster hunting after them.

"So, you're saying this thing—*this Entity*—it's destroying your universe, and now it wants to destroy mine as well?"

"I wish it were that simple," Zoe responded, sucking back more tears.

"What do you mean?"

"It isn't just *my* universe he intends to destroy. He wants to wipe out *all* of them. *All universes.* Every last one of them." She paused a moment, allowing what she just told him to sink in before continuing. "This creature—this *multiversal-apocalyptic abomination*—is the *only* thing capable of traversing across each timeline. It's probably just as easy as it is for me and you to walk from one side of the street to the other. To pull this off, to tear apart the fabrics of time and space, it needs to unify its attacks. *It needs to—at the same time and location across the multiverse—initiate its armageddon.*"

"Jesus Christ," Kelly said aloud, unintentionally, not knowing whether to believe the absolute madness Zoe was telling him, or to knock her out and get as far away from her as humanly possible. The second option seemed more welcoming, but he held a gut feeling that the first option was the one he should be going with, as crazy and unbelievable as it seemed.

"I know," Zoe said, reaching into her breast pocket and pulling out a pack of cigarettes.

"I didn't know you smoked." Kelly said, surprised at the sight of the pack.

"I don't. But Jessie did, and I need something to calm me down." Her hands shook as she tried to light the cigarette. "Want one?"

He hesitated—*but only momentarily*. "Hell with it." Kelly reached out and lifted one from the pack, borrowed the tiny red lighter and ignited the butt, coughing as he struggled to suck back his first cigarette since before the academy.

Together, they enjoyed their smokes as Kelly tried to put together all the pieces.

This spectre-like creature had the power to traverse time and space.

Somehow, Zoe had been sent across impossible boundaries, shifting from one universe to the next.

And as for Kelly, he had the ability to bend time, a power only cursed upon him after his encounter with the Entity.

It was no coincidence.

Not believing in coincidences was a symptom of his profession.

But he still couldn't piece together how it was all connected, nor why the creature was so obsessed with hunting him down across the city. Once their cigarettes were spent, as thin smoke rose in the storage unit, accompanied by the dim hum of the single lightbulb, it was time to figure out what else remained in this lunacy of a story. He *needed* to piece this all together, at risk of possibly losing his sanity.

"There's one thing I don't understand." Kelly tossed his butt onto the floor, the faint orange glow dying under his boot. "If this *Entity* is so powerful, as if the devil himself, then why— *if he needs to begin his attack at the precise time and space across universes*—is my timeline still intact? Why weren't there armies of twisted puppets roaming the streets, tearing apart everything good in this world?"

Zoe looked up at Kelly, her eyes red but absent tears, and against all the odds, she managed a half-smile, the first one since seeing the little girl with the pink backpack earlier this morning. "Do you believe in fate, Kelly Christopher?"

Kelly didn't crack a smile. His thoughts were too exhausted and bothered to do such a thing. "At this point, I'm ready to believe just about anything."

"Good," she said, looking down at her watch.

Kelly knew he wasn't going to like what followed.

She looked back up at him, the rain pounding harder outside, the wind howling against the now-rattling garage door. "You better. Because sixteen hours ago, in what would be the future, with two shots from your gun, you inadvertently stopped the *Entity* and prevented the apocalypse."

28

* even hours ago—in the future—*the words rattled around in Kelly's brain, as did the security footage showing him shooting down Zoe in the Halifax Ferry Terminal. He wasn't anywhere near the ferry station when the shots were taken, yet there was no denying that he was in the video. The way he held the gun in his left hand, the clothes he was wearing, and even the scruff on his face all pointed the finger toward Kelly.

But how?

He couldn't travel back in time, could he?

That was impossible.

Kelly had slowed time on a couple of occasions, but it required a great deal of energy, draining the shallow forces around him each time he tried.

But everything else that happened today was impossible, wasn't it?

Who knew what was possible and what wasn't.

Everything was impossible until it was attempted.

Suddenly Kelly flashed back to the first words Zoe told him, right after she bashed Frank in with the truck.

"If you want to save her, get in".

Kelly processed the words again, tumbling around in his tired brain like a washing machine.

Was there a way to save Donna?

Did he really hold that power?

He needed to know more. He was about to ask Zoe for more information when he heard faint moans coming from Frank, who was handcuffed to the chair next to Kelly.

"W-What happened..." Frank said as he slowly drifted back into consciousness—*into this hell Kelly found himself in.*

"Frank..." Kelly stood tall, knowing that he was going to go ballistic when he realized where he was. He knew Frank well enough to know how he reacted to most situations.

"Kelly?" With sudden alertness, Frank snapped back to reality, like a switchblade snapping open. Upon recognizing his surroundings, Frank's confusion turned swiftly into rage. His breathing grew heavy, and he fought like hell to break through his cuffs, Zoe and Kelly having to hold him to the chair so he wouldn't sprint at them with his over-sized frame—*chair and all.*

"What the *hell* is going on!?" His glare was fixated on Kelly, not even noticing Zoe as he head-butted Kelly right in the nose, sending him tumbling backward into the sofa. "I'll kill you, you backstabbing traitor!" Frank kicked, bit, and swung his free hand around as much as he could, Kelly and Zoe using every ounce of energy to keep him pinned down.

"Frank, stop! Look!" Kelly tried to point over toward Zoe, but the enraged brute was having none of it. He stomped a few more times, blindly shoving Zoe off to the side as his glare remained fixated on Kelly, whose nose was bleeding profusely.

Frank thrashed. Frank punched. And Frank cursed.

Then without warning, Frank dropped to the floor, his hand still cuffed to the chair.

Kelly rubbed the water from his eyes to see Zoe standing over him, a taser in her hand, and Frank down on the floor, shaking, trying to catch his breath.

"Thanks," Kelly said as he grabbed a loose rag and wiped the blood from his face. They lifted Frank back into a seated position. This time, Kelly bonded his legs with some rope he found lying in the back of the storage unit, making sure it was tied tight around Frank's ankles.

"Frank?" Kelly whispered, bracing himself for whichever version of his partner would confront him this time—the hate-filled rage-monster, or a more submissive version. It turned out it would be the latter, if not for any other reason than fear of being tazed again.

"How…" Frank muttered.

"How *what*, Frank? We're not here to hurt you." Kelly looked up toward Zoe, motioning for her to holster the taser.

"How did you escape?" His breathing was heavy. Kelly grabbed a bottle of water, feeding it to him like he was a tortured prisoner-of-war.

"I'll tell you everything," Kelly said, knowing he wouldn't believe any of it without hard proof. "But first, there's someone you should see."

Frank scanned the room, his eyes locked in on Zoe in the corner of the room. Kelly could have pinned the exact moment Frank realized who it was.

"No way," Frank said, visibly confused and cautiously weary. "You're dead. I saw your body. I was there. You're not real. You can't be."

Zoe responded this time, choosing her words carefully as she tried to explain the impossible to someone entirely in the dark. "It's me, Frank. And it's damn good to see you."

"I don't understand, Zoe. You were shot. *He* shot you. I saw it!"

"Yes, there's no denying you saw Kelly shoot someone. But it's not what you think. He had no choice."

Kelly watched as Frank struggled to grasp the twisted reality. Kelly wasn't even sure if he believed it himself, and he had seen the *Entity* with his own two eyes. There were some things that the human mind just wasn't meant to see—*some things that were meant to be left behind the veiled curtain.*

"So," Frank said to Zoe, choosing his next words with care, "if Kelly didn't shoot you, then who did he shoot?"

Zoe cracked a smile, and Kelly knew Frank wasn't going to like the answer. "Zoe Stevens."

Frank just looked up at Zoe, the rage slowly starting to slither back in, his face turning shades redder as he swallowed the desire to fight. "Fuck off."

This time it was Kelly's turn to butt in, not really knowing where to start, but he had to try something. "Listen, Frank, we go way back, and I know that you know when I'm lying. Look into my eyes. Everything we're about to tell you is the truth. I swear on it. I promise."

Kelly knew Frank was going to resist their explanation at every corner. That's what a good detective did. And their story— *as horrific and real as it was*—was anything but believable.

"Fine," Frank snorted. "I'll listen. But don't expect me to believe any of it."

Kelly broke a small smile. It was nice to have his friend back, even if he was tied up in a storage unit while they were hunted by a spectre moulded from time and space. At least there was some familiarity left in this horrid day. "Don't worry," Kelly said. "We don't expect you to believe any of this. But you need to accept it. Our lives might depend on it."

For the next twenty minutes, Kelly recounted the events occurring over the past few hours. Zoe listened as well, hearing for the first time about Kelly's ability to bend time to his will.

Kelly explained that up until the jail cell he was as blind as Frank was, and that his ability to slow time was the *only* reason he was able to escape the *Entity*'s grasp. He told his tale of the confrontation at the regional library, how he was forced to fight his way out of another scenario. He even told Frank what had happened to his wife Donna, the knife sticking from her skull, and how Kelly was forced to shoot two innocent police officers under the *Entity*'s control. Kelly didn't expect Frank to believe a single word, but at least he was listening, and it felt good to be able to share this with a friend.

Once Kelly finished his story, it was Zoe's turn to share hers. She tried her best to explain the multiverse theory. She revealed how she had been somehow sent from her universe to theirs, and how Zoe Stevens from this universe was indeed shot on the morning of October the 8th as an effort to stop the expansion of the *Entity*'s power.

With reluctance, she described Jessie's demise, of how the *Entity* forced Jessie to kill himself, and how she narrowly escaped with her life just as Kelly had. Tears broke across her face as she explained Jessie's death in detail. This was the first time Kelly heard about Jessie. Zoe and his story were similar in many ways.

The two detectives listened as she explained the visions cursing her, and how she witnessed the death of every person she came across, and how there was some sort of intertwined destiny that led to Kelly saving their entire world from utter chaos.

It took about forty-five minutes to explain the full story to Frank, who hadn't asked a single question, listening intently as each of them told of their encounters with the *Entity*, and how it was up to them to stop the apocalypse.

After concluding their explanations, they each took a seat, sipped some water, and waited for Frank's response. In the last forty-five minutes, they had told Frank about multi-universal travel, time-bending, an evil ghost-like *Entity*, twisted puppets, dead cops, and the end of the world as they knew it.

Kelly wasn't sure if Frank could accept their story, much less join them in the coming fight. Still, he held out the smallest sliver of hope that he would somehow come to his sense and believe that his best friend of many years wasn't a cold-stone killer, and that everything he did had some sort of divine purpose. *It was hope in vain.*

Immediately Frank burst into manic laughter. His erupting roar filled the tiny storage unit as he choked on his own spit, laughing uncontrollably, the entire story a complete fabrication of their minds from Frank's point of view. It took about forty seconds of Frank sitting handcuffed on the dusty wooden chair before he returned to normality, his ribs throbbing from the amusement.

It made Kelly angry, that the best man at his wedding was laughing aloud as he told him of his wife's gruesome death. Of course, Frank didn't believe a word, but that didn't make it any better.

Frank was the first to cut the tension, furthering his laughter by bombarding the two storytellers with questions. "Alright, let me humour you for a second. Let's say I pop whatever pills you both are taking and believe you for a moment. What in the world— no, what in the *universe* would a creature as powerful as that want from two cops from mainland Nova Scotia? And what on earth does '*multiverse*' even mean? You expect me to believe there's an infinite number of universes with an infinite number of possibilities, all of which are being destroyed by this universe-jumping monster you call '*The Entity?*' It's a bunch of nonsense if you ask me; some kind of wild story to try and divert me from whatever else is going on. And believe you and me, I'll figure out what it is. I promise you that."

Frank continued to ramble on as Zoe and Kelly listened to him mock their stories and their loved ones' deaths. Kelly didn't even look at him, resisting the urge to confront him physically. Any physical altercation wouldn't help their cause, no matter how badly he wanted to knock out his teeth.

But Kelly *did* understand where Frank was coming from. There was no way a soul in the world would believe their story without proof. Not even Kelly himself would have believed it if he were sitting in Frank's position.

If it was proof that he wanted, then it was proof he was going to get.

Kelly closed his eyes, concentrating on the room around him, and as he felt a faint energy begin to form around him, Frank's words began to slow, coming to a standstill as time itself slackened to a snail's pace. Kelly opened his eyes, looking over at Zoe, the water from the bottle suspended mid-air as she poured it into her mouth. To Kelly's right, Frank's mouth was wide open, speaking some sort of nonsense to them, sounding better now, silent in time, than he did when he had volume.

He knew if he walked over and punched Frank in the face now, that he'd have the strength to knock his skull clean off his spine. Such a large force exerted in such a short amount of time meant Kelly was basically Superman, at least in terms of strength and speed. He had to be careful about where he stepped. A single mistake would be enough to kill his best friend, or Zoe. Kelly stood, his indent lingering firm into the couch. Carefully, he stepped to his left toward the closed garage door, keeping his distance from Frank and Zoe, both frozen like statues. He turned, feeling the rage grow from Frank's contemptuous comments, clenching his hands into fists.

Then, channeling the force of a heavyweight boxer, Kelly pounded on the steel garage door, giving it four or five solid blows, the cold steel scratching his knuckles. Once Kelly's rage was released, and temper had cooled, he sat back down in his blue butt-print, closed his eyes, and released time from his grip.

In an instant, as a result of his time-stalled blows, the garage door exploded outward, smashed into the front of Zoe's truck and landed onto the pavement behind it. The cold wind immediately rushed inward, the roof still protecting them from the night's heavy rain. Kelly had prepared himself to watch both Zoe's and Frank's reactions, wondering if they would have even seen him move. Zoe seized her pistol, aiming it toward the empty door. Frank had utterly shut up, his eyes wide and mind blown as he tried to explain what had happened.

Kelly tapped Frank's shin to regain his attention. "Believe me now, Frank? You wise-cracking a-hole."

Frank looked like a deer in the headlights. "That was you?"

Kelly nodded, a small amount of satisfaction flowing through him.

"Dude, what the *hell*?" Zoe cursed at Kelly at the sight of her truck, which was now decorated in a few deep scratches and dents from the garage door slamming into the hood of her Ford F-150.

To be honest, Kelly didn't even think about what was on the other side. He was so amped up in rage when he pounded on the garage door that he didn't even think about it, like a racing greyhound equipped with blinders, eyes focused solely on the mechanical hare. Kelly realized he needed to be more careful. His newfound power was as dangerous as it was miraculous.

"Sorry, Zoe. It isn't like it's your truck anyway, right?"

Zoe looked at him, puzzled.

"I mean, if you're not from this Universe. Then that's *this* Zoe's truck—*the one that's no longer with us*—am I right?"

"I suppose…" Zoe responded, cursing at Kelly under her breath. "*Still*…it's a nice truck."

"Fair enough," Kelly replied, diverting his attention back toward Frank, who looked as if about to speak.

"Did you really just do that?" Frank asked, his eyes bugging out of his head.

"Uh-huh."

"Do something again. Show me." Frank seemed more intrigued than confused, like the entire story had just clicked.

"I can't," Kelly responded. "It takes a lot of energy to stop and start time. It takes some time to—*well, for lack of a better word*—recharge."

Frank glanced over toward Kelly, the anger and mockery wholly gone, replaced by expressions of concern and amendment. "Kelly, if that's true…*then Donna*…"

"She's gone, Frank. I couldn't save her." It felt more real every time Kelly spoke of it out loud, like she would still be alive if he blocked the incident from his mind altogether. Of course, he was a fool to think such a thing.

Donna was gone. And it was his fault for not protecting her.

"Kelly… I'm sorry…"

He could see that the regret in Frank's eyes was real, that for the first time since Kelly was arrested this morning, Frank was showing sympathy for him. For the first time in what felt like an eternity, Kelly had gotten his partner back.

29

Frank McDowell stirred awake on one side of the blue sofa from a well-needed nap, the handcuffs around his wrist no longer a requirement. After an hour or so of intense Q&A between Frank, Kelly, and Zoe with their bizarre stories, they decided to try to get some sleep and reconvene at first light. All three were visibly exhausted, so not one of them was opposed to getting a little shut eye.

Frank may not have believed every aspect of their outlandish tale, but he had seen enough to know that at the very least there was something supernatural going on, and from the look on his partners face—*well*—that was enough to at least keep him by his side for now. They had allowed Frank to text his wife, telling her he wouldn't be home tonight, that he'd be sleeping at the office to try to catch up on work. She didn't like it, but agreed, considering the severity of the case.

They found extra blankets in a dusty box near the back of the storage unit and distributed a few among themselves. They smelled of must and mould, but none of them cared, all too exhausted to mind the stench. Kelly was fast asleep on the other side of the couch, and Zoe was keeping watch from the storage unit's edge, a thick beige blanket wrapped firmly around her shoulders.

The group had agreed to take watch in one-hour increments, allowing the other two to grab some well-needed slumber before trying to figure out what their next move would be. Frank's turn didn't start until 3:30 AM, but sleep was barely coming to him as it was, so he decided to take his shift a bit early. He rose from the sofa, careful not to disturb Kelly on the other side, and walked over toward Zoe, plopping down on a chair next to her.

He must have startled her, because she jumped slightly, clearly startled. Zoe looked up toward Frank, and he could have sworn for a split-second that her eyes were as black as night, but after she blinked, her eyes looked normal, and he figured it was just his early-morning weariness taking its toll.

"You're early," she said, gazing back toward the fresh air.

"I'm an old man now," Frank replied. "I hardly sleep as it is. See anything?"

"Nothing. A few sirens in the night, but nothing else."

"Good," Frank replied, slightly doubting if there was even anything to keep watch for. He'd humour them for the time being, at least until he saw something with his very own eyes. He didn't know whether to trust them, or to call the station and reveal their location. They trusted him enough to release the shackles off his wrists, so he figured he'd wait it out a while, to see if the rest of their story ended up being true. It wasn't that he disbelieved Kelly, it was simply a difficult concept to accept. A little caution never hurt anybody. "Why don't you take my place and close your eyes. Only a few hours of darkness left."

"I'll stay up a bit," she said, smiling. "Keep you company for a while. Cigarette?"

"No, thanks." Frank only smoked Cigars, and that was for special occasions only. He was never one for cigarettes. They were silent killers.

Despite Zoe's second-hand smoke, Frank welcomed the cool night air. The smell of mould lingered heavier and heavier the deeper you stepped into the tiny storage unit, so he was happy to be closer to the fresh air.

A few weeks ago, the song of crickets would have played deep into the night, but it was too cold for them now, most of them dead or dormant. Winter was on their doorstep, and it wouldn't be long before he'd be finishing his nine-to-five shifts in the dark. One of the perks of living in Canada, he mused, listening to the cars drive on the highway in the distance.

He looked over toward Zoe, alive and breathing, as if the footage he watched yesterday was all a big sham—*as if there wasn't shooting in the first place.* "I have to admit, it's a relief to see you here, alive and well."

Zoe smiled at him, *forced*, but a smile, nonetheless. "Thanks," she said. "It's nice to be alive. If only for a little while."

"What do you mean?"

"Nothing." She shook off the thought, but Frank was interested. Besides, what else was there to talk about? Nothing would ever be interesting again after the tales he heard today.

"No, go ahead. I'm listening." Frank pushed.

"It's just…*this Entity*…I don't know if there's any way to stop something like that. You know?"

"Didn't you say Kelly stopped it? In the future? Or in the past? Honestly, I can't keep track anymore."

She laughed, her smile a nice sight for anxious eyes. "I'm still trying to piece it together myself. But if I were to guess, by killing Zoe, it stops the *Entity*'s connection to this universe somehow. Saving it."

"I get that," Frank said, not entirely sure if he did. "But after he kills Zoe, why doesn't the ghost, *the Entity*, whatever you call it, just move on to the next person, then the next? If it's all-powerful, why doesn't it just kill everyone and get it over with?"

Zoe pondered the thought as Frank pulled the blanket tighter around himself, his breath visible in front of his face. "I think—*and this is purely speculation*—that the *Entity* needs to coordinate his invasion. In my universe, he took over *my* body, he chose *me*, for no other reason than that I was the closest to him when he materialized. Now, and I may be wrong about this, I feel that there was some version or another of myself across every universe, in the *exact* same spot, at the *exact* same time. And in some sort of connected and parallel attack, the *Entity* possessed them all, connecting each and every universe in one coordinated strike. *Every universe but this one.*"

"That's quite a speculation," Frank said.

"True, but we *do* know that he didn't grab any foothold in this universe, at least not strong enough to bring the end of times along with him. I think it has something to do with Kelly, and the fact that he somehow figured out how to stop the connection, *if only by accident.* It's hard to explain, but it's what I saw when the *Entity* sent me to this universe."

Frank looked back at Kelly, sound asleep on the couch, wrapped up in a bright pink comforter, snoring away. "Maybe. But you said there were infinite universes. Infinite timelines. Doesn't that mean that something was bound to happen sooner or later, something to stop the *Entity*, whether it be this universe or the next? You know, infinite possibilities and all that nonsense?"

"What happens when an unstoppable force meets an immovable object?" Zoe asked, catching Frank slightly off-guard.

"What?"

"Nothing. It's an old phrase."

"What's the answer?"

Zoe took another puff of her cigarette before flicking it out into a puddle that had formed by her dented truck. "Guess we'll find out."

After a few moments of late-night silence, Zoe stood up, stretching her arms and making her way toward the couch. "I'm going to try to get some sleep. Although I doubt it'll come. Don't forget to wake Kelly at four-thirty."

"I will. Goodnight."

"Night."

The night had grown quieter. The sirens had become few and far between. They were most likely out there looking for himself, as well as Kelly. Frank considered sneaking away and calling in the force to arrest the two until they figured out more, but nothing other than a gut feeling forced his hand, holding him firmly in place in his chair, keeping watch for a creature he barely believed in, waiting for any sign of the unbelievable events they had described. He had one last question, though, something that just didn't sit right with him, although he couldn't really pin why.

"Zoe?" he asked, hoping she hadn't yet fallen asleep.

"Yes?" she whispered drowsily.

"You said you barely got out of your house alive, right? When the *Entity* forced Jessie to...*you know*?"

"Yeah. What of it?"

"Well, you mentioned arriving near your home wearing only a jacket. When did you have time to change into your police uniform?"

Zoe paused, leaving Frank hanging a moment before giving a response.

"I have a bag in the truck. I managed to snag the keys during my escape. I changed once I slipped away. Night, Frank."

"Night, Zoe. Sleep tight." Frank had been a cop for a long time—longer than he'd like to believe. He had seen a lot of lazy cops and a lot of great ones, more of the former than the latter. But Zoe had always been one of the good ones, always keeping to the book, doing things *exactly* as they should have been done. That's what made her such a terrific officer. It seemed unlike Zoe to leave her pistol and armour lying unattended in the backseat of her truck, completely against protocol.

Every firearm not holstered to their hip was to be always locked up, with no exceptions. The same goes for the armour. Every rookie knew that.

But given the day's odd events, his mind was already overexerted with thoughts. Yet, as he sat in the silent darkness of the October night, the persistent unease that something was amiss wouldn't subside.

30

When Kelly woke up on the morning of October the 9th, it was no gentle emergence back into consciousness. He sprang from the couch, sweat pouring down his frigid body, his hand at his hip where his pistol would typically be.

All night, he had dreamed of the *Entity* and visions of his wife reaching out to him, a seven-inch knife embedded in her eye, the shadowy creature lurking behind her, moving her limbs with white dangling strings, the ominous marionettist controlling her every move as she stood twisted in the darkness of their bedroom.

In his dream, it was as if Donna was trying to speak, trying to tell him something, her jaw grinding back and forth as if searching for words in the silent movie of his dream. Donna reached out to him with her twisted arm, and without the touch of her hand, slowly reeled him in toward her and the *Entity*, like a fish on the line. Kelly tried to resist but was helpless to withstand the temptation of darkness. He mindlessly marched forward toward the *Entity* and his butchered wife, unable to divert his gaze from the seduction of the void, stopping only a foot before his wife, the knife's handle halfway between their noses.

Without defiance or resistance, Donna reached up, grabbed the handle of the knife and slowly slithered it out of her skull, blood rushing down her cheek like a waterfall, the strings still dangling from her arm and wrist as the *Entity* forced her hand. Once the knife was free, Kelly could see the deep gash across Donna's face where her eye had been, the stainless steel of the blade covered in blood and slaughter. Then, with the single flick of the *Entity's* translucent hand, Donna turned the knife around and pointed the jagged end toward Kelly, who was destitute to watch as his body remained out of his control.

Slowly, Donna glided the chef's knife forward through the stench-filled air, inching it closer and closer toward his face as he watched. Then—*unable to even wince under antagonizing pain*—she slipped the knife through his eye, deep into his skull. In his dream, Kelly's vision somehow remained unobstructed, looking down at the steel blade now sticking from his face like the barrel of his gun. It was at that moment he heard the only sound played throughout his vivid nightmare. It was a single whisper breathed by Donna's dead lips, but he knew it was the *Entity* speaking through her.

"*...no...time...*"

Then as if the pain had all set in at once, Donna began to scream, shrieking at the top of her lungs as her jaw open wide, the blood trickling over her lips and into her mouth as she nearly burst Kelly's eardrums, the room vibrating like a powerful earthquake.

Then he was awake, continuing the screaming into reality as Frank and Zoe jumped from their seats at the startling cry. It took only mere moments for Kelly to realize it was all a nightmare as he reached up to touch his eye, feeling no knife, incision, or any other abnormalities.

"Jesus Christ, Kelly," Frank said, settling back down on his chair to face the parking lot. "Did you have an aneurysm or something?"

Kelly didn't respond, trying to remember the dream as it slowly fluttered away from his mind, the words' *no time'* the only memory remaining in its wake.

"Well? You alright?" Frank pushed.

"I'm fine. Just a terrible dream." Kelly returned to his spot on the sofa, trying to calm his nerves as his tremble began to wither. He looked toward the open garage door, where a faint light from the sky was starting to shine through in the morning's greeting. He had slept right through the dark, missing his allotted hour of night-watch. "You were supposed to wake me, Frank."

"Yeah, well, you look like you needed the rest. Besides, I wasn't sleeping anyway. Not after what you crazies told me."

Kelly grumbled, frustrated that Frank had shouldered the burden of watch, yet relieved for the rest. He still felt like a ton of bricks, but at least the bags under his eyes had faded.

Zoe reached into her duffle bag and pulled out a few protein bars for the three of them. Kelly received a *'Peanut Butter Parfait'* power bar, although it tasted more like sawdust and starch. It was something, though, and he'd wash down the taste with what was left of his water.

They had made it through the night without any intrusions—*both the cops and the Entity nowhere in sight.* Kelly was confident they wouldn't see daylight without a threat to their lives or freedom, but he was happily mistaken as the morning breeze blew in from the ocean as the sky got brighter and brighter by the minute. After a few stretches and some splashes of puddle water in their faces, it was time to decide where to go from here. Up until now, his plan was just to survive, to escape the clutches of the prick that tore his whole life apart. But he was tired of running, tired of watching his world go up in flames. It was time to do something about it. It was time to go on the attack—*even if it was impossible.*

Even if it was suicide.

He thought again about what Zoe had said, about there being a chance to change all of this.

If you want to save her…

Was there really a chance to go back and change everything?

Did Kelly truly possess that power, not just to slow time, but to reverse it as well?

It sounded like absolute insanity to him, but so did everything else that occurred over the past twenty-four hours, and he wasn't about to just brush away even the slightest possibility of saving Donna, the officers he shot, and even the lady he shouldered off the library balcony. *Kelly didn't know if it was possible, but he believed in it, and that was enough.*

He turned to Zoe as she fastened her body armor back on and slipped her holster back on her belt, looking ready to return to the office as though none of this had happened—*as if she wasn't from a different universe.*

"How do we fix this?" Kelly asked, hoping she had some sort of insight as to what they should do next. Besides, it was Zoe that had a connection with the *Entity*, giving her all the haunting visions and whatnot.

Frank cut in before Zoe could speak. "Fix what?"

"How do we fix yesterday? How do we save Donna? How do we stop the apocalypse? You name it. Yesterday, right after she hit you with the truck, she said to me, '*if you want to save her, get in.*' Right Zoe?"

"I did," Zoe responded, her voice hoarse with the remnants of sleep.

"You mean there's a way to—to stop all of this?" Frank stammered out, still half-lost in the chaos.

"Not just stop it," Zoe said, "To go back and reverse it all together, as if it never happened."

"I don't follow," Frank replied, Kelly sharing the same sentiment. It seemed that Zoe was the only one who had any sense of what was going on, her mind-meld with the *Entity* giving her insights beyond human comprehension. The two men waited for her to explain her master plan of saving the world and stopping the *Entity*, hoping against hope that it was even possible.

It was her turn to speak. "Listen, I don't even know if I'm right. This is just my working theory, but from what I've seen, it's the best we got. Are you ready to hear it?"

"We're ready," Kelly and Frank said in unison.

"Alright. When the *Entity* and I crossed paths back at the ferry terminal, he didn't just share his intentions with me, but he also shared, for lack of a better word, his consciousness. It was like our minds became one—it learned everything I knew, and I it, if only for a moment. Now, it comes and goes in fragments, but I remember some parts clearly, one in fact, that had stuck with me ever since I crossed over to this universe."

Kelly and Frank allowed her to continue.

"This creature—*this Entity*—it had the ability to not only jump through space, but time as well. It's like an inter-dimensional being. And what's interesting is that it doesn't perceive time like you or me. We see it as a linear path, going from point A to point B without ever going backwards. We're born, we live, we grow old, and we die. But what if—what if it wasn't that simple? What if all of those moments existed simultaneously, an entire life lived within a singularity."

Frank was the first to voice his confusion, matching that of Kelly. "You're going to have to be clearer than that. Especially if this leads to where I think it might—*with our lives on the line*." Kelly nodded in agreement.

"Fine. Put simply, there is no single direction of time. It's not linear. It exists all at once."

"Okay, but what does this have to do with the *Entity* and us?"

Zoe thought about it for a moment, visibly looking for the right words to try and make them understand. "What happens when your car runs out of gas? You drive to the gas station, fill up, and go back home. You're able to move to any point in space, back and forth freely. You choose what direction you go. What if the same could be said about time? What if—and I realize these are big conclusions to jump through, but this is what I saw when the *Entity* took control—what if you could travel to any point in time simply by choosing the moment, and you'd be there?"

"Are you saying that this...*Entity*..." *Frank said,* carefully constructing his words, "...has the ability to travel across not only space, but time as well? Like a time traveler?"

"In a sense, that is exactly what I'm saying."

"Then why has it been chasing Kelly around the city like a *damn* fool? Why doesn't it just zip-zap to an exact moment and time and wipe us all out in an instant? Clearly, the *Entity* possesses enough power."

Kelly thought about it, imagining the *Entity* simply appearing in front of him, taking over his body and disappearing in a matter of nanoseconds. It was a terrifying thought, and an encounter he was thankful hadn't yet happened.

"I've pondered that too," Zoe said, her gaze falling to the floor. "That part remains unclear to me."

Kelly thought back about his dream, vaguely remembering the image of his wife yanking the knife from her eye and driving it into Kelly's face, the *Entity* lingering behind her, controlling her every move. He thought about what it said to him, using Donna's voice as his means of communication.

No...Time...

Kelly thought the *Entity* meant it as a threat to him, saying he was out of time and that it was going to find them and kill them.

But that's not what it meant at all.

He wasn't chasing Kelly halfway across the city just for the sake of torturing him. Somehow, in some way, Kelly had absorbed the *Entity*'s abilities to bend time. That's why the *Entity* tried to kill him back in the jail cell, and again at the library, and once again at his own home.

The creature was attempting to reclaim its power.

"I think I can take a guess," Kelly answered.

Go ahead," Frank said. "Because I sure as hell can't make sense of it.

"The *Entity*, I think I know what it wants from us. And more specifically, I think I know what it wants with *me*." Kelly hopped out of the couch, pacing around the storage unit as he tried to explain his theory to Frank and Zoe. "Think about it. You said it yourself. What would this multi-universal travelling *Entity* want with an inner-city cop like me? It doesn't make sense. *Unless*, I have something it wants—*something belonging to him*. Something like its ability to travel across time."

Frank appeared skeptical, trying his best to connect the dots. "That would explain his infatuation with you, but how did you get the power in the first place? Why you? Isn't that quite a leap to make?"

"I'm not sure, Frank, but I suspect we're about to discover the truth, whether we're ready or not."

"And why do you say that?" Frank asked, still perched on his wooden kitchen chair.

"Because precisely twenty-four-hours ago—*in the future*—" Kelly nodded over at Zoe as he stole her line. "I believe I was the one who shot and killed Zoe Stevens—*Zoe Stevens from our universe.*" He corrected himself. "I think that man in the video, was in fact, me."

The three of them sat in silence. They could hear the morning traffic starting to pick up as the sunlight began to creep over the horizon to the east. The crows cawed overhead, perched on the power lines, scavenging for their morning meal of garbage and worms. And somewhere out there the *Entity* prowled, waiting, wandering — *trapped in time.*

31

regory Davis arrived early for work on the morning of October 9th, pulling into the driveway as the local news played on the AM radio. A full-on manhunt was underway for ex-detective Kelly Christopher, practically shutting down the entire city as the search intensified for the man held responsible for the deaths of three officers and his wife, reported radio anchor Craig Clarke. Apparently, the shooter at the ferry terminal had escaped custody, made his way home, and killed two cops and his wife before fleeing the scene. There had been roadblocks set up across both bridges after that, as well as a few on some of the central veins leading into the city. Two helicopters were constantly on patrol overhead, scouring the surrounding forests and neighbourhoods while armed officers scouted the neighbouring streets, searching for any signs of Kelly Christopher.

Gregory himself had to pass through two roadblocks to reach the storage facility where he worked. A young couple, planning to move to Alberta, had arranged an early morning appointment with him. They wanted to fetch their belongings early in the morning and hand over the keys, so Gregory volunteered to show up a little early and meet them, possibly give them a hand if they needed it. Typically, the couple could have deposited the keys in the drop box, but recent vandalism by hooligans had compelled Gregory to change some of the locks, ensuring no unauthorized access.

He was a little early reaching the open gate to the storage facility, having left a little bit early on account of the roadblocks.

It was only five-to-seven, and he did not expect the couple to arrive until about 7:15 AM this morning. He was relieved the rain had held up. It would have been unfortunate to watch them move their belongings in a downpour.

He took a sip of his steaming coffee, black, just as he liked it, rolling his car up to the main booth where he kept his file-folders and other documents. Exiting his Buick, Gregory entered the small office building, opened the door, and searched for the spare keys to unit number seventeen, along with the documents for the couple to sign, which would release their unit ownership. It took a few minutes to find—*he wasn't the most organized old fellow*—but he found them as always, setting them out and prepping them for the young couple's arrival.

By the time all was said-and-done, he still had about ten minutes to spare before he expected them to arrive. It would give him enough time to walk the aisles of the facility for a quick inspection, making sure the hooligans weren't back to destroy any more of his property.

Gregory started with the higher-numbered units, inspecting units forty through fifty-nine followed by sections twenty through thirty-nine.

All was quiet.

Everything was in order.

He expected the same for sections one to nineteen but was baffled to see one of the garage doors of his units smashed open, lying on the pavement next to a green Ford F-150. Gregory marched ahead to investigate, furious that someone would to that to his property but halted when he saw a man and a young woman emerge from the open doorway, tossing a duffel bag and several items into the truck's bed.

Gregory retreated to the corner of the long semi-detached building, peeking out around the edge of the sidewall.

His eyes were not as good as they used to be—*and the unit was a few dozen yards away*—but it didn't take long for him to recognize the man hiding within the destroyed unit. He had seen his face on CBC last night, during the intermission of a Pittsburg Penguins game in their loss to the Jets. They displayed mugshots of the murderer—*of Kelly Christopher.*

The gruesome story had made national news, everyone across Canada sending their prayers to the officer gunned down in the ferry terminal. He forgot what *she* looked like, but was almost certain that the man currently residing in his storage facility was indeed the man everyone was looking for. And if that *was* the man, then he wanted to go nowhere near that murderous devil.

Instead, Gregory retreated to his Buick, hopped into the cab, grabbed his cellphone, and immediately dialled 9-1-1.

He wasn't going to let that killer getaway.

He   was   going   to   be   a   true   Canadian   hero.

32

Kelly didn't realize how close the sirens were until it was too late. The cops had shown up in droves. Several police cruisers had blocked each side of the entrance to .the storage units, their sirens blaring, their red-and-blue lights flashing brightly. Following soon after was the police chopper, hovering loudly overhead, shining a colossal floodlight down atop the green ford as the sun rose over the horizon on the dim, cloudy day. The noise was nearly unbearable, the sounds of shouting, chopper blades, sirens, and boots shuffling as the police force took their positions surrounding storage unit 15.

Zoe, Kelly, and Frank all retreated to safety within the storage unit, careful not to give the officers an easy shot, should they decide to open fire. At this point, Kelly wasn't convinced that they wouldn't. He was the most hated man in the country and knew a vengeful cop with an itchy trigger finger wouldn't think twice about gunning him down.

Kelly knew *exactly* how these situations went down, having been around a few of them himself over the years. It wasn't often that the Halifax Regional Police department needed to use their tactical equipment and strategies—but they were certainly well equipped if the moment arose.

And arisen it had.

Kelly attempted to anticipate how the police would close in on their position. There would undoubtedly be several snipers posted, each with direct viewpoints of their heads should they pop out of their hiding spot— each shooter waiting for the order to take the shot if they have even the hint of suspicion that a gunfight may ensue. The remainder of the force would set up a full F.O.V. perimeter around the entire facility, ensuring there was *no hope* of escape, leaving Kelly and his companions with two options.

One, they could lay down their weapons and surrender.

Two, they could go out guns-a-blazing, a battle they'd lose in a matter of seconds—not that the three of them had any intention of firing a weapon. Most of these fellow officers were their friends—*their family*. The last thing they wanted to see was any of them get hurt.

Before long, the commanding officer, who Frank assumed would be Commander Clemons, would grab the microphone, reading their restrictive options for everyone within a quarter mile to hear.

They were cornered.

There was no doubt about it.

Together, Kelly, Zoe and Frank took cover against the thick concrete walls of the storage unit, quickly trying to decide what their next move would be, keeping their eyes peeled for any snipers lining up the shot from the storage-unit roof on the far side facing toward them.

Frank was the first to speak. "Let me go out there. Let me reason with them, tell them this is all some giant misunderstanding."

"Frank—*no offense*—" Kelly said, knowing that if his partner walked out there, he wouldn't be returning a free man. "—but as far as they're concerned. I'm a cold-blooded killer of three cops. Even if we show them Zoe's still alive, there are two more bodies lying riddled with shotgun shells on my bedroom floor. I highly doubt we'll be able to talk our way out of this one. Those boys out there are itching for a fight."

"But—" Frank tried to speak again, but Kelly cut him off. Kelly had no intention of letting anyone surrender at gunpoint.

"Look. It might work in the long term. But even if we walk out there, at best we're all getting arrested. And if you two are locked up inside a jail cell, I don't know if I'll be able to get you out using my power. You'll be easy pickings for the *Entity*. It will take you to get to me. That's what *it* does. I can't have that happen again. I just can't. Not on my account."

Greg Clemons' voice came over the loudspeaker. "*Kelly Christopher, come out with your hands up. We know you're in there. Your companions too.*" He paused a moment, the sound of the sirens and chopper filling the sky, then he started again. "*Come on Kelly. We don't want any more dead cops.*"

If things proceeded as they had in the past, Kelly figured they had about five to ten minutes before the swat team started tossing tear gas into the storage unit, flushing them out into firing range. If caught in the smothering smoke, it would be impossible for a shooter to distinguish Kelly's body from Frank's or Zoe's.

They'd be an open target.

They needed to get out of this.

Zoe suggested an unconventional solution. "Use your power, Kelly. Slow time down."

"That only works for me. You two will be stuck here, and I won't be able to get you out." Kelly had slowed down time only a few times now, but it was relative to him and only him each time. He couldn't slow down time for someone else, not that he was aware.

"How do you know? Have you tried?" Frank was speaking now, clearly not used to being on the other side of the barrel, a hint of fear in his voice. It was a feeling Kelly was starting to become accustomed to.

"Well, no, but..."

"Then what are you waiting for. Get us *the hell* out of here."

Kelly knew Frank had no idea how this worked, not that Kelly had any better inclination toward whatever was happening to him. This power—*somehow stolen from the Entity*—was his curse, leading to the deaths of too many people already, whether directly or indirectly. He was tired of it resulting in misery. It was time to start trying to use it for good—*if that was even possible.*

"Alright, fine. I'll try it." Kelly said. It wasn't like there were any other options, so what the hell.

Kelly closed his eyes, focusing on the energy building within him, feeling it envelop him, as if he were standing at the bottom of a deep well rapidly filling with water. He felt as if a boundless ocean flowed around him, the pressure against his skin rising while he focused on the sounds of Frank and Zoe's breaths, picturing them alongside him in the empty chamber that was his mind.

Suddenly, the sounds of the world around him began to slow…

The heavy winds rushing off the chopper's blades faded to a standstill.

The sirens grew deeper and deeper until they ceased altogether.

The entire world had stopped entirely as the pressure around him began to wither, the energy surrounding them emptying into a vacant nothingness.

He looked over toward Frank and Zoe, who were—*to Kelly's astonishment*—moving and breathing as if their relative world had not changed. Both stared at Kelly with puzzled expressions, as if they were expecting fireworks, or for an alarm to signal the end of his process.

"Did it work?" Frank asked.

Kelly smiled at Frank. The familiar silence was answer enough. "Have a look."

Cautiously, Frank peeked his head around the corner, staring toward the fleet of police cruisers and officers pointing their rifles and pistols toward them. Each of the surrounding officers stood like statues, unblinking and unwavering as Zoe, Kelly, and Frank stepped out into the wide open.

Above, Kelly could see the helicopter, suspended mid-air, the blades barely rotating as it hovered high above. On the far end of the storage units, he could see a man with a scoped sniper rifle strapped across his back, wholly paralyzed enroute to his elevated position.

Except for Kelly, Zoe, and Frank, time itself had been halted for the entire world.

"My God..." Frank said aloud, giving the only appropriate response to the situation. "...this isn't possible."

"Yet, here we are," Kelly responded, recognizing in Frank's bewilderment his own initial reaction upon facing a world brought to a standstill.

"How did you do that?" Frank said, his eyes never veering from the dozen rifles pointed their way.

"I have no sweet clue," Kelly answered truthfully."

The physics of it made no sense.

The reality of it was nonsensical.

Yet, here they were, trapped between seconds.

"Pretty neat, eh?"

"Messed up is what it is." Frank picked up a large stone from the ground and whiffed it high into the sky, narrowly missing the helicopter above.

"Careful, Frank, you're a lot stronger than you think. Everything operates differently in this state, and you must be cognizant of that. It's this strength-in-time that allowed me to break out of my cell and knock down the garage door. Even a slight bump into someone could be more than they can withstand. If you hit them hard enough, the blow could be lethal.

"Right. I'll be careful."

Kelly was unsure if Frank fully grasped the extent of their newfound power now that he was moving at inhumane speeds relative to the rest of the world, but Frank was smart. Kelly knew he'd be cautious.

Frank turned over to Zoe, who was acting surprisingly calm, given the situation. "What do you think of all this?"

She holstered her pistol, shifting her gaze back to Frank. "Yeah, it's pretty neat."

"*Pretty cool?* That's it? You're not amazed by all this?".

"Sure, it's amazing. We should get out of here before Kelly loses his grip and we're caught in a bullet storm. We don't know how long he can hold them like this."

Kelly agreed. The power was a complete mystery to him. It was uncertain how long he could maintain this. Should his hold on time falter and normalcy return, they'd be standing right out in the open, and all it took was one confused officer to end it for them all.

Together, the three of them walked away without resistance, navigating effortlessly between the dozens of offers, all of which were still aiming their rifles toward storage unit *fifteen.* They were careful not to bump into anyone or anything—*the slightest impact was enough to break bones or worse.* Within a few steps, they had cleared the perimeter, quickly distancing themselves from the scene in case Kelly lost his stranglehold on time.

Yet, Kelly couldn't help but admire the stillness of the world around him. It was the epitome of tranquility, almost enough to make him forget about the horrible and chaotic events of the last day.

Almost.
Every car was motionless...
Every bird hovered mid-flight...
Every leaf was frozen in the non-existent wind...
Everything had come to an absolute standstill...
Everything but the Entity, which still out there, prowling...

Together, the three of them marched a few kilometres down the main drag of Dartmouth, each of them utterly silent as they spectated the paralyzed universe surrounding them. It took them about a half-hour—*relative to themselves*—to make it back toward the residential area where Frank's house was located—*and only a few seconds relative to the rest of the frozen world.*

Frank's wife would have been already at work, riding the Halifax Regional hospital's early shift, so his house would be empty and safe. Kelly would be able to relinquish his power to let it charge back up, and Frank could call into the station, telling them he'd be working out of the house today to try and deter suspicion, not that there was any. Frank was pretty sure they didn't see his face at the storage-units, so his home provided the perfect cover to hide a woman from another universe, a supposed cop-killer from this universe, and himself.

And as an added bonus, Frank had several beers in the fridge, and even though it was still barely the crack of dawn, he could sure go for a nice cold-one right about now.

Once they stood in the backyard, shielded by Frank's tall wooden fence, Kelly released his grip on time. Sustaining suspended time was draining, an ability he preferred to use only when necessary. Allowing time to resume its course, the sounds of nature and urban life surged back into existence, as if there had been no interruption.

The birds began to chirp.

The leaves rustled in the wind.

And the sounds of distant sirens echoed across the sky.

They took asylum within Frank's empty home, all of them slumping down in his living room, taking a much-needed breath of relaxation. Kelly sensed his powers recharging, feeling the familiar pressure build around him, and Frank cracked open a very early-morning Keiths and began to sip. Zoe sat quietly on the couch, leaning forward with her elbows on her knees, her head cradled in her hands.

"What are you thinking, Zoe?" Kelly asked, noticing her deep in thought.

"I think I've come up with a plan."

"Have you figured out a way to save Donna?" Kelly perked up, rising from his slouching position, eyeing Zoe intently as he listened.

"Not just her," Zoe said as she raised her eyes to Kelly, her eyes momentarily appearing dark as they caught the edge of the sunlight. *"I think I know how to save your entire reality."*

33

Frank's home phone had been ringing off the hook as Zoe, Kelly and himself took refuge in the familiar comfort of his living room. Typically, Kelly would be relaxing on Frank's Chesterfield, watching the game and nursing a beer as they made simple conversation. On a typical visit, there would be finger-food. In the winter, they'd enjoy hors d'oeuvres like nachos, pigs-in-a-blanket, or some takeout like pizza or chicken wings. In the summer, they'd be surrounded by home-grilled hamburgers, hotdogs, corn, potatoes, or whatever Frank could find in the depths of their downstairs freezer.

But this was no routine visit.

The curtains were drawn so no passersby could peer in and see the most wanted fugitive in recent Canadian History. The food was limited to sliced bread, peanut butter, and some early-morning beers. The company included an out-of-dimension police officer and the overwhelmed Frank, and not to mention somewhere out on the streets, tracking Kelly down like a supernatural hound, *was the Entity.* And on top of it all, Kelly was battling the recent loss of his beloved Donna, butchered in their own bedroom less than twelve hours ago.

Today was no ordinary day.

Not in the slightest.

The persistent ringing of Frank's home phone interrupted Kelly's scattered thoughts for the fourth time, the sound grating on his nerves.

"You should answer it, Frank."

"That's a terrible idea." Frank said as he returned from his kitchen, carrying butter knives and a tub of peanut butter for them to share as Zoe revealed her masterplan.

"No, he's right." Zoe said, sitting opposite Kelly on a loveseat in the living room, facing the 52-inch flatscreen. "The last thing we want is a few cops showing up to make sure you're alright."

Frank considered it and agreed with the reasoning. "What should I tell them? 'Hey boys, I'm sick today and won't be coming in?' I doubt that'll be well received considering everything that's going on. I've already missed too much time already." Frank tossed the peanut butter next to the bread on the glass coffee table. Kelly dove right in, his stomach running on nothing but a protein bar and fumes.

"Just tell them you're looking into a lead this morning and will be in shortly."

"But what happens when I'm not? We can't expect Kelly to keep using all his so-called 'regenerative energy' to freeze time." He looked over toward Kelly, who was already slathering peanut butter on his first slice. "Can we?"

Kelly nodded against it. Holding time at a stand-still was exhausting, like holding your breath on the bottom of the ocean. After escaping the library, Kelly was drained, talking a few hours before he was charged and ready again. He didn't want to use his powers unless it was necessary.

"It won't matter," Zoe said, also digging into the multigrain bread. "If my plan works, all of our worries will be gone. They'll be no reason for the cops to chase us down in the first place."

Kelly and Frank exchanged looks.

They were both in the dark. Whatever insight Zoe had from her multi-universal dance with the *Entity*, they clearly didn't have it.

"I'll explain it all, " she said, "but first, answer the phone before I go insane."

Frank conceded.

He walked over to the black home-phone, hovered above it for a second trying to come up with a quick, yet believable lie, then answered. Kelly and Zoe listened quietly in the background, carefully not to make a peep.

"Hello...speaking...I see...And you don't know how...I see...any idea who? Well, listen, I'm just following up on a lead, then I'll be in as soon as I can. Just give me a few hours. Yeah. Sounds good. Thanks, Pat." Frank hung up the phone.

"Well? What'd they want?" Kelly asked impatiently.

"Pat was telling me about your grand escape. They have no idea how you got away. They also know you're not alone, having spotted an unidentified woman alongside you."

"Then they don't know you're involved? Or that Zoe is—for lack of a better explanation—*alive*?" Of course, the Zoe from *this* universe was dead. Frank had seen her with his own eyes, but how could you explain that to people who thought the most confusing thing in the world was taxes?

"If they had any suspicion, there would be a swarm of cops scouring every inch of my house. They couldn't have seen me. I was well-hidden in the storage unit when they arrived."

"Good," Zoe said. "Then we have time to discuss the plan."

"You care to share this master plan with us?" Frank responded, sitting down next to Kelly on the sofa, digging into the bread and peanut butter as the two partners awaited Zoe's proposal.

"Alright. I don't even know if this is possible, but something tells me it'll work."

"What tells you that?" Frank skeptically asked.

"Let's just call it a woman's intuition," she said, not putting either of their minds at ease. "You ready?"

They both nodded. Kelly was becoming impatient. Ever since Zoe hit Frank with her truck, he had been operating on the promise that there was a way to save his wife. She was his entire world, and he had little desire to fight on without her. If there was a chance to somehow—*within the confines of his newly-found abilities*—bend time and save the only woman he'd ever loved, he'd take it.

No matter the cost.

No matter the odds.

Zoe glanced toward Kelly. "You're our only shot at this. At saving your wife. At stopping the *Entity*. It's all up to you."

"And how am I supposed to do that?" Kelly asked.

"You already know, don't you?" Zoe called him out.

He did.

Kelly had been harboring a notion for some time now.

How does one save someone who's already dead?

There was only one way that was possible, an idea that, before the events of yesterday, Kelly would have thought to be absolute and utter nonsense. But what is and isn't possible cares not about the reality one has come to understand, but the reality that truly exists.

To save her, Kelly would have to do the impossible.

Kelly would have to go back in time.

"I do." He said, acknowledging her crazy idea. She smiled, nodding back.

"Well, I sure as hell have no idea," Frank said, cutting through Zoe's and Kelly's mutual understanding. "So please, start explaining."

Zoe began to detail her plan.

"Kelly can't just slow time, Frank. He can also reverse it." Zoe spoke calmly, as if she were an expert at all this. Kelly wondered for a second how much the connection she had with the *Entity* affected her when she swapped universes. He didn't care, though. He just wanted to get to the plan and save Donna.

"You mean, like time travel?" Frank said, bluntly. On paper, it was obvious, but said aloud as part of a serious discussion, it was a concept no one was ever truly prepared to face and understand.

"Pretty much," Zoe responded. "Like I said before. Time isn't linear. It exists all at once, just like the space around us. All Kelly needs to do is pick the moment in time he wants to be in, then travel there. It's that simple."

Kelly disagreed with that.

There was nothing simple about it at all.

He barely even knew how to control his power, let alone manipulate it to a specific point in time.

But he'd learn.

He had no choice.

Then there was the butterfly effect theory. However, he hadn't given it much thought. Things couldn't possibly be any worse than what they were right now.

"And you know he has this ability, how?" Along with his straight-to-the-point attitude, Frank was also a healthy skeptic. Part of the nature of being a good detective.

"Because," Zoe said with a gentle smirk across her face, "we have proof."

"The security footage," Kelly reaffirmed, becoming more and more confident he had *actually* seen himself on the video shown to him in the interrogation room.

"Exactly," Zoe responded. "You told me that some sort of look-alike shot and killed Zoe Stevens from this universe. But it was too much of a coincidence that she died right before the *Entity* should have appeared, as he did in my universe. It didn't add up. But once I learned about your ability to bend time, somehow stolen from the *Entity*, I pieced it together quickly. I'm surprised you didn't."

"It's not exactly the most believable story," Kelly replied, aware he would never have guessed that it was himself from the future, having travelled back to the past and getting caught doing it on security footage at the Halifax Ferry Terminal. "But at least it's an explanation."

"And you're just going to accept this *explanation?*" Frank said, with a heavy emphasis on 'explanation.' "It's out there…"

"You saw me slow down time just by closing my eyes, Frank," Kelly said, staring directly at Frank from across the dimly lit living room. "Is this truly so hard to believe?" Frank always made sure every detail fit within the story and would never be convinced of a conclusion unless all the arrows pointed the same direction. Kelly knew it would be a long shot to get him fully on board, but if they could get Frank even to step one foot on the platform, he'd consider it a victory.

"I suppose not," Frank said, placing one step forward. "But the Kelly I saw in that footage was a murderer. He killed an innocent woman—*our friend*. If you haven't done it yet, then you're *about* to. If that's how this time-travel nonsense even works. I can't be a party to that."

"Even if it means saving the world from the *Entity*?" Zoe asked as if that were remotely a normal sentence.

"And how do we know that?" Frank said, his temper rising a little. "Besides what you told us, what evidence do we have that shooting an innocent woman in an open crowd is the answer to the end of the world?"

A valid question, Kelly thought to himself, knowing better than to jump into the middle of one of Frank's tirades. Kelly was no murderer—*even though the events of the day would suggest otherwise.* He couldn't just walk up to an innocent officer and shoot her in the face without just cause, even if what Zoe was telling him was true. Just like time travel, the end-of-the-world was something one didn't truly believe unless witnessed firsthand.

"Because you're still alive," Zoe said, interrupting Kelly's thoughts. "I know it's hard to believe. But you didn't see what I saw. It's real, *and it's coming,* whether or not you choose to believe it."

Frank was unconvinced. Kelly knew it. He could see the inquisitive look on his face as he finished his second slice of bread and peanut butter. Frank would continue his barrage of questions, as if any of this could ever make sense to a regular human being.

"But didn't he already stop it? Yesterday morning Zoe was shot and killed, wasn't that the connection across the multiverse? She's dead. What reason would Kelly have to go back to redo what's already been done?"

Zoe paused a moment, as if she were trying to come up with an answer, *or a way to explain it in a way that Frank and Kelly could understand.*

It was hard to argue Frank's point.

Their Zoe *was* dead.

Besides going back to save Donna, why would they need to go back?

"Do you believe in fate?" Zoe asked open-endedly to them both.

Frank shrugged; he wasn't the type to think of those sorts of things. Nor was Kelly. He didn't care about trying to answer questions there was no way of explaining. He was an evidence-based decision maker. He responded, though, interested to see where this conversation was going. "Sure. Why not."

"As much as the next person," Frank said, a similar mindset to Kelly.

Zoe analyzed both of their answers, deeming them satisfactory enough to continue her point. "What if you could see your fate laid out before you? Your next move printed as clear as day in your mind. What would you do?"

Kelly knew where this was going, and he didn't like it. Fate didn't make him a murderer, his decisions did, and he had control over those.

Didn't he?

"If it meant shooting a friend," Frank answered before Kelly had the chance, "I'd cut and run."

"I don't think it's that simple," Zoe responded, as if she knew more about fate than the two detectives in the room with her. "I don't think it's simple at all."

Finally, that was something Kelly could agree with. Out of everything he was cursed to endure over the past twenty-four hours, not a single bit of it was simple. And he sure-as-hell didn't like the idea that his future was predetermined for him…even if his future resided in the past.

But there was one thing he was even more sure about, and that was he would do whatever it took to save Donna. And that meant he *needed* to go to the past. He would go along with Zoe's mad plan for now because that was the only way he was going to save his wife.

The three of them sat in silence for a few minutes, each of them contemplating the insanity Zoe had just explained to them as if watching a science-fiction movie they didn't understand. Kelly knew Frank didn't believe it. He had seen the time-bending powers for himself, but the impossible was always hard to grasp until it was rolled out like a red carpet. And even if he knew something beyond his comprehension was real, it didn't make the next inconceivable event any more believable. Frank may not have believed any of it, but Kelly was starting to come around.

"I'll do it," Kelly declared, answering an unasked question. "I'll go back in time. I'll try. *For her.*"

He didn't have to define what *'her'* meant. He knew that Zoe and Frank understood. If Frank couldn't believe in anything else, he could believe in Kelly's pain. That was a demon well-understood, a power not-so out of grasp.

No one responded, the sound of Frank's wall-clock ticking in the silence as the three of them reflected amongst themselves. Kelly watched as the second-hand of Frank's clock spun around and around, never standing still—*never going back.* He thought back to the security footage, seeing his future-self fire a bullet directly through the eye of a friend.

Was he capable of such a thing?

Even for Donna?

Was that truly his fate?

He remembered Zoe's gun, already being drawn before dropping to her death, the P226 landing beside her in her pool of blood and gore as the rest of the crowd panicked and retreated out the main entrance doors.

The whole thing felt uneasy, like he was missing something right in front of his eyes. Every bone in his body felt askew, his gut was turned, and his head throbbed in warning.

Kelly was no murderer.

Yet he had seen the footage as clear as day, and the more and more he thought about it, the more and more he began to realize that it *was* him on that video screen—the matching outfit, the gun held in his left hand, the badge on his belt, it all fit too perfectly together.

Was he really going to give in to fate?

Now that he knew his future, couldn't he just put a gun to his head and pull the trigger?

Wouldn't that end his so-called 'destiny?'

Of course, he couldn't do that. That wouldn't help Donna or stop the apocalypse.

Not a single piece of this made sense.

Destiny, time travel, the multiverse, fate.

How could one man possibly come to terms with everything unfolding before his eyes?

It was impossible.

It was pure and utter nonsense.

Yet he had to believe.

Belief was all he had left.

34

Sirens had been blaring back and forth all over Dartmouth and Halifax as Kelly Christopher remained out of sight behind the curtains of Frank's window, listening to them drive by one by one, each passing siren indicating that the station still had absolutely no idea where they were, nor how they had escaped. It had been over an hour since Frank's phone call from the station, and he knew it wouldn't be long before someone got suspicious and came over unannounced to check out Frank's place. They knew Kelly and Frank were close friends, and if one detective could go rogue, who's to say another couldn't do the same? *It didn't matter*. The three of them wouldn't be here when the cops came knocking. They'd be in the last place anyone would ever suspect, a place no living officer could investigate.

They'd be in the past.

Frank was upstairs gathering his things while Zoe sat patiently in the darkness of the living room, waiting for him to get ready, and for Kelly's power to recharge to its full potential. Kelly had felt fully recharged for a little while now—*it didn't seem to take too long for his ability to come back*—but he was taking it easy just to be sure.

This next step, traveling back in time, was uncharted territory for him. While slowing time was draining, reversing it to return to yesterday seemed even more daunting, like it would require a great deal more energy to pull off. Of course, that was all hypothetical. Kelly had no idea what to expect. It wasn't like he was learning to ride a bike.

But somehow, he knew it would work.

Whether it was the sight of himself on the security footage, Zoe's unwavering confidence, or the chance to save Donna, Kelly felt compelled to proceed. He was grateful for whatever was fueling his courage to attempt the impossible. He would need all the courage he could muster.

There was eerie anticipation as Kelly mentally prepared himself to travel back in time. Zoe sat across from him, staring at Kelly, almost as if studying him, watching every move with acute observation. Realizing her intense focus, she looked away once Kelly caught her eye, shifting her attention to the ticking clock on the wall instead.

Kelly considered the ordeal Zoe had endured over the last twenty-seven hours, coming face-to-face with the *Entity*, getting torn across the multi-verse, only to go to an identical copy of her home to see the man she loved already taken from her by the shadow's grasp. Despite it all, Zoe seemed composed. Zoe had always been a tough officer, though Kelly would have expected some signs of fragility given the circumstances, even for someone as rough-edged as her. Zoe's unexpected confidence helped ease Kelly's own head as he tried to shoo away the sorrowful presence of mind stalking his every thought. If Zoe could get through all this with a straight head, then he could as well. Plus, she seemed adamant that all was not lost, that there was a way to save their loved ones. Her assurance provided the impetus he needed to forge ahead and block out the images of Donna getting murdered in their bedroom.

Things were going to be alright.

"So," Kelly said aloud, trying to break the silent tension lingering in the air, "Once we're in the past, what's the plan? What then?"

Zoe drew her gaze away from the ticking clock and glanced back at Kelly. "We save Jessie and Donna," she said, as if it didn't come with a heavy anchor tied to it.

"By killing you...*I mean the other you*...Zoe?" What was one life against billions? If what Zoe told them was true, that killing the other Zoe was the only way to prevent the end of the world, which she seemed ever adamant that it was, this had to be the only logical option. Right? Who wouldn't pull that trigger.

"And to stop the *Entity* from connecting to this universe," she responded, the sentence sounding crazier and crazier every time she said it.

"Even though she's already dead?"

"And who took her out?" Zoe asked.

"My future self, the one who already traveled to the past." This time loop was not doing any wonders for his sanity, the idea of a future and past version of himself was tearing across his brain like a heavy migraine. Kelly's future version was the man who pulled the trigger, which, in a way, laid out the footprints for what present Kelly needed to do next.

Did that mean there was an endless loop of Kelly's, murdering Zoe Stevens over and over again?

He didn't want to think about it. But one question did pop into his mind, one that even Zoe hadn't been able to answer. "Where is the future version of myself? And you and Frank, for that matter? Where did they go?"

Zoe shrugged. "My knowledge stops with you and the *Entity*. But he's likely out there, ready to assume your place in this timeline once you leave."

Kelly shuddered at the thought of another version of himself replacing him once he travelled back. And if the 'fate' nonsense that Zoe talked about had even a hint of truth to it, then theoretically, he would be doing the same to the next version of him, and so forth—*if that's even how this all really worked.*

It was a paradox alright...

Fortunately, his spiraling thoughts were interrupted by Frank marching down the stairs. In his hands were two black standard-issue P226 pistols, a police badge, and a holster. "If we're going through with this," Frank said, handing Kelly one of the guns and the badge, "then we're not going empty-handed." He looked over at Zoe, who was already packing her firearm. "You full up?"

"I'm good," Zoe responded.

"Thanks, Frank," Kelly said as he fastened the holster on his left hip and tucked the pistol into its sleeve. "But why do I need the badge?"

"Who knows," Frank responded truthfully. "Might help you get through security. Maybe it'll bring good luck. Just take it."

Before the initial shooting had occurred, Kelly was still an innocent man., so maybe the badge *would* come in handy. Plus, he was wearing one in the security footage, although the camera wasn't decent enough to capture the numbers on the front. Perhaps the badge Kelly wore in the footage wasn't even his. That would be at least a hint of evidence on his side. If they got through this, he resolved to remember that detail. *And the gun,* Kelly thought as his mind booted back to detective mode.

"Hey Frank, did you ever check the serial number of the pistol used in the shooting?"

"I think one of the boys did, but I didn't get a chance to follow it up."

"Might be a good idea," Kelly pushed, slightly frustrated. He shook it off. It didn't matter anymore, not with everything else going on. He was focused on one thing and one thing only, saving Donna.

Kelly had just clipped on his holster when Zoe stood up from her chair. "Are you boys ready?"

Frank laughed, snorting at the remark. "Not a chance. You ready, Kelly?"

Kelly smirked, Frank's humour a nice relief in the tense atmosphere. "Not a chance. But we're going anyway. You sure you're up for this, Zoe?"

"I've been ready for an eternity," she responded, joining the madness alongside Frank and Kelly. The three of them were about to do something never thought humanly possible. They stood, forming a circle around the coffee table that held an open jar of peanut butter and an empty bread bag.

"Assuming this is even possible," Kelly said, trying to steady his nerves, "How far back should I take us?"

"Why don't we go back to 1939 to blow Hitler's head off and stop a war while we're at it. Neither Kelly nor Zoe found humor in his jest.

"Maybe next time," Kelly answered, focused on the task at hand.

Zoe interjected, firmly focused on the mission. "Let's focus on a specific day and time first. How does 5:00 AM yesterday sound? That should give us enough time to head over to the Halifax Ferry Terminal and—"

"—kill Zoe Stevens," Kelly interrupted, loathing that this was the only way.

"Yes," their Zoe responded. "Unfortunately, yes."

"Remind me again, why we have to kill her?" Frank asked. "I mean, you're clearly still alive. Why should *our* Zoe suffer a worse fate?"

"Because I'm not from this timeline," Zoe repeated, no hesitation in her answer. "And trust me, her fate is much better than the universe I left behind."

How could he respond to something like that?

How could he even argue?

To argue something, you needed a platform to stand upon, and neither Frank nor Kelly had any experience whatsoever with anything of the sort. Their course of action was based solely on Zoe's recounted experiences and twisted memories they were perfectly happy not to possess in their own minds.

Kelly was done with talking. His brain had already met its capacity for insanity and madness. It was time to experience it for himself. It was time to act. "Shall we?" Kelly asked, already beginning to absorb the energy around him, the shallow pressure starting to trickle across his skin.

"Let's do it," Frank said. "Let's save the world."

Kelly closed his eyes and fixated on the room around him. He allowed the energy to build-up against his skin, as though the air thickened with electricity. He focused on Zoe and Frank, listening to their breaths as they waited for Kelly to do his thing. Kelly listened to the clock beating away like a heart nailed to the living room wall.

The swelling pressure intensified, as if he were sinking further and further into the depths of the deepest ocean, an invisible force pressed against his chest. Kelly envisioned their destination, imagining himself with Zoe and Frank passing through a vortex of time…

…like an arrow reversing its flight…

…a bullet retreating into its barrel…

Suddenly the ticking of the clock began to slow, each tick elongating, pressure mounting to an almost unbearable intensity.

Tick... Tick ....Tick .... Tick

The clock slowed to a standstill, the thoughts inside his head the only sounds that remained.

Tick ...the electricity reached its. Kelly clenched his hands into fists, fighting the growing discomfort as he sank deeper and deeper into his mind, time around him fading.

Tick......although his eyes remained tightly shut, his eyeballs felt as if they were squeezing into his sockets. Frank and Zoe's breaths began to fade into oblivion, and their presence vanished in parallel.

Tick.........the pressure became too much to bear as Kelly succumbed to the dominating forces closing around him, his thoughts dissolving into nothingness, his mind a barren void latched within time's grasp—but time no longer had meaning. And Kelly had blacked out.

...Tick...

    ...Tick...

        ...Tick...

            ...kciT...

                ...kciT...

Part VI
The Beginning of the End

35

Kelly, come on man, wake up. Don't do this to me." Frank's voice echoed around in Kelly's head, spinning and gyrating as his consciousness slowly slipped back from the dark. His entire body felt weak, a pervasive pins-and-needles sensation spreading across his skin, akin to a wave of anesthesia. It felt like he was coming out of the freezing cold, as if stepping in front of a warm fireplace, with his perception returning slowly in the heat. Opening his eyes, he found himself staring up at the ceiling, Frank hovering over him like a nurse tending to their patient.

"Jesus Christ, Kelly. You scared me there for a second."

Kelly still didn't fully understand where he was, the mental haze clearing like morning fog in the rising sun. He pushed off the hardwood floor, forcing himself to a seated position as he fought the urge to collapse again under instability. His elbows wobbled and his muscles trembled, but with Frank's assistance, Kelly was able to rise to see he had collapsed in the middle of Frank's living room. It took a few more seconds before his memory came rushing back to him, realizing what they had just attempted wasn't a dream, but was in fact, *real*.

"Did it work?" Kelly whispered, his voice as weak as his limbs.

"I don't know," Frank responded, helping Kelly to the sofa. "Are you alright?"

Kelly honestly wasn't sure how to answer that question. It felt like every ounce of energy had been zapped from his body, leaving nothing behind but a numbing deficiency. He could feel his strength slowly seeping back, but not nearly as fast as he'd like.

"I'm okay. I need—*food*." Sometimes after waking up in the morning from a long night of drinking Kelly would feel a similar weakness, like his mind had woken up, but his body had yet to follow. Donna would always make a warm breakfast of bacon, eggs, sausage, home-fries, and a few cups of coffee. That always rejuvenated him.

"Here," Frank reached for the peanut butter tub on the coffee table, only to find it missing. The coffee table was bare. There were no crumbs, no empty bread bag, and no peanut butter covered kitchen knife.

"*Huh.*"

Frank's gaze shifted to the ticking clock on the wall, his face looking like that of a flabbergasted audience member at the Cirque du Soleil. Kelly also looked at the clock, sharing in Frank's moment of awe. The hour hand was just passing the half-way mark between the five and six, and the minute hand was on its way to making another rotation around the clock, marking forty-two minutes past the hour.

5:42 AM.

It worked.

Kelly could hardly believe it, but it actually worked.

"No way," Kelly said, bewilderedly, "Frank…"

"I know. Incredible." It was not exactly 5:00 AM as they had planned, but his new-found power wasn't an exact science to begin with.

Kelly looked over to where Zoe had been standing before they made the jump through time to find her missing. Only Frank and Kelly were there to witness the spectacle of reversed time.

"Zoe's not here," Frank observed, as Kelly's gaze quickly scanned the room.

"Where did she go?"

"I don't know. She was here one moment, and after your time reversal, she was gone."

Kelly didn't understand. Had he failed to bring her back in time with them? Why did it work for Frank but not Zoe? Maybe she appeared somewhere else? He had no idea the reach of his power, or the ripple-effect it could have if he misused it. It was not a power humankind was meant to wield.

Zoe could be anywhere.

Or any-time, Kelly thought.

"We'll find her," Frank said in an assuring manner, Kelly knowing there was no possible way he could provide any credible pledge. Still, it was good to hear. "For now, let's get you on your feet." Frank returned from the kitchen with a can of Dr. Pepper, crackers, a banana, and granola bars, setting them on the kitchen table. Immediately, Kelly promptly opened the Dr. Pepper, drinking half the can in one go. He then dove straight into the crackers, stuffing down four or five before devouring one of the granola bars, washing it away with the remainder of the soda. He saved the banana for later, not knowing if this diminished state would return.

"Thanks," Kelly said, his energy already starting to shift back to normal.

"Don't mention it."

Kelly got to his feet, wobbled briefly, then steadied himself, Frank by his side to catch him if he fell. He looked back up at the clock, expecting it to be back at around nine o'clock as if his eyes had just played a trick on him. They didn't, and it was still the early morning of October the 8th.

"Well, what now?" Frank asked, as if Kelly had any clue.

"We should head to the ferry terminal. If our Zoe is here, she'll likely go there."

"To confront herself—*her other self*, that is."

Kelly didn't respond. He wasn't given the chance. Suddenly, a shuffle from upstairs caught their attention, the sound of footsteps walking above them on the second floor of Frank's house.

They hadn't considered the implications of their arrival time. If they had travelled back to the early morning of October the 8th, then the Frank of the past hadn't yet gone to work, nor had his wife.

They were still home.

"Frank, think." Kelly turned his attention to the Frank standing beside him. "Early yesterday morning—*this* morning— did you come downstairs in the night…?

Frank paused, his mind slowly grasping Kelly's implication. "Oh shit."

"Quick, follow me," Kelly's whispered urgently, leading his partner across the living room, through the kitchen and out the back door. He could hear footsteps on the stairs behind them, seconds away from reaching the bottom and turning toward the main level. They unlocked the back door, stepped through, and quietly closed it behind them, then snuck their way into the backyard and hid under the kitchen windowsill just as the light flicked on in the morning darkness. Kelly pressed a finger to his lips, signaling Frank to stay silent as the kitchen tap turned on inside.

It wasn't often one had to hide from one's own self.

Frank tried to resist the urge, but no amount of reasoning could overwrite his curiosity. Slowly, he lifted to his feet against Kelly's silent hand-gestures, trying to stop him. The gestures were useless, the inquisitiveness too strong. Frank peaked up through the windowsill, facing inward into his own kitchen as he watched the past-version of himself fill up a glass of water from the kitchen sink.

He only watched for a few seconds before the kitchen light flicked off, indicating that *past*-Frank had made his way back up toward the bedroom to catch another half-hour of sleep before his entire world flipped upside-down.

Frank joined Kelly back on the ground, amidst the cold and dirt, his mind clearly trying to process what he had just witnessed.

"You know…" Frank said, his words carried by the misty wind of the early morning, "…I need to lose a few pounds."

"More than a few," Kelly quipped before his mind jumped to the task at hand. "Come on. We should move."

Frank nodded.

They had time to spare, but today wasn't the day to show up late. Kell's energy was sapped, rebuilding slowly, but not quickly enough. He wasn't sure if he'd be able to pull off another time-jump anytime soon. If they failed, he would try, but he didn't want it to come to that. There was just too much uncertainty surrounding his abilities—*so much that he didn't know.*

Together, Frank and Kelly left the backyard, hopped the fence, and made their way toward the rural streets of Dartmouth. There was a bus stop only a few blocks away where they could grab a ride across the MacDonald Bridge toward the Halifax side of the harbour. Then from there, it would be a short stroll to the ferry station along the boardwalk.

The fresh misty air was soothing against Kelly's skin, the empty neighbourhood roads and buzzing streetlights stood as an eerie calm before the storm ahead, almost as if it were warning them of the impending calamity. He was thankful not to be alone, Frank once again standing by his side, no longer a prosecutor, but a companion. It almost made Kelly feel like things were going to work out, that they were going to get through this unscathed.

Almost.

He still found himself trying to piece together the puzzle, trying to understand the entire picture, as if he were on the case of a serious double homicide. But his usual work had knots that were tied together, strings that always came to an end. He could follow the sequence of motives from start to finish, each action flowing into the next like a long chain of dominoes. But in the case of time-travel, it wasn't like that at all. It was like an endless loop of dominoes, where each action led into the next until he was right back at the beginning again to the initial domino.

The action of killing Zoe was what got him accused of murder, which led to his contact with the *Entity*, which progressed into a giant super-natural goose chase across Halifax. These events—*and his meeting with Zoe from another universe*—are what allowed him to learn about the nature of each event, and the apocalyptic-purpose of the dark spectre, which in turn, forced him to go back in time in the first place. Kelly imagined this is what would lead to the eventual death of Zoe Stevens in the Halifax Ferry Terminal, although every bone in his body prayed for a different outcome. It was an endless cycle from which there was no escape, and he couldn't help to think of what part he played in the old phrase; *Which came first, the chicken, or the egg?* Of course, that could be answered with evolution. But this endless time loop, there didn't seem to be a reasonable answer in sight.

Frank and Kelly walked halfway to the bus terminal in silence, each detective lost in their own thoughts before Kelly felt his thoughts on time loops were too burdensome to keep to himself.

"Frank, there's something on my mind—a thought that no matter how hard I try, I can't seem to shake."

"You too, eh?" Frank responded, confirming he was also trapped inside his own head.

"You want to share first?"

"Nah, you go ahead."

"Alright." Kelly wasn't sure if it would make sense aloud, but he figured he'd give it a shot. "Zoe—*the Zoe that time-travelled with us*—she seems determined that killing the version of herself from this universe is the *only* way to stop the *Entity* from grabbing a more permanent foothold in this universe. You know, aligning the multi-verses or something like that." Frank simply listened to what Kelly had to say. "She says that it's because each Zoe across the multi-verse was at the same time and place simultaneously, which allowed the *Entity* to somehow align its power across the multiverse, infecting everyone all at once. At least, that's how I understood it."

"Sure. It sounds nuts, but that is what she said."

Kelly nodded. "Well, why do we need to *kill* Zoe? If we're able just to get her away, to misalign her from the other universes, wouldn't that be enough?"

"Are you asking me or telling me?" Frank said, somewhat sarcastically.

"Just thinking aloud. I mean, If I can misplace you and me in time, couldn't I do the same for Zoe? *Our Zoe?*"

"Maybe," Frank responded. "But is that a gamble we really want to take?"

"Do you want to shoot and kill a friend because someone told us it was the only answer? Even if it was herself?" Kelly was capable of many things, but shooting a fellow officer, he didn't know if he had it in him.

"Kelly, you've seen the footage yourself. You did it, and as far as I can tell, the world didn't become '*consumed in darkness,*' or whatever she said happened."

"Perhaps,' Kelly mused. "Or perhaps not." It was hard to argue with Frank, but something wasn't sitting right. Maybe it was exhaustion. Maybe it was the delusion of it all. Whatever it was, it was eating away at him like acid on steel. "What's on your mind, Frank?"

"And follow *that*? Are you kidding?"

The two detectives were only a block away from the bus station, the glass capsule coming into their field of view. Kelly found himself always looking over his shoulder, his twenty-four hours of being a captured criminal and wanted felon catching up with him, not to mention the *Entity*, who hadn't shown his absent face in quite a while now.

"Go ahead," Kelly said to Frank, not wanting to listen to his own wandering thoughts any longer. "Let's hear what you got."

"Well, I've been piecing together Zoe's story alongside everything that happened to you and me in the past little while. Aside from how she managed to don her entire police uniform amid her escape, everything seems to add up. Everything but *one* thing."

"And what's that?" Kelly asked. He had been continuously tying together everything that Zoe had told them without much friction, *even if* it was utterly unbelievable.

"When she nearly ran me over with that truck of hers, what was it exactly she said to you? The first words that left her mouth when she revealed herself?"

"She said, '*If you want to save her, get in.*'" Kelly wasn't sure where Frank was getting at, but he was one of the best detectives he knew, rarely missing a beat during any case they worked. If he had something to say, it was almost always worth listening to.

"And she was referring to Donna, right?"

"I don't know who else she'd be talking about. Frank, what are you saying?"

The two arrived at the bus stop, the mist waving across the slight breeze as they took shelter inside the glass box to wait for the next ride across the bridge.

"What I'm getting at is, Zoe had just arrived, racing onto your lawn and nearly killing me in the process." Frank paused a moment, choosing his words carefully as he unveiled his perception to Kelly, *"How did Zoe know Donna was dead?"*

36

Frank and Kelly stepped off the transit-bus with barely twenty minutes to spare, inhaling the fresh air blowing in from the harbour on the Halifax side of the water. It was now twenty minutes before the moment when Kelly's life would be turned completely upside-down. It was a strange feeling, knowing precisely what was about to happen.

Kelly always believed he was a being of his own free-will, yet he felt compelled to follow the path seemingly laid out for him, presumably making the same decisions he had watched on the security footage a mere twenty-four hours ago. It made him wonder if all the moments of his life were rolled out for him like a carpet on a runway, his decisions a sheer illusion merely waiting to be caught on the nearest security camera.

Had Kelly not seen the security footage, would events still lead him to right here, pursuing an impossible task to save the world, or were it his decisions leading him to this moment?

It was a question he couldn't answer. Kelly doubted there was a single person alive on Earth that could. But still, it was a question that cycled around in his mind, over and over like a tumbling washing machine as he and Frank made their way down Lower Water Street toward the Halifax Ferry Terminal on the hunt for their friend and prey, Zoe Stevens.

They were only about a half-click away from the terminal, dim mist cutting across the glow of the orange street lights. They had no plan of action, no strategy. They simply wanted to find Zoe before 6:53 AM, the moment the *Entity* would try to grab a permanent foothold in this universe.

"Which way?" asked Frank as the bus rolled away from the stop and disappeared around the corner.

There were two paths they could take. They could either make their way down Lower Water Street and cut across the Tim Horton's parking lot toward the terminal, or they could head across the boardwalk, following the harbour-side path, which would also lead directly to the dock. The Water Street direction was faster, but Zoe was known for patrolling the long section of boardwalk that stretched from one end of Halifax to the other. It was a picturesque walk, particularly serene in the early morning hours, the majority of locals still sound asleep in their beds.

"Let's take the boardwalk," suggested Kelly. All he could envision was himself pulling out his gun and shooting Zoe. Even now, on the precipice of human existence, Kelly found it hard to believe he was capable of such a thing. And even though he knew it was going to happen—*having seen the security footage himself*—he still held on to the minuscule chance that there was another way, that destiny had nothing to do with it.

He prayed they would run into Zoe on the boardwalk and pull her as far away from the terminal as humanly possible. He prayed that would somehow be enough. Kelly hoped her absence would be enough to disrupt the spatial link across the multiverse. It was a long shot, and Kelly barely knew what he was talking about, but *anything* sounded better than cold-blooded murder, and he knew that Frank would be thinking similarly.

Together, the two detectives cut to the right, heading off the main drag and making their way onto the Halifax boardwalk. A gentle breeze blew off the harbour, a thin fog hovering lightly above the water in the cold morning air. Sitting across the dark barrier rocks separating the water from the wooden boardwalk were dozens of perched seagulls, waiting for the morning commotion so they could dig into the waste and scraps left behind by the humans on their morning trek.

Across the water, toward the Dartmouth side, Kelly could see the ferry getting ready to make the short trek across the harbour with its morning passengers making their way to work within the business sector of Halifax. The ferry accommodated walk-on commuters only, not intended for cars or vehicles. It resembled an oversized hockey puck topped with a command bridge, painted in blue, white, and yellow, able to hold hundreds of passengers and crew. There were a couple of matching ferries that made the trip back and forth, but Kelly could only spot one operating at the moment. He seldom used the ferry, preferring to drive across the MacDonald Bridge. Occasionally, he would take the ferry home after a night out, but those instances were rare.

To Kelly's right, a few pigeons picked away at a candy wrapper blowing around in the breeze next to a children's playground shaped like a giant submarine. It was strange being on the boardwalk so early in the morning, completely barren of life, tourists, and buskers. Every other time Kelly had bothered to take a stroll along the boardwalk in the warmth of a sunny day, it was always filled with a smiling crowd enjoying the pleasant views, ice-cream stands, outdoor patios and various snack-shops. Usually, there'd be people riding bikes, walking their dogs, or taking a casual jog up and down the long boardwalk. Instead, replacing the busy crowd was a few hungry pigeons devouring garbage on the barren path. Kelly knew the tranquility would soon be shattered, recalling from the footage people fleeing in terror after the shooting.

Would he really shoot Zoe Stevens?

In fifteen minutes, he would have his answer.

Somewhere far from sight, a ship's horn blared twice, cars flooded into the city from the rural outskirts, and businessmen and women boarded the ferry on their way to work, as if today were an ordinary day like any other—as if their decisions were their own, as if time travel wasn't real, oblivious to Kelly's dire mission.

Thoughts of the imminent shooting triggered a torrent of questions in his overwhelmed mind. Questions about time, the multiverse, fate, destiny, *the Entity*, and whatever else decided to pin itself at the forefront of his mind. And no matter what questions raced through his thoughts, he could never find a confident answer for any of them. He wished Zoe was here—*the Zoe from the other universe*—to answer his enigmas and bring peace to what he was about to do, but she wasn't, and his anxiety grew like a water balloon ready to burst.

Where had she gone?

He thought he brought her back through time just as he did with Frank.

Why did it fail for her but not them?

More questions he had zero answers for. There was only one question he could articulate that wasn't overwhelming, one that Frank might be able to answer definitively, offering some solace.

"Are we really doing this?" Kelly asked, breaking the silence between the two as they quickened their pace.

When Frank looked over to him, Kelly could tell he was also lost in distress and worry, the idea of what they were about to do becoming more and more real as their moment drew near. He had known Frank long enough to be able to detect stress and concern by merely looking at him, like an unmistakable poker-tell at a high-stakes table.

"Do we have a choice?" Frank said.

"Did we ever?"

"Huh?"

"Never mind," Kelly had always been a more introspective person than Frank. Frank held a *'this-is-how-it-is'* approach, so it wouldn't surprise Kelly if his partner were contemplating the physical steps about to happen that would lead to Zoe Stevens' murder, while Kelly pondered over the idea of destiny and fate. That's what made them such a good detective duo. Frank focused on *how* a crime was committed, while Kelly focused on the *why*. Together, they would always find the motive *and* the means to pull it off. But now, they were struggling to determine either as the Halifax Ferry Terminal came within view.

Kelly and Frank halted, staring at the familiar building they had frequented over their years in Halifax and Dartmouth. It wasn't an overly impressive building, its faded panelled siding and tacky concrete base making it look like a structure straight out of the eighties. Atop the main double-door entrance, a sun-spent sign read *'Metro Transit Halifax Ferry Terminal'*. A stairwell led up to the second level, serving as a lookoff for tourists to get a better view of the harbour and boardwalk surrounding the station.

The sight of the terminal made Kelly's chest tighten, as if only now everything had become real, fate coming full circle, leading him to this moment in time once passed. He took a precious minute to fully comprehend where—*and when*—he was standing. It was surreal—*unbelievable*—like living in a looping nightmare that had no end.

Somewhere out there in the world, his wife Donna lived and breathed, Zoe Stevens had no bullet in her skull, the HRM police station was intact, and a previous version of himself was about to wake up and greet the *shitstorm* he himself faced. Kelly contemplated his power of choice, aware he could simply walk away from the irrational situation. If he wanted to, Kelly

Christopher could simply turn around and leave, evidence that he had power over his fate.

Was that true?

As much as Kelly wanted to turn-tail and run, to see if Zoe's story was true, he knew he couldn't. If there was even a sliver of a possibility that this apocalypse was going to happen, he *had* to face it—because after all, *it was Kelly's destiny.*

"*I'll* ask again," Kelly said to Frank in the quiet calm of the morning mist, "Are we *really* doing this?"

Frank stood beside him, equally anxious, confused, and skeptical, with as much desire as Kelly to turn around and leave. But they'd come this far and seen too much to be able to wave this moment away as false veracity. He looked over at Kelly, offering an answer he could scarcely believe himself, yet he felt it to be true. "Something tells me we already have."

Kelly nearly laughed, his unease breaking through his composed facade.

Was there some sort of endless loop circling over and over again?

Was there a version of himself continually travelling back in time to this very moment?

And now it was his turn to play through the endless sequence?

Kelly had no idea.

He didn't want to think about it, wanting nothing but to get this over with.

"Shall we?" He nodded to Frank, resisting the growing impulse to flee.

"Let's do it."

Frank and Kelly stepped forward, the ferry terminal in their sights under the morning glow.

It was time to play their part.

Like rats trapped in a circular maze.

But in a future as predictable as theirs–*where Kelly's fate had been literally played out before him on a computer screen*—even destiny had a way of throwing a wrench into the spokes. They had barely made it a few steps when a familiar voice called out from behind, halting them in their tracks.

"Frank? Kelly? Is that you?" The voice was instantly recognizable by the two detectives, who didn't even have to look to know who it was that stood behind them.

Turning around, standing atop the wooden planks of the boardwalk, dressed in full police attire, holding an oversized Tim Hortons coffee cup in her hand, and utterly oblivious to the events about to unfold, was their friend and colleague, *Zoe Stevens*.

37

The two inner-city detectives didn't respond to Zoe's friendly gesture. They simply stood there on the Halifax Boardwalk's wooden planks, a hundred yards away from the ferry terminal, staring directly into the woman who, in mere minutes, would be at the epicentre of the greatest event in human history.

Kelly could immediately tell that the Zoe standing before them in the misting rain was the Zoe from this timeline, and not the one from the other multiverse. This Zoe had no bags under her eyes, held a bright glimmer in her eye, and greeted them as if today was a typical day like any other.

He didn't know what to say.

He didn't know what to do.

He only knew that Zoe was standing before them, and they were running out of time.

Kelly didn't know the *exact* time, but he *did* know he had until the ferry docked and passengers disembarked. That's when *it* would happen—*that's when the end of the world would begin.*

But it didn't make any sense.

They weren't meant to encounter Zoe on the boardwalk. This isn't where she was gunned down. He had seen the footage for himself.

Something wasn't right.

"Uh...*hello?*" Zoe said, snapping her fingers in a facetious gesture to grab their attention. "Anyone home?"

Kelly still had no idea what to say or do. It was one thing to let a plan roll out in your head. It was another to execute it altogether. Should he greet his friend and colleague with a handshake or fulfill the grim future he had seen?

Was that truly the only option?

The other Zoe told him it was, but his instincts rebelled. He still had time to figure things out, so he decided to keep his pistol holstered, leading Frank to do the same.

"Hey, Zoe. Sorry, it was a long night. We're both a bit tired," Kelly tried his best to scramble together some words that made sense without sounding like a complete lunatic.

"I'd say. You both look like you were run over by a semi."

"That's about right," Frank responded, following Kelly's lead and not putting a bullet in Zoe's skull.

"What are you guys doing down here so early?" Zoe asked. "You working a case?"

"Something like that," Kelly responded, trying not to act too ominously. "It's sort of a hush-hush case. We'll fill you in later," he lied smoothly, hoping to avoid any follow-up questions.

"Alright. Well, I won't hold you boys up too long. Let me know if you need assistance." Both Kelly and Frank nodded, forcing a terrible smile as she cut between them, walking directly toward the ferry terminal.

Kelly's internal monologue resumed, weaving together the threads of reality.

Was this proof that destiny was his own doing?

Did he have complete control over what he did next?

Wasn't it his choice whether to act now and alter the reality he'd seen on the security footage? Zoe would have never walked into the ferry terminal, he wouldn't be captured on security footage, and the loop would end, *wouldn't it*?

Wasn't it Kelly's decision to make?

And if that was true, then did he really have to shoot her in the first place?

He knew that he'd never be able to do it, even at the gamble of facing the *Entity*'s apocalypse. He was no murderer, no matter what that security footage showed, and no amount of predetermined nonsense could convince him that shooting an innocent woman in the head was the right decision.

"Hey," he called out to Zoe. "Come here for a minute."

"What're you doing?" Frank murmured as Zoe started marching back toward them—*and away from the ferry terminal.*

"Getting her away from there." He said, nodding toward the dull facade of the terminal, "*Alive,*" Kelly added just in case he wasn't making his intentions clear.

"But we know what happens if we don't...*you know...*"

"We don't know shit," Kelly responded. "Just some insane prophecy from someone we've already expressed our doubts about. You want to do it? Be my guest." Frank's lack of response indicated what Kelly already knew. "I thought as much."

Zoe stopped a few feet in front of the two detectives, not nearly as far away from the ferry terminal as Kelly would have liked. "What's up?" she said, taking a slow sip of her oversized coffee.

The first move was to get her away from the terminal, making sure she never stepped a single foot inside. If the *Entity* required her to be at the same time *and* space across the multiverse, then the first step was to get Zoe away from the origin-point as fast as humanly possible.

"Follow us for a minute," Kelly directed, leading both Frank and Zoe toward Murphy's Restaurant, a spot alongside the boardwalk that would give them a little bit of privacy away from prying eyes.

"You mean I get to join Frank and Kelly on one of their exciting adventures?" Zoe said half-mockingly in a light-hearted fashion. If only he were just as naive as Zoe, Kelly thought, walking under the low overhanging roof of Murphy's Restaurant.

They turned the corner just out of view from the ferry terminal, still within sight of the ferry itself, which was already half-way across the harbour and making its way toward the end of the line.

Without Frank or Zoe noticing, Kelly unclipped his holster, holding the gun and casing firm in his left hand. He turned to face them both, trailing behind in the cold as a thin fog slowly crept through the air around them as it seeped off the harbour water in the early morning breeze. He knew if he told Frank what he was about to do, he'd disagree. And if Kelly tried to explain the situation to Zoe, she'd never come close to even remotely comprehending the dreadful circumstance they found themselves in—not without proof of the *Entity* at least, and he had no plans on letting that *thing* get close to her.

"Alright, Zoe, let me fill you in." Kelly lowered his hand to his left hip. "See that building over there, across the harbour?" With his right hand, Kelly pointed out over the water toward a random building barely noticeable through the hazy air.

"Which one?" Zoe asked, stepping forward to get a closer look.

"That one right there," Kelly lied, waiting for her to take just one more step forward. Then, seizing the moment of distraction, Kelly grabbed his pistol by the barrel and struck Zoe on the back of her head with all his might.

Frank caught her as she fell and placed her gently on the edge of the boardwalk.

"What the hell was that, Kelly?" Frank said.

He supposed it was Frank's instincts, stepping in to protect her as she lay undefended on the wet ground, a small bump on her head already starting to form on her hairline.

"I had to make sure," Kelly replied, sliding the gun into his holster and securing it.

"Sure of what?"

"That she wasn't going to be *there*," Kelly said. "And this is far better than killing her, wouldn't you say?"

"If that's the case, then all we needed to do was lure her away, why did you need to knock her out?" Frank kneeled alongside Zoe, caressing her head with his hand, putting pressure on the point of impact.

"We don't know that. This is the only way we can be certain."

The ferry was three-quarters across the harbour, cutting over the calm waters with ease as its arrival drew near. Kelly watched the water churn at the ship's bow, a small white wake forming behind it as it crossed. He prayed that what he just did would save the lives of every passenger on that ship—*their lives, and everyone else on this God-forsaken planet.*

"Listen," Kelly said. "With everything going on, all the unexpected events happening, I needed to do something that was in our control. We took her away from the terminal, away from the connection with the *Entity*. And now we know she's not going back."

"I get it," Frank said bluntly. "I just don't like it."

"I don't like any of it either," Kelly replied, never saying a more accurate statement in his life. "But it's better than killing her, Frank. You have to agree with me there." There was no argument from his partner. Kelly knew it was the right thing to do, but he wasn't yet convinced that this would do the trick. He needed certainty that the *Entity* couldn't gain a hold on Zoe in this timeline. What were a few hundred yards to the *Entity*, a being that could jump across the multiverse.

Taking her out of the exact point in space wasn't enough.

They also needed to get her out of this exact point in time.

And that was something only Kelly could do.

"Frank. There's something else." Kelly said, his eyes still focused on Zoe's still body. "I'm going to send her back."

"Back?" Frank asked hesitantly.

"Back," Kelly stopped for a second, realizing the ironic reference he was about to make, the words sounding like utter nonsense when spoken out of context. *"Back to the Future."*

"You can't be serious?" Frank responded.

"I am. The other Zoe said it was this exact place *and time*. If that's true, this is the only way I can be sure." Sending Zoe to the future meant sending her to a world where her husband was dead, Kelly was a wanted criminal, and every person on the east coast thought she was murdered. It would be a world entirely incomprehensible for her, a world that could only be explained by one other person other than Kelly. "And you're going with her, Frank."

Frank examined him, alarmed as though he'd been greatly insulted. "Like hell I am."

Kelly knew he would respond as such. He was a loyal friend, and an even better partner, and there was no way Kelly was going to drag Frank any further into this.

"You dragged me into this mess," Frank said, fuming. "You sent me back though time to face us off against some twisted abomination with the power to destroy everything *I love*? And now you want to send me away, just like that? I've barely helped at all!" Frank's temper was rising. He always had a short fuse.

"I never wanted any of this," Kelly almost yelled, before catching himself in the act. He took another breath, trying to deescalate any further feud with his friend. "I don't want any of this," he repeated, quieter, calmer. "But what happens if I send her back alone to a world where Jessie is gone, the station is half-collapsed, and I'm the suspected criminal in the most covered crime in Atlantic history? It won't make any sense to her. She'll be lost. You're the *only* person who can fill in the details—the only person who can clear my name. There's no-one else. No one. Only you, Frank. Only you can do this for me."

Frank was silent for a moment, considering Kelly's words as he searched for a response. After a few-seconds pause, he came up with one. "Come back with us then. It's over, isn't it? We have Zoe. She never made it to the ferry terminal. Isn't that what we came here to do?"

Technically they came here to kill her, but neither of them was capable of such a thing. "Maybe," Kelly answered, wondering if it was truly over or not. But something still wasn't sitting right with him—*a feeling*, like they weren't yet out of the woods. The *Entity* wouldn't give up that easily. It still had one more play to make, Kelly was sure of it, and he had no intention of letting it slip through the cracks as he made his premature escape. "I'm going to stay behind, just to make sure. And if all goes well, and we truly did stop it from emerging in this timeline, then I'll just travel back to the moment I sent you, and it'll be as if I never left you in the first place. Besides, if I'm wrong, I don't think I can take any more people I care about being killed on my account."

"That's not your decision to make, Kelly," Frank stated.

"I know," Kelly responded, staring down at Zoe's unconscious body. "But it's one you're going to have to live with."

There was a pause, but after a few seconds, Frank nodded in hesitant agreement. None of the time travel stuff made any sense to Frank, but he trusted Kelly, and even though he felt bitter, frustrated, and slightly abandoned, he would follow his partner's plan.

For a moment, the two partners stood in silence on the boardwalk, the misty rain and cool breeze blowing in their faces, the hushed morning lull saying all there was to be said. The ferry was nearly at the dock, leaving only a few more minutes for Kelly to reach the terminal and confirm that they did indeed stop *The Entity.*

Kelly reached out his hand as Frank did the same, a final firm handshake between partners...friends...*brothers.*

"Thank you for everything," Kelly said, hopeful that it wouldn't be long before they were back together again sipping beers and watching the game on Frank's couch.

"Be careful," Frank responded, his hand firmly placed in Kelly's.

Kelly nodded, realizing this could be the last time they ever saw each other, increasingly hopeful that wasn't the case.

After a few moments of pause, Kelly closed his eyes to concentrate, allowing the familiar pressure to build as he prepared his friends for their return.

He envisioned the moment they had left.

He imagined the boardwalk as it would have been this time yesterday.

And he let the invisible electric sensation consume the air surrounding him once again.

It only took a few seconds—*almost as if Kelly were getting more acquainted with his supernatural power*—because when he opened his eyes, both Frank and Zoe were gone.

Kelly prayed he'd be able to join Frank and Zoe in the future as soon as possible. He hated being a person out of time. It made him uneasy, like holding the world's most significant secret with no one to share it with.

Somewhere in the distant fog, a ship's horn blared, seagulls squawked, and people awoke from their morning slumber. Kelly turned to face the terminal, the ferry just now pulling up to the dock, seconds away from releasing its passengers so they can make their way to their routine office chairs and school desks.

It was time—as time once was—for Kelly to face his destiny.

38

...Time slips the knot of realities bound together...

Kelly burst through the doors of the Halifax Terminal just as the ferry passengers disembarked from their brief trip across the harbor. And although it hadn't happened yet, he knew this was the spot where the *Entity* was destined to emerge. There was something about the air, a stagnant air marking the imminent corruption that would cut its way into this reality one way or another. It felt almost familiar, the ever-present maliciousness filling the air like stagnant electricity, ready to strike.

But Kelly had stopped it, right?

Zoe was no longer around, gone to their own time with Frank. *Wasn't that the key?* Kelly prayed it was because if that wasn't the case, he had no idea what he'd do. For now, Kelly just needed to focus on the task at hand, making sure everything was as it should be, and not how the *Entity* would have wanted it.

About a hundred people walked toward him, passing through the gates toward the entrance, all following their routine weekday morning, most of them dressed in business-casual and formal attire, some in jeans, others braving the cold in shorts. In the centre of the crowd, facing the opposite direction as everyone else, was a beggar in an oversized green coat and toque, holding an aluminum tin can and a cardboard sign that Kelly couldn't quite see. He didn't need to view the front. Kelly had seen the security footage himself. He knew exactly what it said. *'Spare a dime, if you've the time.'* Kelly also recognized the little girl running alongside her mother on the left side, wearing a pink backpack with a rainbow design printed along the side. To his right, a man talked loudly on his cellphone, as if he were brokering the most significant deal of his career.

Kelly recognized everything as if a film unfolded before him, the bland brown walls, the faded floor tiles, and the rotating gates letting people pass through to go on their merry way. He'd reviewed the security footage repeatedly during Frank's thorough interrogation. And from what Kelly could tell, everything was playing out exactly as it had in the footage, right down to the last mannerism.

He looked up at the camera, feeling as if he were part of the scene, not just an observer. And if that was the case, if the film was indeed playing out exactly as it had when he watched it, then he was only a mere few seconds away from shooting Zoe in the eye, dropping her dead amongst a screaming crowd.

But that couldn't be true.

He had already sent Zoe to the future along with Frank. If all had gone to plan, then there should be no-one standing over by the vending machines. Zoe should be long gone and—

No…

Impossible…

It couldn't be…

Ahead and to his left, leaning against the blue vending machines, stood Officer Zoe Stevens…and she was staring directly at Kelly—*grinning.*

Kelly stopped dead in his tracks staring back, trying to make sense of the impossible. In full uniform, Zoe stood precisely where she had in the security footage, surveying the crowd, intermittently obscured from Kelly's view by passersby.

If the Zoe of this timeline had been sent to the future, then who was…

…of course.

It was their Zoe.

It was Zoe from the multiverse.

But what was she doing here?

Was she searching for her other self? If so, then Kelly had some good news for her. Yet, why was she grinning at him, as if privy to something he wasn't? It made him uneasy, his instincts shooting off like sparks in a fire.

"You've...come..."

A darting whisper shot across Kelly's mind like a bullet rushing from ear to ear, Zoe still grinning at him with a crooked smile. The voice was scratchy, nefarious, and broken, swelling in Kelly's mind like an oozing infection. He didn't have to look around to know what was speaking directly to him.

"It's ...time..."

The *Entity* hissed, whispering into his mind while those around him remained utterly unaware. Kelly had no idea how the spectre was communicating with him. The whispers seemed to come out of nowhere. All he knew was that the *Entity* was there, which meant everyone around him was in danger. *Everyone around him was also a threat.* Kelly searched for any signs of the shadowy spectre but didn't have to look long before realizing where the monster had been secretly lurking all along.

Up ahead, as clear as the moon on a cloudless night, Kelly watched as Zoe's eyes faded into a soulless black, fixating upon him as if Kelly was all they saw.

That's when he grasped the grim truth that had been hiding in plain sight all along.

The Entity hadn't been hunting them.

It had been with them all along, hiding inside the shell of their multi-dimensional friend, Zoe, pulling her strings, tricking Kelly into taking it back through time to the exact time and place it needed to be.

It hit Kelly like a ton of bricks.

How could he have been such a fool?

He couldn't believe the mistake he had made, a mistake that was going to bring death and destruction to everything worth fighting for.

"What do you want?" Kelly yelled, getting a few anxious looks from strangers passing by, unsure if the *Entity* possessing Zoe's body could even hear him. As soon as the words left his mouth, he regretted them.

The entire crowd around him came to an immediate halt, freezing in their tracks as the whole foyer became deathly silent. The beggar standing before him with trembling hands no longer showed a hint of waver, standing perfectly still in the air as his aluminum can plummeted to the ground, a few coins rolling away on the cracked tile floor. A hundred souls in the room, none moving, each person as paralyzed as the last, each person no longer under their own control, but trapped under the power of the *Entity*.

The Entity had control of everyone.

Everyone but Kelly.

Then they began to scream.

One by one, each captured soul let out a terrifying screech, as if their hearts were being torn from their chest.

A man at the back of the crowd let out a deafening roar, quickly echoed by a woman standing just a few feet from him. One-by-one, scream-by-scream, each person shrieked in agony, the *Entity* tearing them apart from the inside as he took telepathic control. Twisted bodies trailed each scream as each person twisted and contorted in inhumane ways while the crowd room lost complete dominion over their bodies.

And at the forefront of it all, hovering above the rest with beady black eyes and a crooked smile, was Zoe—*the Entity's shadowy essence hidden somewhere within her body*—staring directly at Kelly as he became surrounded by the spectre's cursed souls.

Kelly turned, seeking a clear path to the exit, only to find a dozen bodies writhing unnaturally between him and salvation. Their jaws were unhinged, their necks were crooked and bent, and their arms convulsed back and forth uncontrollably. The eyes of every man, woman, and child standing helpless within the foyer had turned a barren-black, relinquished of any life or hope they once held. But Kelly wasn't looking at the businessman to his right, nor the twisted little girl standing to his left. Instead, his focus was on Zoe, who loomed above as if captaining a sinking ship.

Kelly was staring at The Entity.

"What do you want!?" Kelly shouted again, louder, his voice barely able to speak out over his trembling despair. He didn't understand how Zoe had come under *its* control. They had been together the entire time, and she seemed completely normal. Was it lying dormant under her skin from even before they met, using her to get to this exact moment in time?

Was that how Zoe knew Donna had been killed?

Then why wait?

Why not just kill them while they slept in the storage garage?

If it did kill them, then maybe there was no getting back to this moment? Kelly was grasping at straws, trying to figure things out as he found himself surrounded in the twisted horde. There was so much Kelly didn't understand, yet, he had a feeling he wasn't going to be given the chance to figure it out.

The entire twisted crowd turned to face Kelly, like watching a perfectly trained platoon perform a choreographed march. Each pair of void-like eyes homed in on Kelly with murderous intent, the horde completely surrounding him.

Each twisted soul took a step forward, closing in on him inch-by-inch until there was barely any room to budge. Kelly reached for the gun on his hip, but two hands seized his wrist, pinning it against his side. A few more hands grabbed his shoulders, one hand clutched tight to his hair, and the rest forced his arms to his side. He tried to turn, to fight, to struggle, but it was hopeless. There were too many of them, the *Entity* making his point that if it couldn't control his mental state like the rest of his twisted puppets, his physical state would have to do.

Beyond the twisted necks and possessed bodies, Kelly could see Zoe Stevens, floating over them all in her police uniform. Her body convulsed uncontrollably, and her skin faded from a fleshy-pink to a rotted-black. It was almost as if severe frostbite engulfed her entire shaking body all at once, her dark eyes matching those of the surrounding crowd. It wasn't long before her ordinarily rosy cheeks turned a sombre charcoal, her waving hair shifting from dark brown to a dying grey, her body resembling that of a decomposed corpse.

Hastily, Zoe's rotted skin began to peel. Her hair dropped to the floor, and her body faded to nothing but dust and ash, going through thousands of years of decay in a matter of seconds, leaving nothing behind but a hovering shadow in her place.

The shadow twisted and drifted, lingering in place, almost as if it was catching its breath after a long slumber inside Zoe's body. A minute passed before the spectre slowly began gliding through the crowd toward Kelly, passing through each twisted soul like a thick sludgy fog. It indolently made its approach, drifting over its puppets until stopping mere inches from Kelly's nose, rooting itself before him, as if mocking him in his defeat.

This was the closest Kelly had been to the *Entity* since it tried to consume him in his jail cell. The air around the shadow reeked of sulphur and rotten eggs.

It had no mouth, yet whispers seemed to emanate from it…

…no nose to breathe, yet it was alive…

…no eyes to see, yet it followed him wherever he went.

Kelly could almost see directly through the spectre as it halted before him, hovering, watching — *waiting.*

"What do you want?" Kelly asked one last time as his voice quivering in anguish. This time, the *Entity* answered, not from his own deep, scratchy voice, but from the uncoordinated whispers of all those possessed around them, each of them speaking a single, unanimous word.

"…*Everything…*"

The *Entity* loomed mere inches from Kelly's face, its swirling, malevolent visage fixed upon him. Kelly sensed his final moments ticking away, his fate converging with the maleficent will of the *Entity* before him. He didn't know how it would kill him. Would it force Kelly's mind to sink within himself, turning him into another mindless pawn like the rest of them? Or would the *Entity* allow its twisted puppets to tear him apart limb from him.

Kelly's time was up.

"Why me?" he asked, hoping to postpone his inevitable demise. He didn't know what was worse, death, or becoming a submissive puppet to the *Entity's* will. He wasn't too fond of either but knew there was no miracle bright enough to save him from this darkness.

The distorted crowd echoed the *Entity's* thoughts, their discordant words piercing the morning stillness.

"…Thief…"

The whispers ended with those of the condemned children in the room, each speaking the word in consecutive hisses, each mind under the *Entity*'s complete control.

Thief?

What did that mean?

The room became silent once more, the whispers fading, the *Entity* remaining still as its clouded face twisted before him. Not a single puppet flinched around Kelly, as if the *Entity* was giving him time to figure out what it was saying. It wasn't like Kelly was a threat to a being so powerful, and if anyone else entered the foyer, they'd instantly be taken under the *Entity*'s control. They wouldn't stand a chance against the expanding darkness.

But what did it mean by 'thief?' There was nothing of this world that Kelly could have possibly taken, *was there?*

Unless it meant…the power to travel through time?

Was that why it had been following him across the city, tearing his life apart like a piece of fragile tissue paper? Was that what led to Donna's death, as well as Jessie's and Zoe's? Kelly had his suspicions, but doubted any of them were true, his exhausted mind barely able to comprehend everything going on around him.

But Kelly never stole the power intentionally. He didn't even know how he got it in the first place. It just happened. It was the only reason he was able to escape the *Entity*'s destructive rampage from the beginning.

"If I give it back—" Kelly said, hesitantly, several pairs of hands holding him tight by his shoulders and arms, "—*your power*—will you leave? And never come back?"

The entire room burst into heinous laughter, each possessed puppet dawning a twisted smile, echoing the *Entity*'s occult response across the ferry terminal.

The laughter then shifted to murderous whispers, repeating a promise Kelly had heard many times before.

"*...Kill them. Kill them all. Kill them. Kill them all. Kill them. Kill them all. Kill them. Kill them all. Kill them. Kill them all. Kill them. Kill them all. Kill them. Kill them all. Kill them. Kill them all. Kill them. Kill them all. Kill them. Kill them all. Kill them. Kill them all...*"

The chant was endless, the twisted voices reciting the *Entity*'s murderous intentions as they slowly began to close in on Kelly step by step. The clutches around his wrist and arm grew tighter, pulling out his hair and tearing at his clothes as the encapsulating mob began to smother him. *Kelly knew he was out of time.* One woman clawed at his face while another tugged at his ankle, each puppet trying to get a piece of him as they chanted in mumbled whispers.

"*...Kill them. Kill them all. Kill them. Kill them all. Kill them...*"

It wasn't until his arm was dislocated, wrenched by the rabid mob, that Kelly realized his folly. Kelly *was* a man out of time—*meaning he had all the time in the world.*

He clenched his eyes shut, endeavoring to ignore the searing pain in his shoulder, the claw marks on his flesh, and the ghostly *Entity* above. Instead, Kelly concentrated on where he stood not but a few minutes earlier, at the terminal foyer's entrance, facing an orderly crowd full of business people and morning travellers rather than that of bloodthirsty, mindless marionettes.

One man bit into his shoulder, while another bashed him in the nose, but Kelly wouldn't budge, praying he could pull off another time-jump before twisted horde ripped him limb-from-limb. He focused on the promise of peace and silence, attempting to block out the whispers to kill. The pain began to slowly cease, the thrashing diminished, and the murderous rampage came to a choking halt—*and with it, the pain, the grasp, and the agony.*

Everything dissipated, but the fear.

The fear endured.

The fear always endured.

It was time to try again—if time would allow.

39

...Time slips the knot of realities bound together...

Kelly found himself facing the doors to the ferry terminal once again. His head spun, his energy seemingly zapped from his body. For a moment, confusion reigned—he didn't know what was happening, why he was here, or how he had arrived. But that sensation lasted only a few measly seconds.

He knew how he got here.

Everything seemed so familiar.

Too familiar...

Suddenly a flood of painful memories rushed back into his mind, and Kelly fell to one knee, barely able to hold himself up as he slowly gained his bearings. The strangers walking by him kept their distance—*as if he were a crazy man about to burst.* He didn't care, the rush of panic and anxiety filling his lungs didn't allow him to care. Kelly clutched at his shoulder—no longer dislocated but still resonating with the agony of the recent assault by the twisted horde. He imagined this was what a phantom pain felt like for someone who recently lost a leg or an arm. Kelly read about it before, about people still feeling a shadowy sensation in areas where their limbs no longer existed—only, he wasn't missing any limbs, and his pain, at one point in time, *was* real. The stabbing in his shoulder was slowly subsiding as he gradually came to grips with his reality.

The time jump worked.

Once again, Kelly had travelled back in time.

He was back at the Halifax Ferry Terminal's main entrance, slightly more drained than before, watching as the crowd disembarked from their journey on the transiting ferry. Standing before him was the same homeless man holding the cardboard sign that read *'spare a dime, if you've the time'*, the same businessman brokering his essential deal, and the same mother corralling her daughter with the pink rainbow backpack.

Then that meant…

…yes…

Across the terminal by the vending machines, Zoe Stevens stood staring at him with glowing black eyes and a twisted grin, her gaze piercing through the crowd, heralding the restart of his nightmarish loop.

And Kelly knew what came next.

Although he had no idea how to stop it.

Kelly tried cutting through the crowd, racing between the incoming bodies to try and reach Zoe before *its* control began—*but it was a futile attempt.* He pushed against the tide of the crowd, jostling with oncoming bodies as irate shoulders jostled him.

He barely made it beyond the homeless man when the shrieks began once again, the crowd becoming still, twisted, and under the *Entity*'s power as it had before. He only made it a few more yards—*barely halfway to Zoe*—when the twisted hands started grabbing at his clothes and limbs, pulling him down and pinning him to the ground as several more bodies piled atop him, trapping him on the floor. More screams pierced the air, along with the murderous whispers of the encroaching *Entity*. Zoe's body, already decayed and peeling away, had reduced to nothing but dust and ash—*a sign of the Entity's ominous reappearance.*

There must have been a half dozen twisted bodies stacked on top of him, like a dogpile atop a quarterback, each of them squirming and withering over him, forcing Kelly to the ground as the *Entity* made its approach from across the foyer. One of the puppets' knees pressed forcefully into Kelly's back, making it near impossible to breathe as he struggled to fight back. Fingernails dug into his wrists and shoulder, and despite his resistance, it was to no avail—*he was trapped once more*. Kelly had barely made it halfway across the room when they took him out, and that was going as fast as he possibly could.

Kelly didn't even know what he would have done if he made it to the *Entity*, but he knew he needed to at least try and stop it, even if it was impossible—*even if it was suicidal*.

He could see a few twisted bodies in front of him from beneath the dogpile, clearing a path, letting the *Entity* float closer to Kelly, the sulfuric stench lingering alongside the approaching shadow.

Kelly braced for the *Entity* to dominate his mind, to plunge him into an abyss of submission from which there would be no return.

Yet, it did not come to pass.

Somehow, Kelly was able to resist the Entity's grasp over his mind.

Perhaps it was the power he wielded, or it might have been sheer luck. Whatever it was, it didn't matter when he couldn't move a single muscle. Though his mind resisted the *Entity's* influence, the creature's control over his surroundings was overwhelming, leaving Kelly with only one avenue of escape.

Kelly closed his eyes, feeling the shallow pressure build up around him once more. Slowly, like water seeping down a clogged drain, Kelly slipped back through time as the clenching hands of the twisted puppets faded alongside the *Entity*. A final whisper reverberated through the waning silence as Kelly once again reversed the flow of time.

"...Kill them all..."

It was time to try again—if time would allow.

40

Kelly once again found himself at the entrance doors of the Halifax Ferry Terminal, standing just inside the entryway, slightly more drained as familiar events unfolded before him for the third time.

The homeless man begging...

The businessman bartering...

The smiling mother guiding...

This time though, Kelly remained in place, not rushing forward through the centre of the crowd, and instead, he kept back, studying his surroundings and surveying all options available to him. For what he could see, there were three paths to the far side of the room.

The first path was a straight line through the middle, where Kelly would need to fend off the soon-to-be-horde. This option had failed twice already, and Kelly doubted any future attempts would be any more successful.

The second option was to climb the stairs to the left, hopping over the railing and making a sprint straight toward Zoe's possessed body across the balcony. There would be less of a fight if he chose this route, but Kelly would still have to be quick, as well as fend off about four or five twisted souls, then the *Entity* itself—*and God knows what he'd do once he reached his adversary.*

The third option was to dip back outside into the misty air, run alongside the glass walls to the right, and smash his way in through the emergency exit. It would be the route with the least amount of opposition, but it meant running twice the distance, and with the time he had, Kelly doubted he could make it to the *Entity* before the creature unleashed his dominance on the world and those around him.

Kelly also thought about going further back in time, but he had sent Frank and the *other* Zoe away just before entering the terminal, and he had no interest in somehow reeling them back into this mess. This left him with a narrow time window to act within—yet countless opportunities to test different paths.

The unique benefit of being Kelly was that he had all the time in the world, as long as the *Entity* didn't choose to finish him off faster than he could use his power to reverse time—and assuming his energy levels remained strong enough to allow him to jump through time.

It appeared that the *Entity* was less intent on killing Kelly and more on capturing him, perhaps to reclaim the power it accused him of stealing. No matter how many attempts it took, Kelly could never allow the *Entity* the opportunity to take back its ability to jump through time. If that happened, it would surely mean the end for every living thing on the planet. But this attempt was a scouting report. Kelly would simply observe, counting exactly how much time he had from the second he arrived, to the *Entity*'s inevitable control over the unexpecting men and women.

It only took eight seconds for the first commuters to walk through the gates and reach Kelly, walking around him out into the city. The bulk of the crowd took about fifteen seconds to reach him, surrounding him as they sluggishly made their way back to their respective business offices and computer desks for another day of work.

Only a few seconds after that, just when the mother and her young daughter were about to make it halfway across the main lobby, the *Entity*'s control began to crawl through the crowd, wrapping its grip over every unsuspecting soul, forcing them to lose complete control of their natural selves, turning them into a horde of twisted marionettes. He watched as the mother emit horrifying cry, her neck and back cracking and bending as her eyes faded from white to black—*along with the rest of the crowd in sporadic fashion.*

Kelly didn't even try to fight the horde, opting rather to conserve his energy. He allowed the contorted hands to slither their way around his arms and tether him in place as he became encapsulated once again by wretched monsters who moments ago stood innocent civilians.

Instead of fighting, Kelly just watched as Zoe's pale body oozed to black dust, dropping to the floor in the form of ash and soot. The *Entity* manifested in its full dark form across the foyer, while the lights flickered overhead, surveying its corrupted horde anew. Slowly, it drifted toward Kelly, its puppets whispering murderous chants in the stale air, the odd broken shriek shouting out over the twisted bodies.

"...Kill them. Kill them all. Kill them. Kill them all. Kill them. Kill them all. Kill them. Kill them all. Kill them..."

Kelly was getting good at drowning out the whispers, shifting from a terrifying threat to a droning silence in the background of the *Entity*'s dark new reality.

"Why don't you just kill me?" Kelly yelled over the sinister mutterings of the *Entity*'s pawns, fishing for any information that could aid him in his subsequent leap.

Suddenly, the whispers shifted, hissing in broken harmony as the *Entity* gave his twisted answer.

"...Already... havvveeee...."

The cryptic words hung in the darkness, leaving Kelly struggling to contextualize them. He hoped it was referencing a version of himself from another timeline, from one of those multiverses Zoe had told them about.

The more Kelly thought about it, the more he doubted any of the things Zoe had told them. They had only been in the presence of the shell of Zoe, inhabited no longer by the loving, assertive, passionate officer they once knew, but instead by the twisted, contorted, corrupted essence that was the *Entity*. There may have been some truth to what she said, but it wasn't Zoe speaking those words. It was the *Entity*, tricking Kelly into bringing the spectre to this point in time. He was sure of it.

"*Screw it,*" Kelly thought as the twisted puppets held him in place by the entranceway of the building. Closing his eyes, he felt the familiar pressure crawl across his skin and initiated yet another leap into the past, restarting the encounter for the fourth time as his energy diminished with each jump.

It was time to try again—if time would allow.

41

...Time slips the knot of realities bound together...

Kelly burst through the entryway doors, disregarding the residual pain shadowing him from his previous encounter, and sprinted left toward the stairwell, Zoe's dark eyes following him the entire way as he dashed ahead, gaining as much ground as he possibly could. *If he could just make it to her before she turned, maybe, just maybe, he could stop the Entity from seizing control.*

It was a long shot, but that was about the only chance Kelly had left, and he would keep trying until he found a way through, even if he was stuck in this loop forever—*although he doubted he had the energy to survive that long.* He was already starting to feel weak on this fourth attempt. His muscles were drained, and his mind was losing focus. This rapid time-travel wasn't going to last as long as he hoped or needed it to.

Kelly raced up the concrete steps on the left side, vaulted the half-railing and landed on the tiles on the far side of the security gates, leaving him with a straight shot to the *Entity*. He could already see Zoe's skin peeling away like rotten fruit, her hair dropping like pine-needles, her entire essence evaporating to black dust and soot. Kelly didn't need to look to hear the agonizing screams to his right, the crowd slowly losing their minds as they shifted under the *Entity*'s power once again.

He wondered how far the *Entity*'s reach was. Were the tormented souls within the ferry terminal the only ones infected, or did the *Entity*'s power extend beyond the confines of the building's walls? Was the entire city lost under its control—*the country, the world? Kelly had no idea.* He only prayed the monsters influence wasn't that strong, not yet anyway. He knew the outcome if he failed—*if he was unable to stop the Entity.* It would mean the end.

He couldn't fail. He just couldn't.

Kelly was mere yards from the specter when a woman clad in a skin-tight hoodie and black leggings lunged at him, plowing him into the sidewall, the two of them crashing down onto the tiled floor below. Kelly struggled to his feet, his head throbbing where it had slammed against the wall, but before he could regain his stance two more twisted souls piled on top of him, pressing their full weight into his chest, forcing him to the ground as several more puppets approached to reinforce their hold, each one of them whispering murderous threats as they advanced toward him.

"…*Kill them. Kill them all. Kill them. Kill them all. Kill them. Kill them all. Kill them. Kill them all…*"

"Piss off," Kelly muttered under his breath at the puppets, shutting his eyes and initiating yet another temporal leap.

It was time to try again—if time would allow.

42

Kelly took the path to the right this time, avoiding the main entrance of the ferry terminal, and instead darting around the building on the outside in the mist. Through .the oversized glass panels, he could see the crowd crossing the foyer, mere seconds from succumbing to the *Entity*'s twisted ensnarement once again.

If only he could tell them what was about to happen, maybe it would make a difference. Perhaps they could shield themselves from the *Entity*'s grip, blocking its instant control over them—*although he doubted it*. Even if they believed him, the *Entity* was too powerful, and Kelly was the only one able to escape the *Entity*'s excruciating stranglehold over his mind.

There was much less physical resistance on the outside, not a single body blocking the way between him and the emergency exit on the right. Reaching the glass door, he realized there was no way to open it from the outside. It was a one-way entrance for emergencies only, emblazoned with '*alarm will sound if opened'* in bold red lettering on the glass. He didn't even have to peek inside to know what was happening, the shrieks already beginning, the *Entity*'s host body already disintegrating to oblivion. But what *did* alarm Kelly was the confirmation that the *Entity*'s reach was indeed beyond the terminal walls. People scattered across the boardwalk and parking area twisted and convulsed as if sharing the symptoms of a severe collective seizure.

Kelly could even see a few twisted bodies up the hill toward the heart of Halifax, standing broken on the sidewalk, twitching and shaking uncontrollably—*not even within sight of the Entity*. This sight affirmed Kelly's relief at having sent Frank to the future, away from the chaos. Kelly was able to withstand the *Entity*'s control, but Frank wouldn't have lasted a second against the overwhelming power of the shadow.

Kelly didn't bother breaking through the glass of the emergency exit door. The outside route offered less resistance but covered almost twice the distance. By the time he reached the door, the entire crowd had become corrupted, a dozen bodies blocking his path between the emergency exit and the *Entity*, which was already hovering in its pure shadowy form.

Instead, Kelly closed his eyes and placed his mind back to the starting point, his body promptly following, the shallow pressure exerting itself once again, his body growing weaker and weaker each attempt.

It was time to try again—if time would allow.

43

...Time slips the knot of realities bound together...

Kelly stood once again at the entrance of the Halifax Ferry Terminal, facing the pre-twisted crowd, barely able to stand. His body had weakened significantly after the last jump. He didn't know how many more hops through time he had left, and he knew if he passed out again, that would be the end. The *Entity* would surely take him, doing with him whatever it pleased—*and Kelly did not want to find out what that was.*

He forced himself forward again, each step growing heavier than the last, feeling as if an anchor had been chained to his ankle as he marched ahead toward Zoe and the *Entity—one and the same.*

Kelly knew he had almost no chance of making it through the crowd. They'd either pin him down or tear him apart long before he reached his target. And even if he did make it, he doubted there was anything he could do to hurt the creature capable of corrupting the entire planet. But again, he would try, because it was the *only* thing he could do.

This time would be different.

Kelly wouldn't blindly toss his body into the horde. Instead, Kelly pulled his pistol from its holster. A few pre-corrupted bystanders witnessed his draw, backing off and letting out terrified screams, as if he were a terrorist about to wreak havoc onto the crowd rather than try and save them. But that wasn't what worried him—*no*—instead, it was that by the time he raised his gun into the air, Zoe's processed body was already pointing her pistol back at him. And unlike Kelly, she was already in a firing stance. She pulled the trigger and a bullet whizzed over the crowd, connecting with Kelly's upper left shoulder, the bullet scraping off his collarbone and lodging somewhere deep within. The entire crowd screamed and panicked, and Kelly dropped to the ground.

Glancing up, he saw Zoe drop her gun as she succumbed to the *Entity*, her eyes oozing from their sockets like runny eggs, her skin flaking off as if grated. Moments later, the *Entity* manifested anew, its corruption spreading rapidly, silencing the screams into a quiet of ensnared, twisted souls, leaving Kelly injured on the floor at the epicenter.

The twisted puppets didn't even bother holding him down this time. Instead, they just surrounded him, forming an inescapable circle around Kelly as he sat impaired on the ferry terminal ground. A small path cleared before him as a twisted figure, a businessman in an expensive suit, stepped aside, allowing the *Entity* to drift forward and halt an arm's length from Kelly, while the corrupted crowd resumed their deathly chant.

"...Kill them. Kill them all. Kill them. Kill them all. Kill them. Kill them all. Kill them. Kill them all..."

Kelly felt his blood begin to pool under him as he struggled to stay conscious, his head becoming light, the *Entity* watching from above as he fought the urge to fall into an eternal slumber. He stared up at the *Entity*, who was hovering inches above the ground in its darkened cloudy form, glitching and twisting like its puppets around him, as if he were not the source of the corruption, but the corruption itself.

"What do you want with me?" Kelly asked weakly, his voice fading.

"Die... return...what was takennnn..."

The voices were discordant, the slurred demands of the *Entity* nearly indiscernible as they echoed off the terminal's walls. Countless black eyes bore down upon him, awaiting his response, each body swaying, ready to pounce upon a single command and bludgeon him to death.

Kelly shouted at the shadow, delirium setting in from blood loss. "I didn't take *anything* from you. I don't know how I got this power." A silent pause hung in the air, punctuated by distant screams outside the building, signaling the spread of the *Entity*'s corruption. Once again, the *Entity* provided its demonic response, the entire twisted horde taking a step forward as they spoke, confining their prey with their gnarled bodies.

"...Die..."

Kelly's consciousness wavered, nearly succumbing to faintness several times, as he fought the compulsion to slip away in the *Entity*'s presence. He knew that if he succumbed to darkness, he would never return, and the world would unravel in his absence. Donna, Frank, Zoe, they'd all become twisted puppets in a hopeless world. And even though that sense of hopelessness had begun to creep under Kelly's skin, he forced himself to fight on, because that's the only thing he knew he could do.

In his debilitated state, clinging to consciousness, Kelly closed his eyes, summoned the now-familiar pressure around him, and willed his mind back through time.

A Shadow in Time

It   was   time   to   try   again—if   time   would   allow.

44

...Time slips the knot of realities bound together...

Kelly didn't burst through the doors this time—instead, he stumbled into the terminal building, barely able to hold himself upright as the energy was all but drained from his waning body. The bullet hole in his shoulder had disappeared, but the phantom pain remained, imprinted in his mind.

Several strangers gave him odd looks as he staggered into the building, Kelly looking more like a hunched senior than a strong middle-aged man. He could barely keep his eyes open against the light, a jagged migraine piercing his exhausted mind. It felt as though he was being torn apart from within, the supernatural power exacting its toll on his psyche. The realization that this power wasn't meant for mortal hands grew clearer as he continued his harrowing battle. He didn't know how much longer he had before it tore him apart, but at this rate, Kelly figured he only had a few more jumps left—*and that was if the Entity didn't get to him first.*

Kelly glanced up once more at the lurking darkness, which had taken its usual spot next to the vending machines in the form of Zoe, her eyes blackened, staring at him from across the room, grinning as though it had already secured its twisted victory.

It wasn't over yet, Kelly thought to himself, pulling his gun from his holster. He was quicker this time, drawing it as fast as he could, the pistol feeling heavier than it usually did given his weakened state. He aimed to raise it quickly, to outdraw his shadowy adversary residing in Zoe's overpowered body.

Unfortunately, with his muscles depleted and mind mentally exhausted, his aim was unreliable, and when he fired the shot, his aim was a few inches too far to the left. The bullet veered away from its intended target and instead struck an older man directly in the cheek, tearing off the side of his face and dropping him instantly as he cried out in agonizing pain. The rest of the crowd panicked and screamed, dispersing rapidly into terrified chaos, while the *Entity* watched from above, as though it had orchestrated the ordeal.

"For Christ's sake," Kelly muttered to himself at the sight of the man on the floor, now getting trampled by the retreating crowd, his face smeared with blood as he tried to protect his head from the stampede. Kelly attempted another shot, but a brave security guard tackled him before he could pull the trigger. Before Kelly could react, he was face-down on the ground with a knee pressing against his back.

Another attempt.

Another failure.

As before, Kelly closed his eyes, felt the familiar pressure encircle him, and drifted back through time, restarting the encounter.

It   was   time   to   try   again—if   time   would   allow.

45

...Time slips the knot of realities bound together...

Kelly's next shot missed again, striking the mother walking with her child, dropping her instantly as her daughter cried out. Three seconds later, the security guard brought him down once again.

...Time slips the knot of realities bound together...

He tried for the stairs to the left again, but was too weak even to jump the railing, and too slow to avoid the crowd of twisted tackling onto the jagged steps, breaking his arm and nose in the process.

...Time slips the knot of realities bound together...

Kelly tried to force his way through the crowd, getting knocked over by a rushing businessman late for an early morning conference call. The man didn't even stop to help him up. He cursed some profanities toward Kelly and marched on his way. Two seconds later, the twisted crowd took him down once again, trapping him in their jagged circle, whispering deathly threats.

...Time slips the knot of realities bound together...

Kelly was brought down before he could even get the gun out of its holster.

...Time slips the knot of realities bound together...

...Time slips the knot of realities bound together...

...Time slips the knot of realities bound together...

...Time slips the knot of realities bound together...

...Time slips the knot of realities bound together...

...Time slips the knot of realities bound together...

...Time slips the knot of realities bound together...

...Time slips the knot of realities bound together...

...Time slips the knot of realities bound together...

...Time slips the knot of realities bound together...

...Time slips the knot of realities bound together...

...Time slips the knot of realities bound together...

...Time slips the knot of realities bound together...

...Time slips the knot of realities bound together...

...Time slips the knot of realities bound together...

...Time slips the knot of realities bound together...

46

Kelly was able to push his limits as far as he could, but his energy was as low as it had ever been. He could tell this was likely his last chance. *He was officially out of time.* His mind churned like a cement mixer, while every bone and tissue in his body screamed with the ache of shattered glass. Meanwhile, his target, the grinning *Entity* in Zoe's body, remained untouched, every bullet missing, every attempt to reach the spectre a complete and utter failure.

He was running out of options.

No matter the path he chose, the *Entity* was one step ahead, beating him at every turn. Kelly had been shot, beaten, tackled, pinned, and nearly killed since his first attempt to stop the end—*and that's not counting the several times he accidentally shot and killed another civilian in the process.* The darkness stood only a building's length away, yet they might as well have been a thousand miles apart, because Kelly was *never* reaching the other side unscathed. No number of unlimited attempts could convince him there was any chance of success, and he knew he didn't have any energy left to try again.

The *Entity's* face, in the guise of Zoe Stevens, mocked him through the crowd, eyes black, teeth grinning in twisted fashion, ridiculing him and his failed endeavours. Hope had dwindled to scattered ash as Kelly thought about all those he'd failed.

Donna was gone, unable to escape the *Entity*'s indomitable clutches.

Frank would follow in the footsteps of the twisted, lost in a world of madness, just another puppet in an ocean of darkness spread across the globe like thick poison.

If Kelly failed, which now seemed the most probable outcome, everything worth fighting for in this world would be lost. There would be no one left to watch an early sunrise over the distant horizon of a hazy sea. There'd be no children to watch their ice cream melt in the beaming sun of a scorching summer day, nor any loving mothers and fathers to watch over them. Darkness would eclipse the light, agony would surpass euphoria, and despair would extinguish hope. Everything worth a *damn* would fade to black, all because Kelly Christopher couldn't defeat the *Entity*—*all because he floundered.*

But he was still alive.

So as long as he held breath, he'd fight on.

Kelly advanced, his feet heavy as lead, fighting the urge to collapse in on himself and surrender to his inexhaustible fatigue. He could see the *Entity* ahead, watching his every move, the two of them in a chess match nearing its end, the stakes as high as they could possibly go. The crowd passed him by, seconds away from mutating into the mindless horde of twisted puppets, ready to bring him down as they had every time before. Kelly took another step, each stride growing heavier than the last, pressing on against the tide of the crowd.

He knew *exactly* how long he had before Zoe's body began to peel and rot to nothingness, marking the *Entity*'s full emersion into the mortal world, as well as the precise moment the shadow initiated his stranglehold on the unsuspecting world. In five seconds, Kelly's window of opportunity would close, and the game would be over.

There would be no more jumps.

There would be no more time travel.
This was his last chance.
He knew it.
The Entity knew it.
This was the end.
Kelly reached into his holster and drew the pistol.

4 seconds…

He raised his pistol in the air, aiming it high into the sky as a few spectators watched in horror. This time would be different.

3 seconds…

Kelly fired a round into the roof, the entire crowd ducking for cover, giving him a clear view of the *Entity* standing on the far side of the room. He could see the possessed body of Zoe Stevens holding her pistol at her side, ready to raise it, but it would *not* outdraw Kelly. Not this time.

2 seconds…

Kelly leveled his pistol, aligning the sights with his left eye, and aimed the crosshairs directly at Zoe, the rest of the crowd remaining low to the ground.

The *Entity* began to raise its own gun, Zoe's oblivion filled eyes focused on the target before her—*but it was too late.* Kelly had already marked his target on the far side of the room, his finger pressed firmly on the trigger.

The target was far away.
The shot needed to be perfect.
Kelly wasn't going to miss.

Not this time.

1 second…

Kelly squeezed the trigger.
The bullet burst from the barrel, soaring above the cowering civilians with fiery intent.
Then, a miracle occurred.

The bullet found its mark, penetrating her eye and dropping her instantly as a shriek of rage split the heavens, shattering every window in the terminal.

There was no time to react as a wave of energy burst through the terminal building, blowing everything back like a sound wave ripping through the clouds. Every person standing was blown off their feet, swept hard to the ground by the invisible force emanating from the *Entity*'s fallen capsule.

Even Kelly was knocked back, landing firm on his back, his weakened state unable to withstand the force of the blast. The back of his head smashed into the ground, the entire room spinning as his consciousness slowly faded to black.

But just before Kelly surrendered to the darkness, before the surrounding cries dwindled and the settling dust, the last thing he saw was the *Entity*, hovering above him, slowly entering his body, absorbing him whole as the light vanished from his eyes.

47

"…Don't let it take you, my love…"

Kelly's eyes snapped open, heart racing, head pounding. It took him a moment to recall where he was, the previous events blending into a stretched blur. Rising to a sitting position on the tiled floor, he pressed his hands firmly to the ground to steady the spinning room. After a few moments, when the nausea had subsided enough for him to focus, he scanned the foyer for the source of the whispering voice that had awoken him.

Yet, the source of the whisper, eerily reminiscent of his wife Donna's voice, was nowhere to be seen. He quickly realized, however, that he wasn't alone. Inches from where he sat lay two corpses, still, silent, and rotting, one adult, and one child, a decomposed pink backpack resting in a grimy puddle next to the smaller corpse. The bodies looked as if they had been decomposing for years, their skin grey and melted, their clothes ripped and torn, their eyes completely absent from empty sockets. Chunks of bone and cartilage poked out of rotting skin, exposed to the cold air. Kelly saw the child's blackened teeth fully exposed, her lips rotted away, her face consumed by maggots and the ravages of time.

Nausea surged once more, and he couldn't hold back as his stomach ejected its contents. Kelly spewed out yellow chunks of acid and bile, filling a stagnate puddle with his vomit.

He looked to the right, away from the mother and her decomposing child, but was met by another corpse, split in two at the waist, withering to nothing but bone and rot—a rusted cell phone lying next to the exposed skeleton. No matter which direction Kelly looked, he was met by a decaying body. The room was filled with them, each corpse looking like they underwent decades of exposure, left to rot where they fell, never given proper peace or farewell. A sea of bodies filled the decrepit ferry terminal, the stench rising through the stale air like a putrid sarcophagus.

Once the bout of vomiting had passed, Kelly struggled to his feet, careful not to step on any of the corpses around him— *which was a difficult task in itself.* Over a hundred bodies lay scattered across the decaying room, each one of them as lifeless and decomposed as the next, and Kelly had no explanation as to why.

Even the building around him looked crumbled and forgotten. The windows were shattered, and dusty glass was scattered over the damp floors. The roof looked as if it were ready to collapse, constant drips falling from exposed holes in the ceiling, dropping onto the abandoned bodies like spring rain. Puddles formed across the floor. Grass and weeds protruded from the edges of the building as nature took back the dilapidated infrastructure. And what made it worse was the utter silence of the city. The usual faint electric buzz was gone. The sound of cars and boats had completely disappeared. The only sound was that of the breeze rustling the leaves on trees that had begun to grow through the cracks of the sidewalk.

Kelly attempted to recall the last clear memory he had, but a foggy haze clouded his mind.

He remembered firing his gun.

He remembered the bullet striking Zoe in the face.

He remembered the explosion.

And he remembered the Entity hovering over him.

Then nothing.

He found himself in a silent world of decay, utterly alone.

And had he imagined the whisper?

Don't let it take you, my love.

Had that been all in his mind?

It sounded so much like Donna, yet, she was gone, just like the world around him.

Kelly made his way toward the shattered vending machines, stepping over the station's rusted turnstile gates, passing by two bodies tangled together in a lovers' final embrace. He couldn't even tell if they were a man or a woman, decayed beyond the point of recognition. Mushrooms and grass had sprouted from their eroded bodies. Kelly looked away, trying his best not to stare at the death that surrounded him — *although it was nearly impossible to miss.*

He managed to block out most of the horror as he approached a solitary body collapsed on the musty ground next to the vending machines, a hole torn from the side of her face, a plate of body armour protecting her deteriorating chest.

"Jesus," he whispered to himself, kneeling next to the body to get a closer look.

Her hair had thinned to nothing.

Her skin withered like a wet newspaper, a single bone poking out of her rotten clothes.

If it weren't for the decayed police uniform and the rusted gun lying next to her, Kelly would have never been able to recognize the body as Zoe Stevens. He could see the bullet marks on the side of her skull, the side of her eye socket broken apart from the impact.

He didn't understand.

He killed her, yet, everything was dead, lost to decay, crumbling back to nature.

It was apparent what had happened.

He had failed.

The Entity had won.

Overcome by defeat, Kelly closed his eyes, ready to lie down beside the decomposing bodies and succumb to the same fate. He was ready to join his wife in the next life—*if there was such a thing*. He looked down at the rusted gun lying on the ground next to him, wondering if it still had one shot left inside, wondering if he even had the courage to pull the trigger—*or would he fail at that too?* He was on the verge of picking it up when a voice echoed from behind him—the same voice that had greeted him upon his arrival in this grim reality.

"Don't let him take you." This time there was no denying her voice.

It was his wife's voice.

It was Donna.

Kelly rose quickly and spun around, and sure enough, came face-to-face with his wife, standing before him, blocking out the rot and decay surrounding this terrible world.

She was wearing her favourite purple blouse.

Her hair was perfectly straightened and tidy, and her smile was strong and bright.

And most importantly, there was no knife protruding from her eye-socket. Her face looked as beautiful and lovely as it possibly could be.

Kelly didn't respond.

He couldn't.

His tongue was tied.

His voice was choked up like that of a blubbering child.

The only thing she could do was reach out and hold her in his arms—only—as he tried to embrace her, there was no contact. Instead of feeling the warm embrace of his wife's loving tenderness, Kelly passed right through her like a cool mist. He tried again, and again, his arms passed right through her like she wasn't even there—*as if she were a ghost.*

"It doesn't work like that here, I'm afraid," she said, speaking as though he hadn't seen her lifeless, bloodied body in their bedroom.

"Am I dead?" Kelly asked, his heart heavy, his mind lost and disorientated.

She smiled, bright enough to lighten even the darkest room on the longest night. "Not yet," she replied, her voice a blend of joy and sorrow. "But if you stay here, you will die."

"I want to stay," Kelly said, ignoring the decaying corpses and rot, seeing now only his wife standing before him, *alive*, but not entirely there.

"Yet, you must go," she said, firmly.

"Where are we?" Kelly asked, more lost than ever before.

"Somewhere in between, I reckon," she said. "This is where you go when *it* takes you. Not quite dead, but no longer truly alive. A world between worlds. *The Entity's domain.* I don't exactly know, but this place—*this horrible place*—it's the world as the *Entity* wants you to see it. Cold, dead, isolated, and most importantly, under *its* control."

Kelly sensed that Donna was in pain. He wanted nothing but to reach out and hold her in his arms and tell her things would be alright.

But he couldn't.

The *Entity* had taken that comfort away from them, as it did all things worth a damn.

"It's too powerful," Kelly lamented, surveying the bodies scattered around him—*a tangible reminder of his failure.* "I can't kill it. I'm just one man."

"No," Donna responded, her voice calm and assuring. "You cannot. But you *can* trap it."

"Trap it? What do you mean? Like in a cage?" Kelly had trapped a squirrel that ate his way into the insulation of the roof of his house once, releasing it miles away in the forest, far enough so it wouldn't come scurrying back. But that was a squirrel, easily caught with a small crate and some peanut butter. How was he supposed to trap a spectre capable of traversing the multitudes of dimensions?

"Not exactly," Donna responded, Kelly noticing the slight transparency of her ethereal form. If the *Entity* was a form of darkness, then she was the light. "You have one thing he no longer has."

"What?"

"You can bend time."

"Look where that's gotten me," Kelly said, feeling beaten, exhausted, and utterly defeated. "How do you even know about that anyway? I never told you."

Donna laughed, a medicine that could lift even Kelly from the hole he dug himself in. It was admittedly a little eerie watching his wife laugh in a ghostly form, hovering over a plethora of rotting corpses, even *if* they were a figment of the *Entity*'s twisted imagination.

His wife continued, her voice as calm and reassuring as ever. "Once the *Entity took me*, I became—*in a way*—one with its twisted consciousness. It engulfs everything you are, and in return, you absorb the knowledge it holds. It's a sort of torture, in a sense. Being trapped inside his twisted world, knowing all I know, yet not being able to leave."

"Then why don't I have that shared knowledge?" Kelly asked, clearly standing in the same world as her. "Where's my 'deeper understanding?'"

"That's the beauty of it," Donna whispered, inching closer to her husband as if someone else was listening in. "He *hasn't* taken you. Not yet at least."

Kelly didn't respond. He just stood silently, a puzzled look on his face. There was clearly something he was missing, praying his wife could provide clarity.

Donna continued. "If it kills you, it loses the ability to bend time forever. The power dies with you. That's your advantage over the *Entity*. That's why you've been able to resist its power for so long. It still holds fragments, but you hold the bulk of its power. It needed to consume you from the inside, but your superior power prevented it from taking control."

"Are you saying he can't turn me into one of his twisted puppets because I somehow acquired part of his power?" Kelly figured it was somehow related to that but wasn't exactly sure why. He was just happy not to be another one of *its* puppets, trapped under the invisible strings of demonic darkness.

"Exactly." Donna smiled again, happy that Kelly was slowly catching on. "That's also why it disguised himself as Zoe. It deceived you into taking it back through time in the form of Zoe, back to the moment where it all began at the ferry terminal."

"It told me there was a chance to save you..." Kelly said, ashamed that he could be so blind—ashamed that he didn't listen to any of Frank's intuitive warnings, curtained by the fact that he had even the slightest chance of holding his wife close again.

"I know." Donna sympathized. "Let me finish. To pull off what it intends to do, the *Entity* needed two things to be parallel across all universes. It needed to enter our plane of existence through the same host, which, just by chance, happened to be poor Zoe. And second, it needed it to occur at the exact time across the multiverse. It's a sort of alignment, no different than an alignment of the planets or stars. By shooting Zoe, you were able to crumble one of the *Entity*'s two pillars of destruction. And normally, it would have just jumped back through time to try again, maybe do things slightly differently, but since you hold its power to do so, you unintentionally thwarted his stranglehold on our universe once again. A one-two punch, so to speak."

Donna stopped for a moment, giving Kelly the chance to filter all the information she had provided him. She didn't expect him to fully understand, knowing there would be questions upon questions to follow, but she didn't care. She was there to give him hope. That was her purpose, the last meaningful act she would ever do with the time she had.

"I know you have questions," she said, cutting him off before he could speak. "But we just don't have the time. The longer you stay in this place, the harder it'll be for you to get back to where you need to go, so listen. I said you could trap it, and you can. But not in the usual sense. You're not going to trap it in a cage, but instead, you'll trap it in *time*. So long as it doesn't have the power you hold, the *Entity* becomes just another victim of time, just like you or me."

Kelly stared at her, standing next to the decomposing body of what looked like a man wearing an old green trench coat, a rusted aluminum tin resting next to his chewed bony hand. "So, you're saying I should run? Stay as far away from the *Entity* as I can?"

"No. You'll last thirty, maybe forty years tops? That's nothing on the infinite scale we're talking about. Then old age will take you. It's a fate no-one can escape, not even you. And when you're weak, the *Entity* can easily swoop in and take it, and he'll just jump back to this exact moment in time and restart the apocalypse as if none of this had ever happened."

"So, to defeat the *Entity*, I need to live forever?" Kelly asked.

"*Or...*" Donna said, grabbing Kelly's attention. "You can pass the power on."

"Pass it on? Pass it on to who?"

Donna smirked, responding with the one person Kelly would never have guessed. "Pass it on to you, silly."

Pass it on to myself?

It didn't make any sense.

"Pass it on to your former self." Donna elaborated. "It's the only way that we know this will work."

"And how do we know that?" Kelly asked, skeptical, bracing for another defeat.

"Because—*it already happened.* You're here. You stopped him."

Kelly didn't respond this time, merely nodding, thinking to himself about the events that had unfolded before him.

Was this some sort of *endless loop*, destined to repeat itself—a perpetual master plan designed to capture the *Entity* within the confines of an eternal day? And more importantly, was this just his turn to play out the events of a boundless trap, ready to pass the torch to the next version of himself in time, forcing him into the same torture he endured the past twenty-four-or-so hours? Were these even questions he was able to answer, or was he just a pawn in a game beyond his comprehension?

He turned his attention back to his translucent wife. "So, by passing it on to the next version of myself in time, we reset the loop, dooming my past self to endure the same events I endured, watching you get...*killed*? Watching my name get tossed to the curb for Zoe's murder? This can't be the only way."

"It is," Donna replied, firmly. "It is the only way. I promise you that. Things need to work out *exactly* as they had for you. No exceptions. No variations."

Kelly's heart sank in his chest as Donna's words slowly resonated with him, understanding what it meant if he continued onward with her plan. "I'll lose you," he mourned.

"Why can't I just stay here with you? I can't bear the thought of losing you. Not again."

"You need to save them, Kelly; only you can. The life of one woman—no matter how dearly loved—isn't worth the lives of billions. Promise me you'll save them. Promise me."

"But..."

"*Promise me.*" Donna stepped closer, passing her ethereal hand over his cheek. He envisioned the warmth of her touch against his stubble—*the softness of her skin.* The *Entity* had taken her away from him, but not the memories. Not even something as powerful as *that* could rip those away.

"I promise," Kelly replied reluctantly, a single tear trailing down his cheek through her incorporeal hand. "I promise."

"I'd come back with you," Donna whispered softly, "But I don't have a body to go back to. Mine is forfeit. Yours is not. Go back to them. Save them all. *Don't let it take you.*"

"I love you," Kelly cried out as Donna's presence began to fade.

"I love you, too," she replied, her voice lingering even as her spectral form dissipated. "*Forever and always.*"

And then she was gone.

The imagined warmth on his cheek gone with it.

He was alone.

It was time to return.

Kelly closed his eyes and envisioned himself beyond the shadowed veil the *Entity* had cast around him, his wife's words echoing around his mind like rekindled hope. He clung to those words in his mind, more tightly than he'd ever held onto anything before, never letting go as the shadow world around him began to fade along with his thoughts.

It was time to return.

It was time to end the Entity once and for all.

Part VII
An Eternal Day

48

elly opened his eyes to a familiar world, lying flat on the
floor next to dozens of unconscious bodies, each one of
them alive and breathing, no decay, no rot, and no
.twisted darkness consuming them whole. Slowly rising
to his feet and holstering his gun at his hip, he surveyed his
surroundings for a better understanding of the aftermath. The
entire room appeared as though a bomb had detonated, the
Entity's shockwave emanating from Zoe's now-still body,
knocking everyone in the room off their feet. The overhead lights
were still swinging back and forth, and every window had
shattered and broken. It looked like a few bystanders were
tending to minor injuries, but as far as Kelly could tell, there
were no fatalities outside of Zoe Stevens. Everyone was alive
and well, completely oblivious to the darkness that had nearly
ended them all.

But more importantly, there was no *Entity* in sight. Kelly
knew it wasn't dead, but with the connection to the other
multiverses broken—as his spectral wife had described—it no
longer held power to corrupt the vast world around it. The
alignment was broken, and for now, the world was out of harm's
way. To his right, a woman held her daughter close, protecting
her in her arms, both looking directly at Kelly, as if he was a
terrorist who detonated a bomb within their peaceful city.

He considered pulling out the badge Frank had given
him, confirming he was an officer of the law, but decided against
it. If Donna's plan was to work, things had to play out *exactly* as
they had for him. That meant playing the part of a mysterious

murderer, ensuring the version of himself from this current timeline was captured and framed for the murder of Zoe Stevens. It was sadistic, twisted, backwards and incomprehensible, yet—as his spectral wife Donna had told him—*it was the only way.* So rather than staying to help and acting the good Samaritan, Kelly turned toward the door, and fled the scene, playing the role of a suspicious suspect, and making sure the innocent bystanders witnessed him doing so. He exited out the main foyer doors, swearing to never step another foot inside that ferry terminal building again so long as he lived.

And only God knew how much longer that would be.

He needed to figure out his next move and decide where to go next. The security footage was his sole glimpse into a future he had witnessed firsthand, nothing else leaving any clues about what the next step in his plan of madness would be. He thought back to the camera footage he watched so long ago in the tiny confines of the station's interrogation room, chained to a table as Frank questioned him about things he had not yet experienced.

Had his actions unfolded exactly as depicted in the security footage?

There were no discrepancies that he could pinpoint from the top of his head. Kelly had entered and discharged a single bullet into the air to quell the morning crowd, then fired the next shot through Zoe's eye, dropping her instantly, her gun landing by her side in a pool of blood, the shockwave blowing out the windows and doors, knocking everyone over like fragile bowling pins.

No matter how hard he tried, destiny had played out exactly as it had meant to, none of his decisions leading to an alternate outcome. It made him both uncomfortable and serene simultaneously. It was an uneasy feeling, seeing firsthand that he had no control over a fate laid out for him. Yet, it was also a sense of comfort, knowing that if he were to pass this power along to the next version of himself in time, then things would play out the same again, over and over like an endless loop of predictable fate.

Hindsight is twenty-twenty, after all.

In the tiny parking lot outside the ferry terminal, a man had vacated his motorcycle, leaving it running and unattended as the motorist ran in toward the building to lend his aid to those caught in the blast.

An altruistic act worthy of a noble man.

No good deed goes unpunished.

Kelly would reward him by hopping on his bike and riding away. He could hear sirens approaching from the distance, the police station less than a kilometer away from the ferry terminal. They didn't know it was him yet, but within the next twenty minutes or so, Kelly Christopher would be the most wanted man on the east coast, and he had no intention of being here when they watched the security footage for the first time.

He looked down at the clock on the motorcycle's dashboard. It was just before 7:00 AM. The other version of himself would be just hopping into the shower right about now, utterly oblivious to the tidal wave about to take over his life. It had barely been after eight' o'clock in the morning when past-Kelly was arrested, blindsided by a few of his fellow officers, with no warning what-so-ever on what was about to happen. That meant present-Kelly had about thirty minutes to get to his house and pass on the power to his former self.

Kelly considered freezing time but questioned whether his body could endure it. He had jumped too many times in his duel with the *Entity* and had plenty enough time to reach his home in Dartmouth without having to resort to powers he still barely understood.

Therefore, instead of resorting to his supernatural abilities, Kelly engaged the bike's clutch, shifted into gear, and tore out of the parking lot just seconds before a pair of police cruisers arrived. It was unnatural to Kelly, leaving a panicked and scared crowd behind, but he knew they'd be okay, so long as he went ahead with his plan to pass the power off to his former self.

Now to get home.

After a few quick turns, Kelly Christopher had made it to the MacDonald Bridge, pulling into the right lane and crossing over toward the Dartmouth side, not a single cruiser on his tail. It had been a while since he last rode a motorcycle, having owned a few dirt bikes growing up, mostly for hitting the trails and backwoods. While Kelly had never owned a street bike, the same basic concept was familiar, and he felt comfortable enough driving it. It was a pleasant sensation, feeling the damp breeze on his exposed face, the cool air rushing back his hair as he crossed over the bridge toward his home in Dartmouth. For a moment, Kelly thought this was going to be an easy mission, a victory-lap to the finish. But a whispering deathly voice echoing from within proved him wrong.

Very wrong.

"*...Kill yourself...*"

The deep, scratchy, nefarious voice was not one unknown to Kelly. He knew exactly what was speaking to him through nefarious whispers.

The Entity.

Kelly nearly drove off the road at the sound of its vile voice, constant threats splitting through his mind like a Gatling-gun, forcing him to grab the handlebars tight and pull the treads back on track, narrowly missing an oncoming Toyota on the other side. The *Entity's* command repeated internally, intruding like a sinister inner monologue fracturing his concentration.

"...Kill yourself..."

Kelly couldn't pinpoint the origin of the voice until he felt his insides squirm and wither, his chest tightening, his heart pounding, every bone aching as if they were being split apart and put back together.

It was inside him.

The Entity was inside him.

Just as it had with Zoe from another multiverse, the *Entity* had buried itself deep within Kelly's body.

Slowly, he felt his body grow numb, the *Entity* slowly seizing control as Kelly's bike began to sway toward the edge of the bridge, Kelly barely able to veer it back to the centre of the road as he fought the spectre's commands. Every automatic biological process had become a desperate struggle for survival. Kelly had to concentrate on breathing, driving, and keeping his eyes open, all while the numbing pain overtook his body, the *Entity* tearing him apart one nerve at a time.

"...Kill yourself..."

Kelly felt an internal urge to steer into oncoming traffic, the *Entity* toying with his natural impulses. The *Entity* was attempting to take not only control of his physical body, but his mind as well, Kelly doing everything in his power to resist the shadowy temptations.

On the other side of the yellow line, a black and silver van drove normally amongst oncoming traffic, and for a split-second, Kelly wanted nothing more than to drive head-on into the chromed grill, the *Entity* internally pulling his strings one at a time. For now, Kelly was able to withstand the suicidal temptations, keeping his head straight, forcing the *Entity* back to the depths of his mind for a few brief moments as he drove completely across the bridge, through the toll, and into Dartmouth.

His home was only a kilometre away, but it would be an impossible struggle to make it that far. All he had to do was make it to his home and pass the power onto his former self without being seen. If he could do that, the rest was written.

"...*Kill yourself...*"

"Go to hell" Kelly screamed aloud, the roaring engine of the motorcycle drowning out his cries. "Leave me alone!"

"...*Kill yourself...Kill them all...*"

The *Entity*'s grip tightened, Kelly's vision beginning to flash in and out of darkness, pulsating as his peripherals began to wither and wane. "You will *not* take me. I won't let you." Kelly's body was growing weak, but he fought through. Every inch he drove ahead was a tremendous victory. He could hear his wife's words echo thought his head, her voice a calming silence holding back the thunderous darkness.

Don't let him take you, my love.

Kelly entered his residential neighborhood, relieved to leave the busy streets filled with oncoming traffic behind, the *Entity*'s voice continuously giving fatal commands.

"...*Kill yourself...Kill them all...*"

He did his best to brush them aside, keeping himself at the helm of his own body—*for now.*

Kelly sped through the neighborhood, well over the speed limit, praying there'd be no officer on duty patrolling the early morning streets. He doubted there would be. On weekday mornings, it was rare for an officer to be stationed in residential areas such as this.

It turns out, he was right, because he was able to make it through his little rural cul-de-sac without any *extra* trouble at all, the *Entity* providing enough of that already.

Pulling in behind his house, Kelly flicked the motor off, the gentle hum of the engine dying, the murderous whispers of the *Entity* holding strong in his mind. He shook his head, using nothing but sheer will to fend off the overpowering spectre infecting his already weakened mind.

The *Entity must* have known his plan to trap it— especially now that they were sharing the same body and mind.

It didn't matter.

As long as Kelly could keep control long enough to pass the power off to his former self, he'd win, and it would lose.

That's all that mattered.

The Entity could not win.

Kelly darted across the sidewalk and hopped their stained fence, landing in the back yard atop a few dying plants already withering from the October frost. It seemed like a lifetime ago since he stepped foot on his property, the last time marking the merciless death of his innocent wife.

He had a feeling he'd be with her soon enough.

Ascending the back of his house was a white wooden lattice, matching their fence and window trim. They had installed it a few seasons ago. The decorative addition was already filled with vines and colourful flowers, adding a bit of natural flavour to their once bland and barren sidewall. The lattice wasn't very thick, but he figured it'd be strong enough to hold his weight, letting him climb up to the second level, assuming he'd have the strength to fend off the *Entity* and reach their bedroom window.

The *Entity* made himself known once again, Kelly's bones cracking and bending from within, the pain nearly stopping him dead in his tracks.

Almost, but not quite.

He would see this through to the end.

It was his destiny, after all.

"...*Kill yourself...Kill them all...*"

"Yeah, Yeah," Kelly muttered quietly, jogging over to the lattice, gripping it tight in his hands. "After you."

He slowly began scaling the lattice, the thin wooden frame bending and shaking, but never breaking. After a few heavy heaves and suicidal threats, Kelly had reached the second level, sliding open the bedroom window—which was thankfully unlocked—and clumsily slid into the room, making sure the coast was clear before he did.

Their room was empty, their bed neatly made, the light flicked off, the former version of Donna and Kelly downstairs unknowingly enjoying their last pleasant moments together.

It was astonishing how quickly life could turn on a dime.

No matter how much time one spent with loved ones, it just never seemed like enough.

Kelly had to be quick, knowing it wouldn't be long before one of them climbed the stairs and saw him standing in their bedroom. He had to make sure events unfolded exactly as they had for him, and as far as he remembered, he didn't see a duplicate version of himself standing in his bedroom on the morning Zoe Stevens was gunned down.

This was just a quick frame job, replacing the former Kelly's personal pistol with the one Frank had given him, the one with two rounds missing. The security footage would be damning enough, but tossing the pistol used at the scene of the crime would be the cherry on the cake, leaving zero chance for Kelly to be released before the *Entity* appeared in his jail cell this evening.

It was a strange thought, knowing that this same thing had happened to him in the previous loop. An exact-carbon copy of himself had broken into his house while he was downstairs, sipping his morning coffee and watching the news, framing him for a murder he had not yet committed.

It was all strange.

Kelly was amazed he was able to make sense of any of it at all.

He placed the *murder weapon* and badge on his bedside table, then promptly unlocked the combination-safe holding his usual pistol, placing it in his holster, the badge in his side pocket.

"…Kill yourself…Pull the trigger…"

The *Entity*'s voice pulled through again, Kelly fighting the urge to draw the pistol alongside his hip, place the cold barrel against his throbbing skull and pull the trigger.

He imagined the temptation was like that of a heroin addict, having to use all his will not to slide that needle under his skin for his next fix.

Kelly could have very easily slipped the gun up to his head under the *Entity*'s suggestive temptations.

In fact, he wanted to, more than anything in the world.

But that wasn't him.

That was the darkness within, pulling the strings of his desires, doing his best to finish him off, break the loop, and gain its powers back.

Kelly wouldn't let it.

He had come too far and lost too much.

This was a battle he had no intention of losing.

Even if it destroyed him.

Kelly was about to slip out the window once again— *making his way to the garage where former-Kelly would be in about fifteen minutes*—but the *Entity* had other plans. A tidal wave of a migraine ruptured across his mind.

It felt as if his brain was swelling like an overinflated balloon, pushing the insides of his skull. The pain was completely unbearable as he dropped to his knee, the *Entity* whispering to him once again, louder and harsher than ever before.

"…Diiiiieeeee…"

Kelly could feel the *Entity*'s strength growing inside him. He was losing more and more control by the second as the creature tore him apart from within. He could barely think as he forced himself not to collapse on their bedroom floor. If he did, it was over. Former Kelly or Donna would find him, breaking the loop, ensuring the *Entity*'s damning victory.

Don't let him take you.

Donna's voice raced across his mind once again, that extra drop of strength enough to force him off his knees, rising to his feet in defiance of the *Entity* tearing apart his body and soul from the inside.

There was medicine in their bathroom cabinet, including Tylenol, Advil, Motrin, and a few other things Donna kept stocked. He didn't even know if it would help, but if he could numb the pain, even by a little bit, then maybe that would buy him the time he needs to pass the torch to the next version of himself, ensuring the loop lives on, trapping the *Entity* in an endless revolution of time.

Kelly crept away from his bedside table, making his way into their en suite bathroom. He had to be quick. He knew it wouldn't be long before someone came into the bedroom and saw him.

He couldn't let that happen.

"...Kill yourself...slit your throat..."

He began to reach down for a pair of scissors resting on the edge of the vanity—*uncontrollably*. The *Entity* guided his fingers over the handle, grasping it firmly in his hand and slowly raising the blade toward his throat, inching closer and closer as he struggled to fight the spectre's stranglehold on his mind.

The cold metal of the scissors pressed tightly into his neck's flesh, the razor edge directed at his jugular. His hand trembled in defiance, an erratic balance of control between the *Entity* and himself. The blade pushed harder and harder into his neck, Kelly fighting with every ounce of energy he held to stop the metal edge from penetrating his flesh.

It took a few strenuous seconds for Kelly to regain temporary control, dropping his hand away and slamming the scissors into the wastebasket next to the porcelain toilet. He took an extra second to catch his breath.

He had to be quick, not giving the *Entity* any time to rebuild its control and end it all. If he let his guard down, even for a second, the shadow inside would surely take his life, and in turn, the life of all those around him.

Kelly slid open the vanity mirror and grabbed both the Advil and Motrin, downing a few pills from each bottle. He washed them back with water from the tap. The pain was almost unbearable, and if the drugs didn't kick in soon, he would surely pass out from the strenuous agony. He wouldn't let that happen, but he needed to get out of there before someone showed up and saw him. Kelly placed the pill bottles back in the vanity, back exactly where they were as not to raise a hint of suspicion, then turned to exit the bathroom—*only to come face-to-face with his wife, Donna, standing in the doorframe, looking as beautiful and alive as ever.*

There was no knife protruded from her eye, and as far as he could tell, she was *actually* there, not existing in some sort of spectral, illusionary form.

For a moment, he thought it was over, his cover blown, the unexplainable standing before her. But luckily for him, the unexplainable also acted as a sort of camouflage, because instead of screaming or calling for help, she simply gave a whole-hearted response, as if she were talking to her actual husband, and not one from the future.

"Jesus, you startled me half to death, I nearly screamed." She smiled at him, Kelly trying his best to keep his cool, to act exactly as he would if everything was normal, as if he were simply getting ready for another day of work. "You must have snuck in right behind me."

He didn't respond. He meant to, but the *Entity*'s internal whispers began to build from within, muttering malicious threats toward his wife standing before her.

"... I'll kill her first... I'll make it lasssttt..."

Kelly fought the urge to curse out, to respond to the spectre threatening the love of his life.

"...A knife in the eye...inserted slowly...she willl suffferr...."

He could tell she was waiting for a response, but he just stood there, silent, a blank look on his face as he did his best to ignore the *Entity*'s odious pledge. Kelly wanted nothing more than to reach out to her, tell her to run as far away as possible, and never look back.

But he couldn't.

There was nothing he could say that would make her believe him, especially without breaking the loop's continuity. It was an impossible decision he had to make—*warn Donna about her impending doom, or save the lives of every man, woman, and child that walked the earth.*

"Well, are you going to get ready for work, or are you just going stand there and gaze at perfection?" she continued.

Her smile was intoxicating, and Kelly knew that in less than a day's passing, she would be lying dead only a few feet from where they stood, a chef's knife sticking out her eye like a jagged spike.

She said something else, but Kelly didn't hear what she said, trying his best to both block out the whispers of the *Entity and* the images of his butchered wife.

"Huh?" he blundered.

"Never mind," Donna replied, placing the brush down on the vanity and grabbing a few pieces of makeup from the medicine cabinet. "What're you doing here anyway? I thought you were all ready?"

The *Entity*'s voice droned in again as she spoke, Kelly barely able to focus on the words coming from his wife's mouth.

"*....Kill her...slit her throat...*"

"Hun?"

Kelly snapped back, his forced thoughts drowning out the *Entity*'s threats for a few moments. "Uh yeah, sorry. Day dreaming." He tried his best to force a smile, looking around the bathroom for any excuse to be in here, spotting his speed stick sitting on the edge of the white sink counter. "I um...forgot to put on deodorant."

He grabbed the stick, giving it a quick rub under his armpits to enforce his lie, praying she wouldn't ask too many more questions. The *Entity* wouldn't stay subdued much longer, Kelly's strength already beginning to wane.

"You alright?" She asked. Donna was always good at identifying when he was down on himself, usually after a hard case or a long day. It was just one of the many reasons he loved her. She was the light on the darkest days.

"Right as rain," Kelly said unconvincingly, repeating himself with a little more enthusiasm. "Right as rain." He wouldn't be winning an Oscar any time soon, but it would be enough to at least get him out of the room.

"Alright," she responded to Kelly's relief, his head still pounding, the *Entity* still tearing him apart from the inside out. "I'm going to finish up in here, but I'll come downstairs and say goodbye before I go. And dear, please don't leave your gun on the nightstand."

"Oh, okay." That was his queue to leave. He wanted to get out of there as quickly as possible, before the *Entity* forced him to choke his wife with his bare hands. "Sorry." He was nearly out of sight before he turned back to her, realizing this would be the last time he ever saw her in the flesh. "I love you."

Donna looked almost thrown off, giving him a strange look as if he had three eyes. "Did you do something bad?"

Kelly laughed, getting one last look at his perfect wife.

If only she knew. If only he could warn her.

"Not yet," he smiled, then he was off, one last task to do to ensure the loop was closed, ending his part in this mission.

It was almost over—the beginning—his end.

49

Kelly crept down the stairs, careful to avoid being seen by his former self. As long as he stayed quiet and close to the wall, he would be able to slip into the garage unnoticed. In a few minutes, the Kelly of this timeline would make his way to the car, speeding off toward his imprisonment, completely oblivious, his entire world to be burned to the ground. It would be there—in the confines of the garage—where he'd slip the *Entity*'s power to him, passing it on to continue the loop, forcing the spectre to repeat the events of the day, and eternity of repetition.

Was this the same way he had unknowingly received the power? How many times had this cycle repeated before him? Was there an origin to this cycle, or was it an infinite loop with no beginning or end? Maybe there was an original Kelly, somehow stealing the *Entity*'s power to travel through time, passing it on and on, cascading an endless snowball effect to which there was no end.

Or maybe there wasn't. He supposed he'd never know.

Perhaps his role was not to know but to play his part in this endless game, guided only by faith. *It didn't matter.* All that mattered was that it worked, entangling the *Entity* in time, breaking its foothold in this universe. If he could just do that, then it was enough for him.

Upon reaching the bottom of the stairs, Kelly detoured into the spare room where they kept their office supplies and a few other random things they didn't want to leave out in the garage. He knew he had a few moments to spare before the other

Kelly rushed into the garage, speeding out to face the chaos. And once Kelly passed on the power, he didn't know if he'd be able to keep the *Entity* at bay. There was a good chance that this would be his final hour, and he wanted to make the most of all the time he had, so he grabbed an envelope, pen, and single sheet of paper from the printer tray, and made his way to the garage to bide his time for the next few minutes.

Kelly concealed himself behind several boxes in the garage's corner, out of view from both the interior entry door and the driver-side door of his car. It was the perfect spot to pass on the power to an unsuspecting self. He wasn't certain if a clear view of the target was necessary, but he wanted to ensure success. This needed to be flawless.

He could also use this short break to try and regain a bit of strength. He was exhausted, the time travel taking its toll. This respite would also allow him to write a brief letter—a message to the only person who would truly understand his words—*his partner and friend, Frank McDowell.*

It wasn't a long note. Kelly knew precisely what he wanted to write as his final farewell. Once he lost this power, he didn't know what would happen, but he figured it wouldn't be good for himself. The power was what repelled the *Entity's* ability to control him. Once he lost it, he didn't know if he could hold back the *Entity* any longer. So, in the musty corner of his garage, hiding behind a few stacked boxes, waiting for his part in this to end, he wrote a short and concise letter to Frank, sealing it up in an envelope and placing it in the glove box of the car.

At some point, the station would probe Kelly's car, and with Frank taking point on the case, it would only be a matter of time before he read it.

Quietly, Kelly slid the envelope addressed to Frank in the glovebox, silently closed the car door, and hid back behind the boxes, waiting for his target to come out so he could finally be free of this torture once and for all.

Just a few more minutes passed before an unsuspecting Kelly from the past stormed out of the house and into the garage in a raging fury, irritated that the station hadn't contacted him about one of the most significant terrorist attacks ever to happen in his city, utterly blind to the dire reality of the situation.

It didn't matter, present-Kelly knew how it would all play out, and that gave him a sense of comfort, knowing that in just over a day's time, the man before him—*himself*—would be in this exact situation, broken, alone, but victorious over the vile *Entity* torturing the world around it. With that thought in mind, and his past self within reach, Kelly closed his eyes, blocking out the murderous whispers the *Entity* continued to express within, and allowed the shallow electric pressure to build up around him one final time. Kelly imagined the power traversing through the air, leaving his body and floating gently over to his counterpart, absorbing slowly into his body. Not only did he imagine it, but he could feel it, almost like a heavy weight being lifted off his shoulders, placed into the next stage of the endless loop, the power of time slowly fading from his body, entering the Kelly from this timeline, completely unaware—*just as it had been for him at the beginning.*

It only took a few seconds, but he knew the exact second the power had wholly vacated his body, the sense of freedom taking over like an overwhelming wave of alleviation.

Additionally, Kelly felt the *Entity* stir within him, squirming, screaming, stampeding, almost as if it sensed its utter defeat, his power fading from his reach, resetting the loop once again, trapping him in an endless cycle in time from which there was no escape.

A few more seconds passed before the garage door opened, past-Kelly pulling out of the drive and out of sight, his part to play in this only just beginning, present-Kelly's part finally ending. And for the first time in what seemed like an eternity, with the *Entity* within and his fate sealed, he was finally free.

Once confident that his past self had driven well away, Kelly quietly left the garage, Kelly quietly exited the garage, making his way back around the block to where he had parked the bike. As he walked, he could feel the *Entity* gradually creeping across his body and mind. *Without the protection of Kelly's time-bending power, nothing could deter the Entity from assuming control.* He didn't know how much longer he had, but it was only a matter of time before his mind was no longer his own, and he was just another twisted puppet like the rest of them. But so long as the *Entity* was trapped inside him, he would drive as far away as possible, giving past-Kelly as much time away from the *Entity* as he could.

Kelly Christopher revved the motorcycle, igniting its roar, the engine vibrating and humming in the damp morning air. He pulled out from the shoulder of the road, pointed the nose in the opposite direction to the police station, and began to put as much distance between himself and the other Kelly as he could.

Kelly had gone further than anticipated, speeding several dozen kilometers down the highway before the *Entity*'s influence began to take hold. He felt his hand begin to shake, his fingers twitching uncontrollably, the *Entity*'s grim whispers beginning to emanate once again.

"...*Time to diiieeee...*"

The threat didn't scare Kelly in the slightest. He had already accepted his fate the second he passed on the power to his former self. His role now was to delay the *Entity* as much as possible, getting the spectre as far away from the station as he could before it took total control. And as far as Kelly was concerned, he had done just that.

Kelly pulled the bike off the main drag, heading down a small dirt trail leading into the distant woods. The street bike struggled with the muddy trail, but he didn't plan on going very far, just far enough that they wouldn't find his body within the coming days.

His vision began to dim, and he felt a sinking sensation within himself as the *Entity* assumed command. He fought against the overwhelming sensation with all his might, but before long, driving the motorcycle no longer remained an option. His fingers and hands were no longer his own, twisting and curling beyond his authority like the twisted puppets he had so many encounters with.

He crawled off the trail, leaving the bike rumbling behind, and made his way into the thick of the woods, alone in the cold, surrounded by nature as his mind began to sink with the dark confines of his captured body.

"...*Diiiiieeee...*"

The *Entity* whispered the word repeatedly, Kelly's mind sinking further and further into his body, his vision growing dark, his body convulsing uncontrollably. He only managed to step a few yards into the woods before the *Entity* gained complete authority, Kelly's entire body twisting and bending uncontrollably, his bones cracking, his muscles tearing apart. The helm of his mind was no longer his own, trapped inside his body just as the *Entity* had been trapped inside his.

Kelly felt his hand reaching down for the gun at his hip, the one he had swiped from his home in exchange for the one used at the scene of the crime. His twitching hands grasped the black metal handle, hoisting it from its holster and raised it slowly toward his head.

Kelly didn't care. He knew what was about to happen. He was scared. But he was ready.

If he still had any motor control over his own body, he would have smiled. He would have smiled because, within a matter of seconds, he would see his wife again, Donna, smiling back with beauty and perfection. The cold metal barrel of the gun pressed firmly against his temple. In the damp darkness of the forest, the click of the safety was loud next to his ear. One final time, the *Entity* whispered to him—a final threat that held little worth in Kelly's seized mind.

"...Diiiiieeee..."

Birds scattered from the distant trees as a single gunshot shattered the silence of the secluded woods. Kelly Christopher was dead. *Kelly Christopher had defeated the Entity once and for all.*

Epilogue

Frank McDowell sat quietly at his desk, with the blinds closed and the lights dimmed, mulling over the events from two days prior, a flurry of papers and evidence resting in chaos on his normally organized desk.

He had shared everything with Zoe, uncertain if she would ever believe him. Although, for the time being, she was too busy planning Jessie's funeral, and promised to keep Frank and Kelly's secret until he was able to dig up more evidence on the case. If he had one duty, it was to somehow clear Kelly's name and prove he stood not the villain—*but the hero*.

At the moment, he was running with a fake story, about someone impersonating Zoe Stevens in order to pull off a terrorist attack in a public area, and Kelly somehow catching on and stopping her in the nick of time. He doubted it would hold up, but for now, it would do the job, at least until he thought of something better. Frank wouldn't give up clearing Kelly's name, no matter what it took.

He prayed that his partner would turn up, backing up his claims and providing more evidence to support his innocence, but it had been over two days since the shooting in the Halifax Ferry Terminal, and he was still nowhere to be found.

Lost in thought, Frank was jolted back to reality by a knock at his door, forcing him to drift back into focus and reality. "Come in," he called out softly.

It was a rookie Officer, Carl Jacobson. He was a new addition to the station, eager to learn, never daring to question the authority of a higher-up detective, the perfect candidate to help Frank try and clear Kelly's name without raising too many eyebrows from the board.

"What is it?" Frank inquired as the rookie stepped into his office.

"We found something. It was in the glovebox of Kelly's car. It's a letter, sir, addressed to you." The rookie handed Frank the letter, then left the room, not asking any questions or overstaying his welcome.

For a moment, Frank stared at the unopened letter, his name scrawled in Kelly's messy handwriting in blue ink.

What did you leave behind? Frank thought, grabbing a letter opener from his desk drawer and popping open the envelope. He picked up his reading glasses from his desk— *reminded of his age, yet grateful for it* —and put them on.

Frank,

I don't have much time, and if you're reading this, I'm probably already dead. But that's O.K. It means you're safe. You're all safe. It's over. You'll never see the Entity again. With some guidance, I managed to trap it in a perpetual loop in time, doomed to repeat the day for eternity.

The perfect prison for such a twisted abomination.

You were right, by the way. Zoe wasn't herself. The Entity had corrupted her all along, using us to jump back in time. It somehow lost its power along the way, sometime at the beginning of all this, long before you or me, tracing back to the very first domino. It tried to use my ability to get back to the moment it all went down, but with a little luck and some good shooting, I was able to take it down. Who would have thought I'd be saving the world.

On a more serious note, Tell Zoe I'm sorry about her husband, and promise me you'll give Donna a proper burial. She didn't deserve any of this.

I couldn't save her.
I tried Frank.
I really did try.

I must go now. I just wanted to say thank you. For everything.
You'll always be my friend, my partner—my brother.

Yours truly,
Kelly.

Frank slumped back in his chair, holding the letter tightly in his hand, a sense of relief growing within in a time filled with utter chaos. He didn't care how long it would take, or what it meant for his name or his career, Frank was going to prove Kelly was a hero.

He had to.

He owed him that much. Because of him, Frank's wife was alive, amongst countless others.

His friends were alive.

Zoe was alive.

He was alive—all of them narrowly dodging death, not even one of them aware in the slightest. Frank would make them aware. He would make sure the whole *God-damn* world knew the name, Kelly Christopher.

He would dedicate his life to it.

He would dedicate his life to his friend, his partner—his brother.

Turn the page for a sneak peek at
Book I of The Twisted Boeman Collection

HIDDEN

A. Ryan MacGibbon

Hidden (Preview)

Debbie Oslo took a reluctant step forward, her unwavering gaze glued to Daray's open office. Then she took another step, this one larger than the last, her fingers shivering in the cold. She slowly crossed the den one dawdling step at a time, making it halfway to the door before stopping once more, her eyes slowly adjusting to the increasing dark. Debbie could barely see into the office, but she could make out the corner of a desk and what looked like a small martini bar with a few glass decanter sets on top. There was zero light emerging from the office, every faint glow emanating from the den's overhead light, which was dim in itself.

Once more, she left a hallowed greeting to the forbidden dark, praying for a familiar or welcoming response. "Hello?"

Zippo.

"All right then," she said to no one but herself. "I'm coming in."

Debbie halted for a few seconds, hesitating to explore the prohibited office. She could just as easily head back upstairs, dash to her car and drive back home.

The job was completed.

All she had to do was leave.

But she couldn't just leave with the office door open. Daray would think she went in. Then he'd surely fire her for breach of contract. And in a town where most advertising was done by word-of-mouth, she would do *anything* to ensure there were never any complaints about her or her business.

So, defying what the chill in her spine warned her, Debbie pushed ahead, stepping over her grey rag on the floor and into the freezing dark of the office. It took a few extra seconds for her eyes to adjust to the darkness, the cold wrapping around her like a blanket. The office was small, not much larger than the storage room. Daray's desk stood in the centre near the back wall, covered in chaotic papers, notes, and a laptop. The floor was a continuation of the living room, and the walls were completely covered with bookshelves. Every wall had a bookshelf on it, Daray's own personal library surrounding every corner of the office. Most shelves had novels and textbooks, a few knick-knacks and ornaments, and a few were filled with office supplies.

But it wasn't what was in the icy room that caused a subtle alarm for Debbie Oslo.

It's what *wasn't* in the room.

There were no windows.

None.

It was completely isolated from the outside world, the glass-framed bookshelves the closest to a window as there was.

Then where was the freezing air flowing from?

Debbie reached for the light switch with her shaking hand, flicking it on, only to be filled with anxious disappointment.

The switch did nothing.

The light was dead, the room enduring the dark.

Debbie flipped it a few more times, wishfully hoping it was a loose connection, but she had no luck. Instead, she reached for her cell phone in her pocket, pulled it out, and used the screen's light to try and illuminate the room. She wasn't technologically inclined, unaware of the 'flashlight' feature on her fancy cellphone, though in such a small room, the screen's light would do, her boney thumb constantly clicking the power button to stop the phone from turning off.

Debbie took another step into the empty office, searching for a hidden window or faulty air-conditioner, anything that could explain the open door and freezing air, but other than the martini bar, wooden desk, green office chair and a lifeless lamp, there was nothing else in the room.

How in God's name did the door swing open then? Debbie thought.

Maybe the floor was slanted, and when she jiggled, it swung open?

Maybe...

More speculation filling the unknown...

Humans were good at that.

Especially when their skin was as tense as polar ice.

Debbie took a deep breath, letting her nerves slowly calm, knowing at the very least that she was alone. She ran her hand through her short grey hair, her other arm holding the phone as a makeshift flashlight. She released a small smile of relief, the anxiety beginning to fade, her heart sinking back to a healthy pace.

"You're going crazy, you old bag," she said to herself in the isolation of Daray's office library.

"You're truly going..."

SLAM.

A deafening noise exploded to her right as Debbie released a howl of a scream echoing almost loud enough for the neighbours to hear.

Almost.

Her heart promptly doubled in tempo, the anxiety racing through her veins as if it were injected by an invisible needle. In a swift motion, she pivoted to identify the origin of the loud sound, the noise still reverberating through her ears as if it weren't totally silent once again.

On the floor behind her was an oversized purple book, lying face up on the hardwood floor. Debbie kneeled and grabbed it, surprised by the weight of the hefty textbook as she lifted it with trembling fingers. The cover read '*Diagnostic and Statistical Manual of Mental Disorders - DSM-5.*' She had no idea what it was, but its contents didn't matter

How in the hell did this fall from its place on the bookshelf?

Debbie had no idea.

But she didn't care.

She wanted the hell out of this house.

Now.

Debbie lifted the book from the ground, rising and placing it back in its spot on the shelf.

And that's when she felt it.

The crisp breath on the back of her neck, matched with the deteriorating smell of blight rising within the teeny office. It filled her nose like swamp water, drowning her airways with a wretched stench. The distinct, concentrated breeze bounced off her wrinkled skin, her eyes watering with malodor. It wasn't until she turned to run did Debbie witness the source of endless trepidation that had corrupted her so effortlessly.

It lingered before her…

Hovering inches off the ground…

A demon mentioned only in the darkest of church sermons…

Floating within the center of the forbidden office, arm outstretched and jaw snapped from its hinges, dangling from the loose thread of rotting muscle, was what Debbie Oslo could have only described as the Devil.

Debbie could see the creature's mid-ridden tongue waggling back and forth in the dark as drool and rotten blood oozed from the gashes where its jaw should have been, black eyes glaring down upon her behind rotten skin.

Debbie didn't scream.

She had no voice to scream.

She couldn't find the will to scream.

Her breath drew shallow as her heart pounded from within her tensing ribcage.

Debbie could only stare with faith-breaking dread as the broken-jawed woman floated before her, as clear as the mist from her lungs, staring directly into Debbie's immobilized soul. Then, after what felt like the longest three seconds of Debbie's life, fear turned to adrenaline, her instincts overtaking any logic that remained within her forsaken mind. Her feet began to tumble forward before her mind could even conclude that that was the only decision available to her. Debbie turned from the woman floating before her, the rotting stench drowning her shallow-drawing lungs, and ran as fast as she could from Daray's forbidden office.

But she didn't make it very far.

Her bones were tense, and her coordination and arthritis could not overcome her panic.

She scooted about two steps before her right foot caught the corner of the grey rag lying at the entrance of the office door, and Debbie went tumbling down, cracking her head off the edge of the IKEA coffee table and landing on the cold floor with a harsh thud her fragile body could hardly handle.

When she came about, the room was whirling, the smell of rotten stench triggering her eyes to water, her mind slowly wavering back into consciousness. Debbie rolled over onto her back, an egg-like bruise forming on her right temple and a large dribble of blood gushing from her broken nose.

It took a moment for her vision to roll back into focus, but when it did, the only thing she could see was the broken-jawed woman floating above her, bone-exposed arm outstretched, reaching down to Debbie as if to rip out her throat, a single abrasive and coarse word splitting from her rotting throat...

"...Releasssse..."

Debbie stared in horror at the monster towering over her, the demonic spectre closing in as the remaining light seemed to slowly wane.

Running was no longer an option, her head spiralling too fast for Debbie to find her bearings.

And at her age, fighting was never a possibility.

This left one last alternative as she awaited her fate in the freezing dark basement of the Horvac household.

Debbie screamed...

She screamed as if her life depended on it...because she was pretty sure it did...

Her screams drowned out the howls of the demonic creature, Debbie's crying voice hollering louder than she ever thought capable.

And this time, the neighbours would hear her screams....

Every house within three blocks would hear the horrid shrieks of Debbie Oslo, under the menacing gaze of the broken-jawed demon in the depths of Daray Horvac's blackened basement.

Debbie   screamed...and   screamed...and   screamed.

The Writer's Embrace

For more up to date information regarding new editions to the series, novels, short stories, and more, visit www.thewritersembrace.com, home of A. Ryan MacGibbon.

The Writer's Embrace is an ever-evolving writing community designed and maintained by the author *of The Twisted Boeman Collection,* and a place where fellow writers, readers, and followers can:

- Find up to date information regarding the release of new books and novels.
- Read blogs and informative pieces written by the author.
- Read raw short stories and poems directly from the author.
- Learn more about A. Ryan MacGibbon.
- Communicate directly with the author through our contact pages.
- Write your own stories and poems and discuss them amongst peers in our **Free Writing Forum**.
- Enter Semi-Regular Contests, offered on-and-off depending on time availability.

The site is entirely free and welcomes writers and readers of every background!

www.thewritersembrace.com

The Twisted Boeman Collection

The *Twisted Boeman Collection*, envisioned by A. Ryan MacGibbon, comprises a series of standalone novels that delve into the diverse and chilling realms of horror. Each book is a unique foray into different sub-genres, crafted to offer readers a pulse-pounding journey from the first page to the last.

Book I - Hidden

Are you afraid of the dark, or is it perhaps what may linger in the shadows that frightens you? Thirteen years ago, Daray Horvac witnessed there is more than what we think exists beyond the veil of death, and thirteen years after, he publishes his work for all the world to see, revolutionizing the way humans perceive the soul—*but not without a ghastly cost*. Follow along as the Horvac family becomes haunted by a creature no longer interested in remaining *Hidden* behind the veil of

Book II – Twisted Shores

Originally released as a stand-alone, this remastered version of Twisted Shores is sure to have the reader at the edge of their seat as Bill Shapely goes toe-to-toe with the *Entity* and his army of twisted maniacs, all under the *Twisted Boeman's* malevolent control, all forced to obey his dark commands. Will Bill survive, or will he lose his mind alongside the rest of Sydney, NS?

About the Author

A. Ryan MacGibbon's roots are deeply embedded in the rugged beauty of Cape Breton Island in northern Nova Scotia, where he was born and raised. His formative years by the elegant Mira River set the stage for a lifetime of curiosity and exploration, leading him to Acadia University for a B.Sc.H. in Physics and subsequently to McGill University in Montreal for a M.Sc. in Particle Physics. A seasoned professional in data science, Ryan dedicates his leisure time to crafting enthralling novels and short stories or enjoying the company of friends and family in the lively quarters of downtown Halifax. His literary debut, *Hidden*, marks the beginning of *The Twisted Boeman Collection*, a series of standalone horror novels that introduce readers to the darkest corners of his mind. Ryan currently resides in Halifax, N.S., where he shares his life with his remarkable family.

Reach out at www.thewritersembrace.com.

@thewritersembrace

:)